"The finest graphic novel of the year."
—*Helsingin Sanomat*

"*The Nightingale That Never Sang* looks at the world through the eyes of a child and an adult at the same time. The end result is an exceptional blend of innocent beauty and miraculous cruelty."
—Ville Pirinen, *Kulttuuritoimitus*

"*The Nightingale That Never Sang* has strength and sensitivity, with echoes of long-hidden secrets and dislocated shame. The best debut in years."
—Ville Hänninen, *Empirix*

Winner of the 2020 Critics' Award,
The Finnish Association of Critics (SARV)

First prize, 2017 Nordic Comics Competition

Juliana Slyrri

The NIGHTINGALE That Never Sang

"The Blue Swimsuit" narration co-written with Elina Johanna Ahonen.
"The Clambox" narration co-written with Myrtillius Kauria.

First published in Finland by Suuri Kurpitsa as *Satakieli joka ei laulanut*.

English translation by Juliana Hyrri and Zach Dodson.

Published by
featherproof books
Chicago, Illinois
www.featherproof.com

First edition
10 9 8 7 6 5 4 3 2 1

Library of Congress Control Number: 2020952702
ISBN 13: 978-1-94-388826-9

Printed in Estonia by Meedia Zone OÜ

Juliana Slyrri

The NIGHTINGALE That Never Sang

featherproof BOOKS

THE BLUE SWIMSUIT

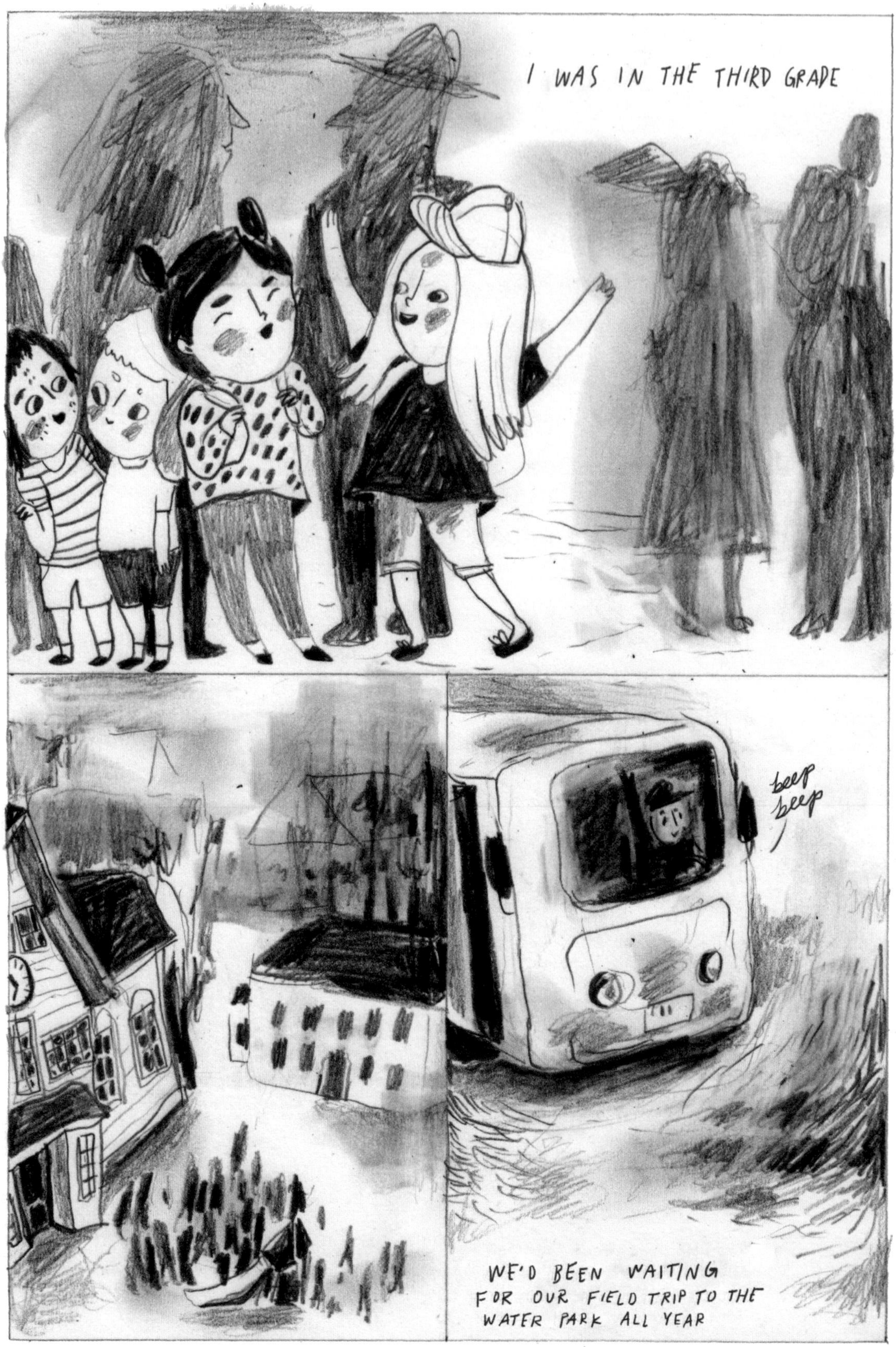
I WAS IN THE THIRD GRADE
beep beep
WE'D BEEN WAITING FOR OUR FIELD TRIP TO THE WATER PARK ALL YEAR

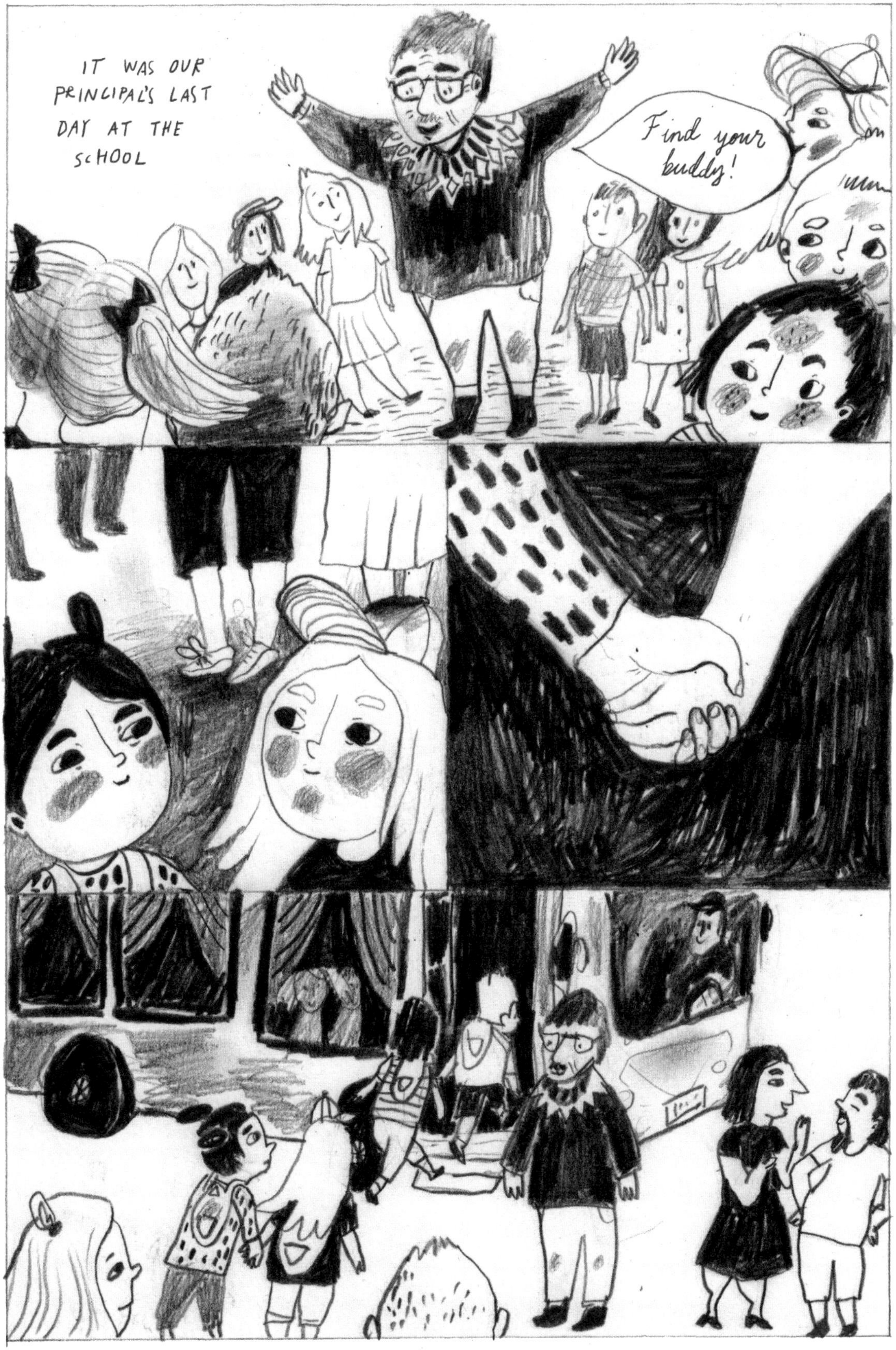
IT WAS OUR PRINCIPAL'S LAST DAY AT THE SCHOOL
Find your buddy!

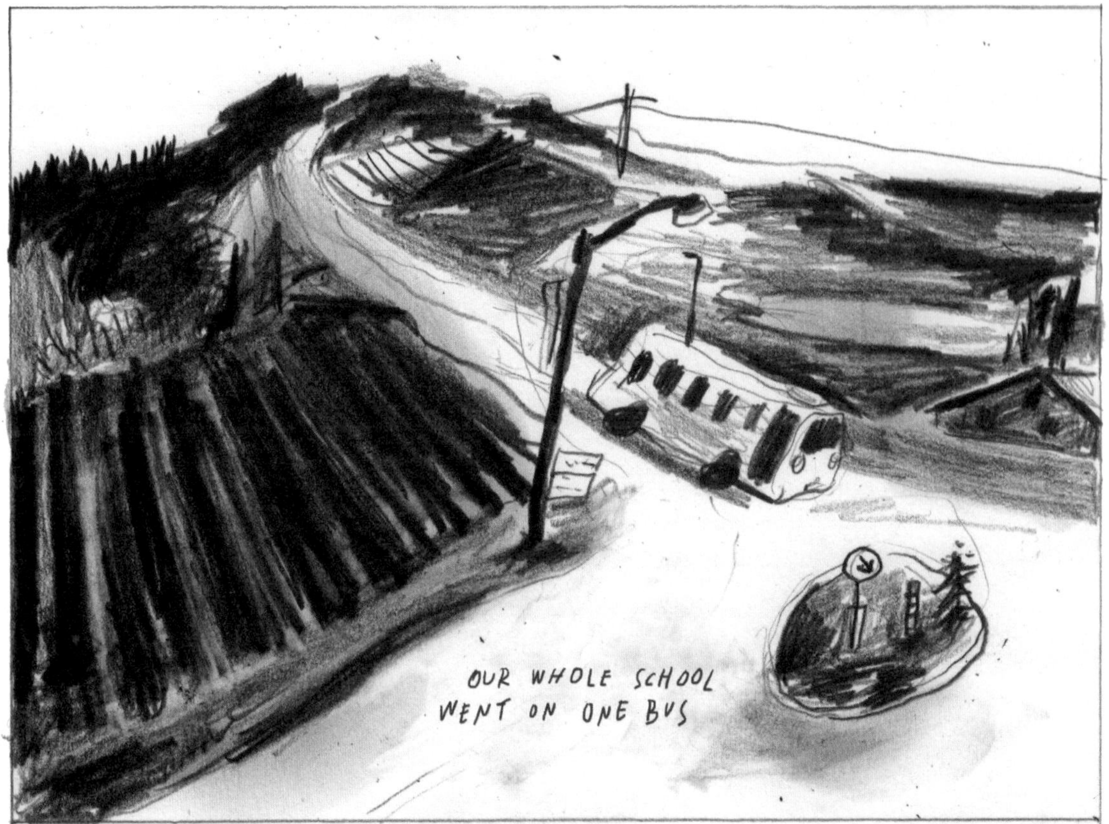
OUR WHOLE SCHOOL
WENT ON ONE BUS

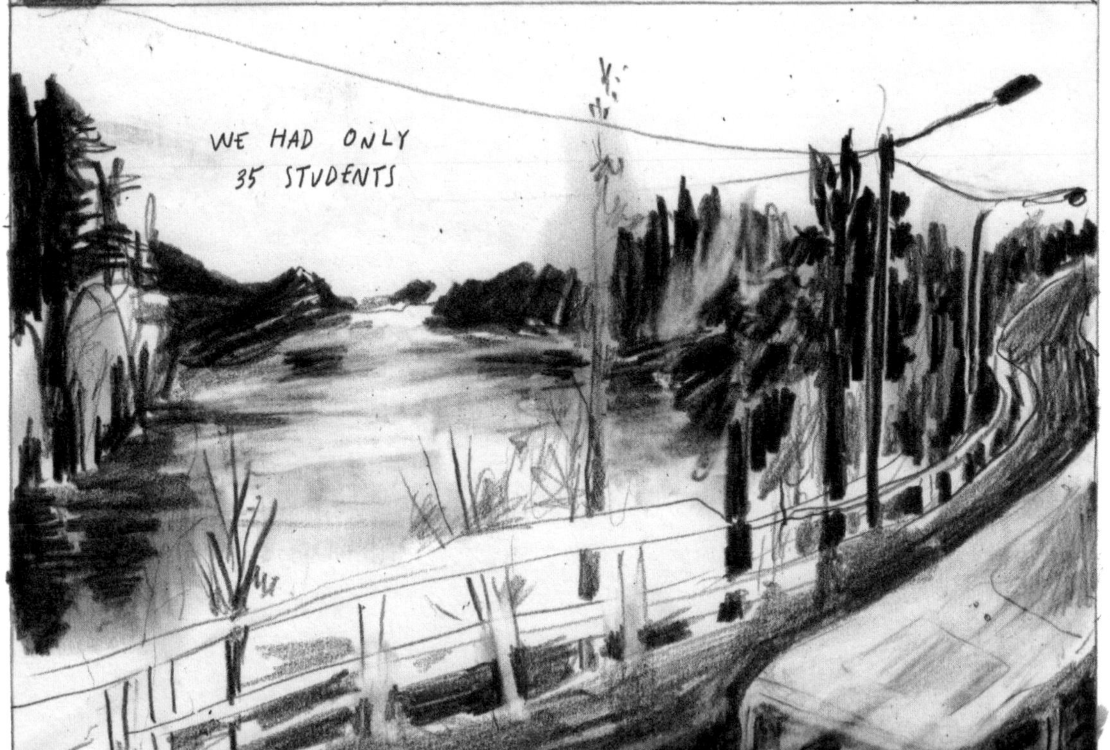
WE HAD ONLY
35 STUDENTS

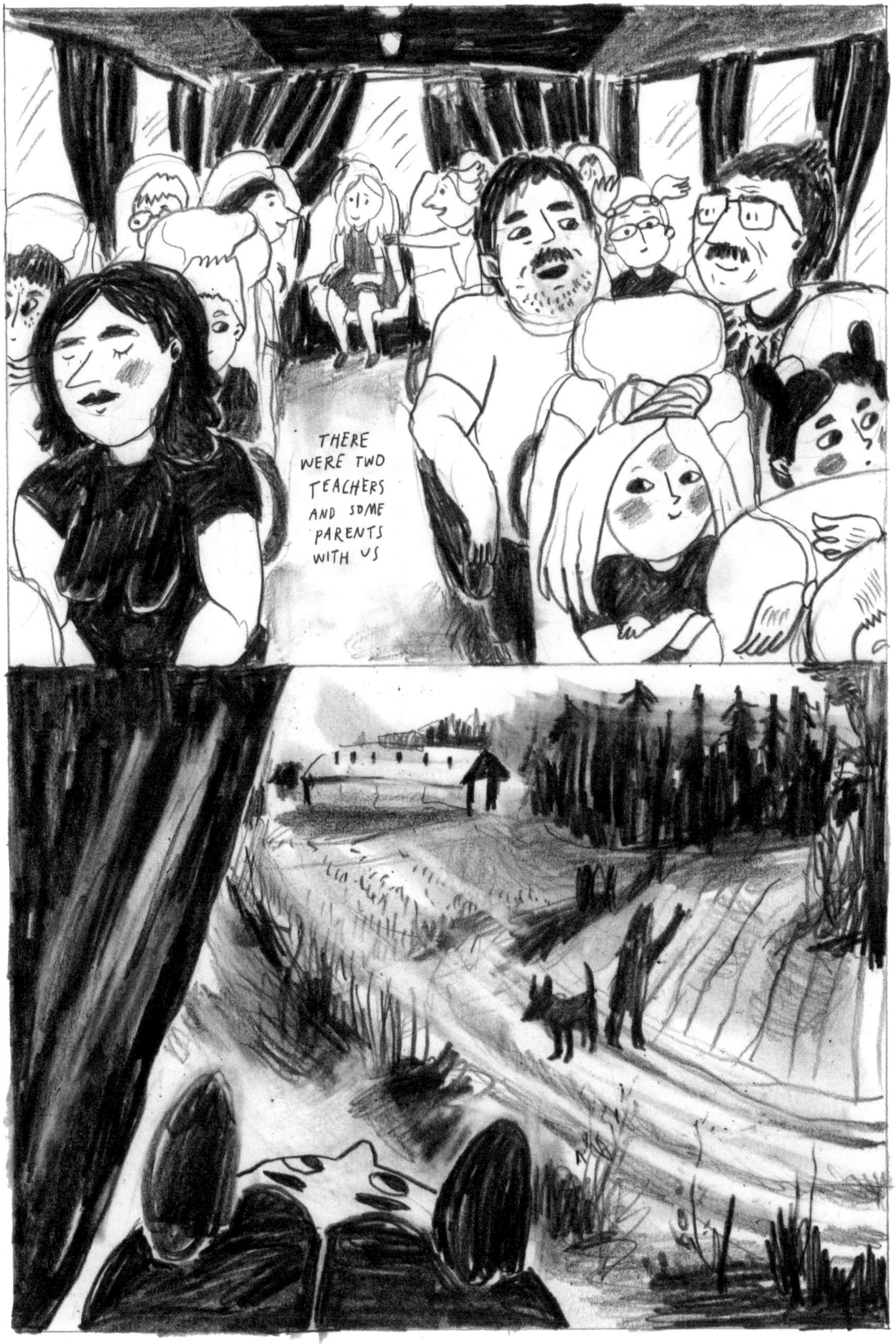
THERE WERE TWO TEACHERS AND SOME PARENTS WITH US

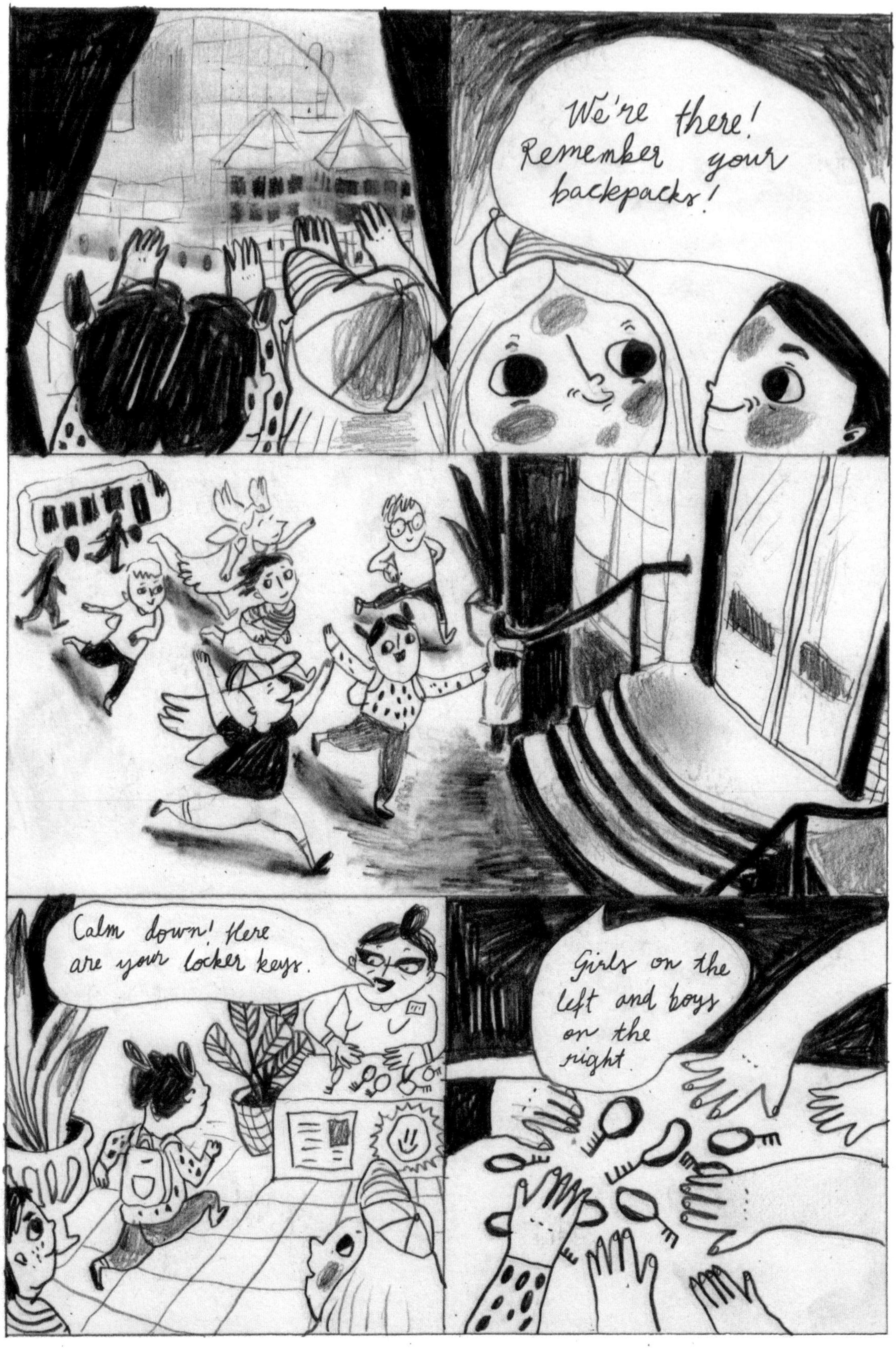
We're there! Remember your backpacks!
Calm down! Here are your locker keys.
Girls on the left and boys on the right.

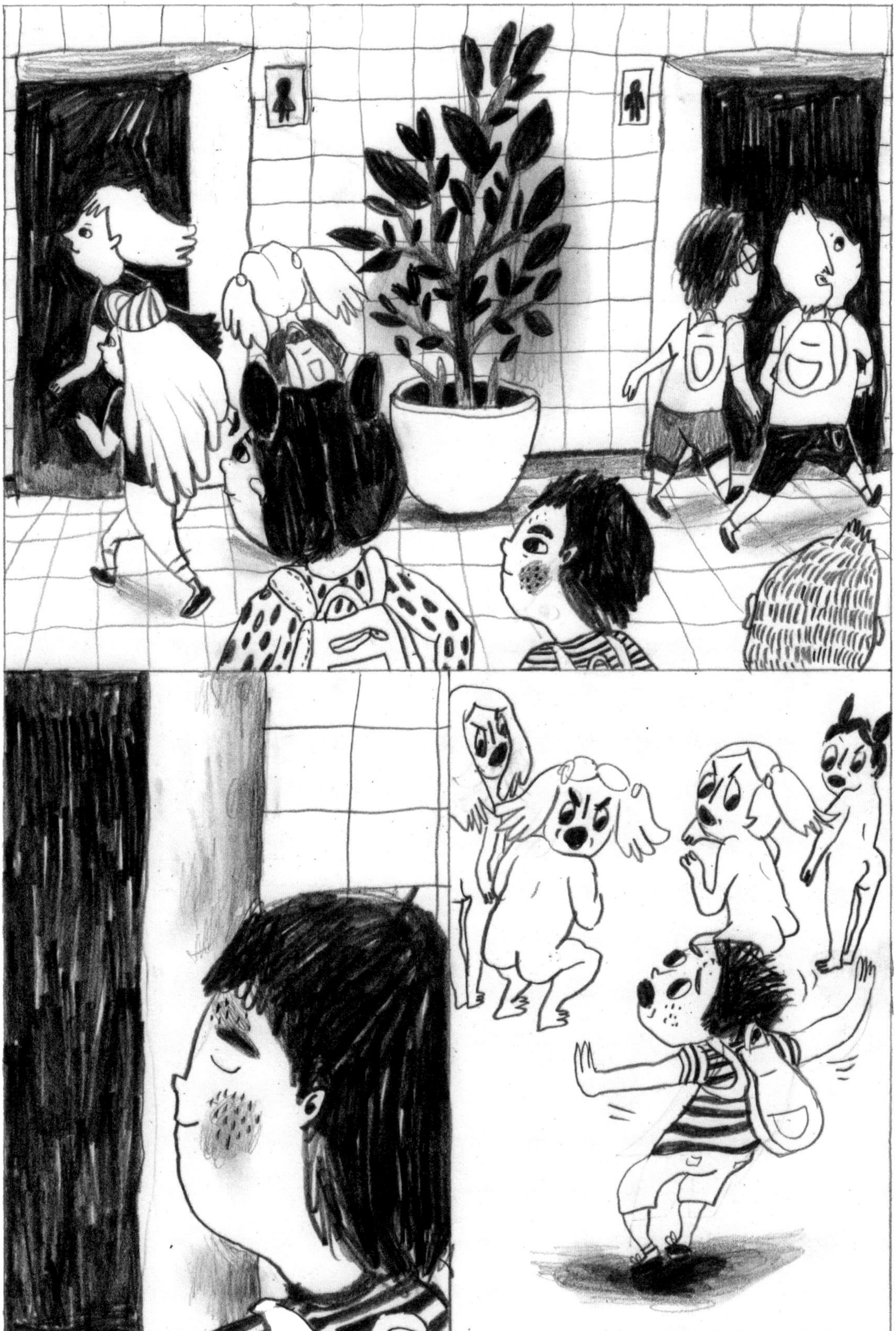

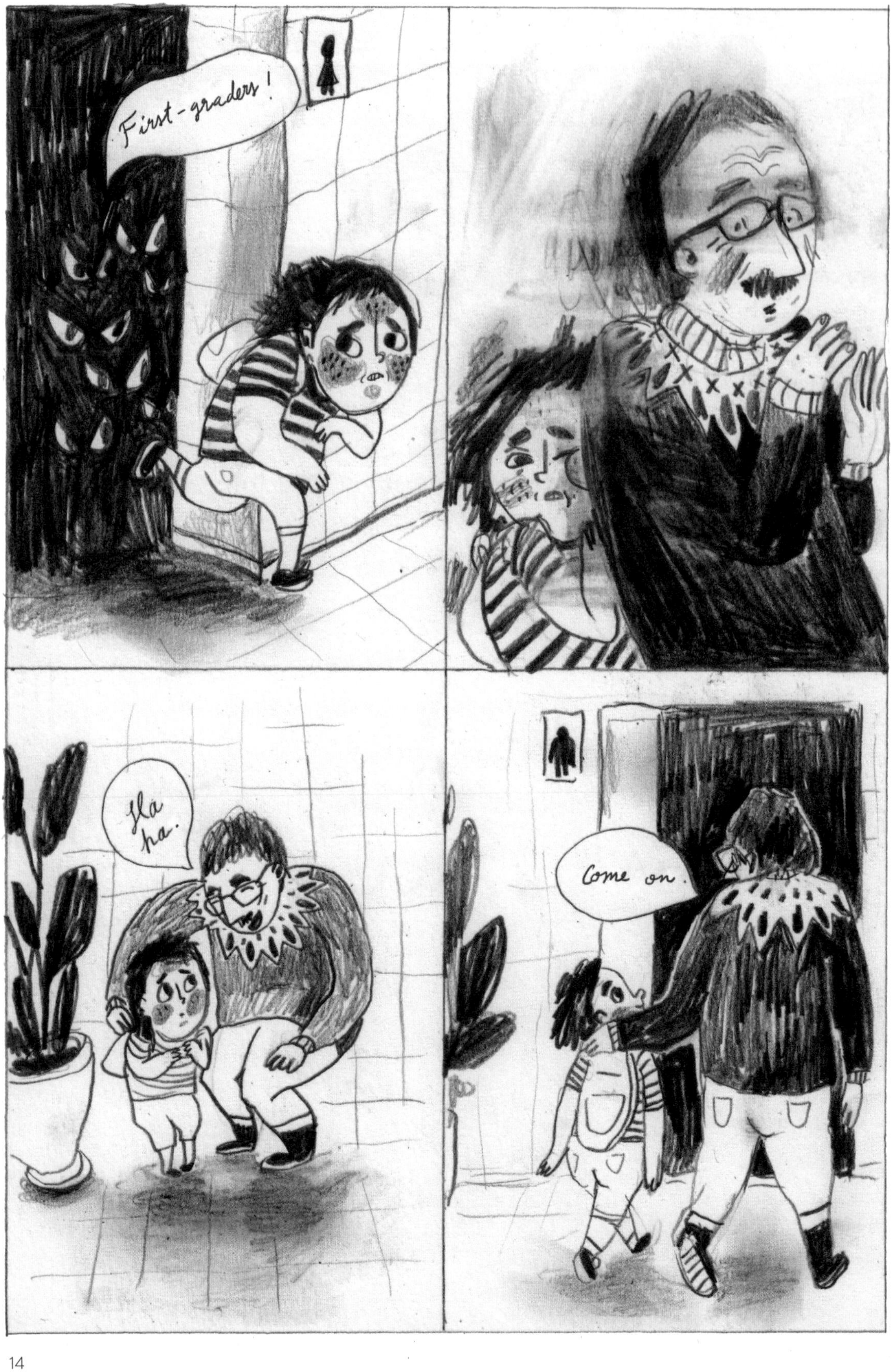
First-graders!
Ha ha.
Come on.

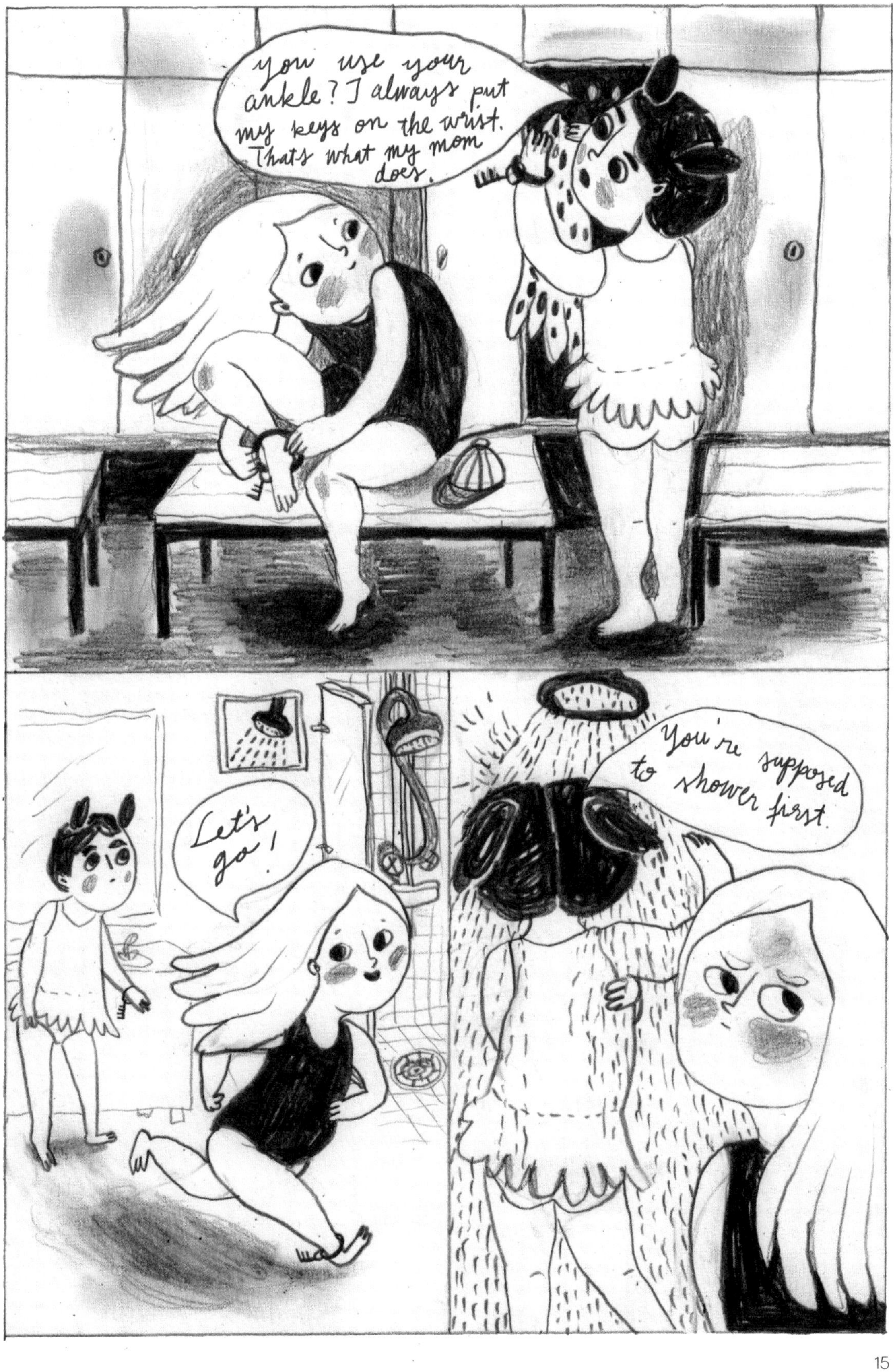
You use your ankle? I always put my keys on the wrist. That's what my mom does.
Let's go!
You're supposed to shower first.

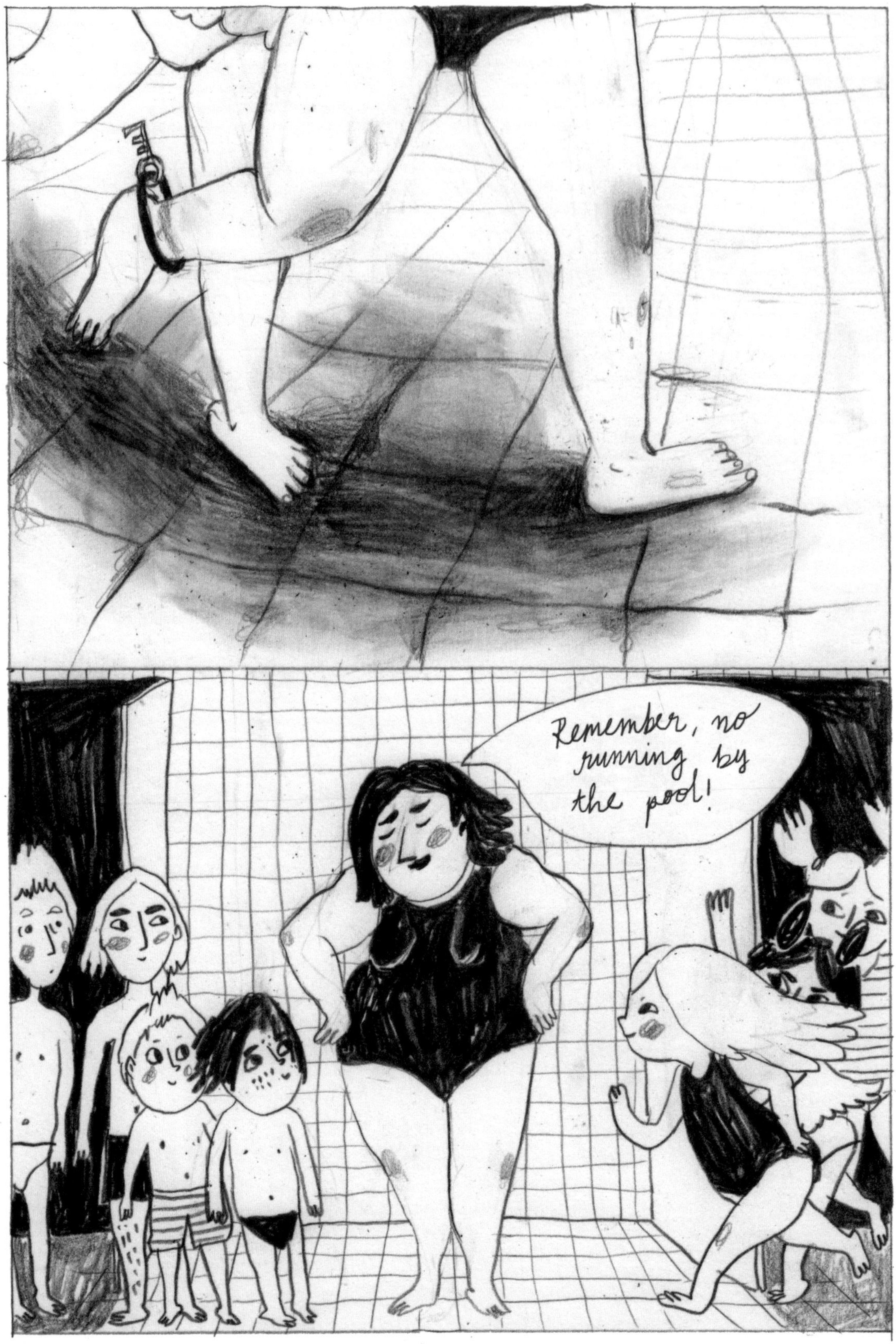
Remember, no running by the pool!

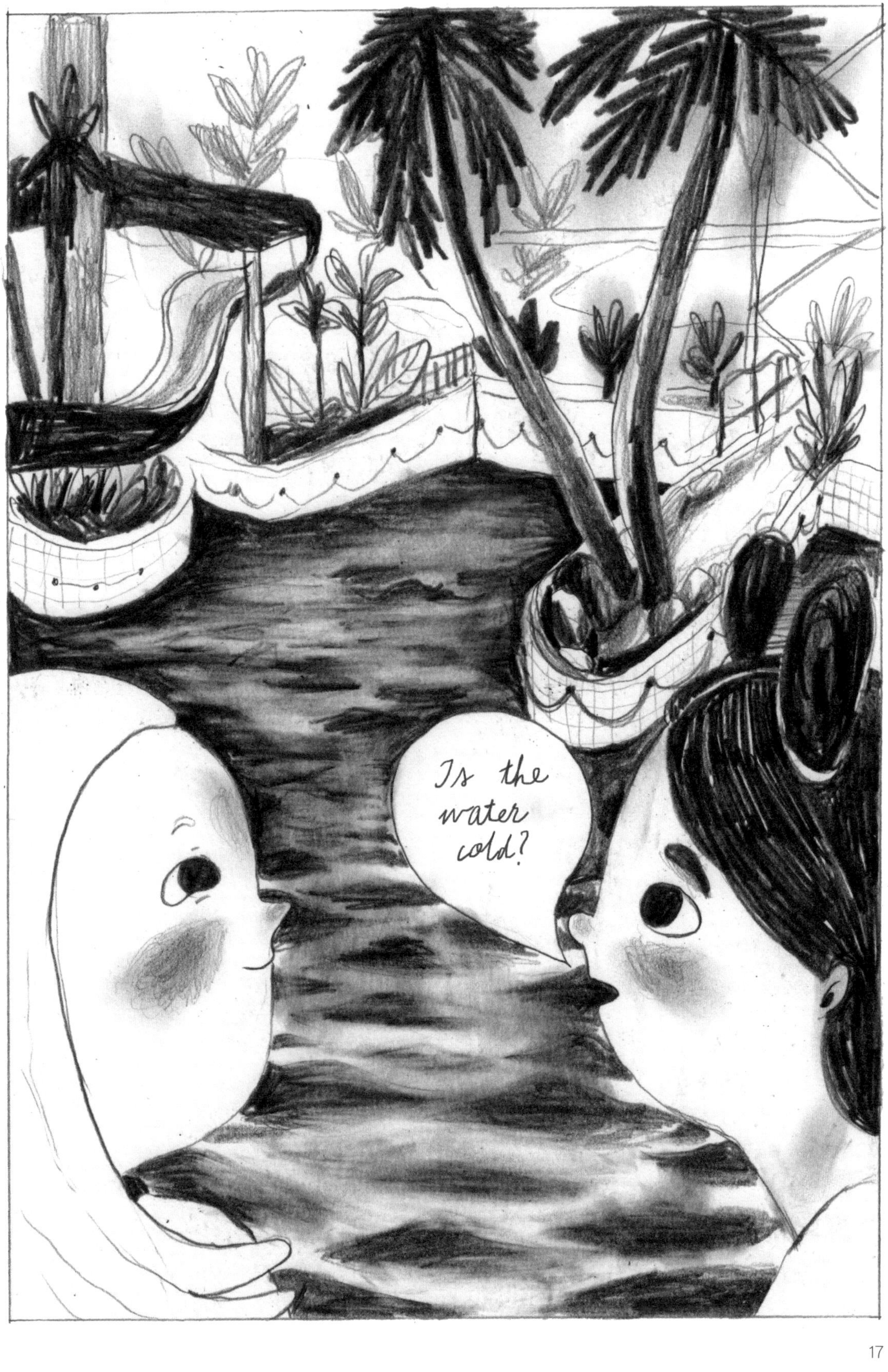
Is the water cold?

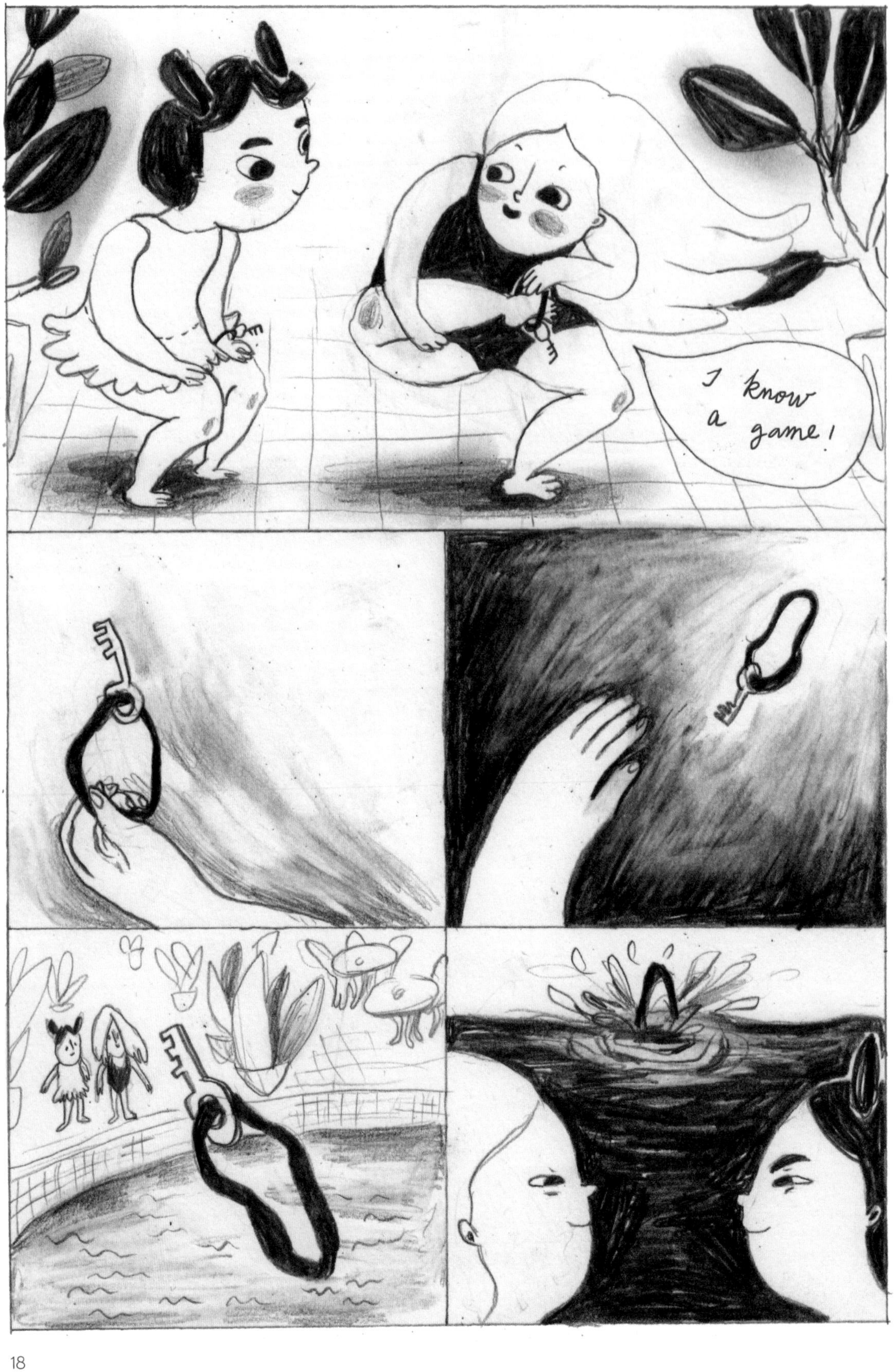
I know a game!

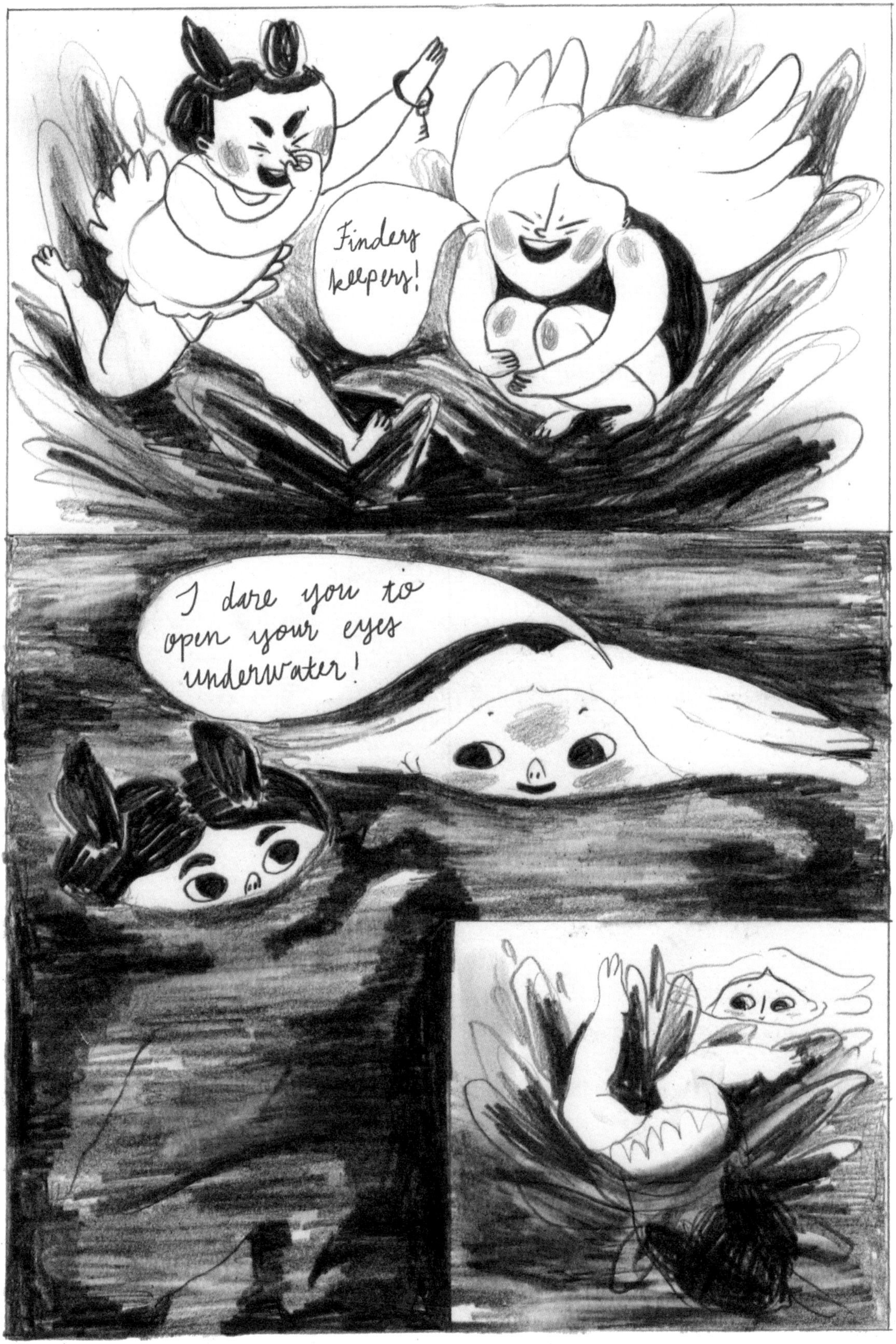
Finders keepers!
I dare you to open your eyes underwater!

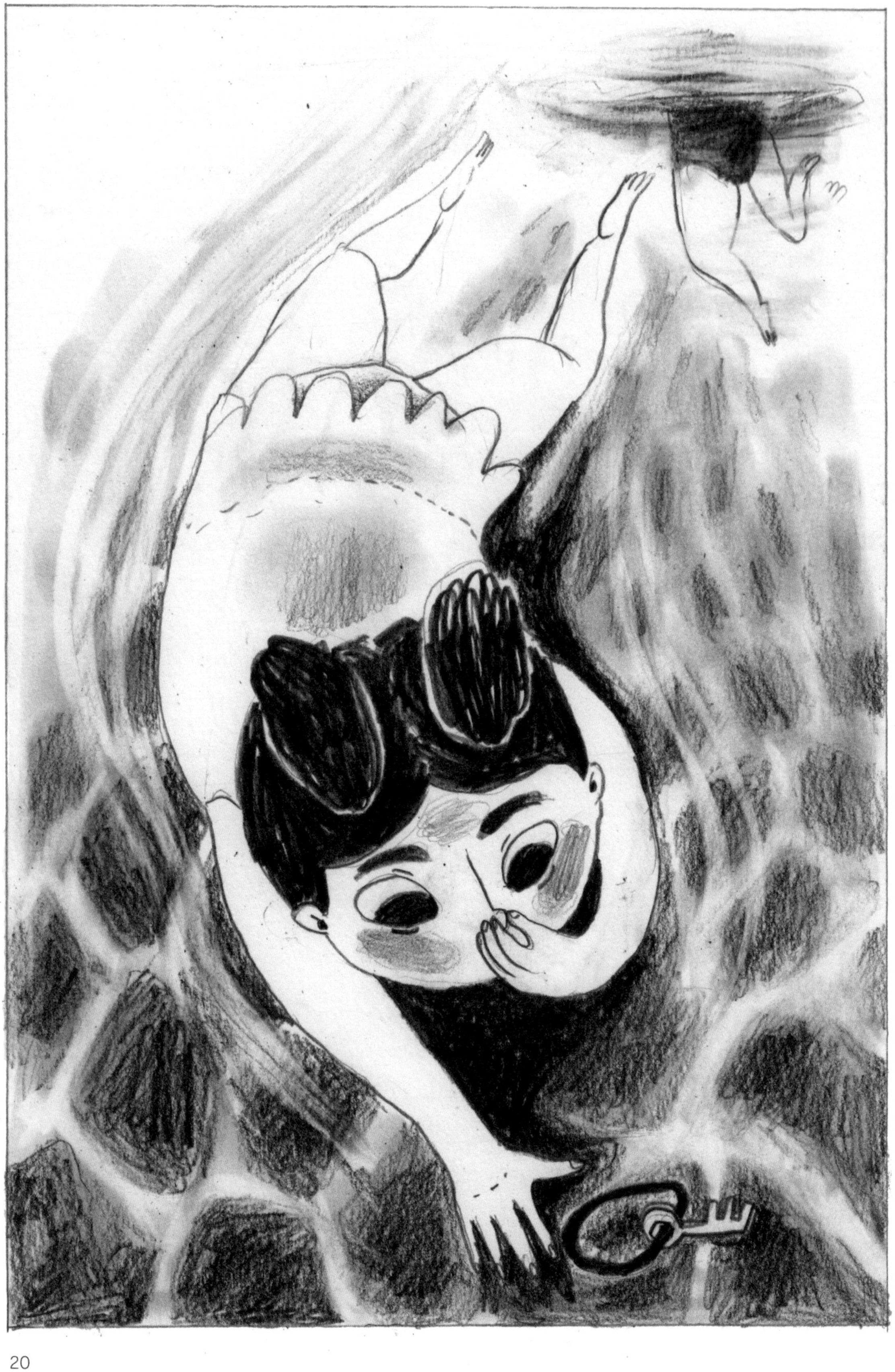

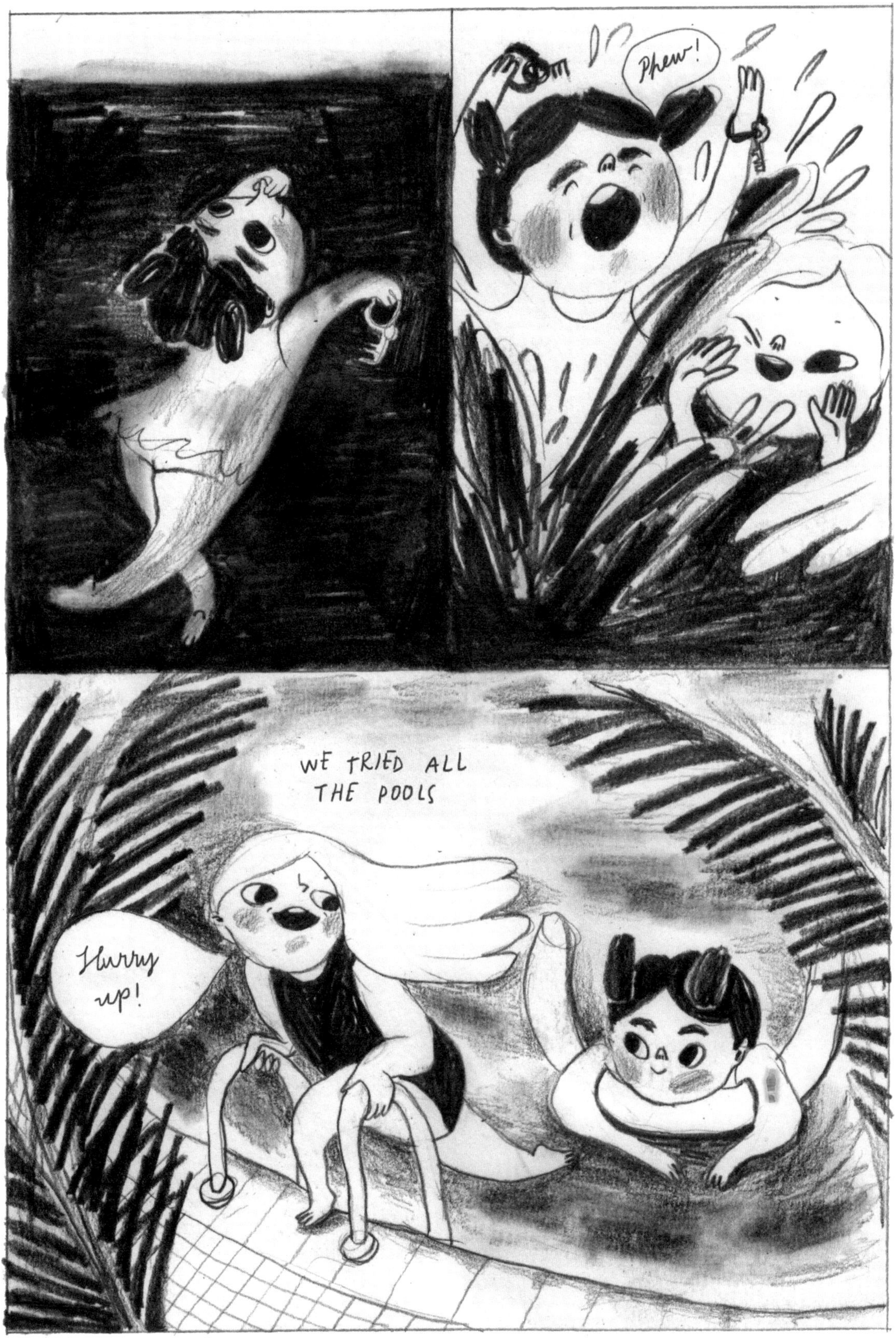
Phew!
WE TRIED ALL THE POOLS
Hurry up!

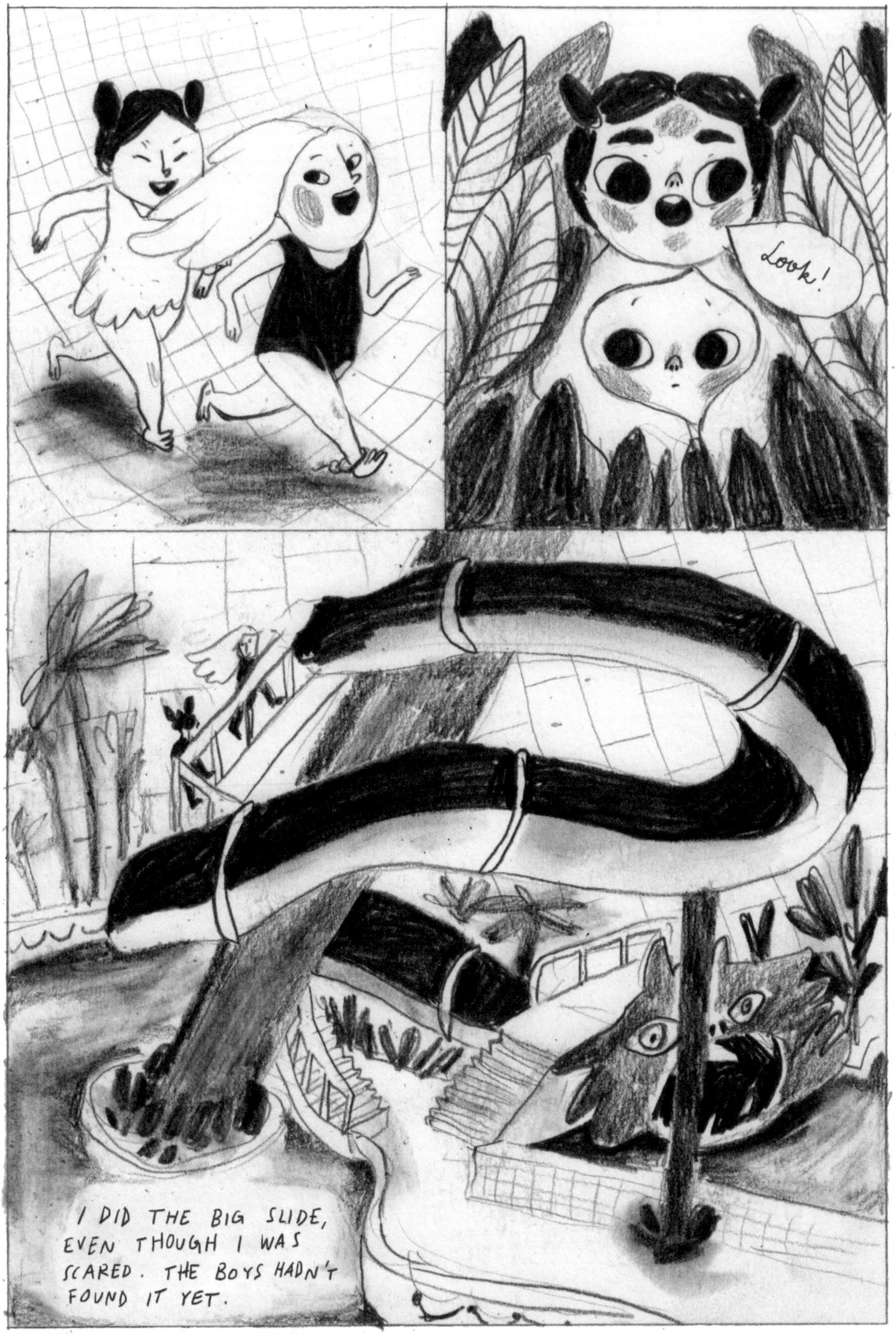

Look!
I DID THE BIG SLIDE, EVEN THOUGH I WAS SCARED. THE BOYS HADN'T FOUND IT YET.

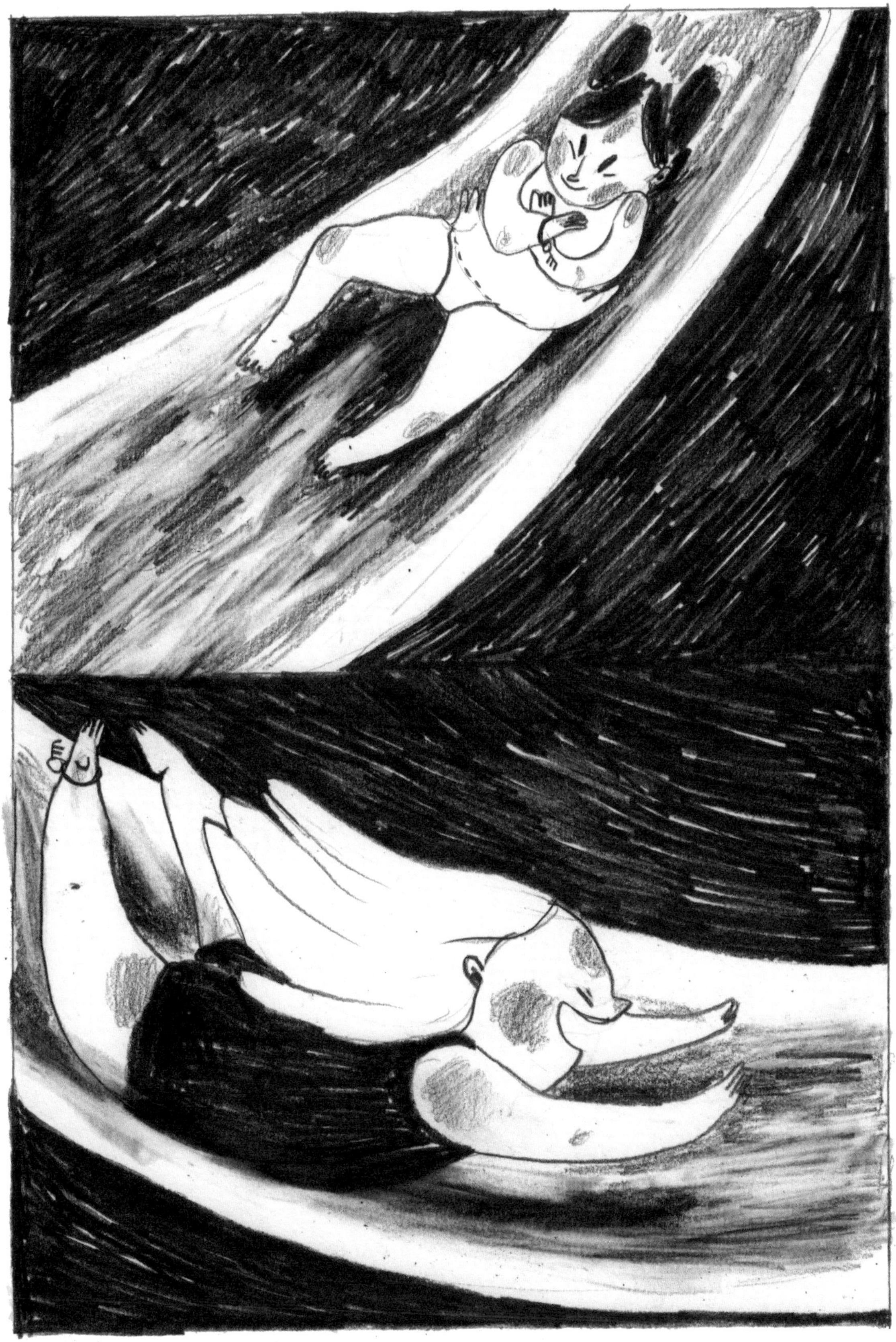

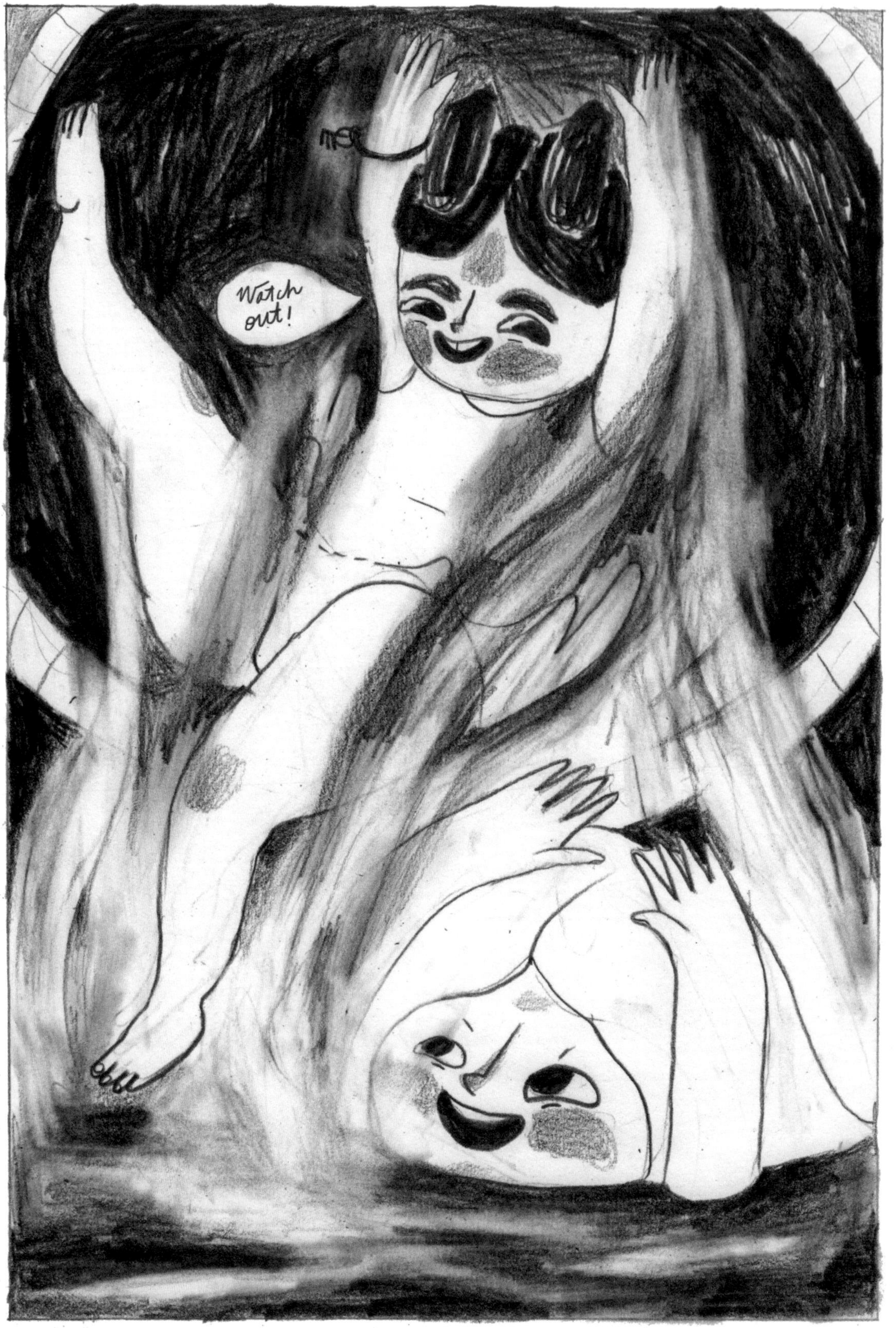
Watch out!

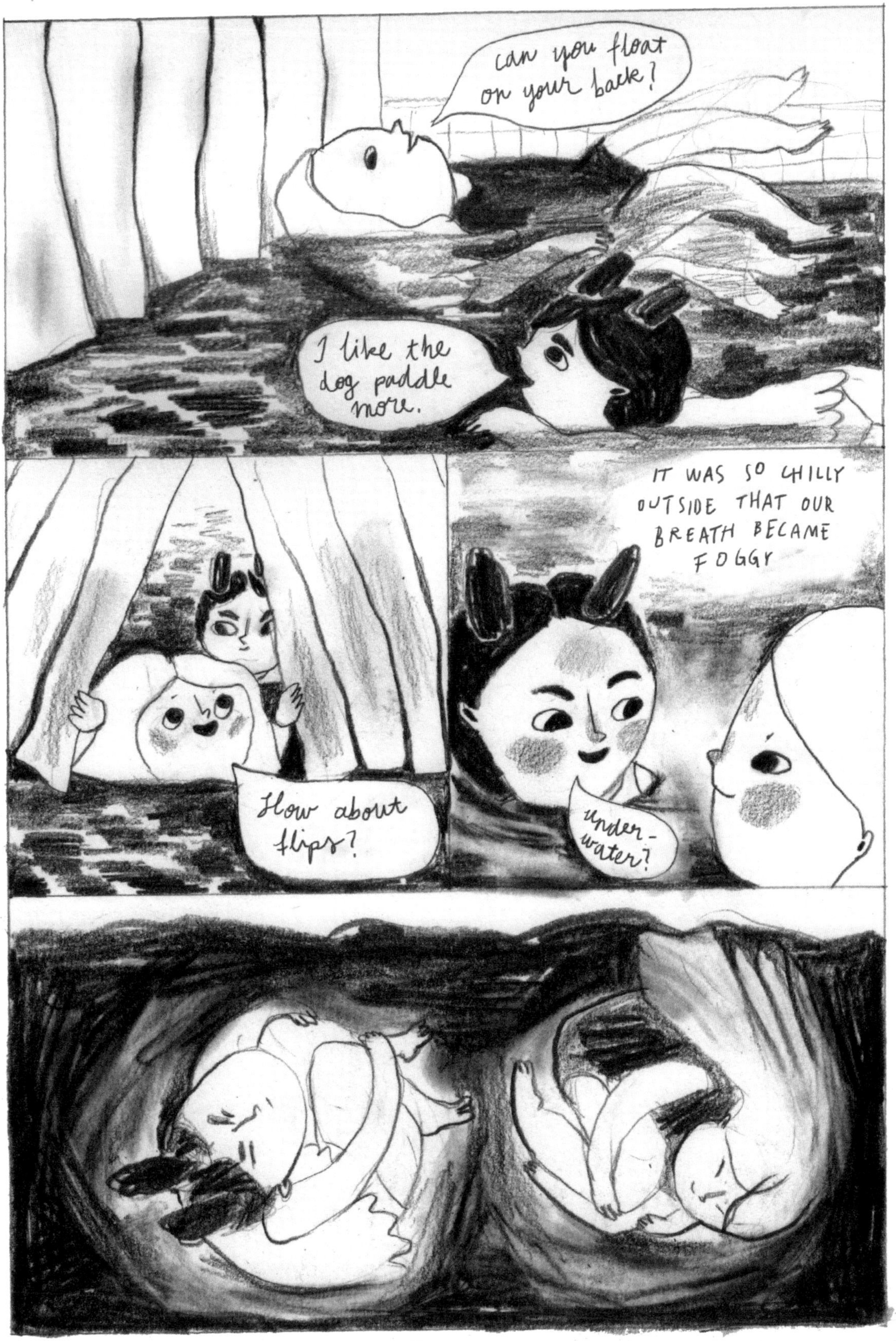
can you float on your back?
I like the dog paddle more.
How about flips?
IT WAS SO CHILLY OUTSIDE THAT OUR BREATH BECAME FOGGY
under-water?

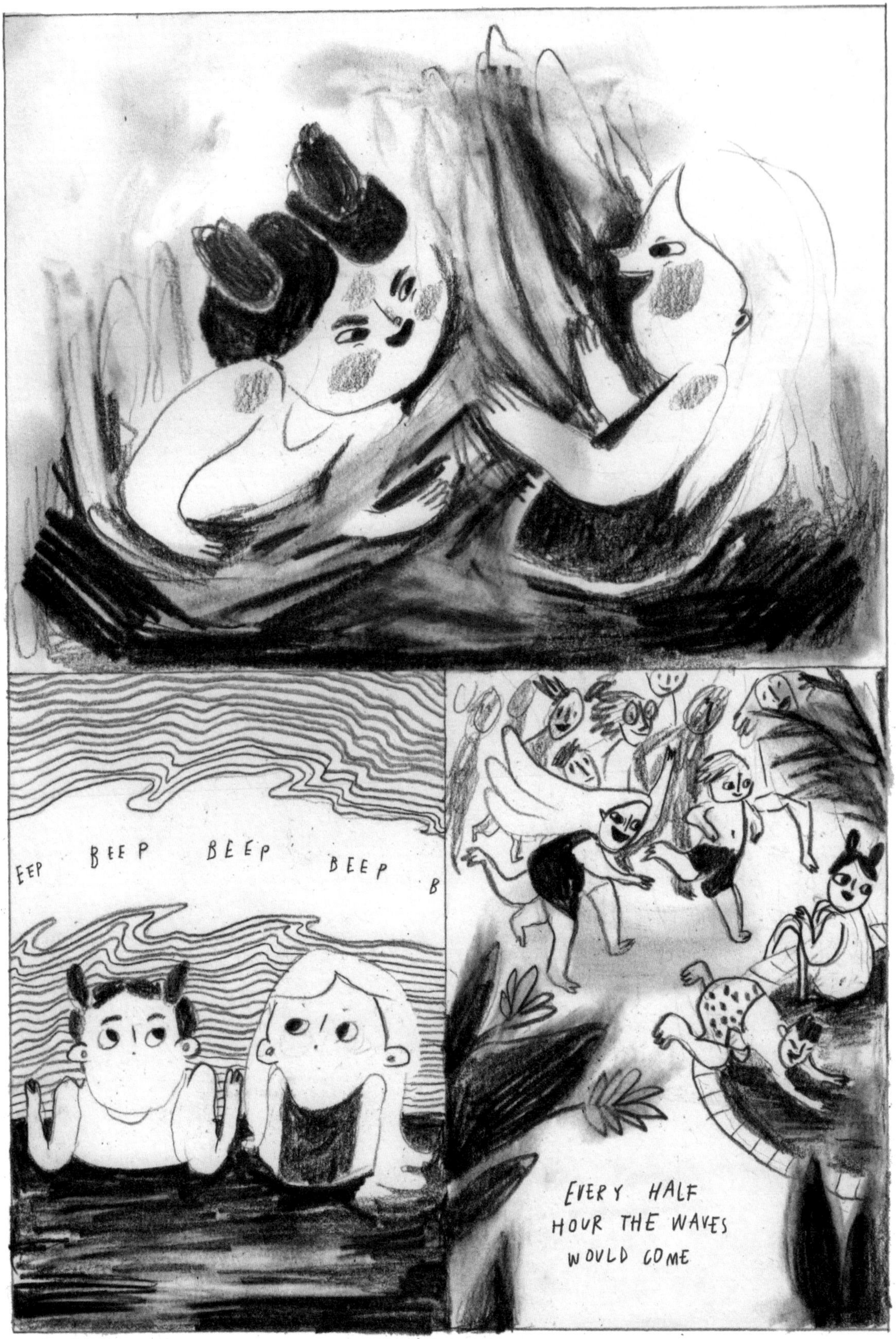
EEP BEEP BEEP BEEP B
EVERY HALF HOUR THE WAVES WOULD COME

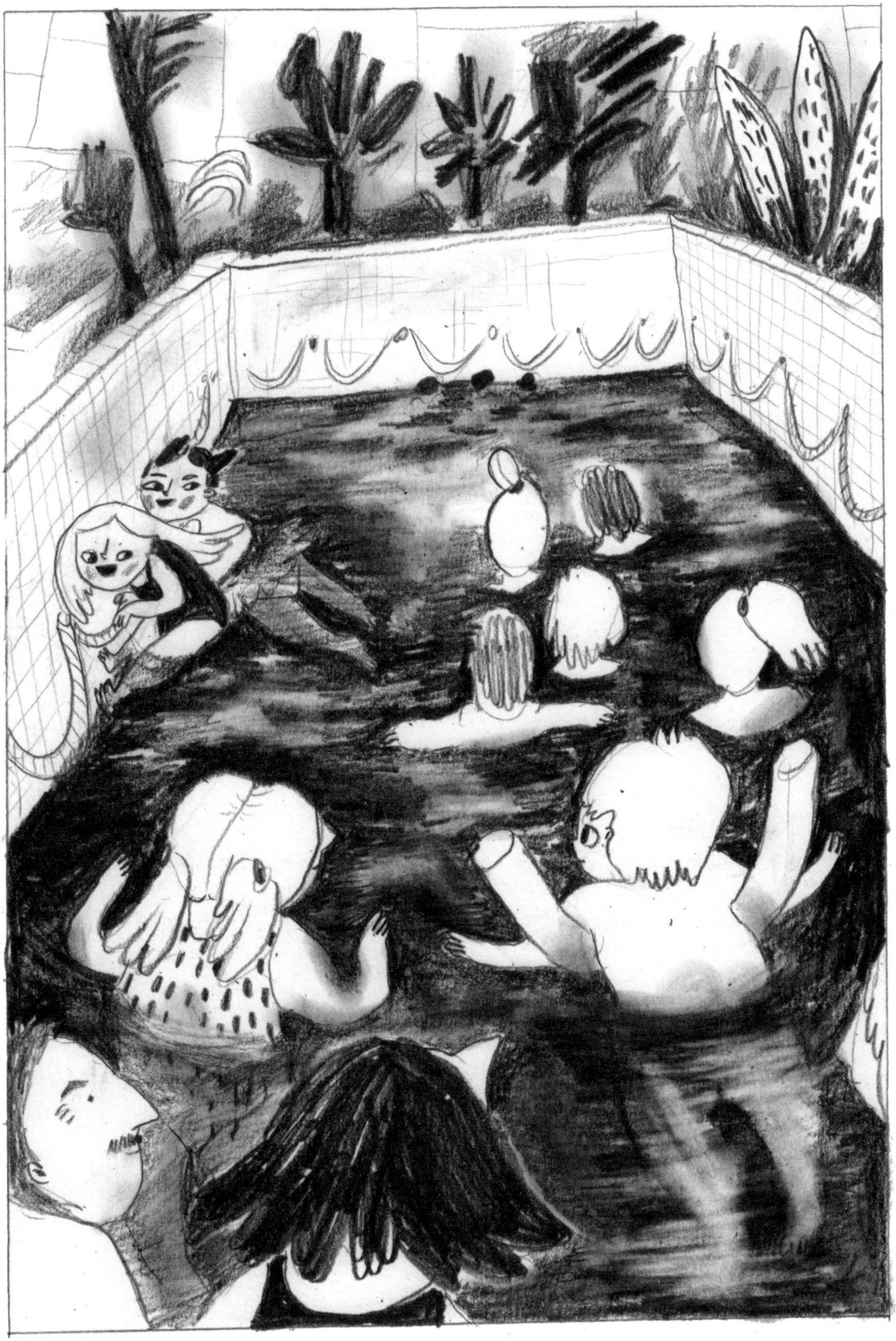

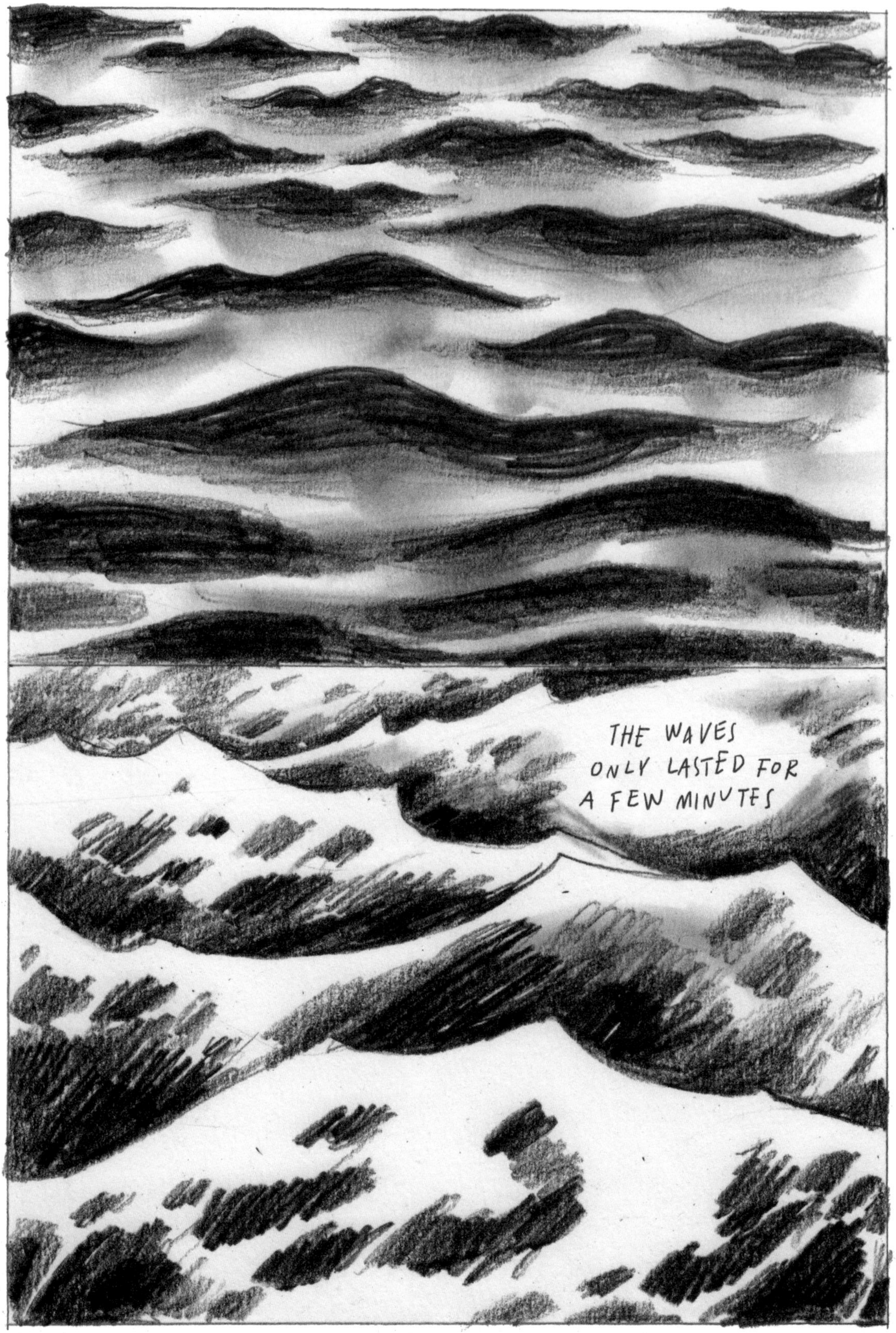
THE WAVES ONLY LASTED FOR A FEW MINUTES

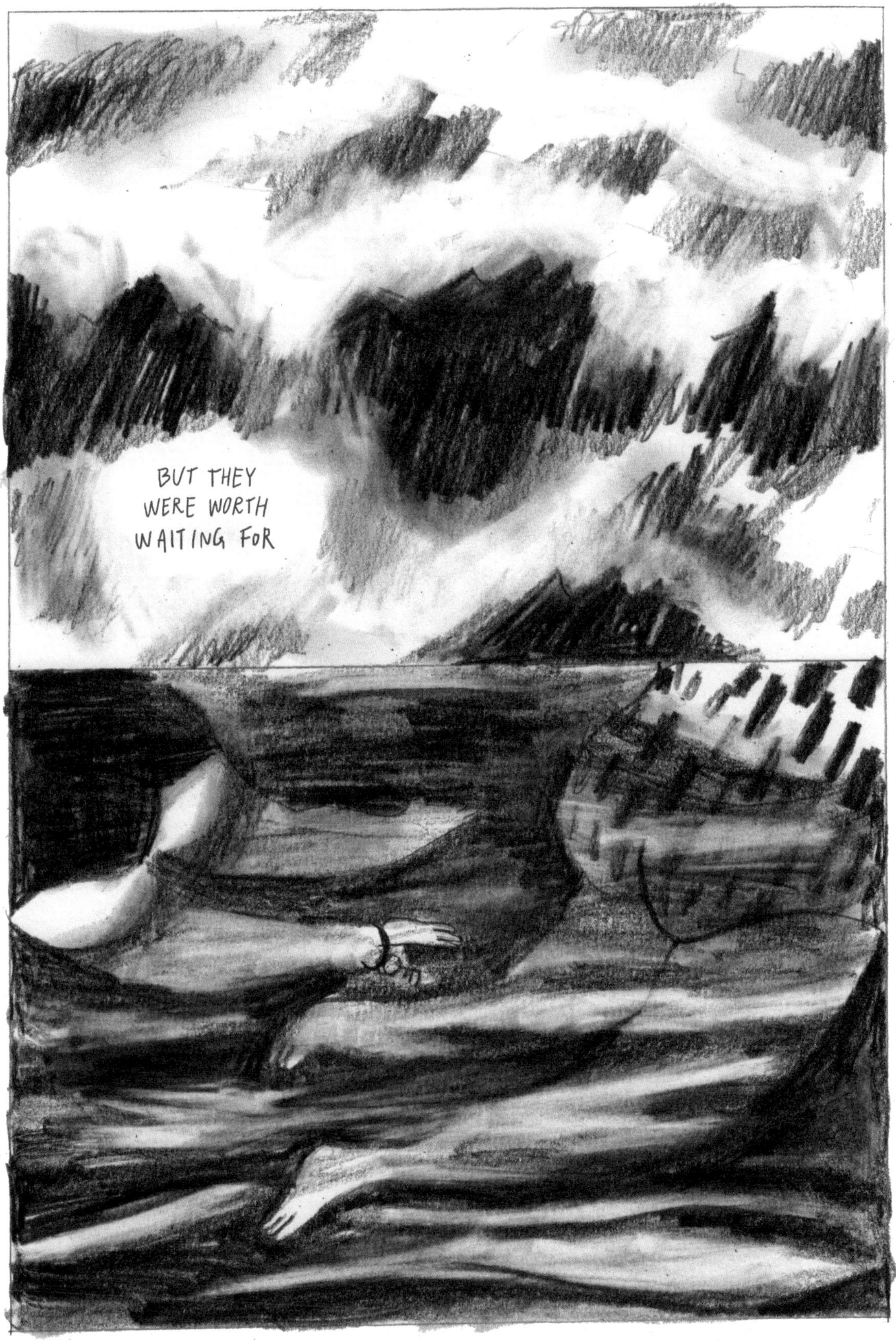
BUT THEY
WERE WORTH
WAITING FOR

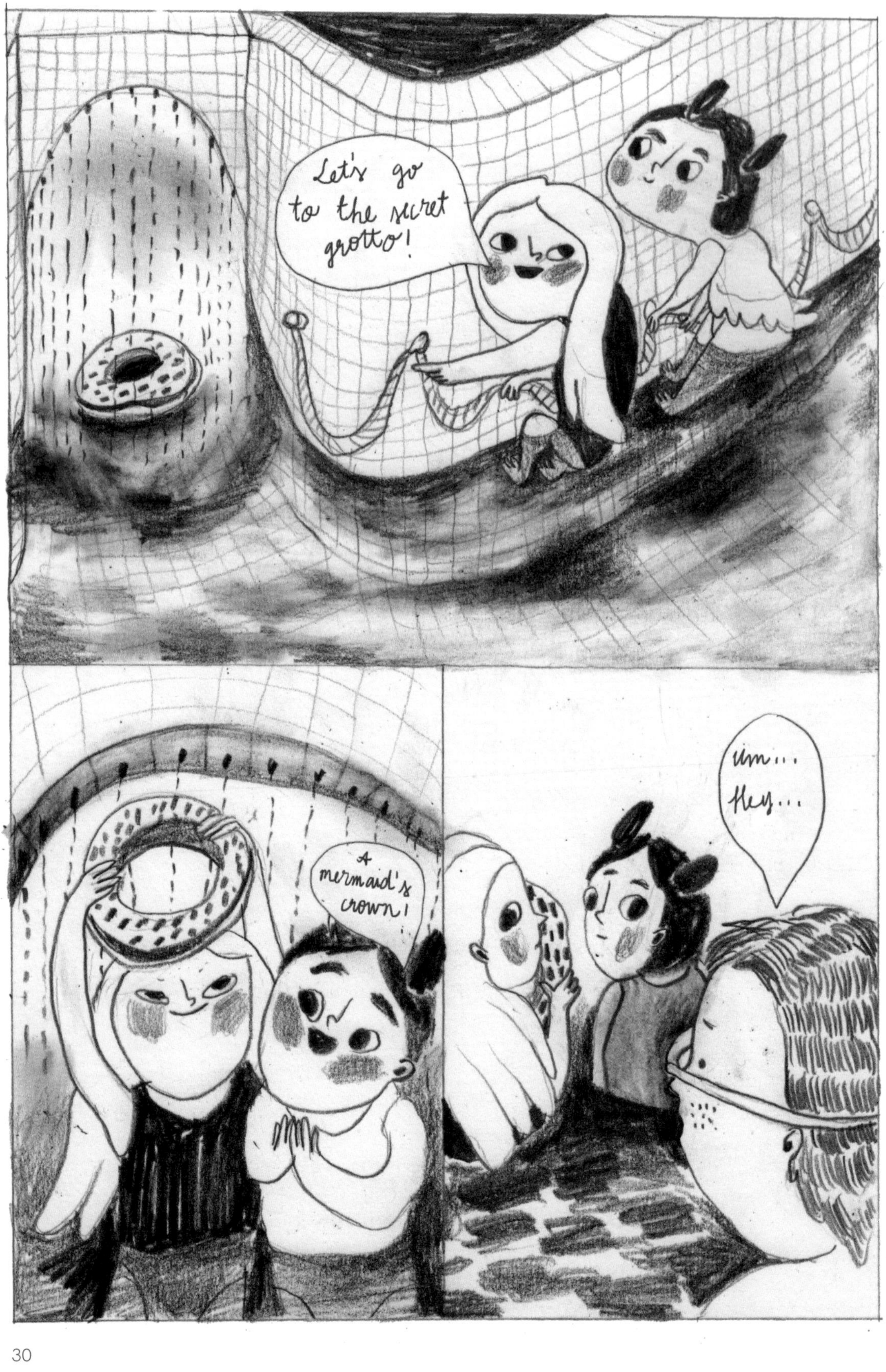

Let's go to the secret grotto!
A mermaid's crown!
um... Hey...

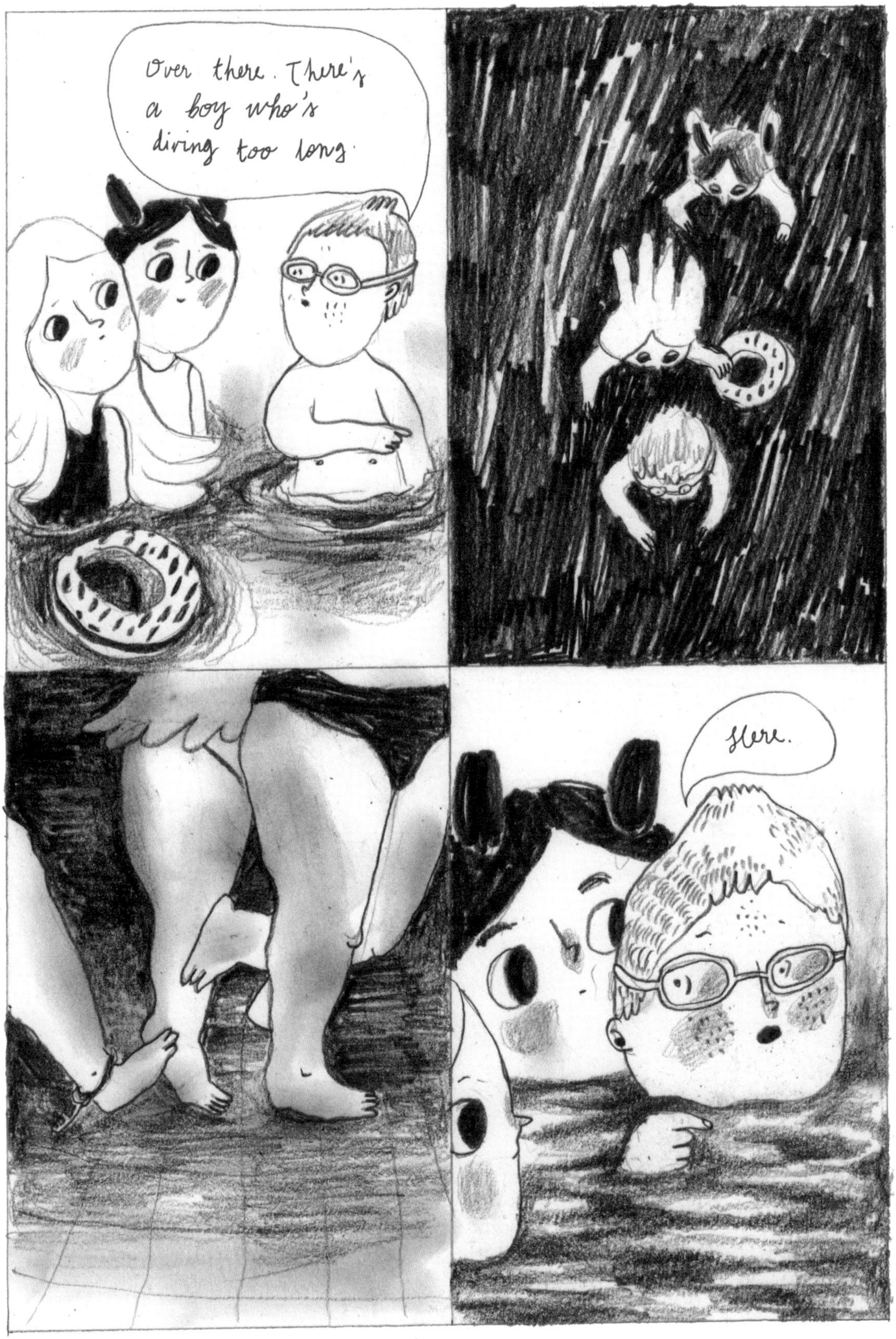
Over there. There's a boy who's diving too long.
Here.

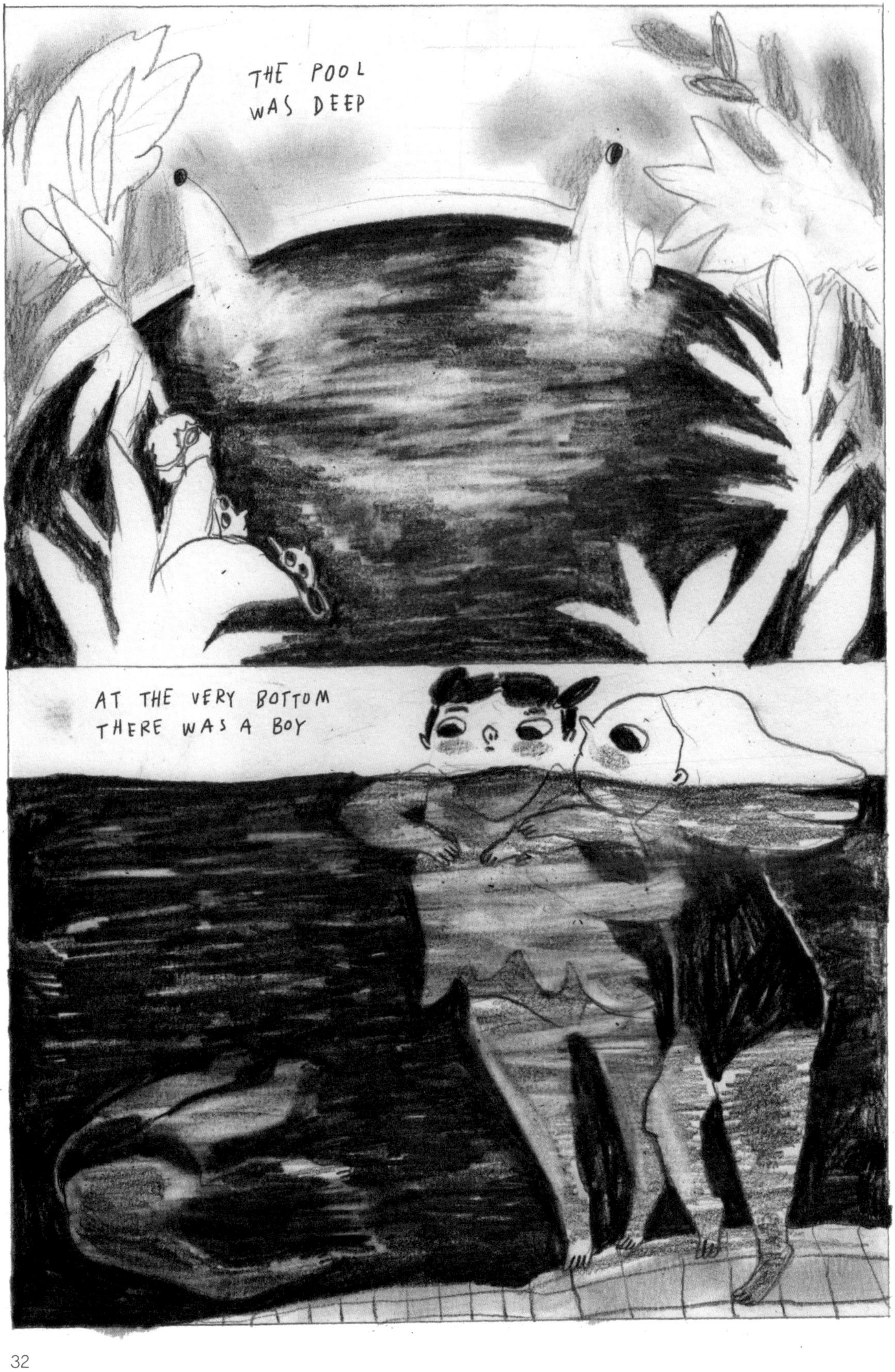
THE POOL
WAS DEEP
AT THE VERY BOTTOM
THERE WAS A BOY

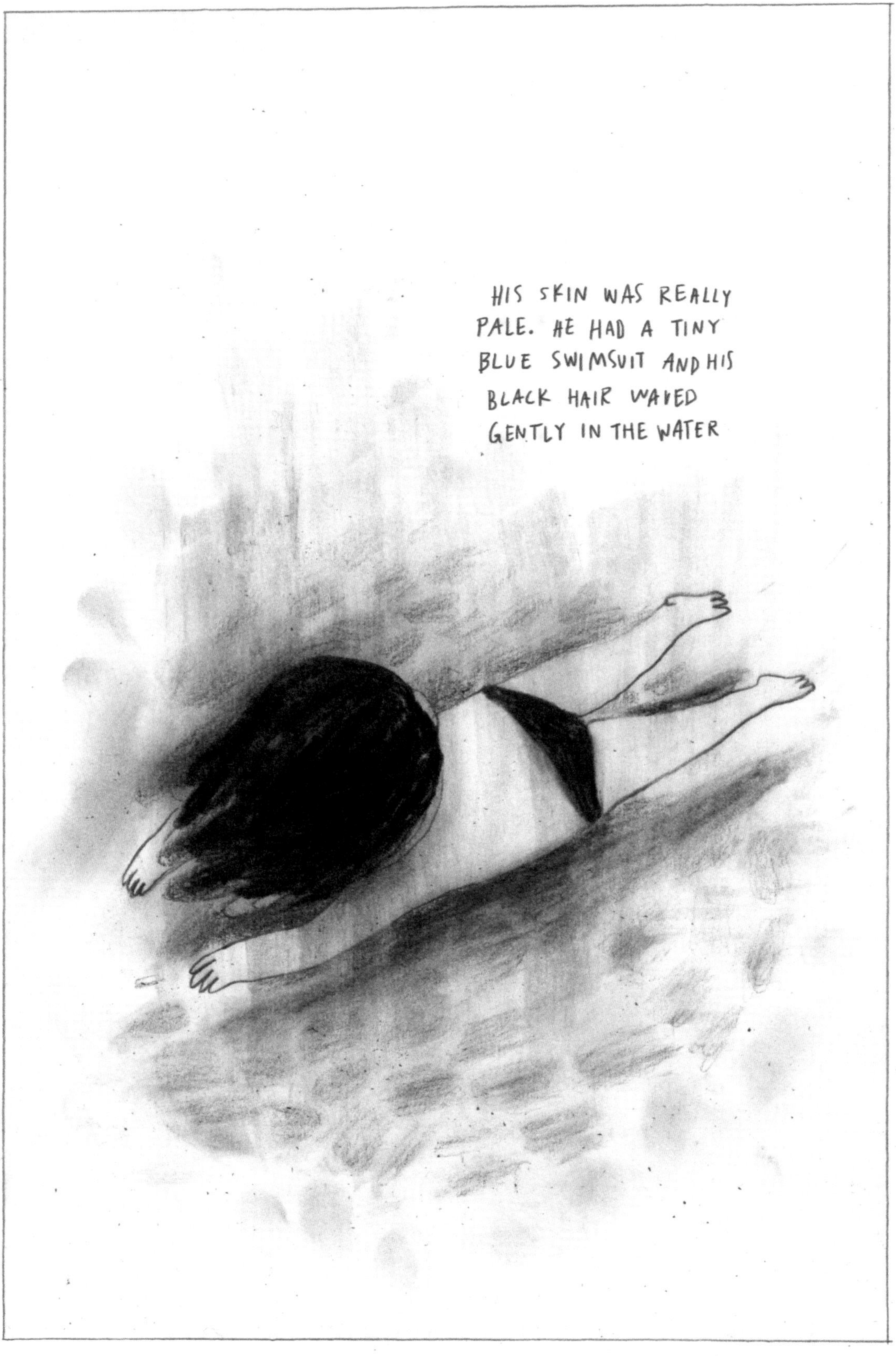
HIS SKIN WAS REALLY PALE. HE HAD A TINY BLUE SWIMSUIT AND HIS BLACK HAIR WAVED GENTLY IN THE WATER

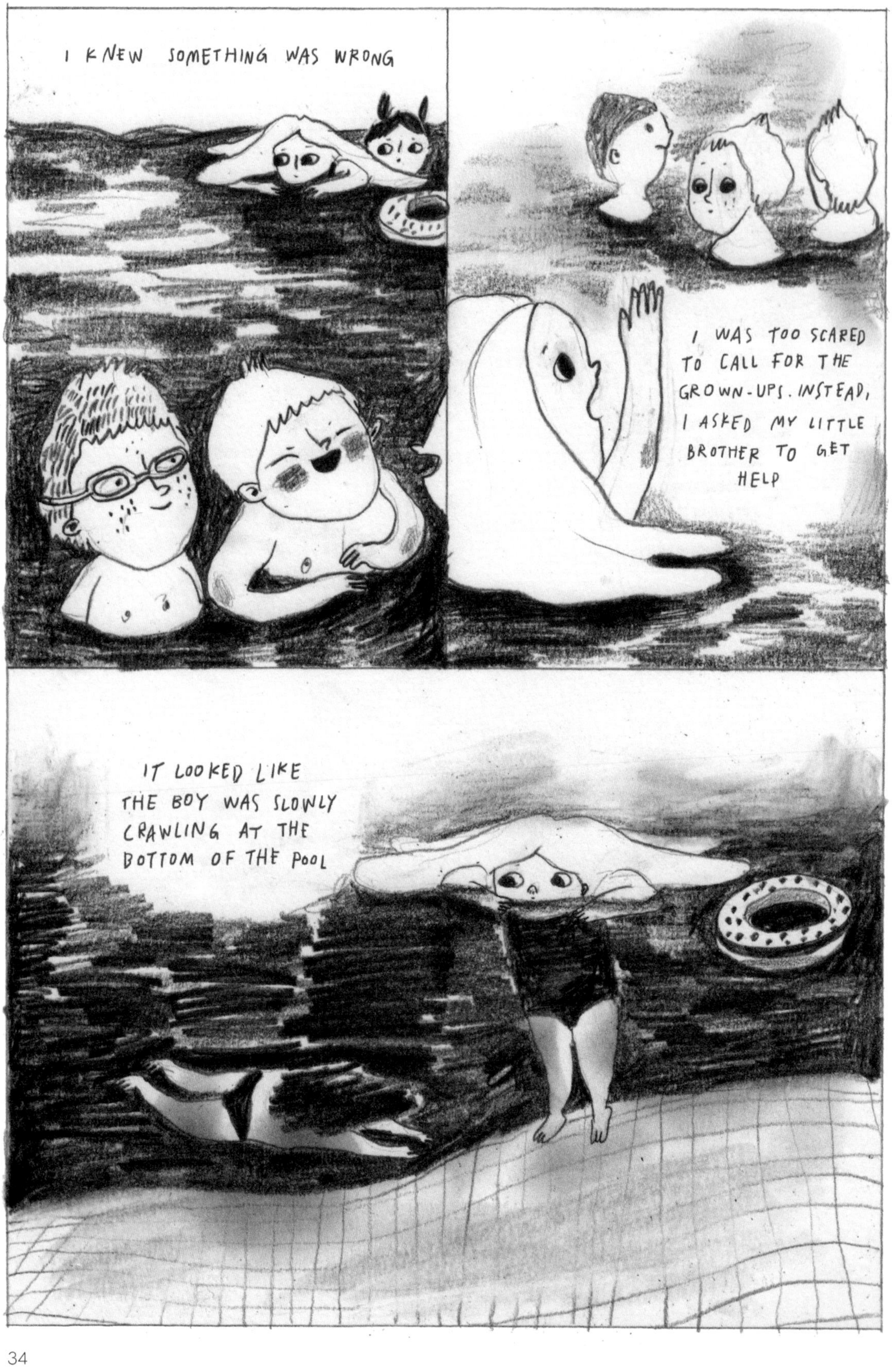
I KNEW SOMETHING WAS WRONG
I WAS TOO SCARED TO CALL FOR THE GROWN-UPS. INSTEAD, I ASKED MY LITTLE BROTHER TO GET HELP
IT LOOKED LIKE THE BOY WAS SLOWLY CRAWLING AT THE BOTTOM OF THE POOL

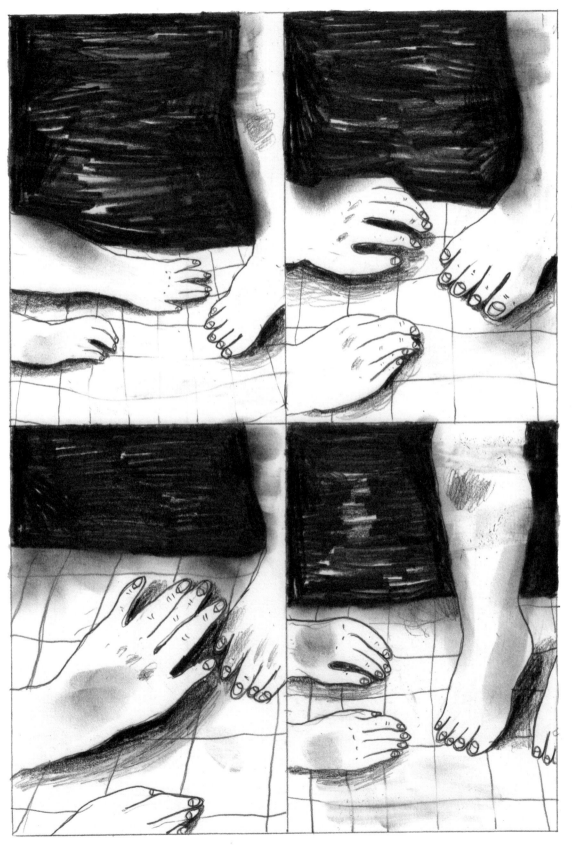

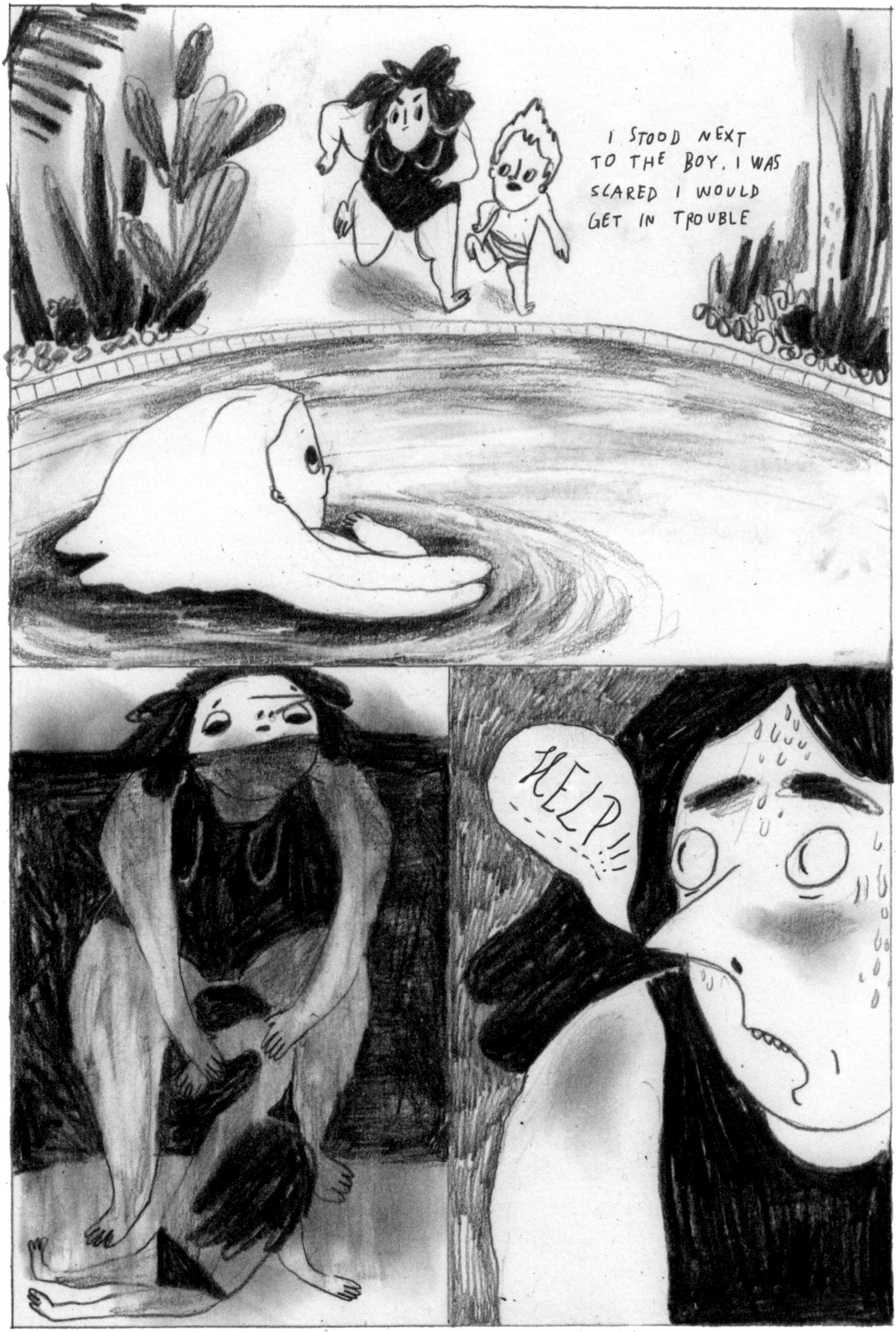
I STOOD NEXT TO THE BOY. I WAS SCARED I WOULD GET IN TROUBLE
HELP!

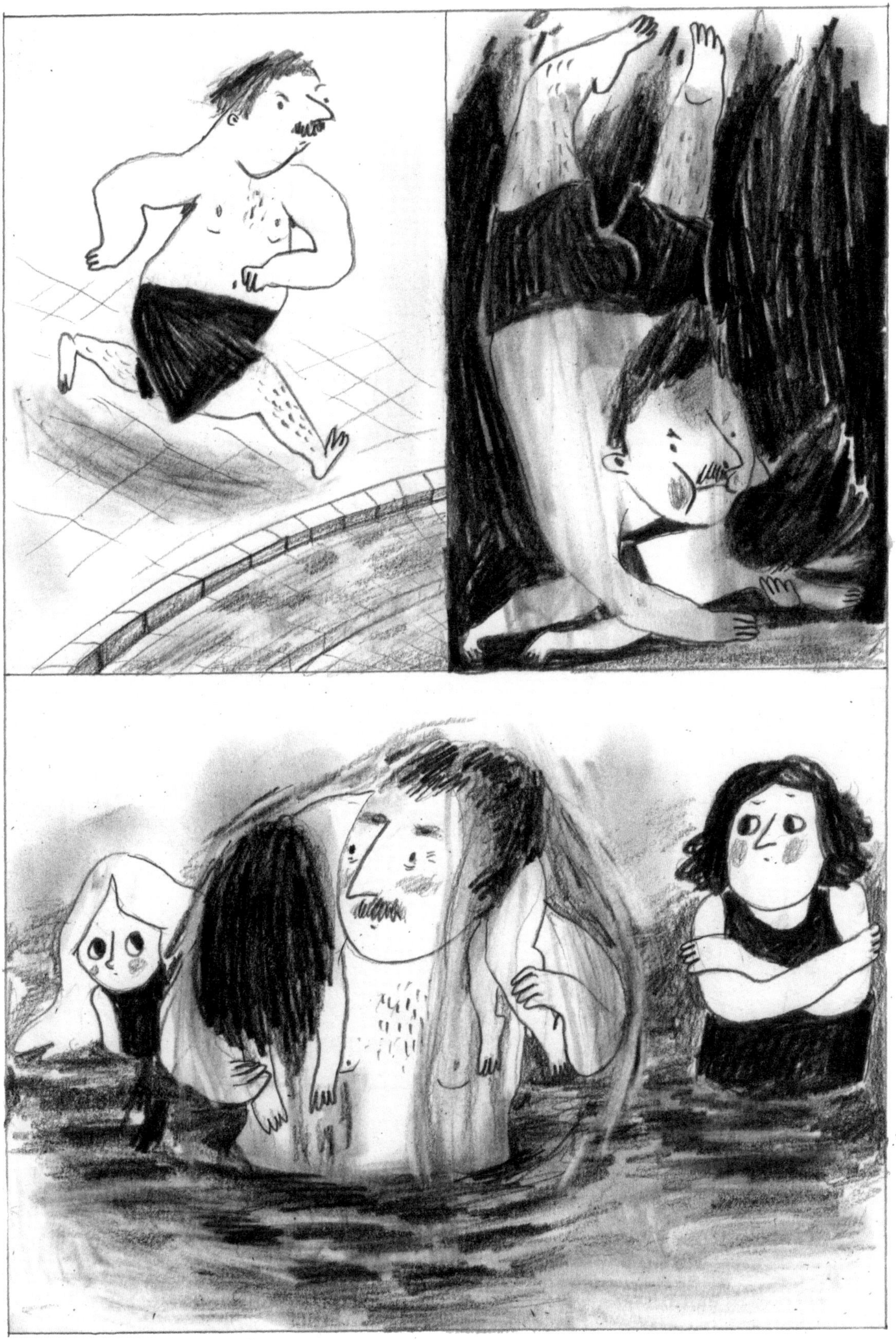

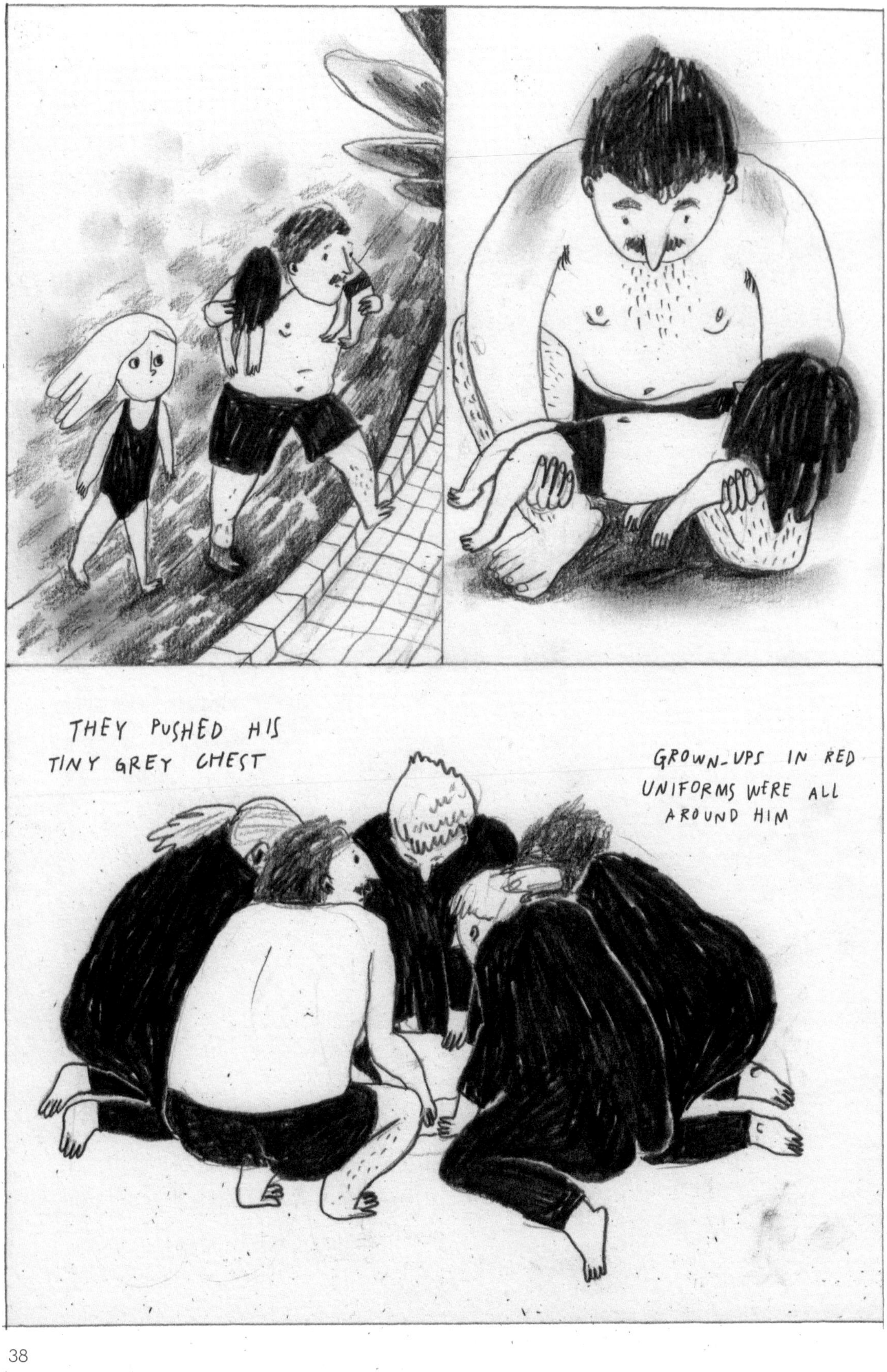
THEY PUSHED HIS TINY GREY CHEST
GROWN-UPS IN RED UNIFORMS WERE ALL AROUND HIM

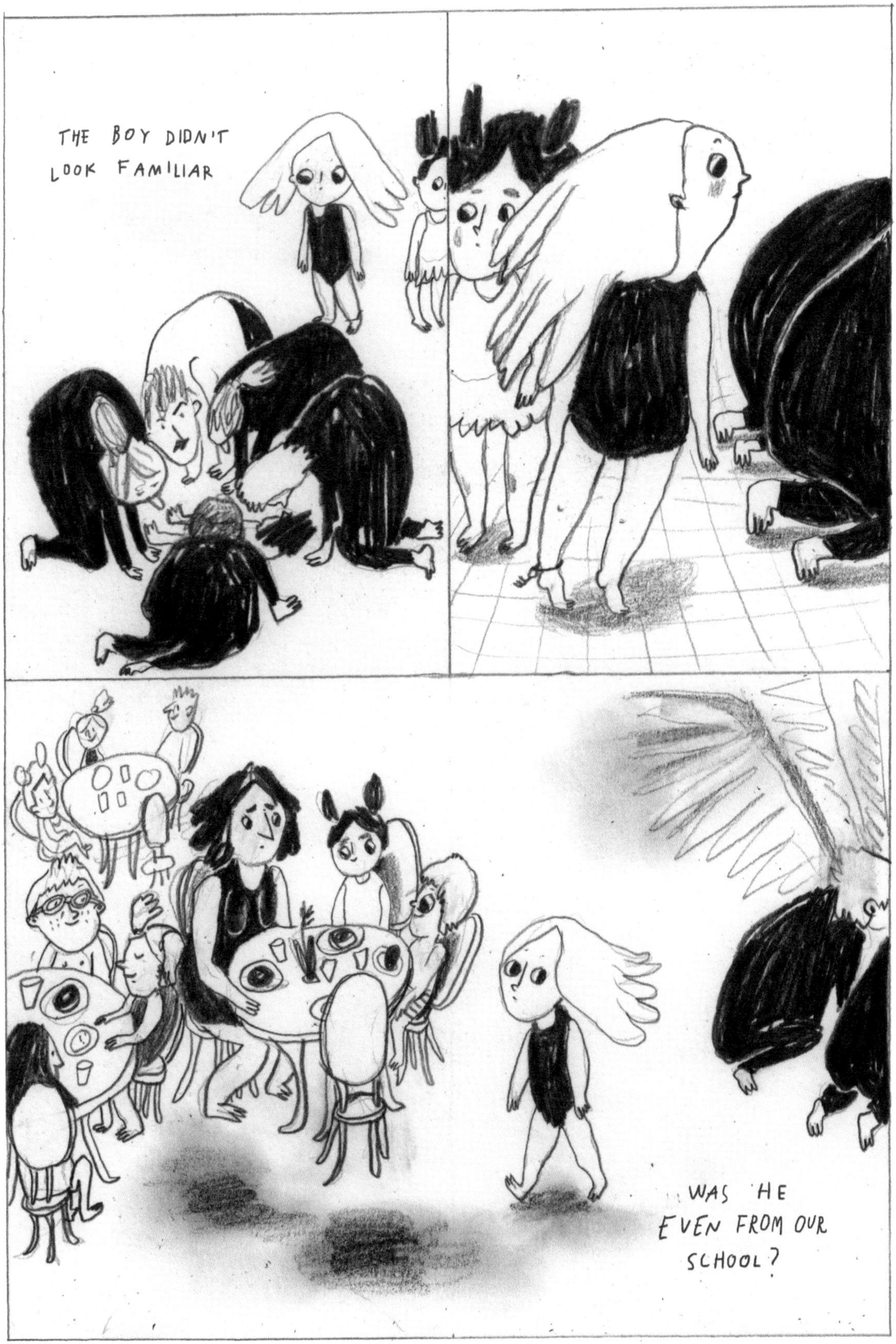
THE BOY DIDN'T LOOK FAMILIAR
WAS HE EVEN FROM OUR SCHOOL?

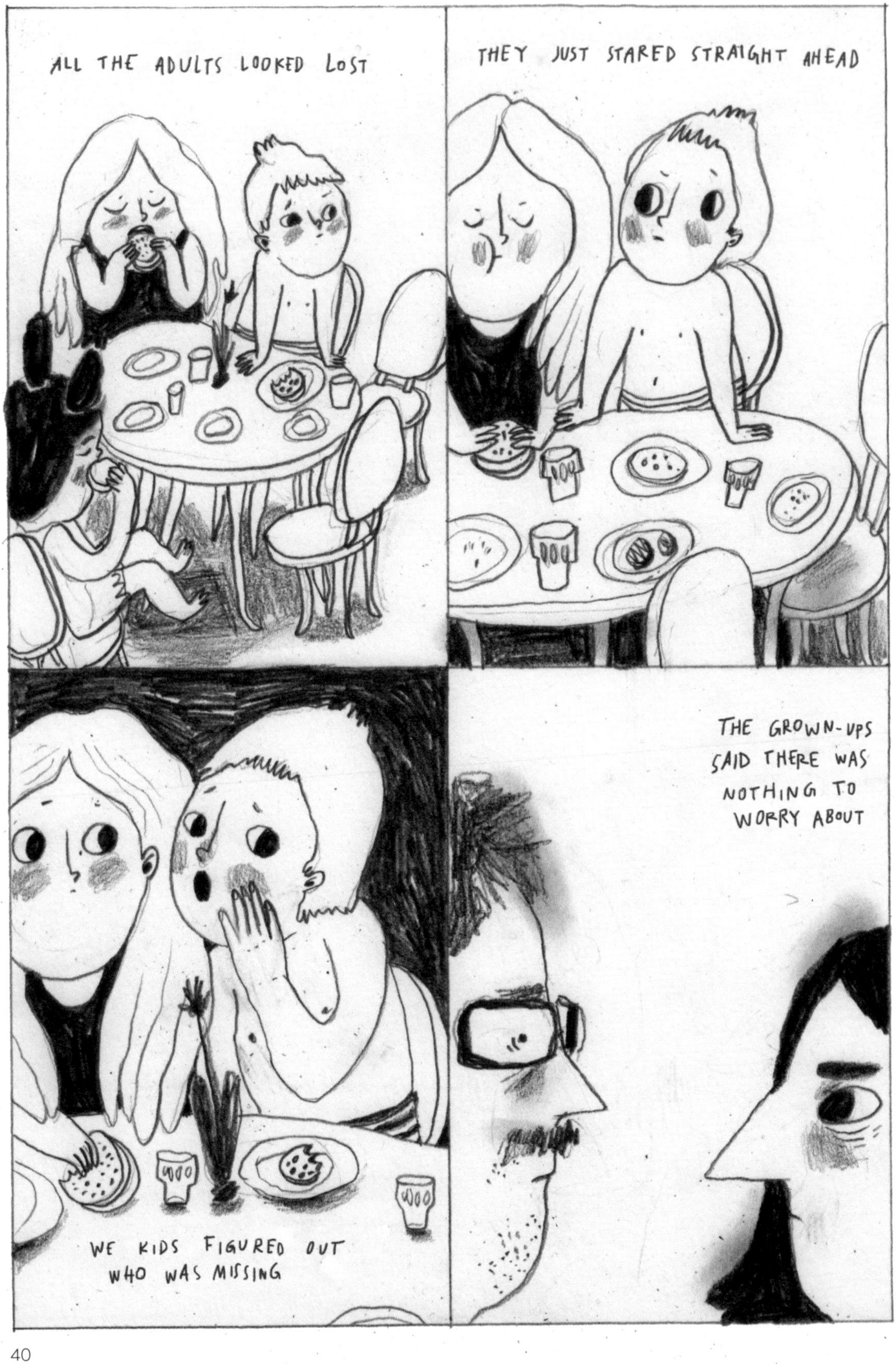
ALL THE ADULTS LOOKED LOST
THEY JUST STARED STRAIGHT AHEAD
WE KIDS FIGURED OUT WHO WAS MISSING
THE GROWN-UPS SAID THERE WAS NOTHING TO WORRY ABOUT

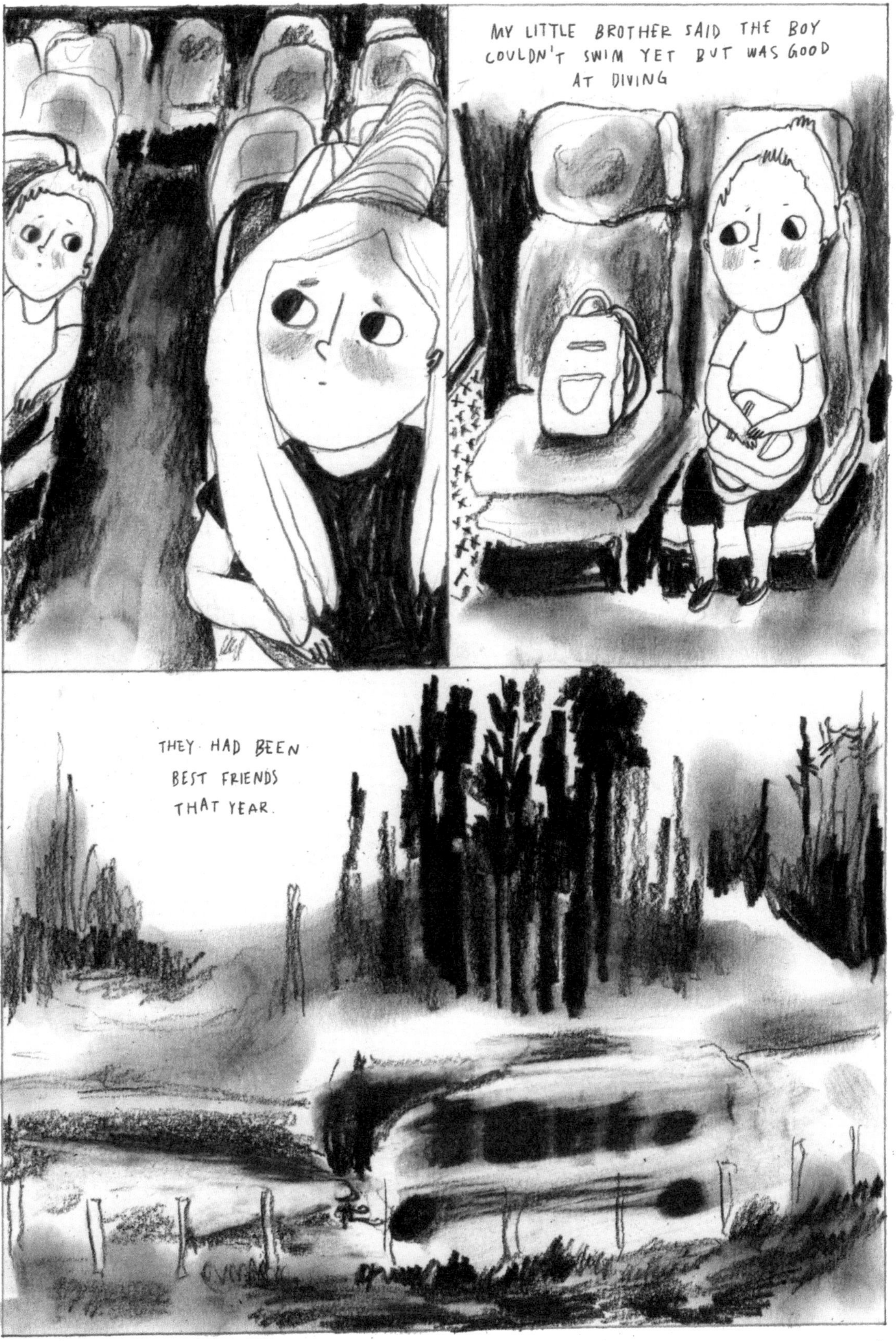
MY LITTLE BROTHER SAID THE BOY COULDN'T SWIM YET BUT WAS GOOD AT DIVING
THEY HAD BEEN BEST FRIENDS THAT YEAR.

WILD ROSES

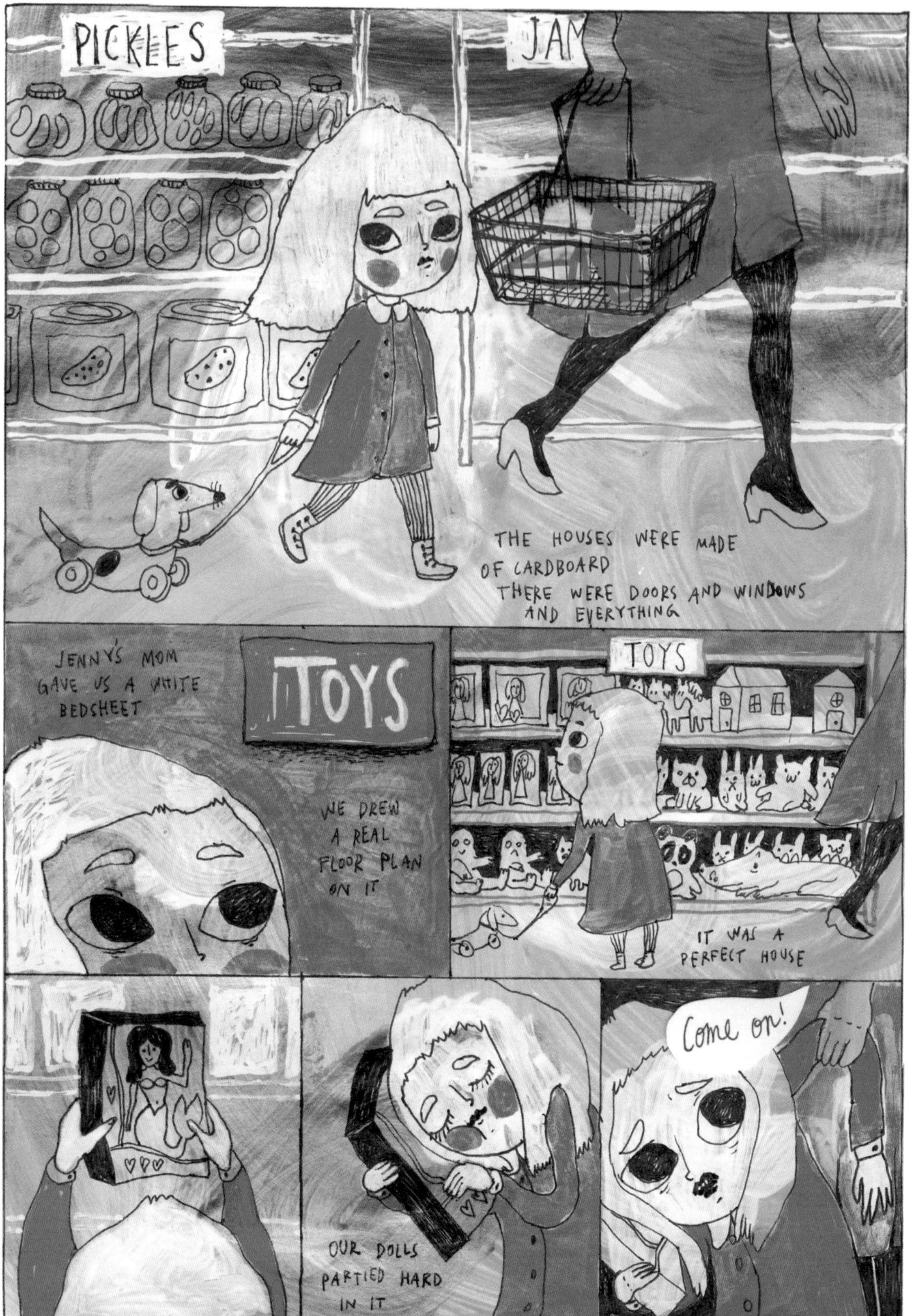
PICKLES
JAM
THE HOUSES WERE MADE OF CARDBOARD
THERE WERE DOORS AND WINDOWS AND EVERYTHING
JENNY'S MOM GAVE US A WHITE BEDSHEET
TOYS
WE DREW A REAL FLOOR PLAN ON IT
TOYS
IT WAS A PERFECT HOUSE
OUR DOLLS PARTIED HARD IN IT
Come on!

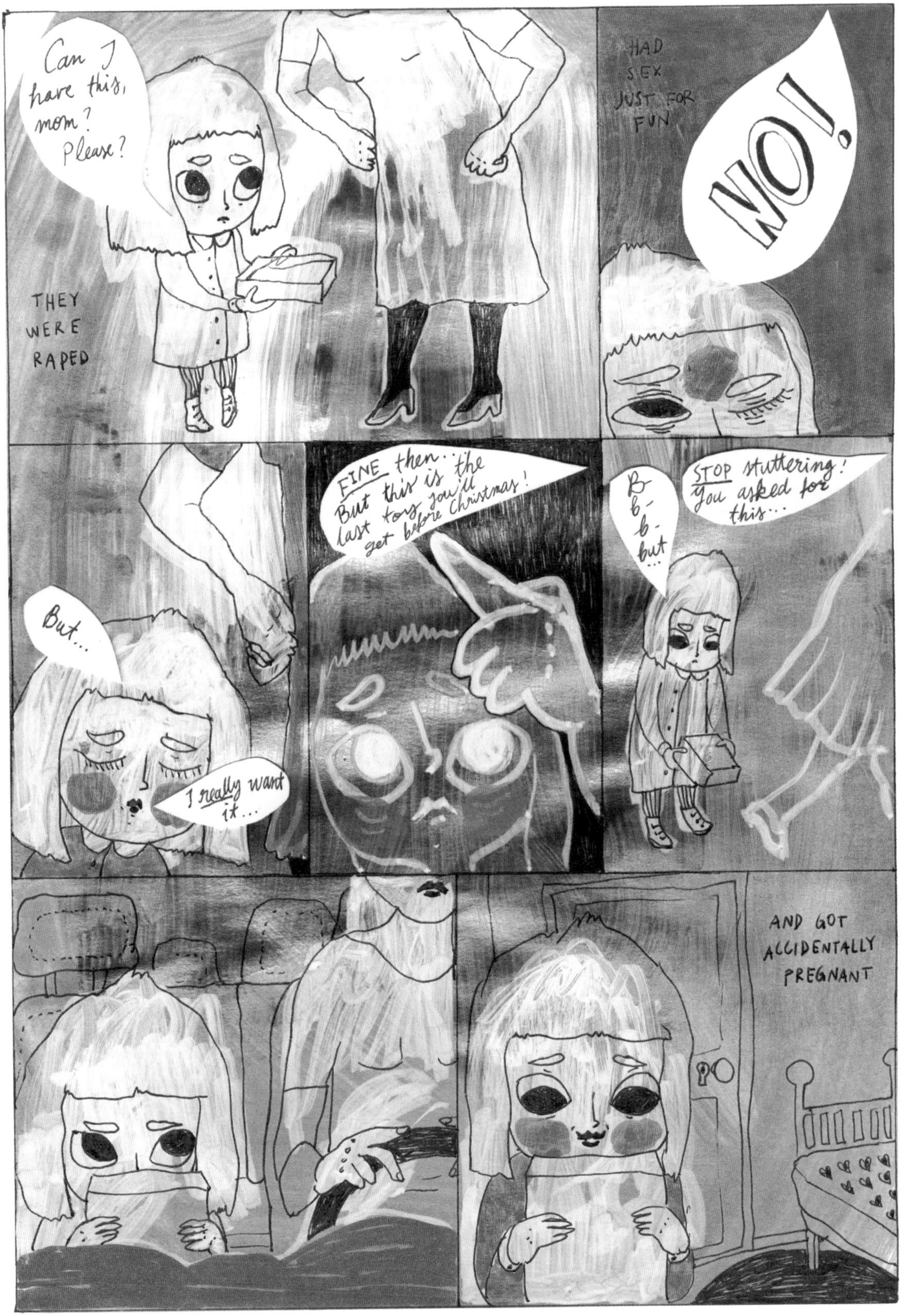
Can I have this, mom? Please?
THEY WERE RAPED
HAD SEX JUST FOR FUN
NO!
But...
I really want it...
FINE then... But this is the last toy you'll get before Christmas!
B- b- b- but...
STOP stuttering! You asked for this...
AND GOT ACCIDENTALLY PREGNANT

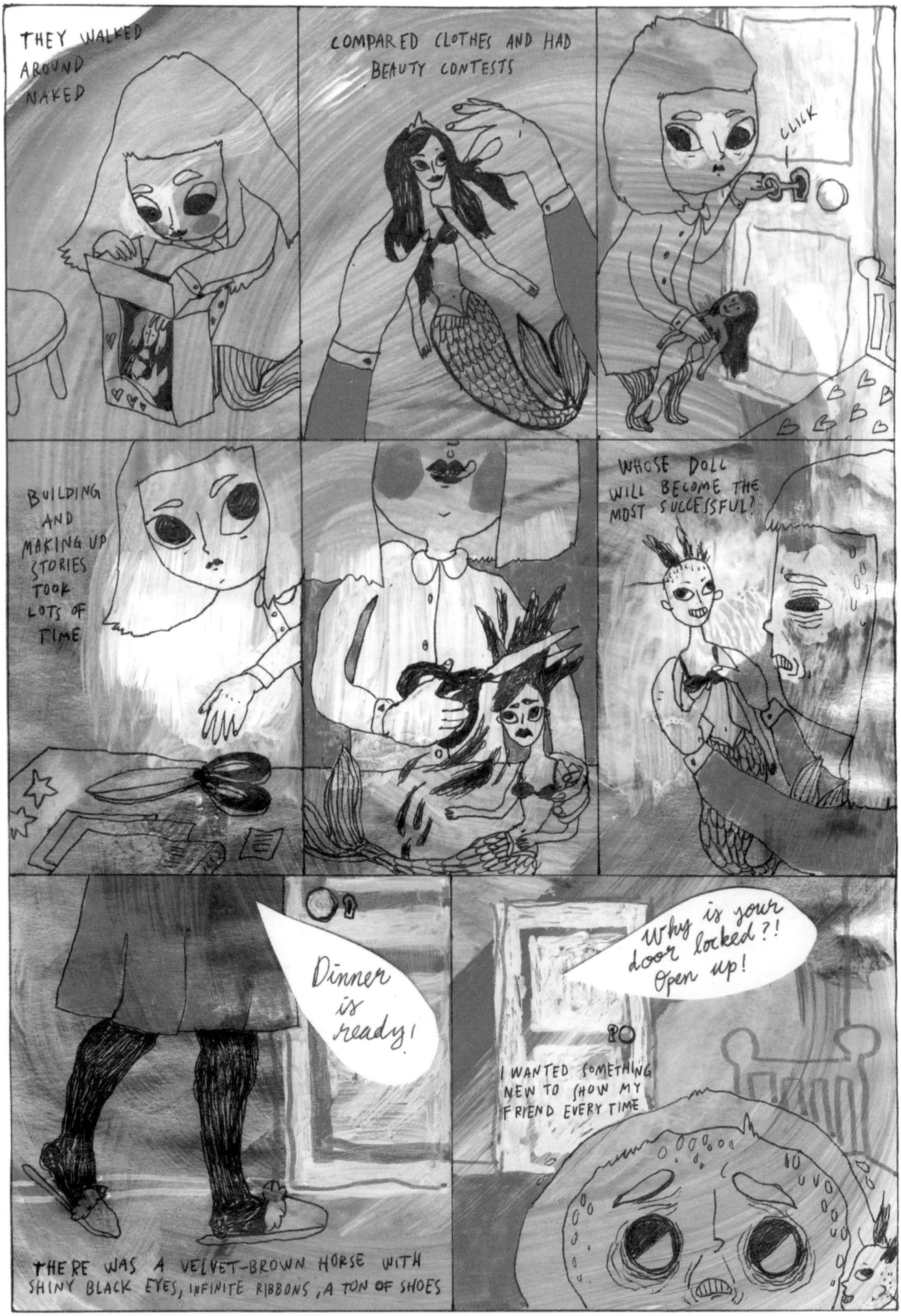
THEY WALKED AROUND NAKED
COMPARED CLOTHES AND HAD BEAUTY CONTESTS
CLICK
BUILDING AND MAKING UP STORIES TOOK LOTS OF TIME
WHOSE DOLL WILL BECOME THE MOST SUCCESSFUL?
Dinner is ready!
THERE WAS A VELVET-BROWN HORSE WITH SHINY BLACK EYES, INFINITE RIBBONS, A TON OF SHOES
Why is your door locked?! Open up!
I WANTED SOMETHING NEW TO SHOW MY FRIEND EVERY TIME

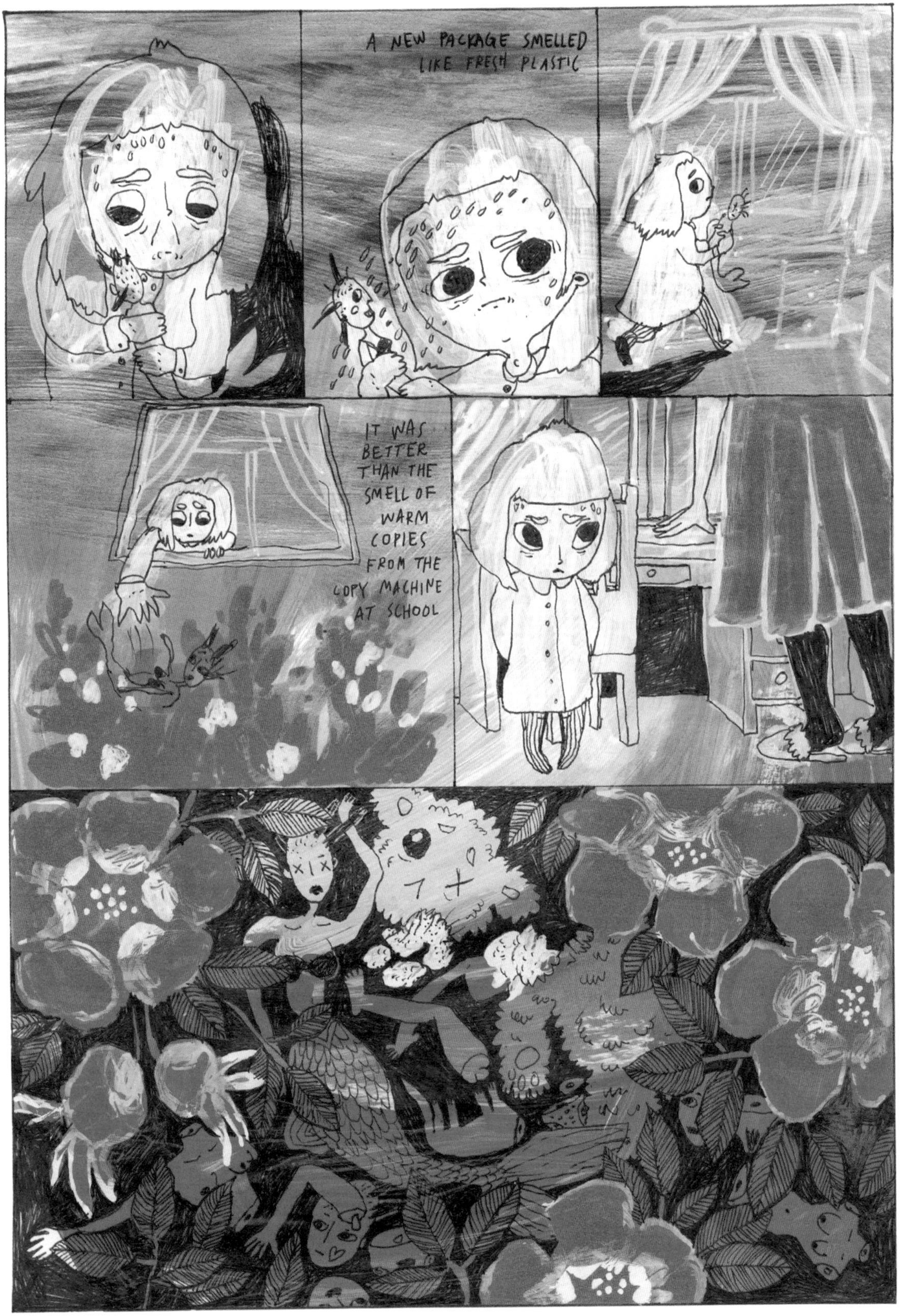
A NEW PACKAGE SMELLED LIKE FRESH PLASTIC
IT WAS BETTER THAN THE SMELL OF WARM COPIES FROM THE COPY MACHINE AT SCHOOL

THE
SLEEPOVER

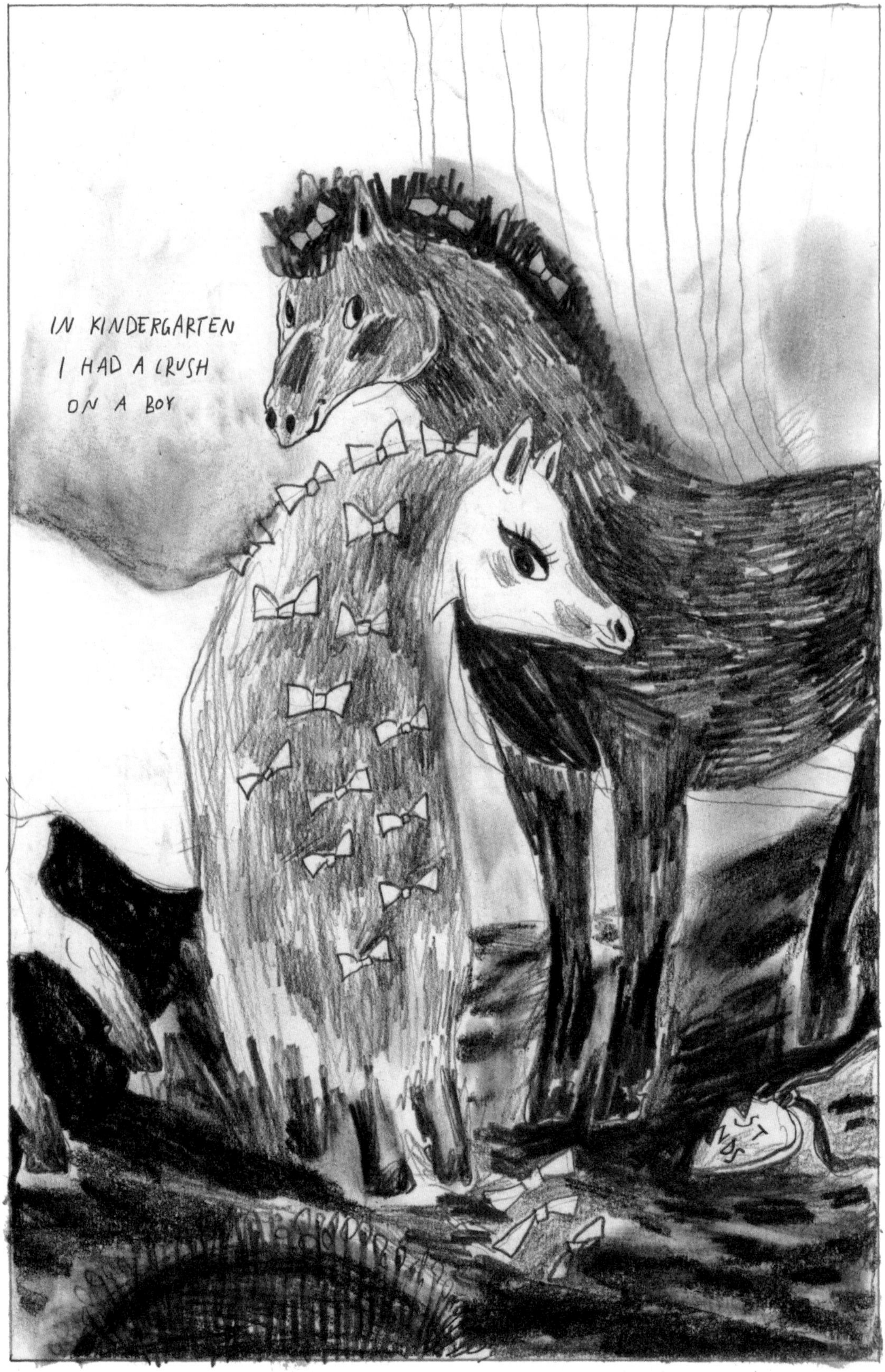
IN KINDERGARTEN
I HAD A CRUSH
ON A BOY

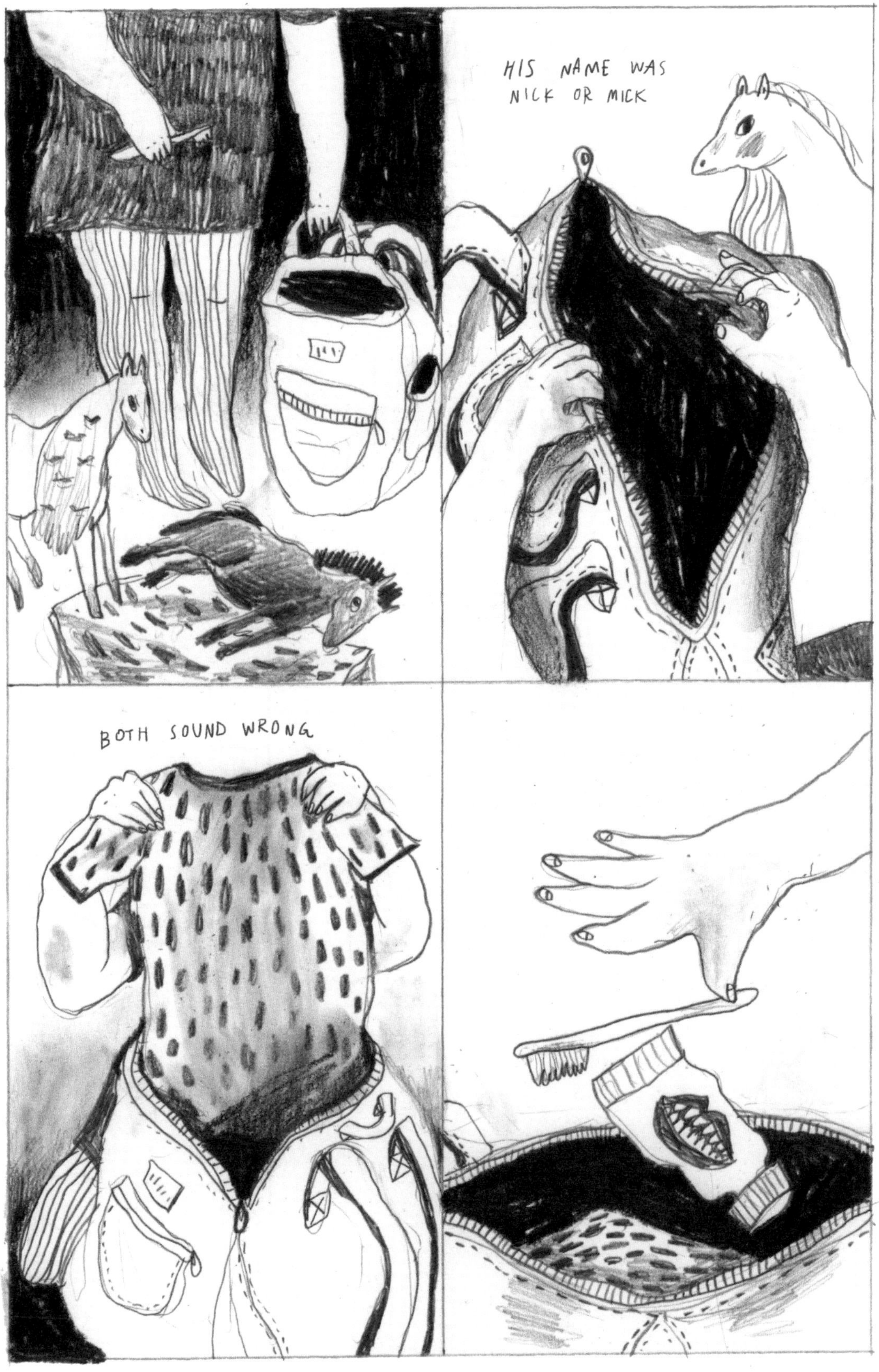
HIS NAME WAS
NICK OR MICK
BOTH SOUND WRONG

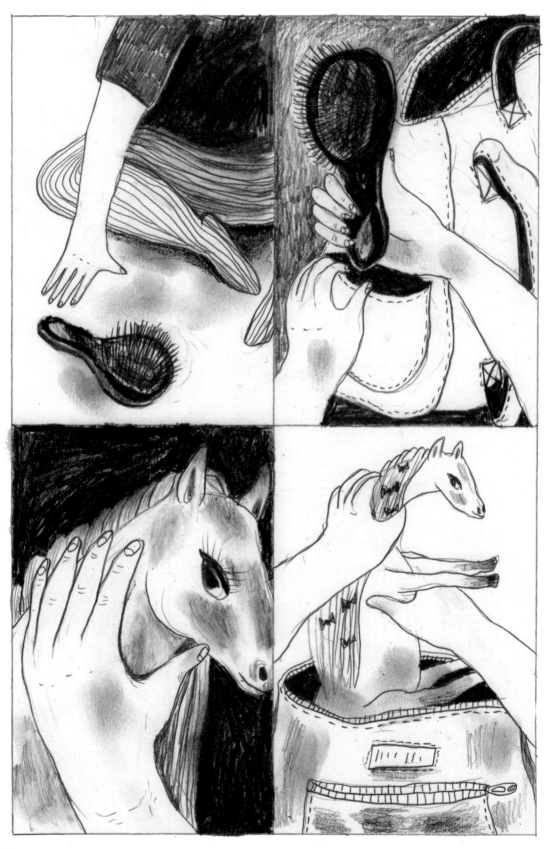

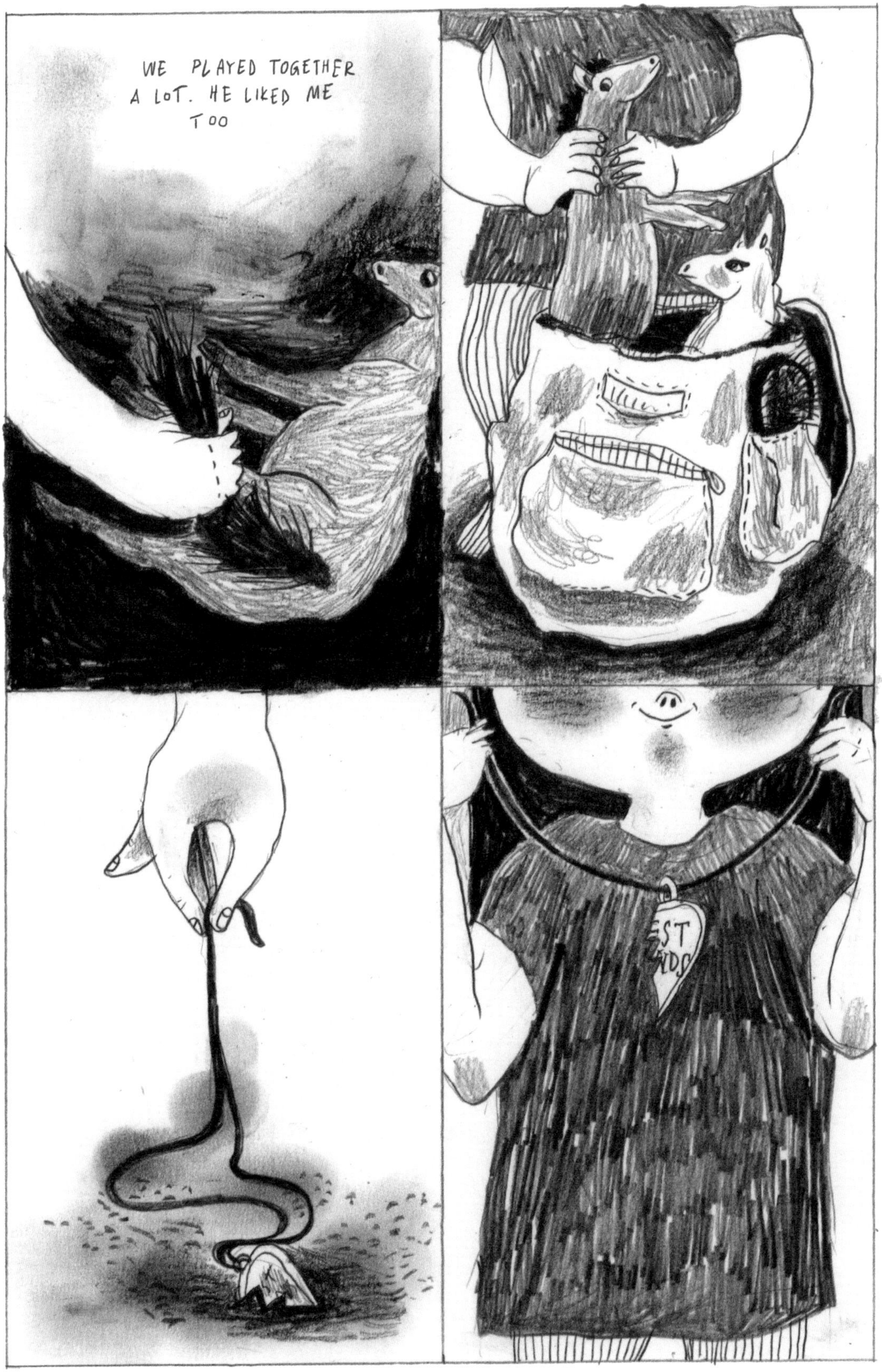
WE PLAYED TOGETHER
A LOT. HE LIKED ME
TOO

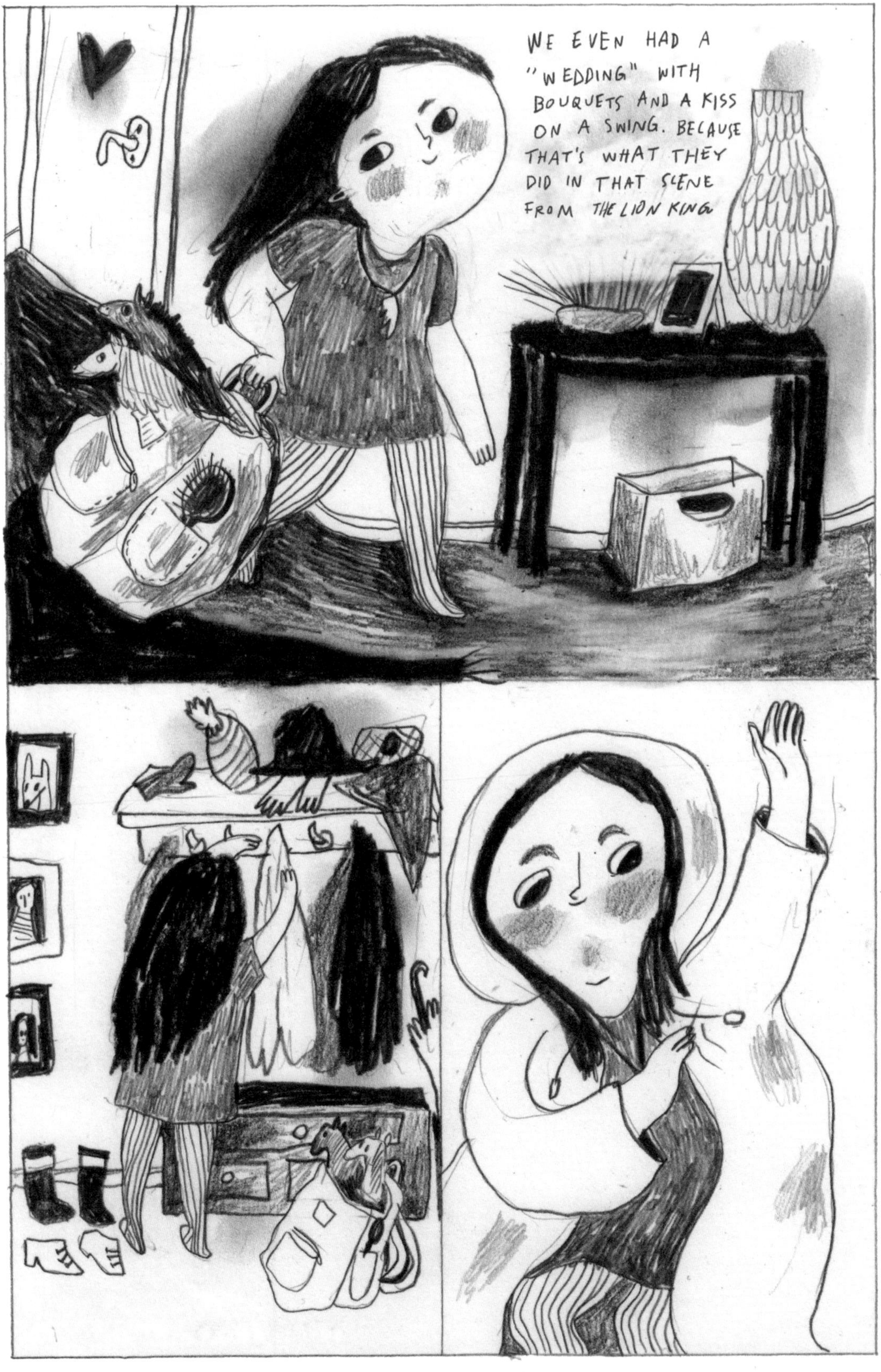
WE EVEN HAD A "WEDDING" WITH BOUQUETS AND A KISS ON A SWING. BECAUSE THAT'S WHAT THEY DID IN THAT SCENE FROM THE LION KING

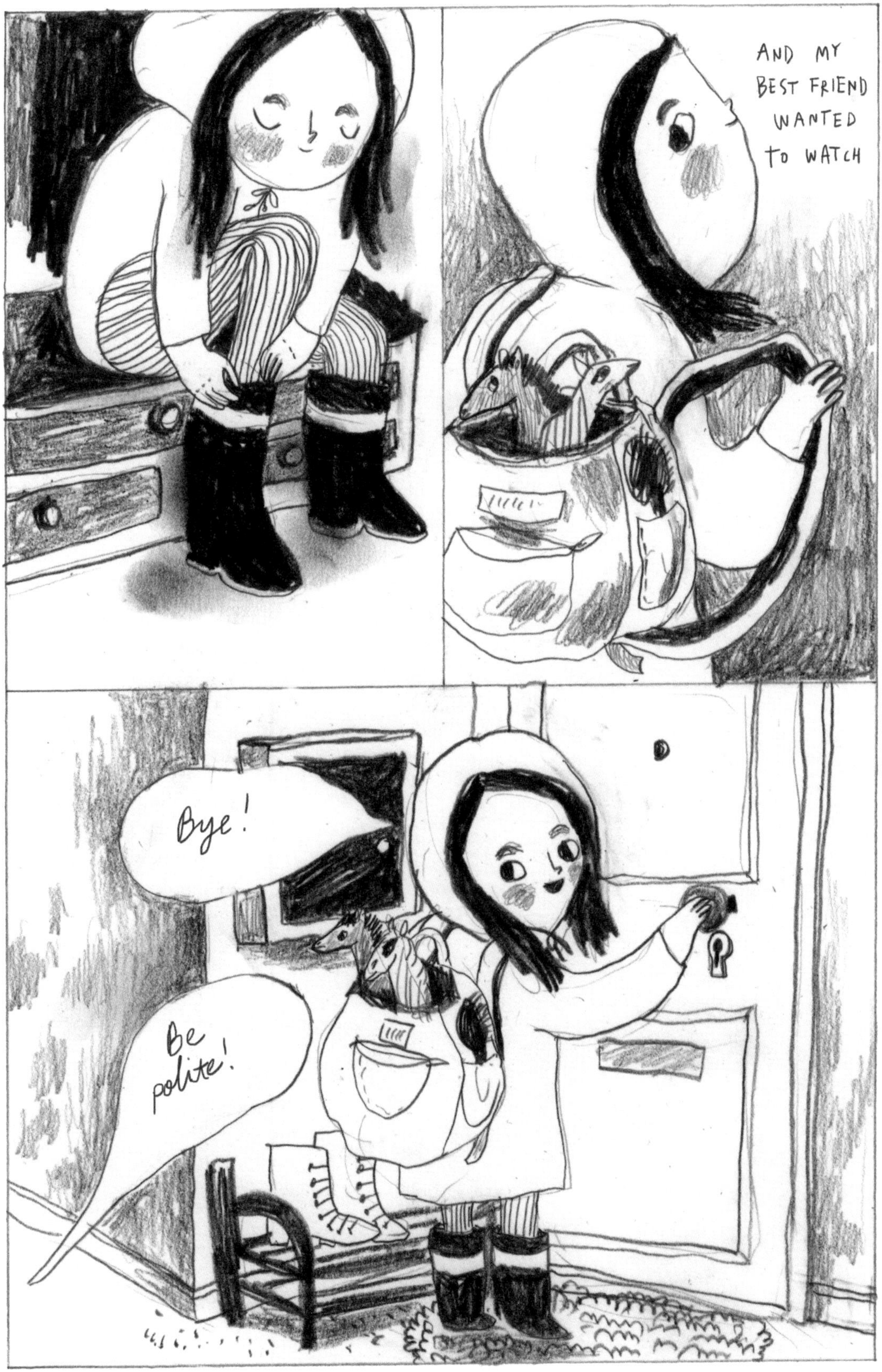
AND MY BEST FRIEND WANTED TO WATCH
Bye!
Be polite!

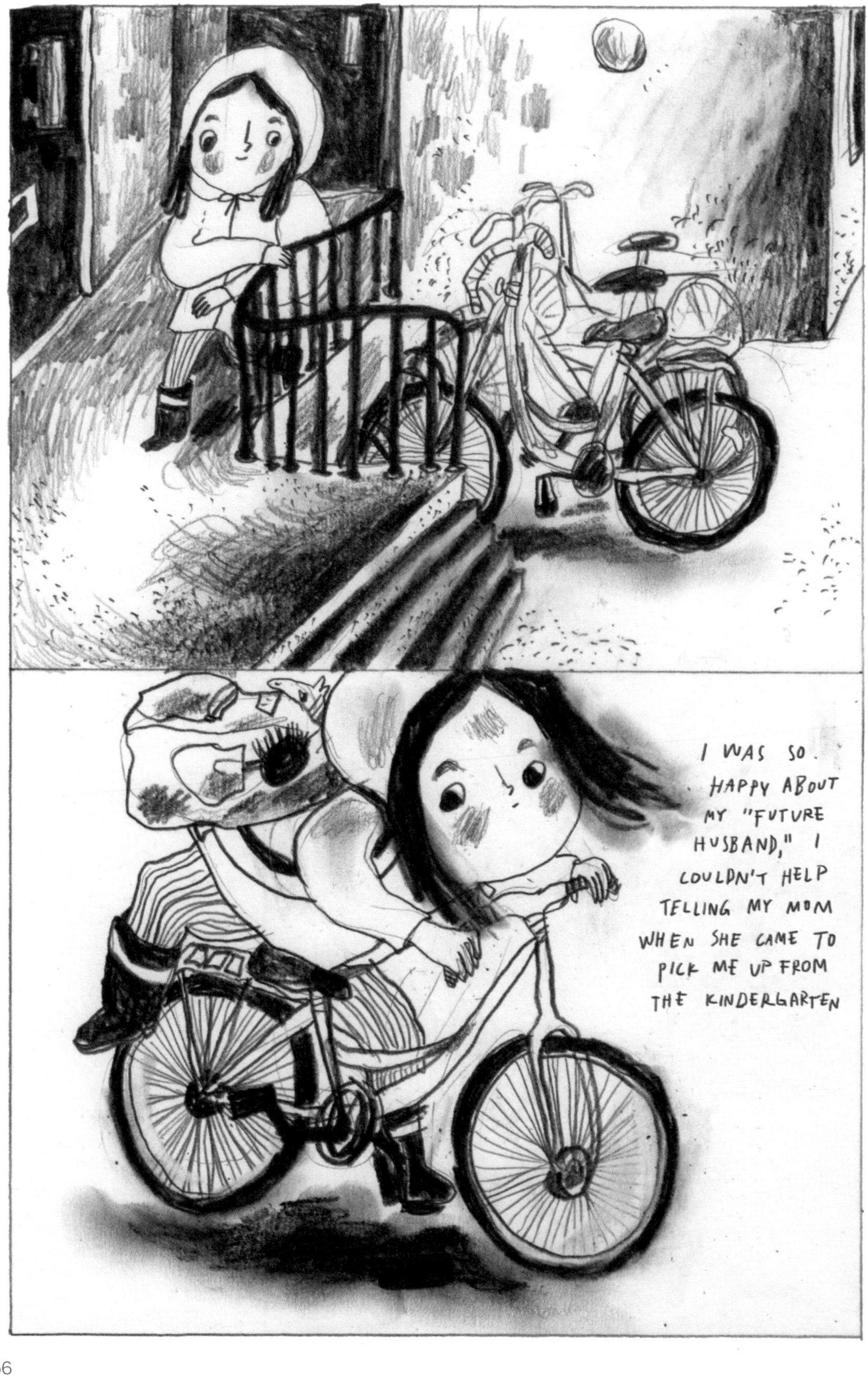
I WAS SO HAPPY ABOUT MY "FUTURE HUSBAND," I COULDN'T HELP TELLING MY MOM WHEN SHE CAME TO PICK ME UP FROM THE KINDERGARTEN

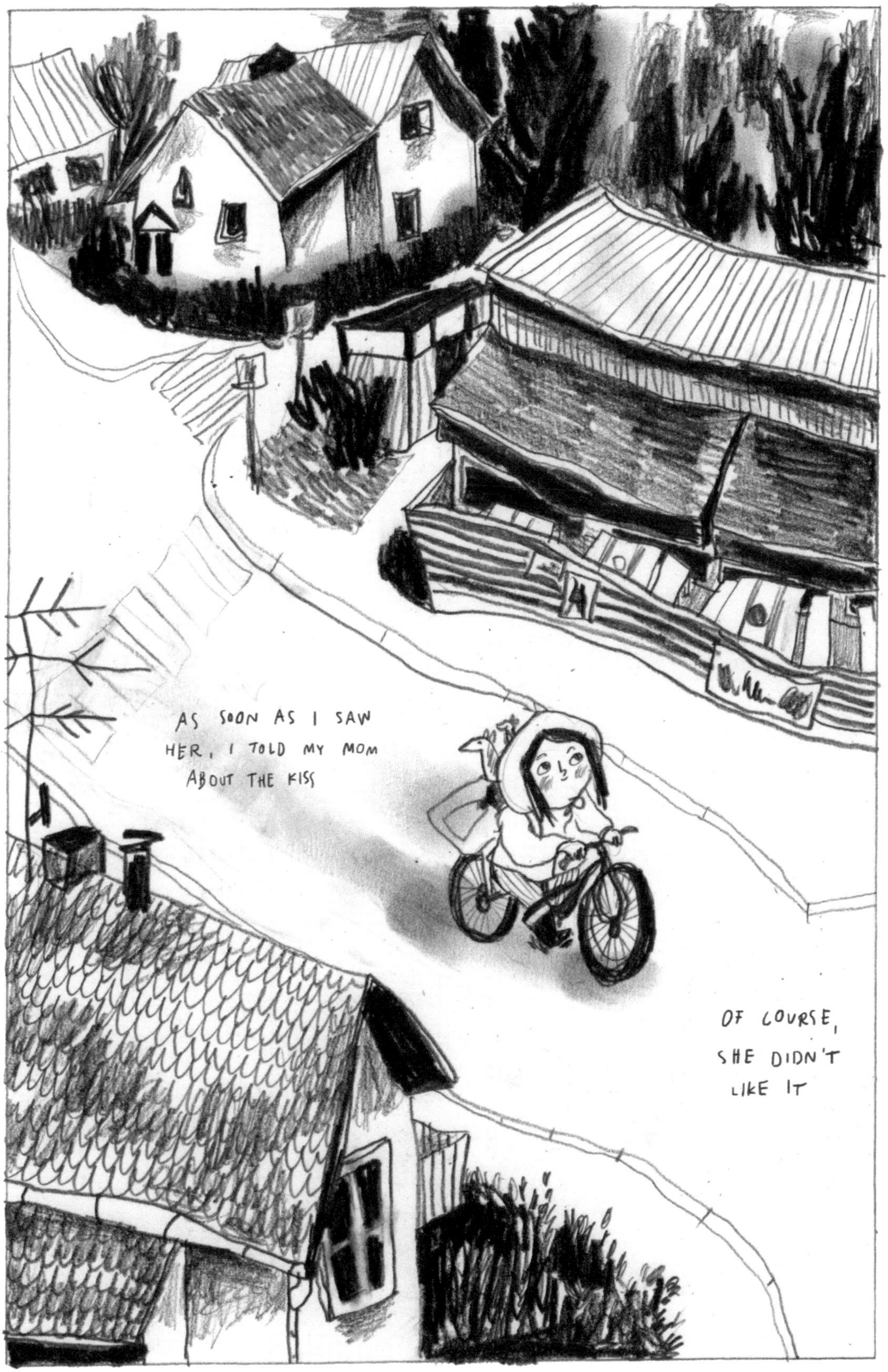
AS SOON AS I SAW HER, I TOLD MY MOM ABOUT THE KISS
OF COURSE, SHE DIDN'T LIKE IT

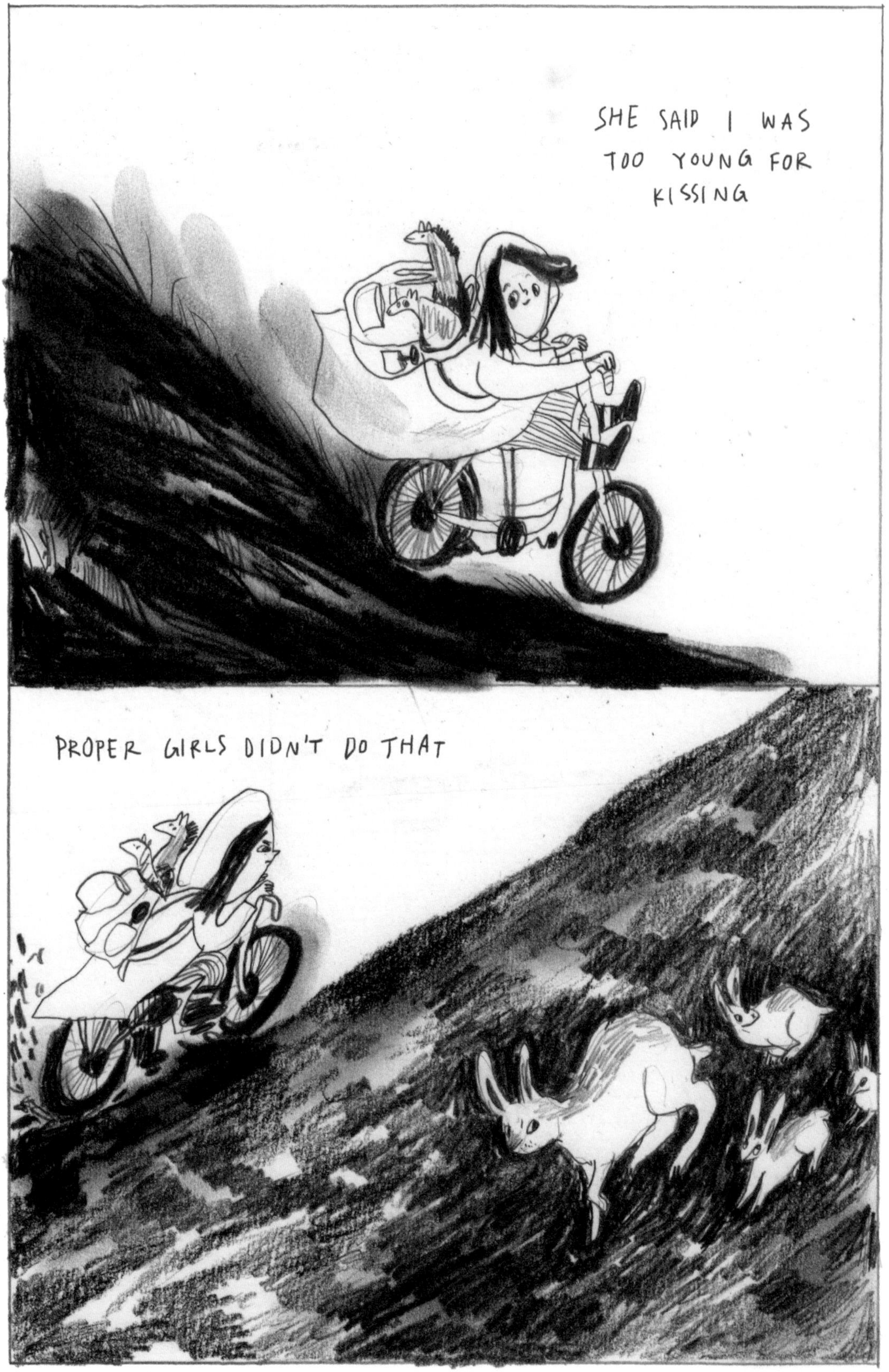
SHE SAID I WAS TOO YOUNG FOR KISSING
PROPER GIRLS DIDN'T DO THAT

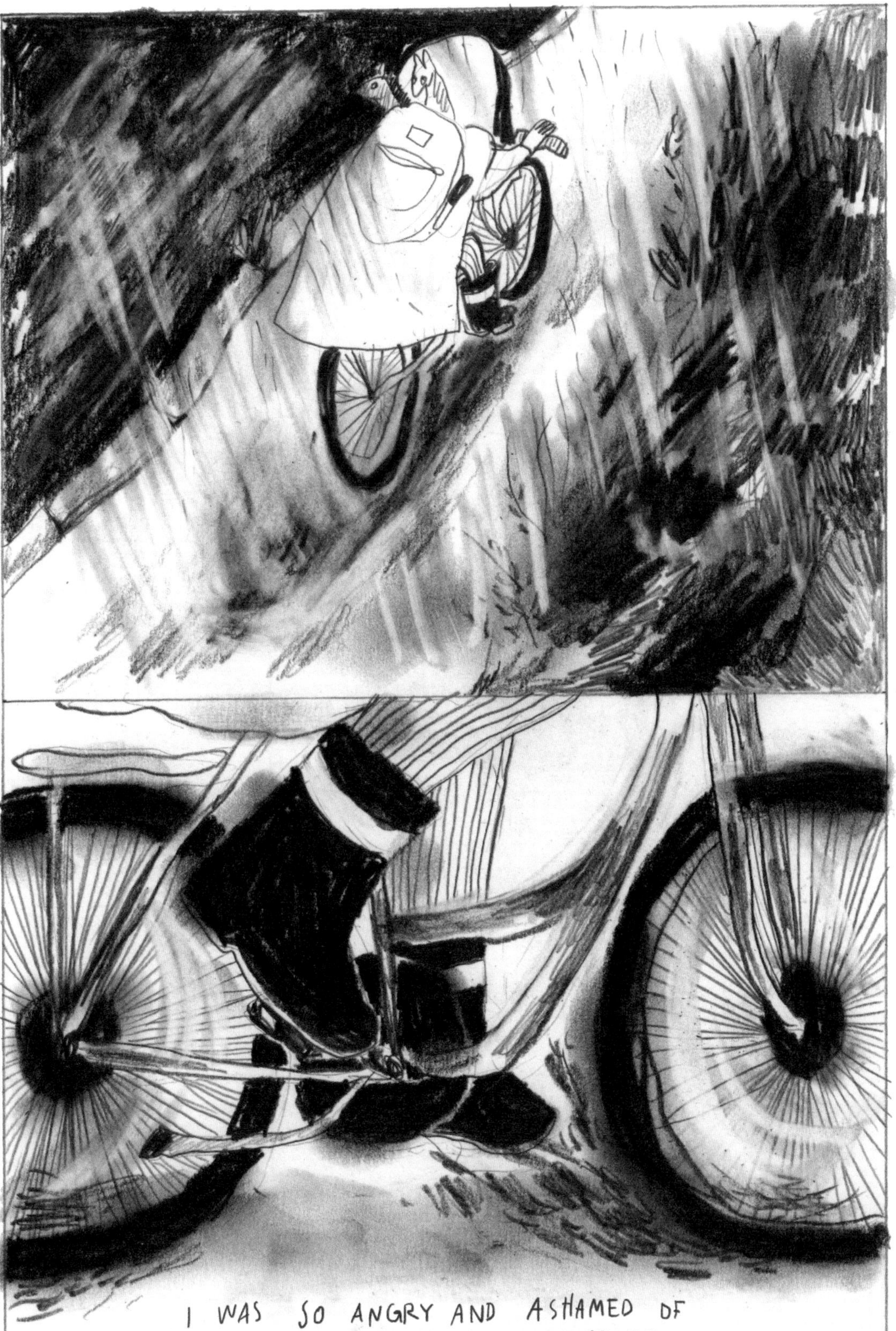
I WAS SO ANGRY AND ASHAMED OF
MYSELF FOR BLURTING OUT MY SECRET

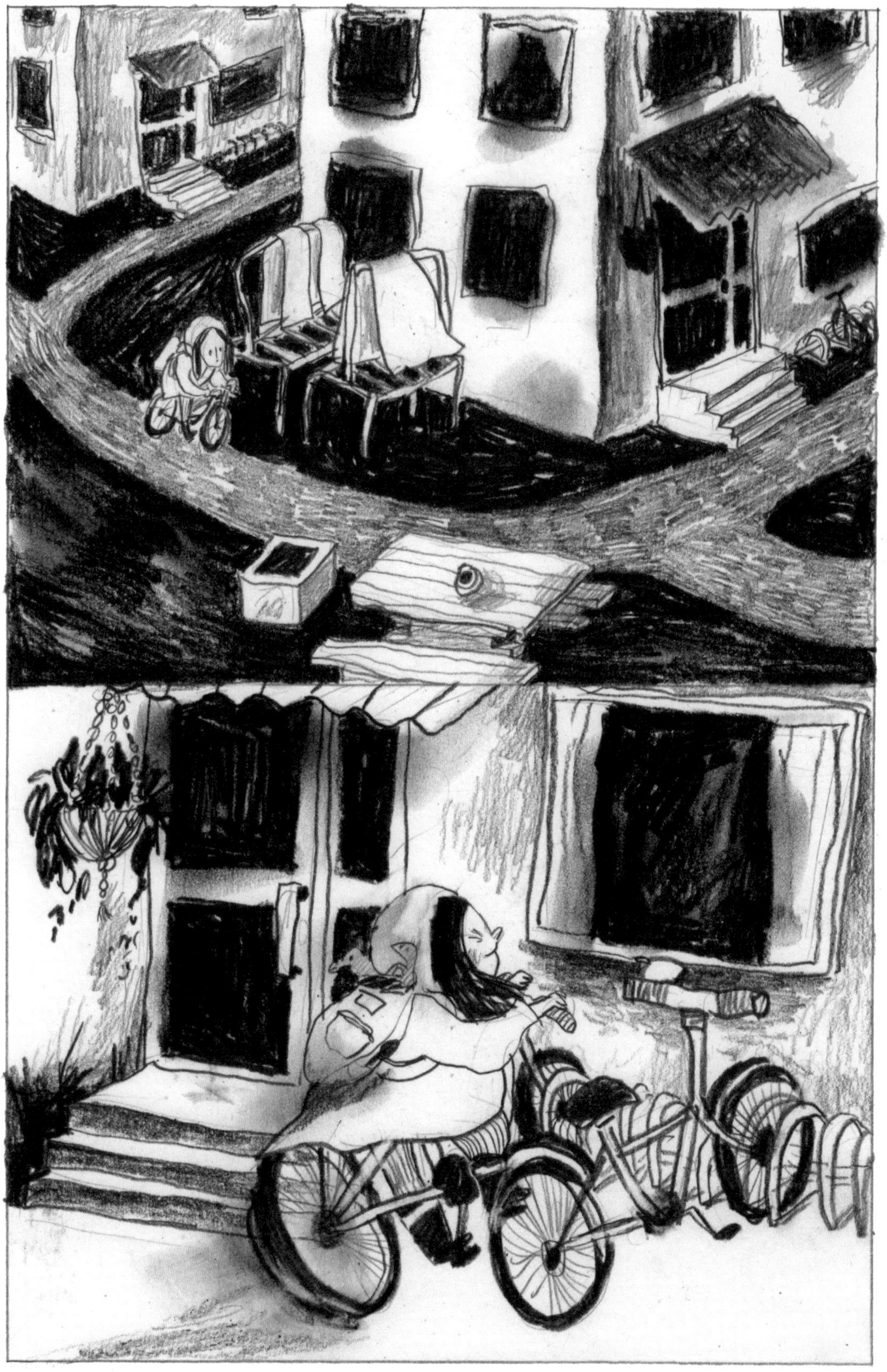

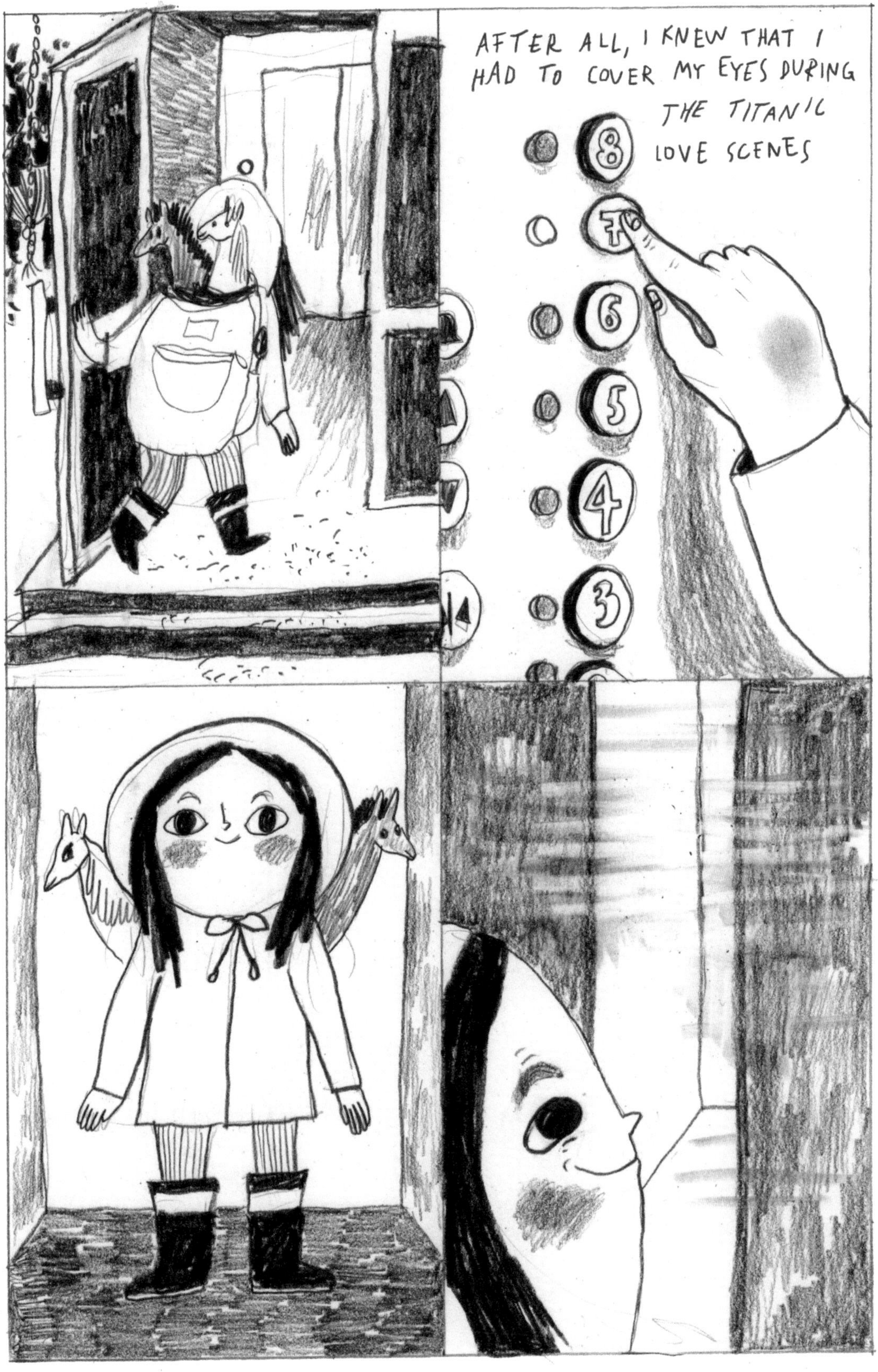
AFTER ALL, I KNEW THAT I HAD TO COVER MY EYES DURING THE TITANIC LOVE SCENES
8
7
6
5
4
3

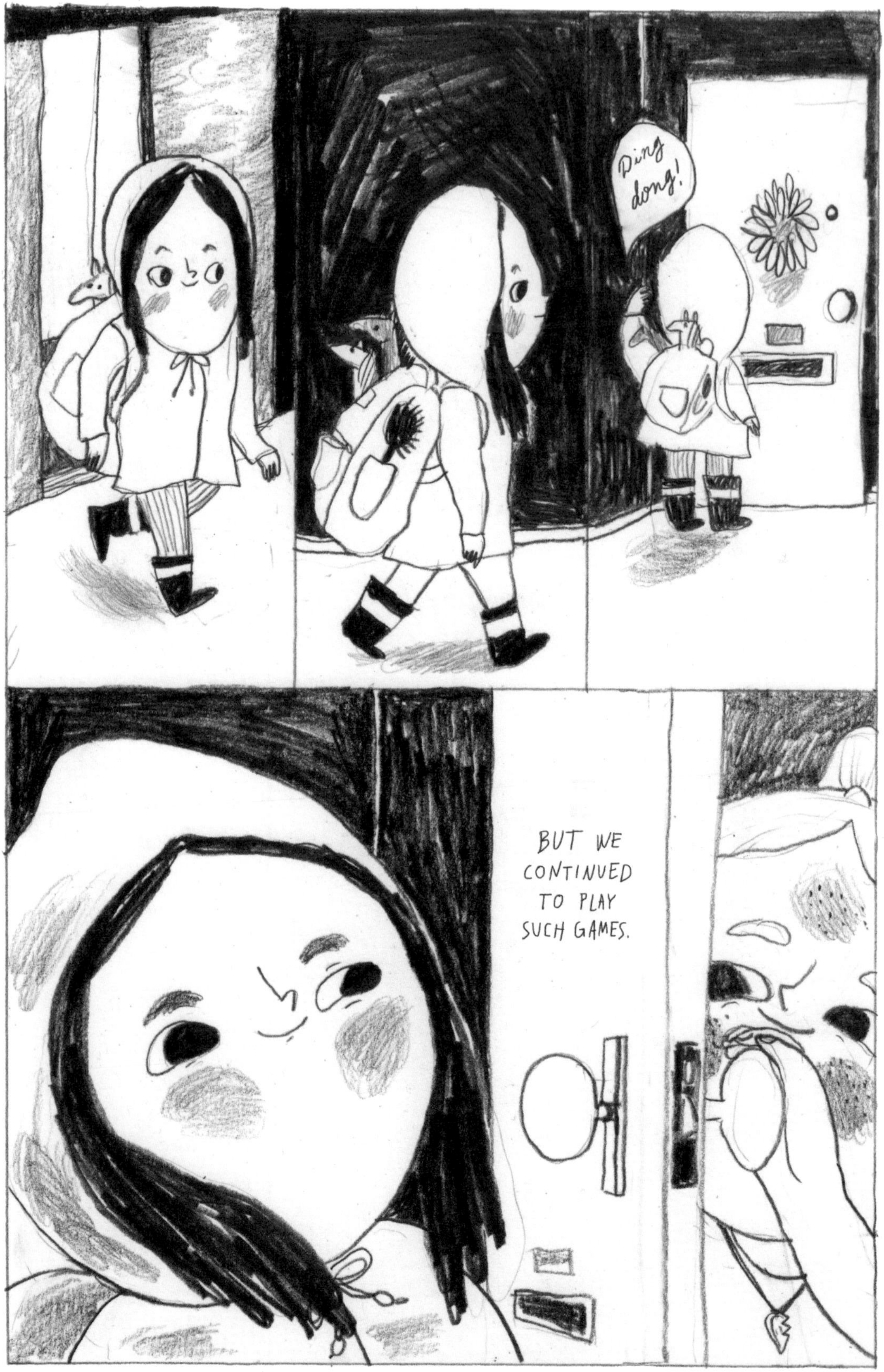
Ding dong!
BUT WE CONTINUED TO PLAY SUCH GAMES.

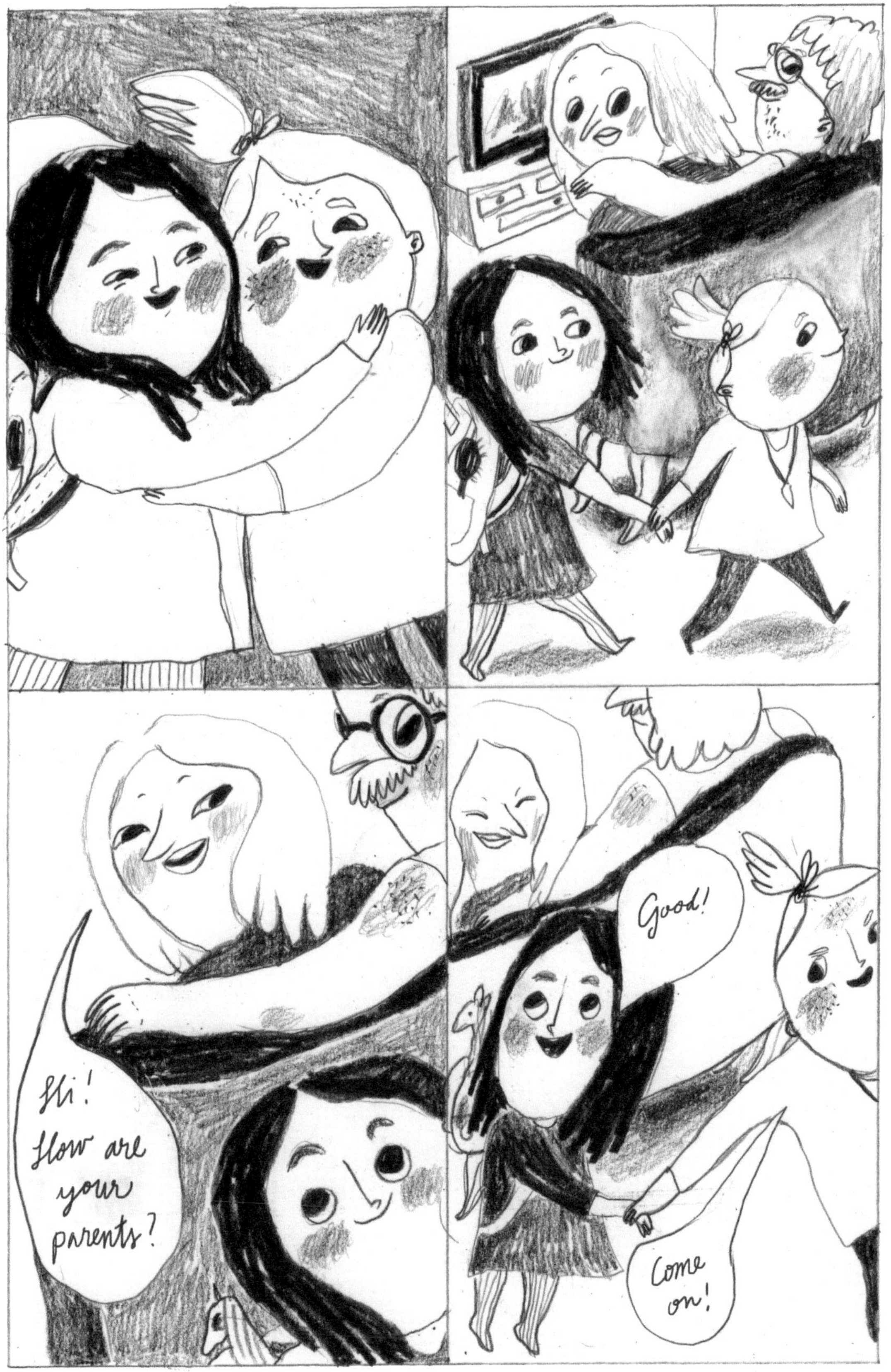
Hi! How are your parents?
Good!
Come on!

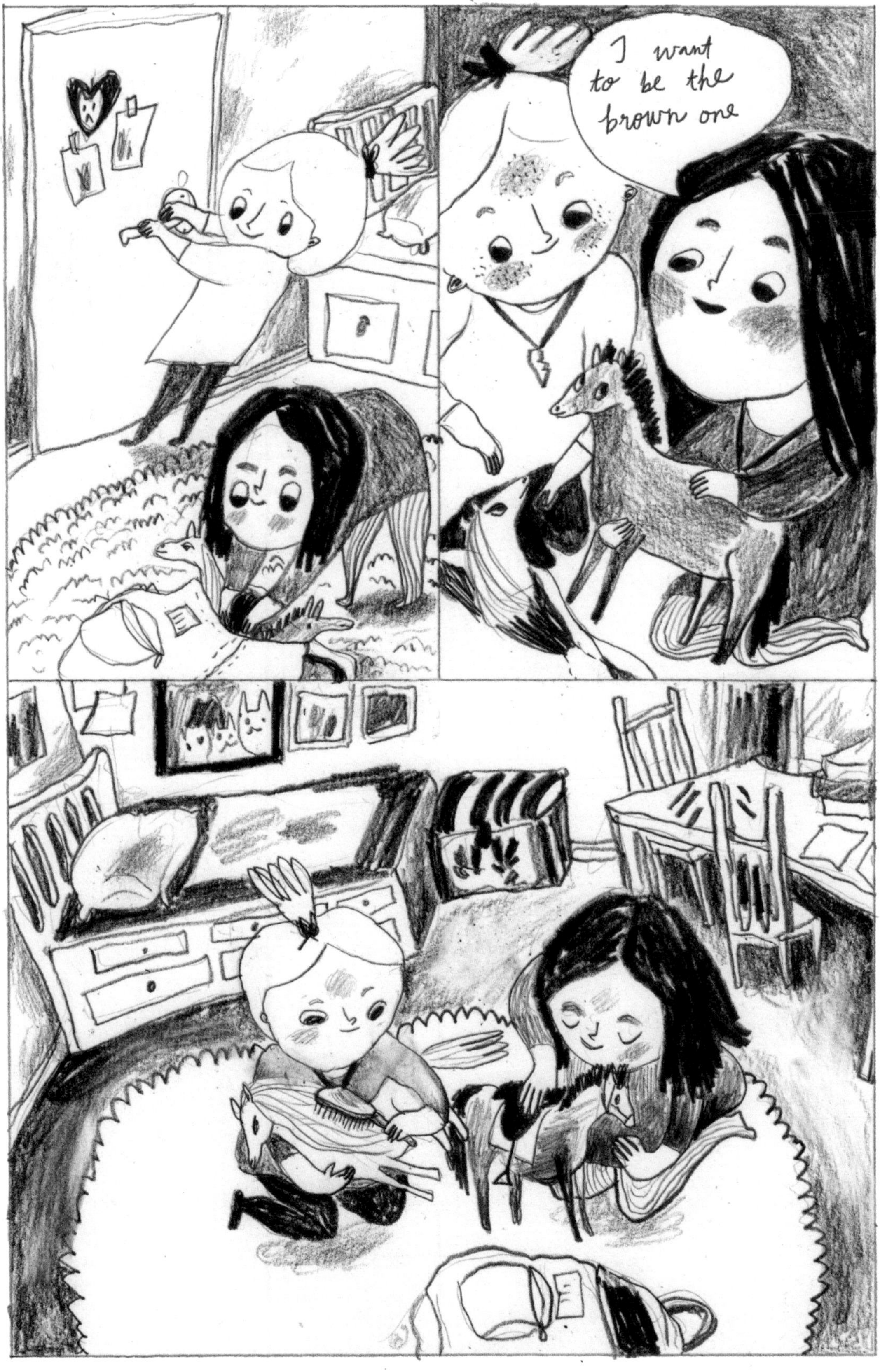
I want to be the brown one

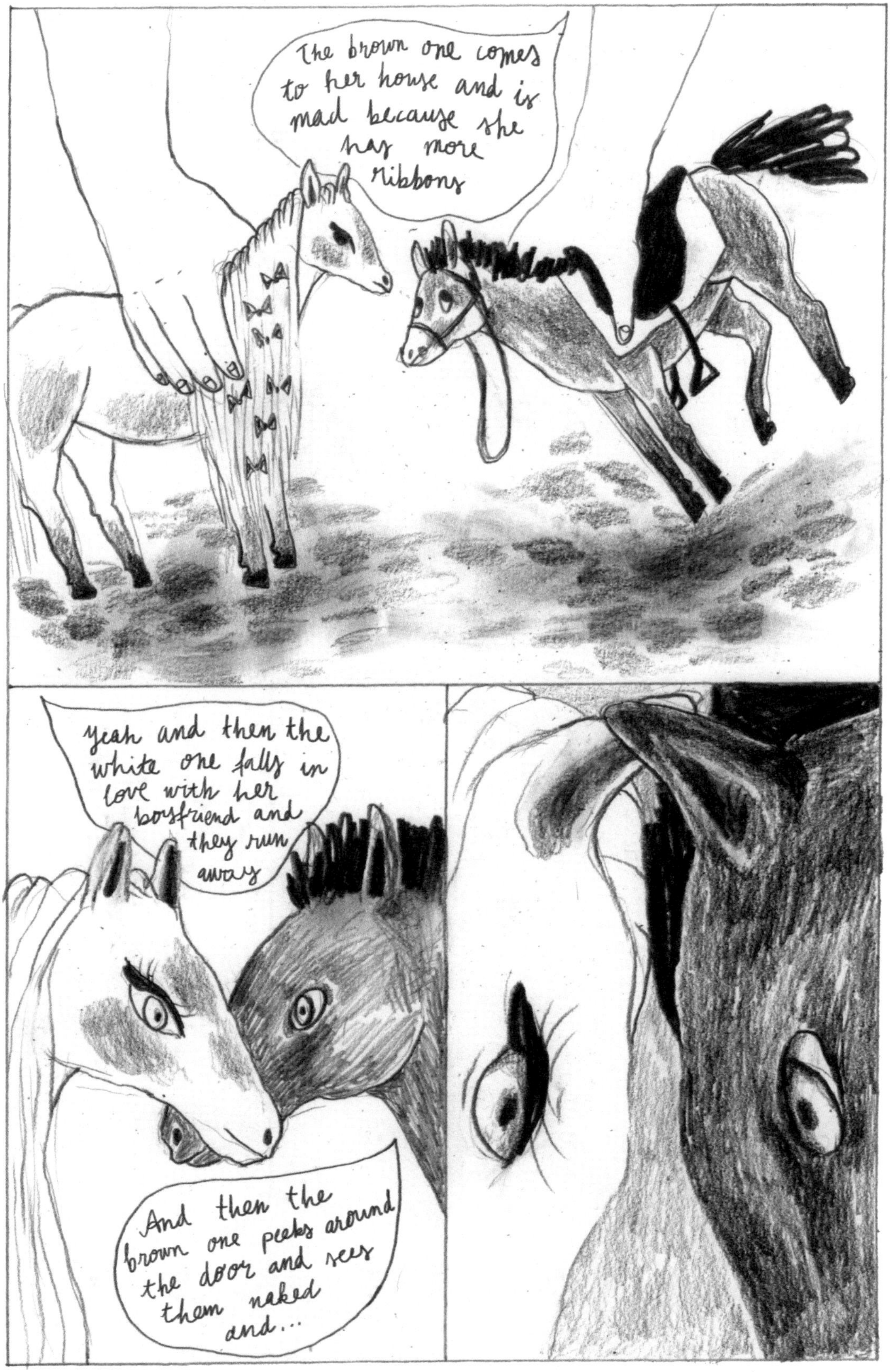
The brown one comes to her house and is mad because she has more ribbons
yeah and then the white one falls in love with her boyfriend and they run away
And then the brown one peeks around the door and sees them naked and...

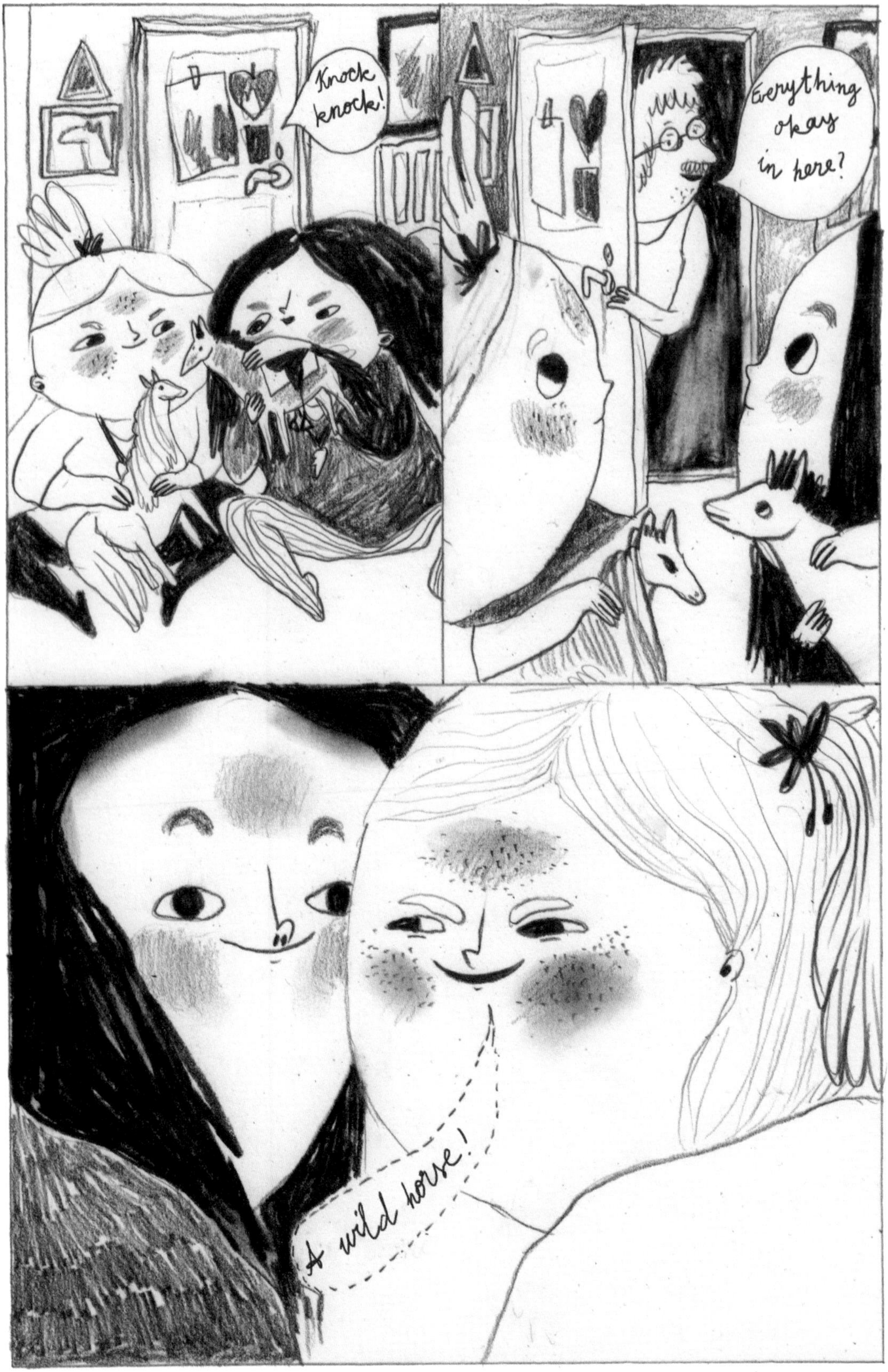
Knock knock!
Everything okay in here?
A wild horse!

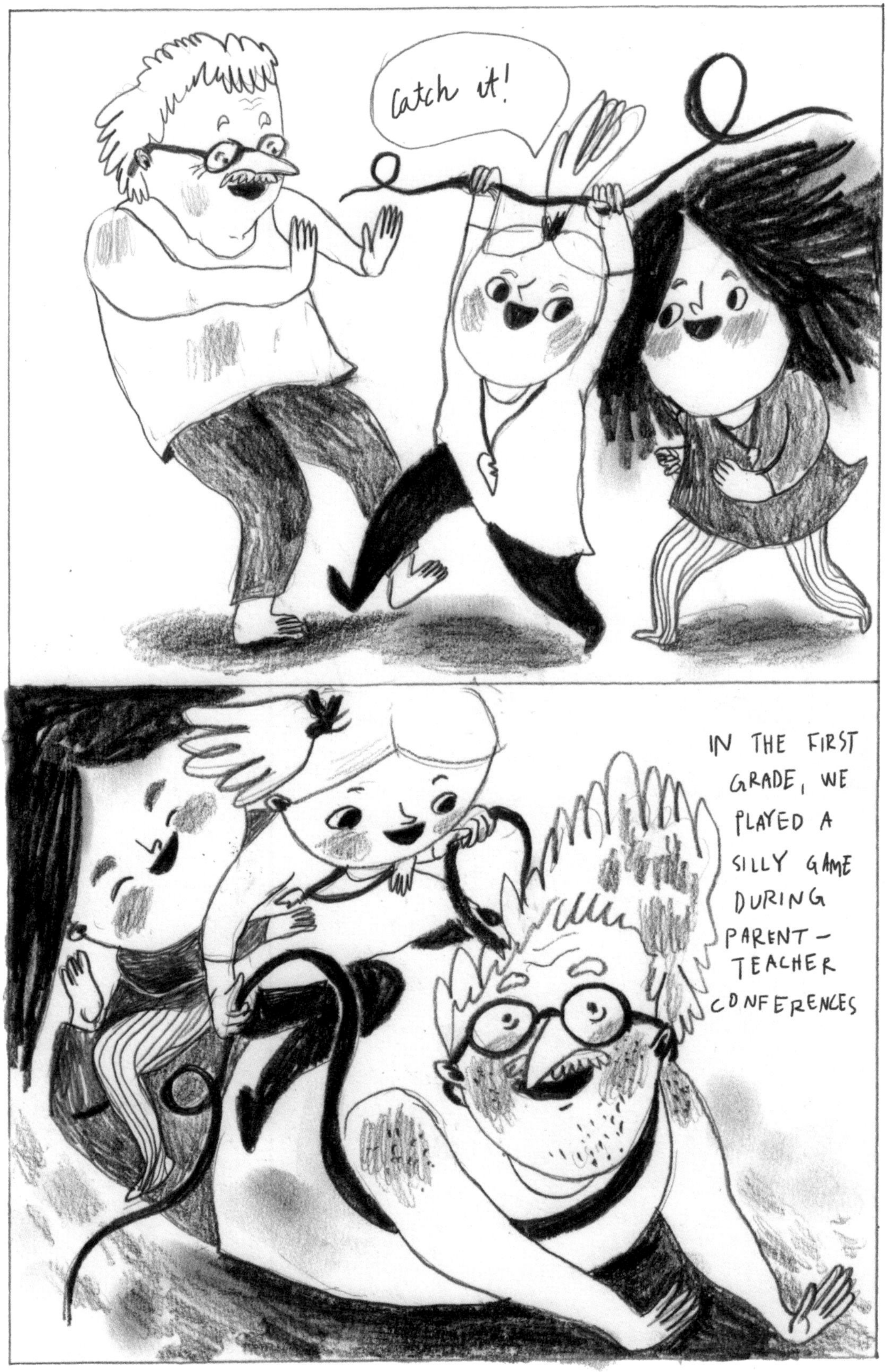
Catch it!
IN THE FIRST GRADE, WE PLAYED A SILLY GAME DURING PARENT-TEACHER CONFERENCES

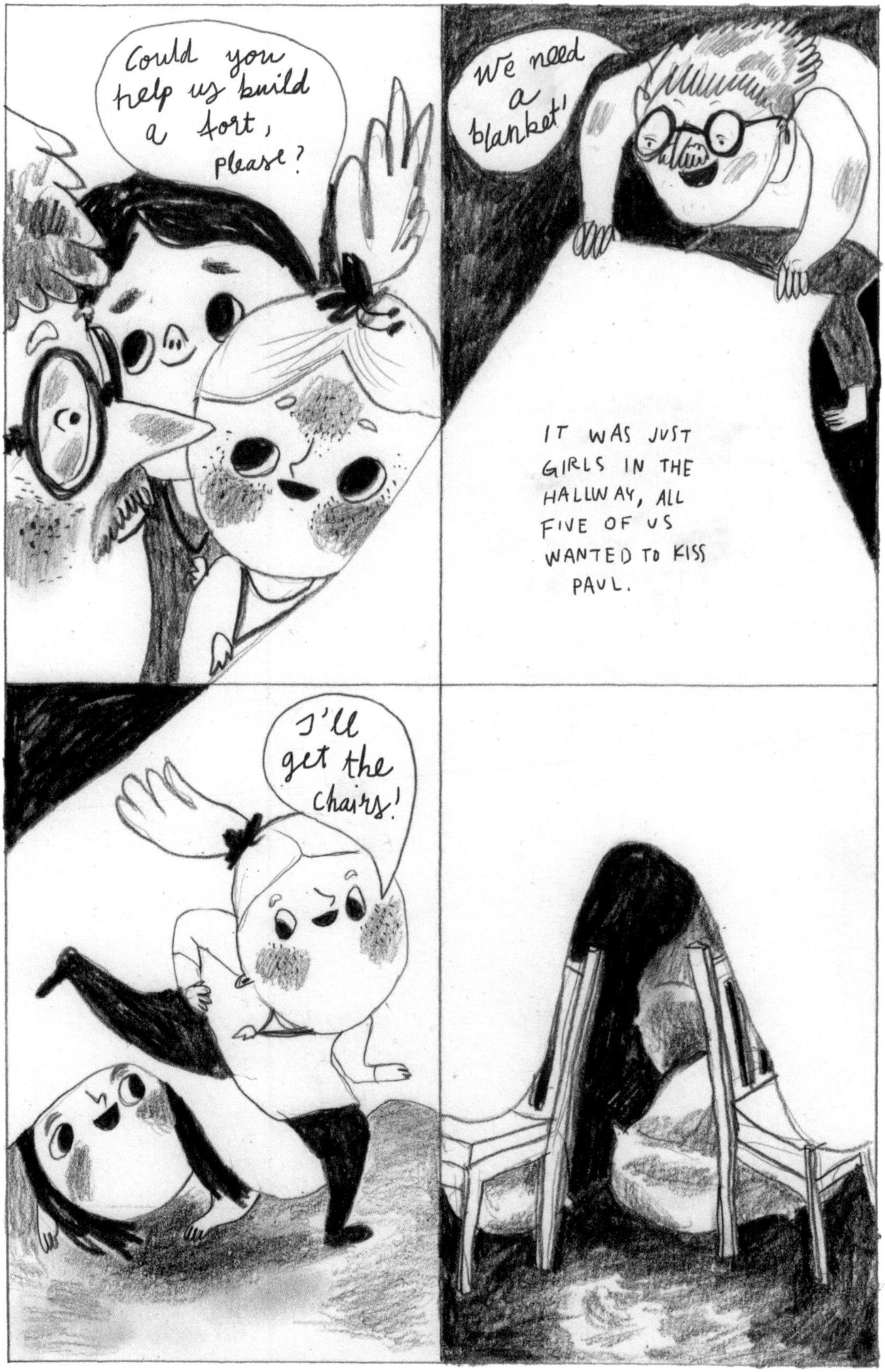
Could you help us build a fort, please?
We need a blanket!
IT WAS JUST GIRLS IN THE HALLWAY, ALL FIVE OF US WANTED TO KISS PAUL.
I'll get the chairs!

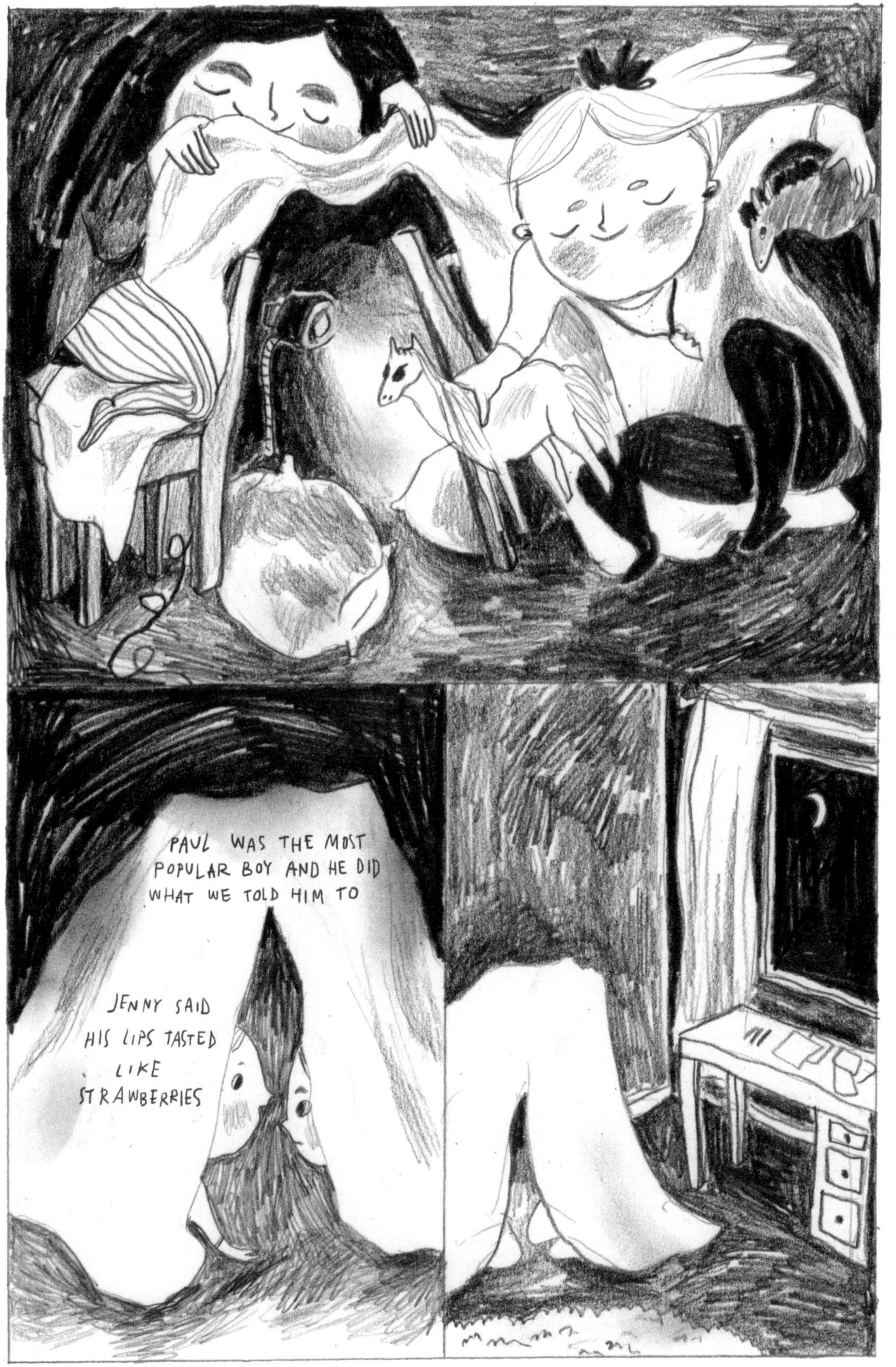
PAUL WAS THE MOST POPULAR BOY AND HE DID WHAT WE TOLD HIM TO
JENNY SAID HIS LIPS TASTED LIKE STRAWBERRIES

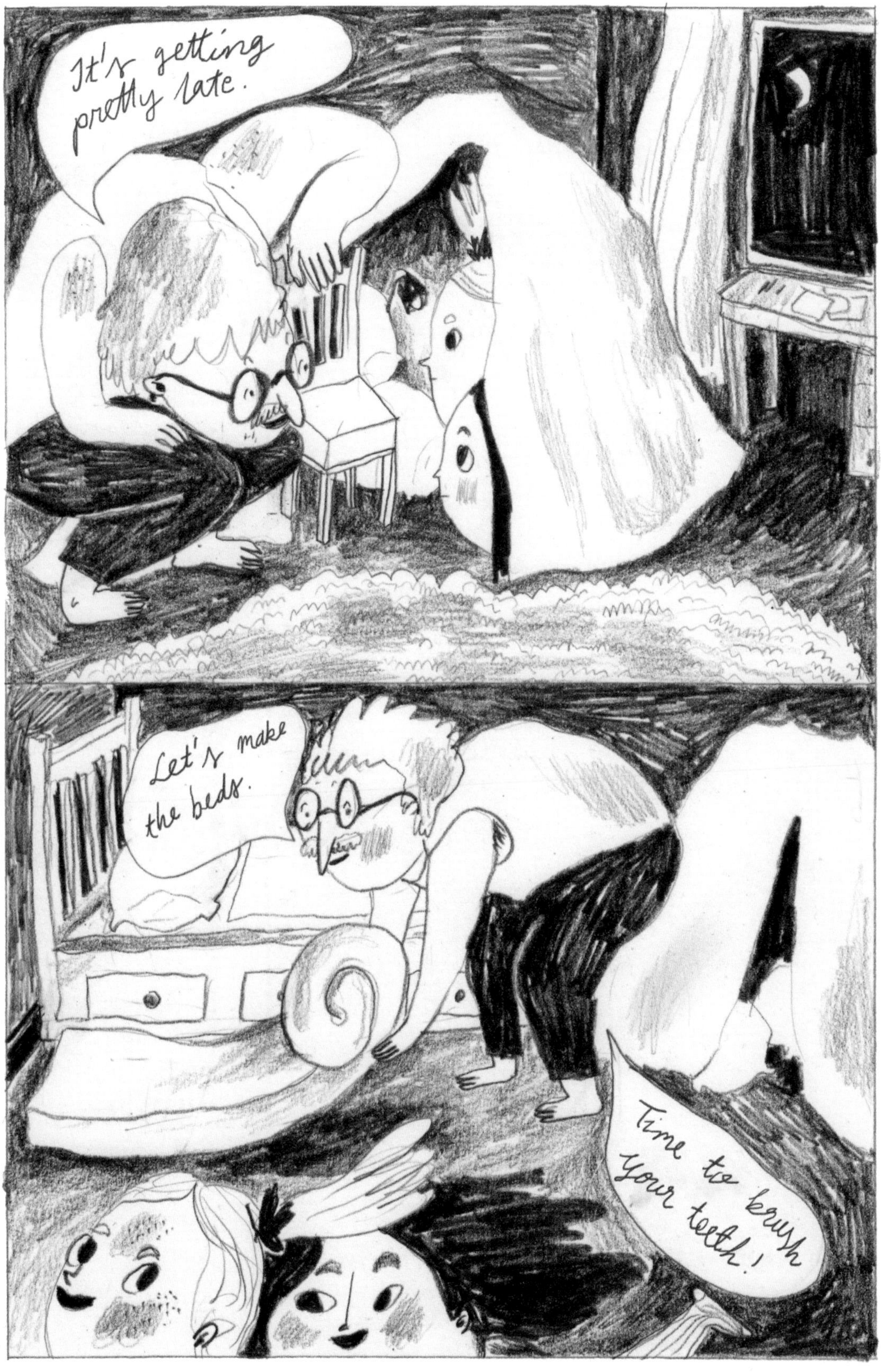
It's getting pretty late.
Let's make the beds.
Time to brush your teeth!

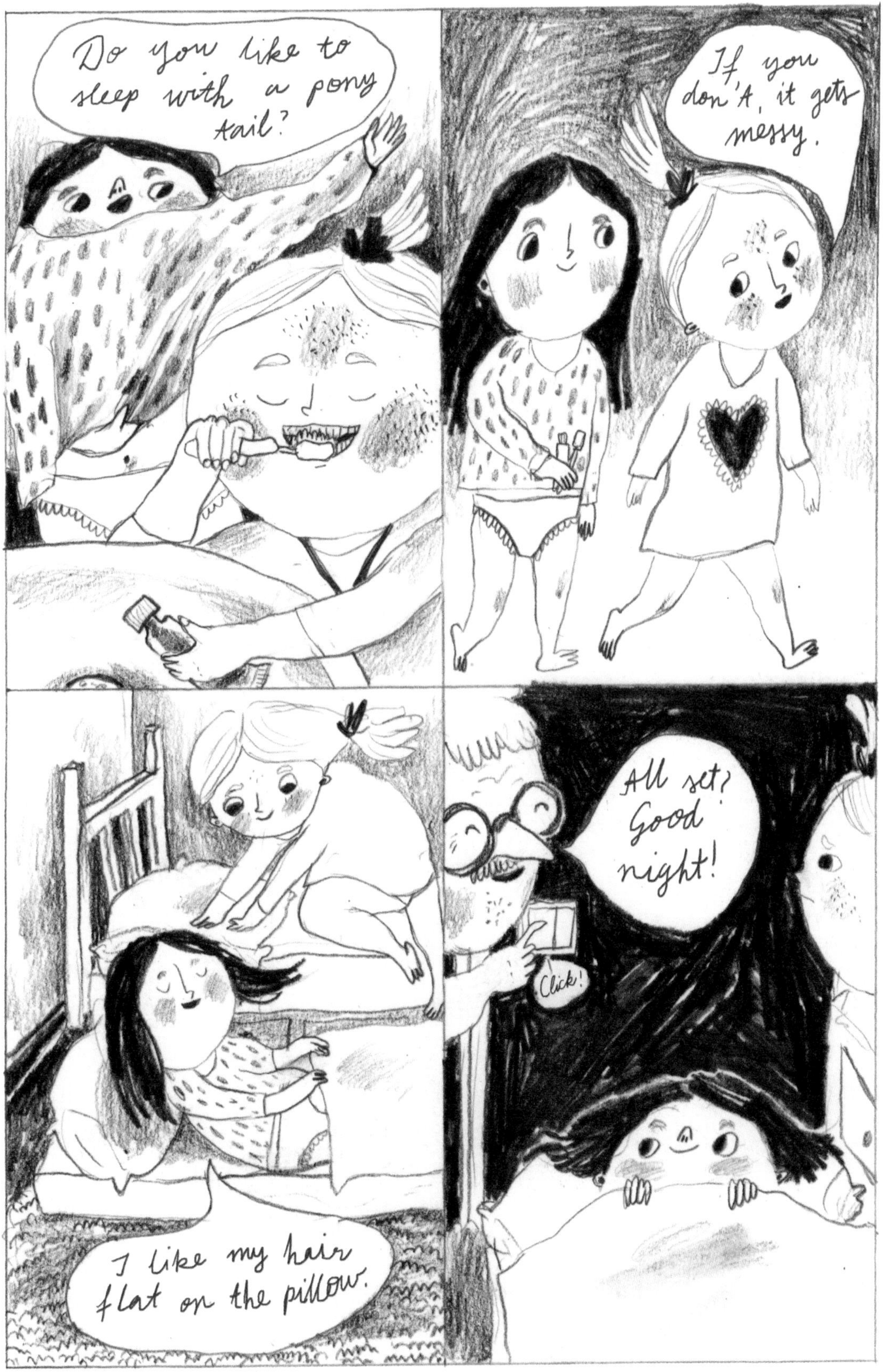
Do you like to sleep with a pony tail?
If you don't, it gets messy.
I like my hair flat on the pillow.
All set? Good night!
Click!

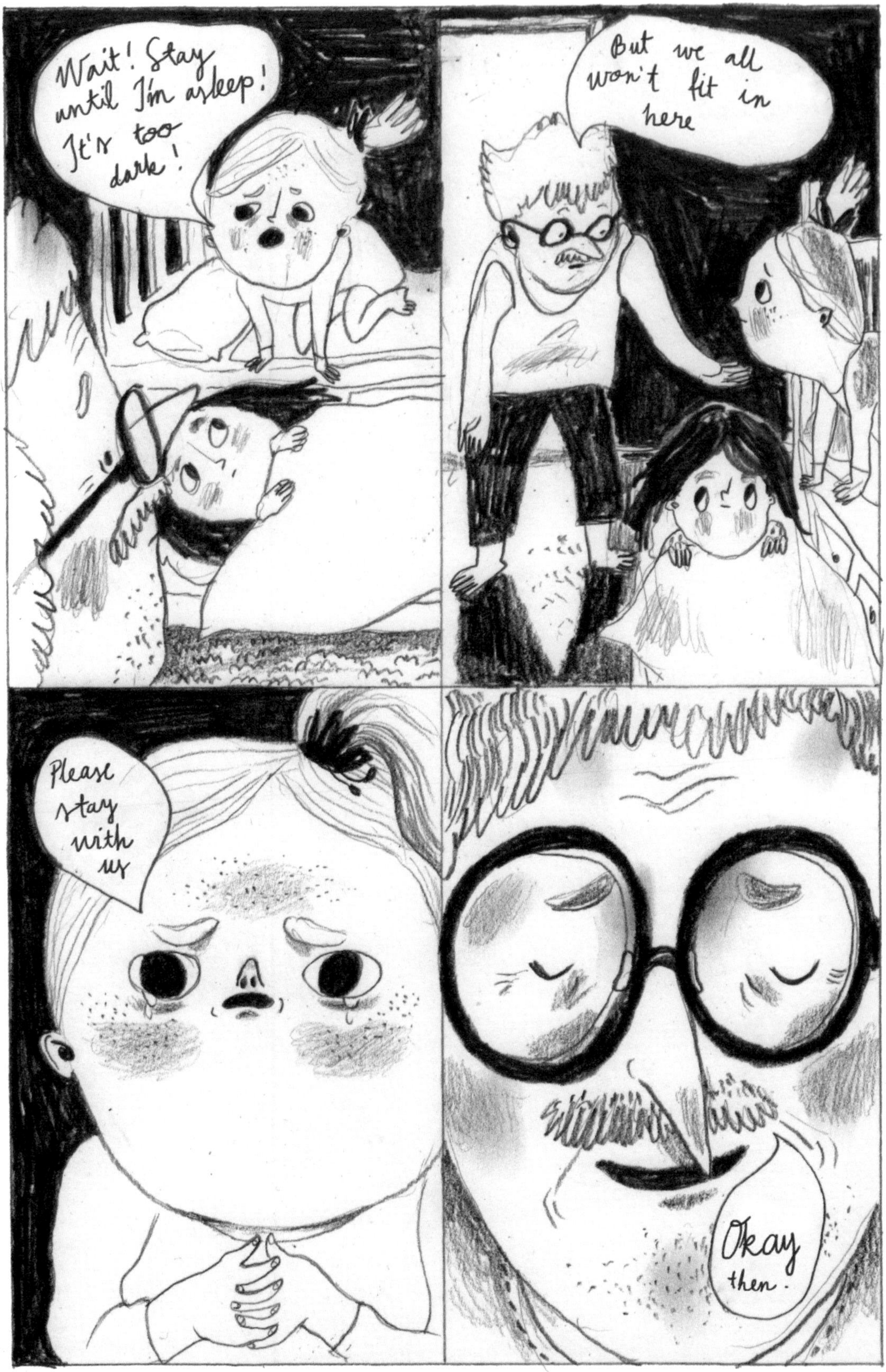
Wait! Stay until I'm asleep! It's too dark!
But we all won't fit in here
Please stay with us
Okay then.

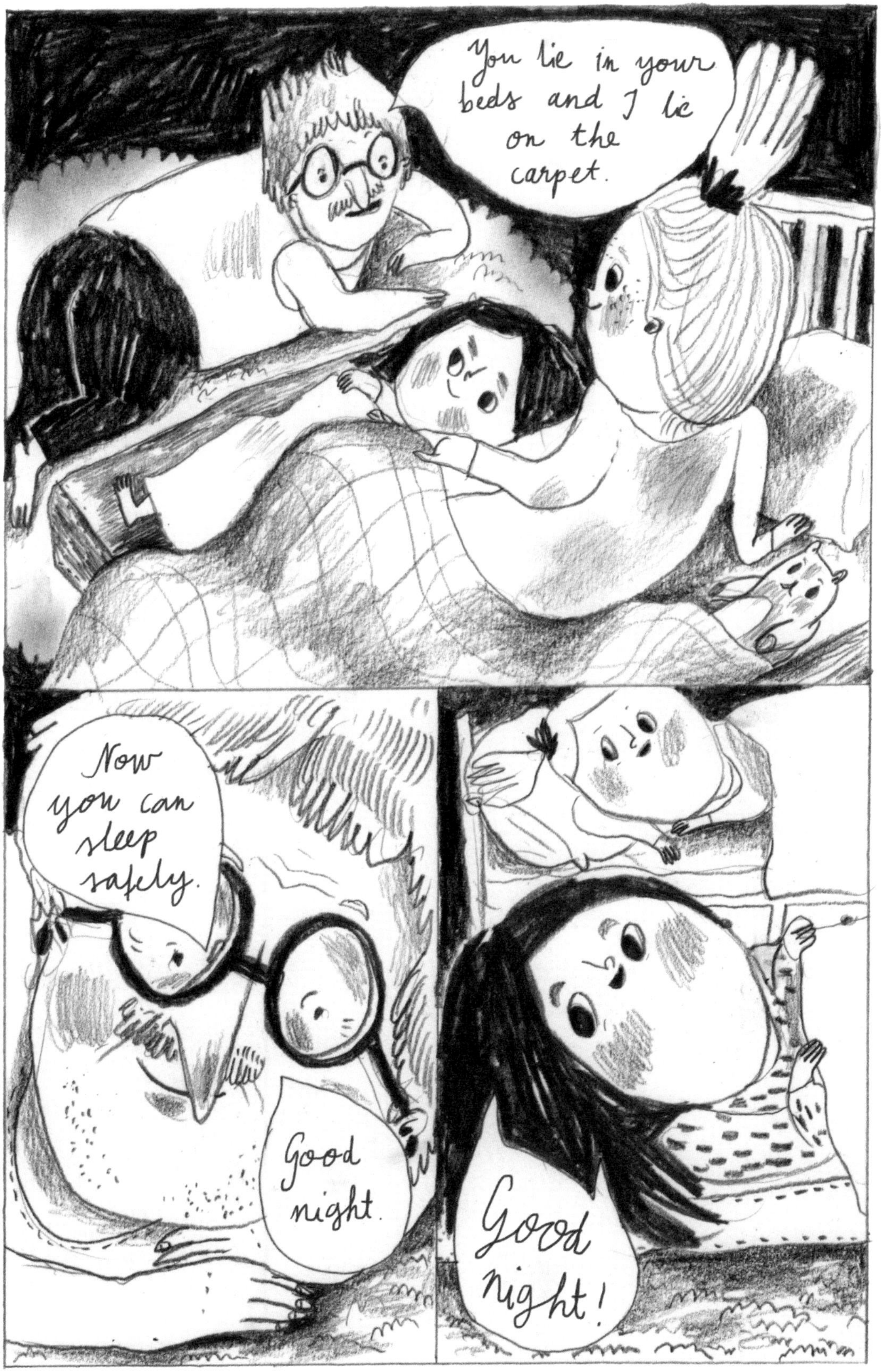

You lie in your beds and I lie on the carpet.
Now you can sleep safely.
Good night.
Good night!

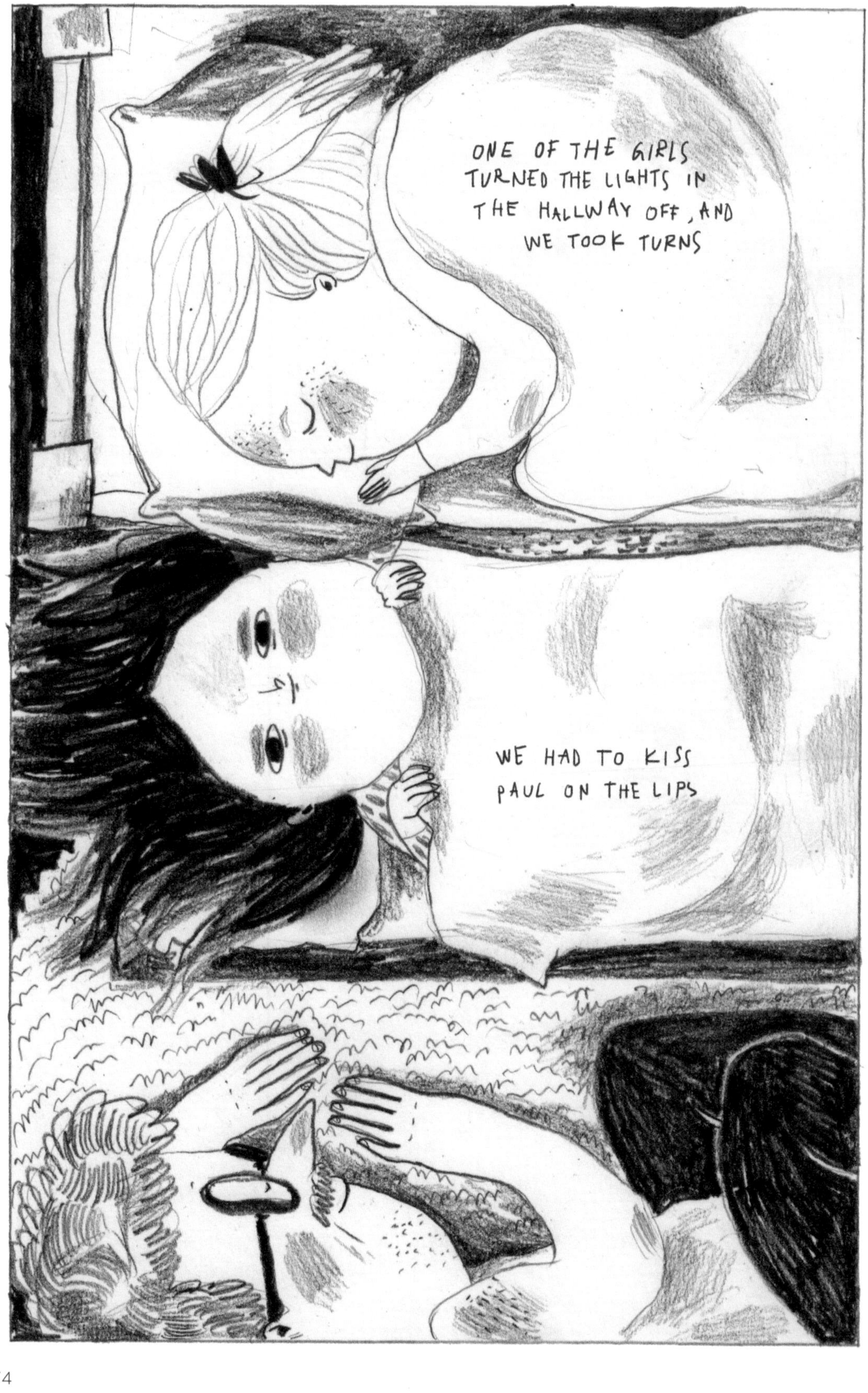
ONE OF THE GIRLS TURNED THE LIGHTS IN THE HALLWAY OFF, AND WE TOOK TURNS
WE HAD TO KISS PAUL ON THE LIPS

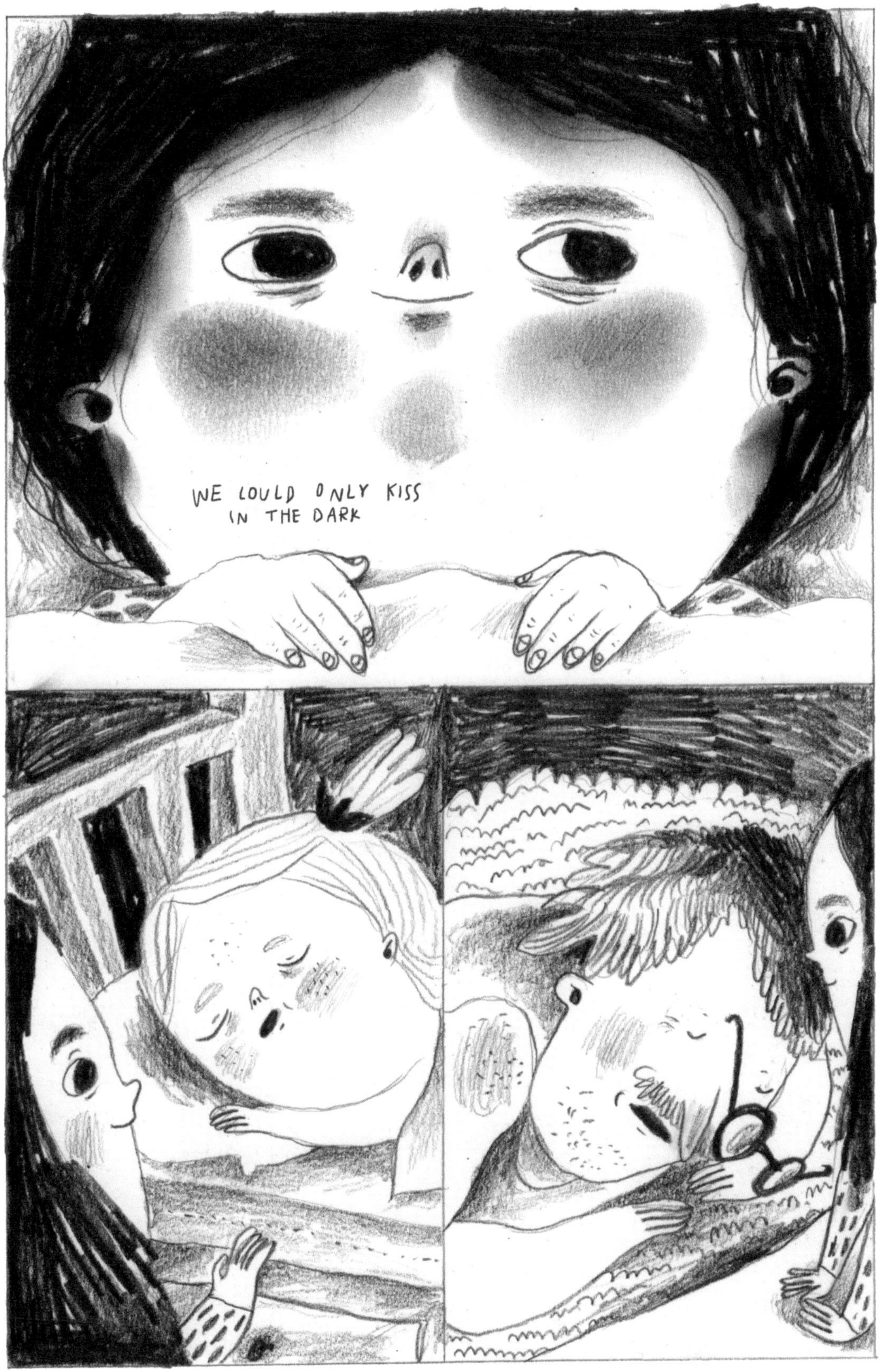
WE COULD ONLY KISS IN THE DARK

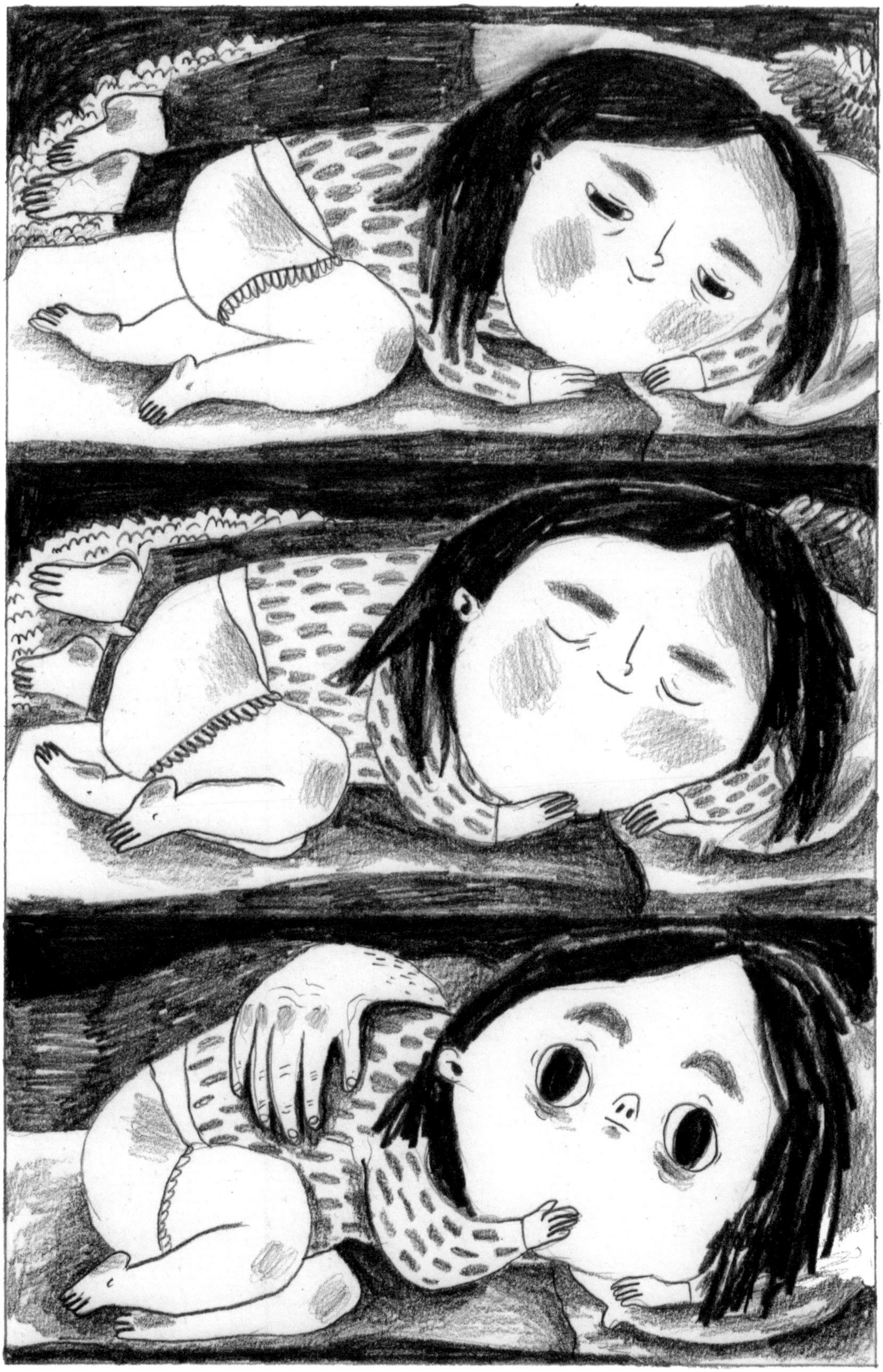

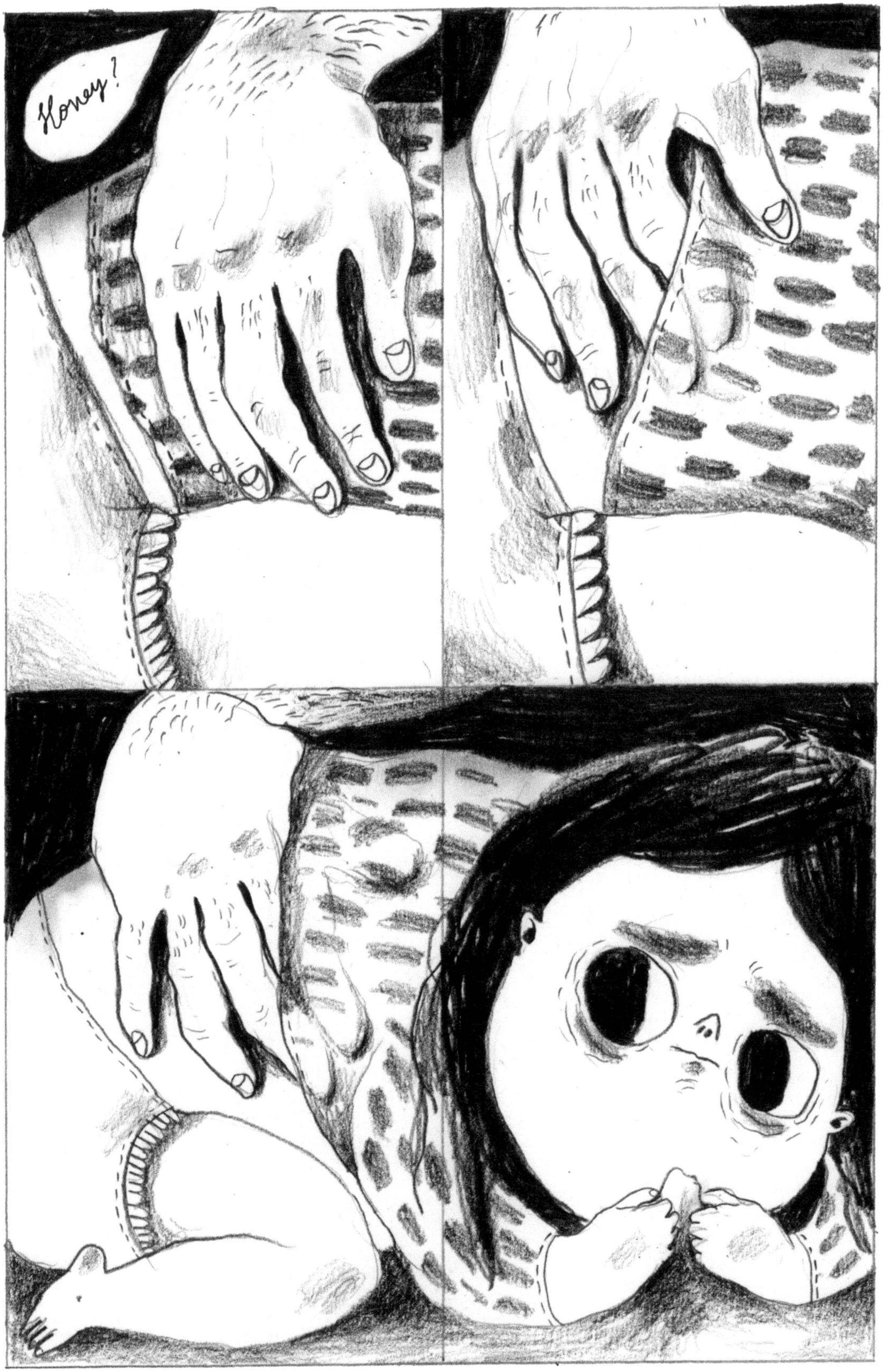
Honey?

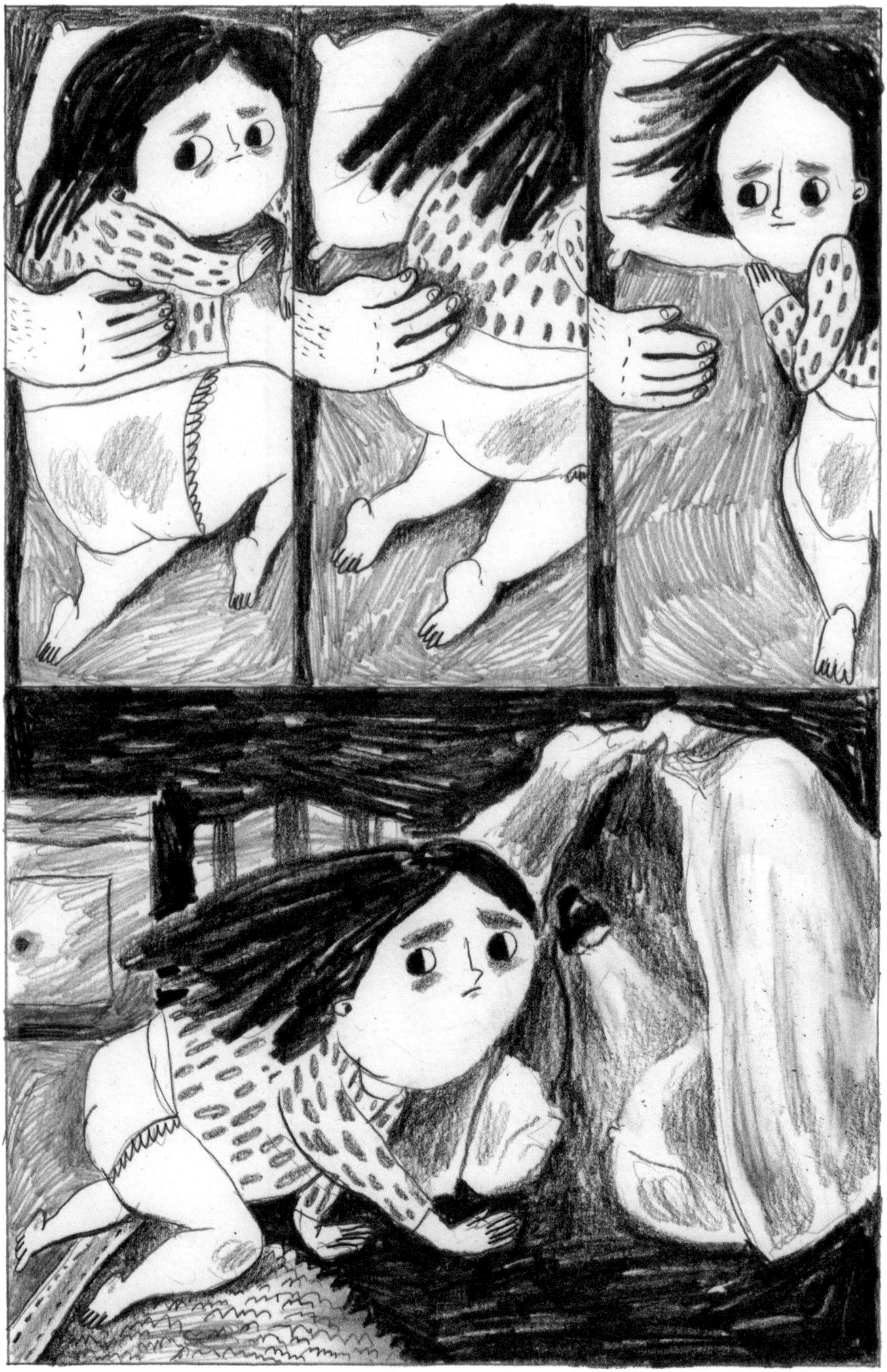

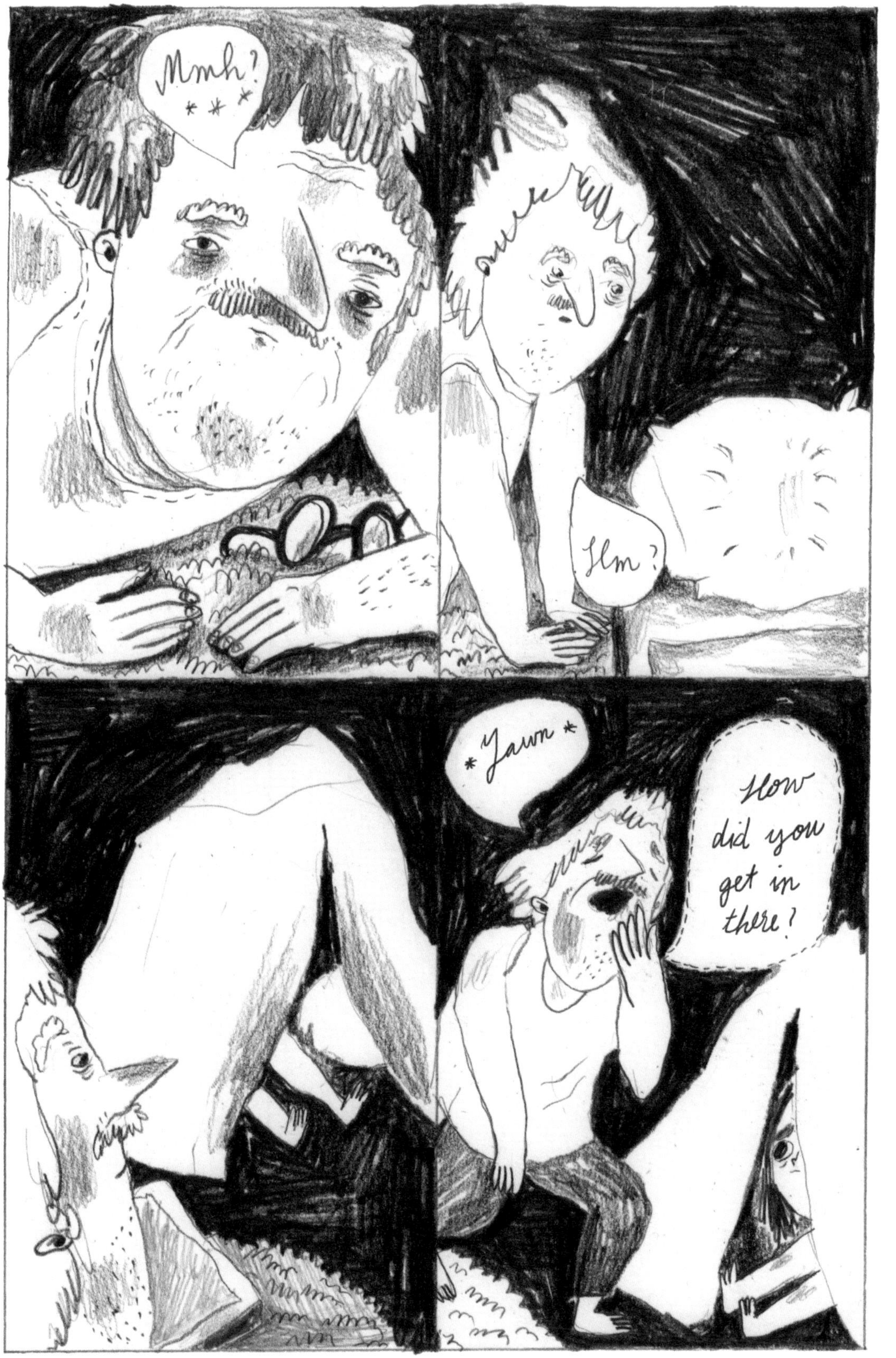
Mmh? * * *
Hm?
* Yawn *
How did you get in there?

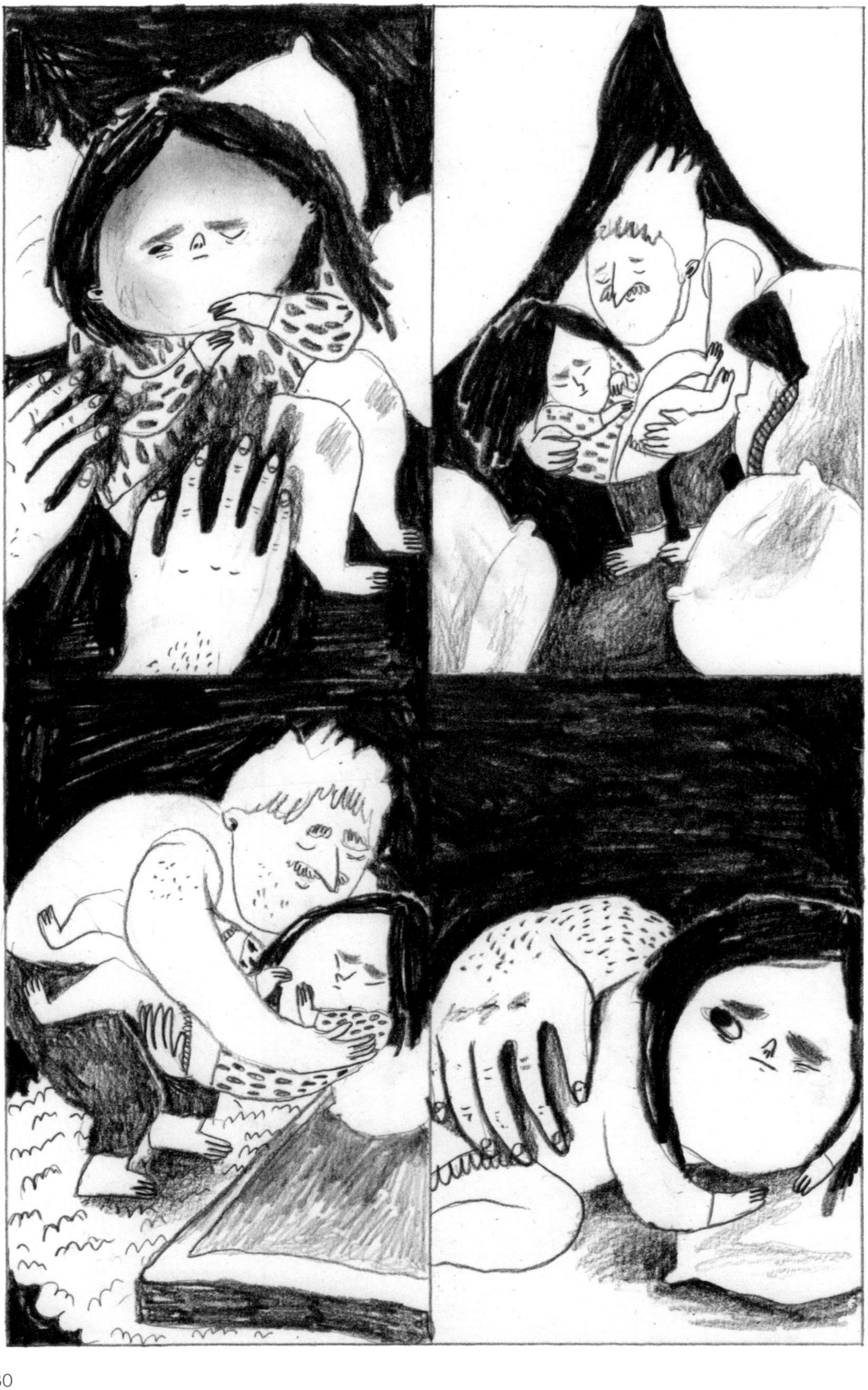

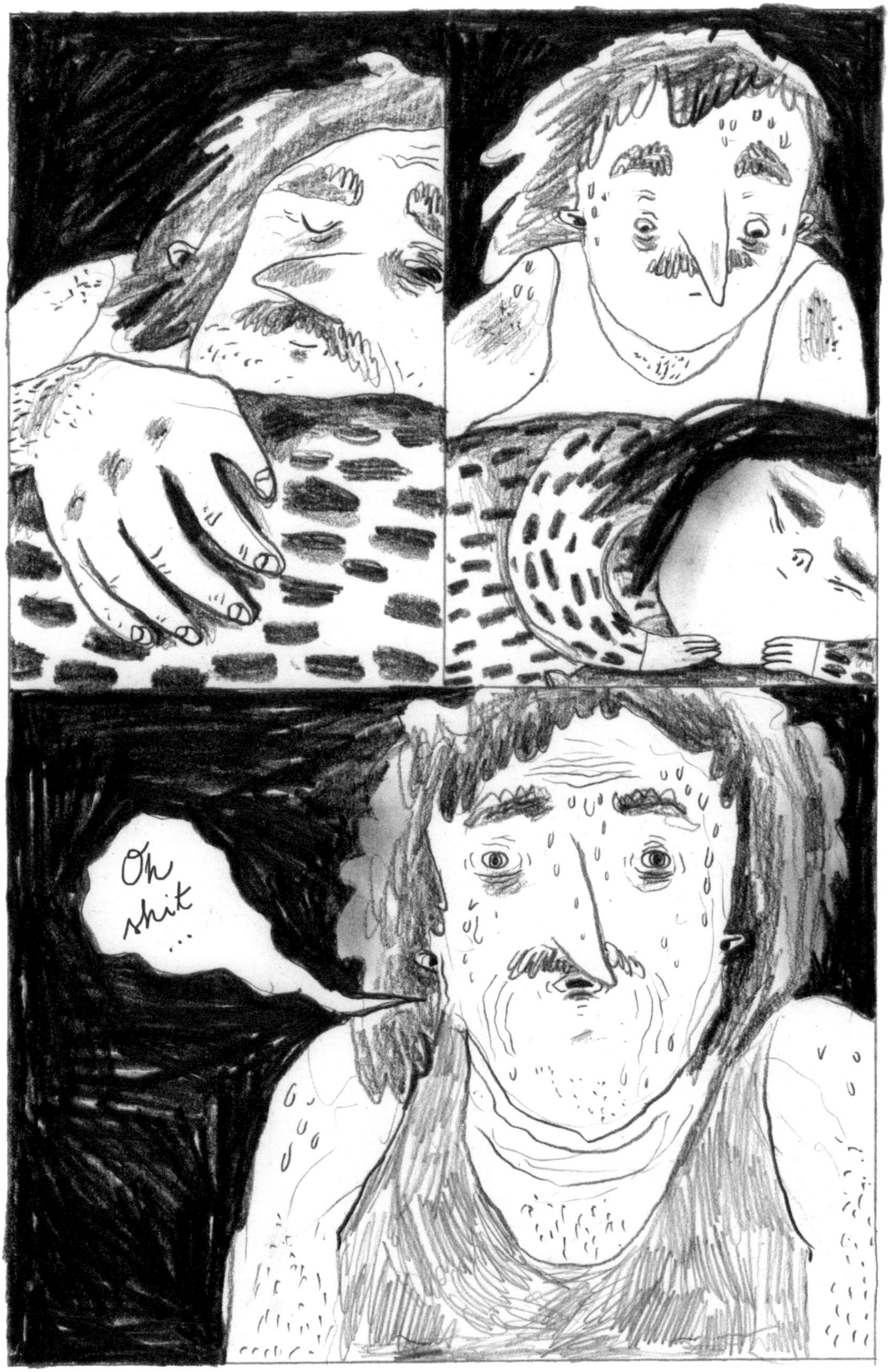
Oh shit ...

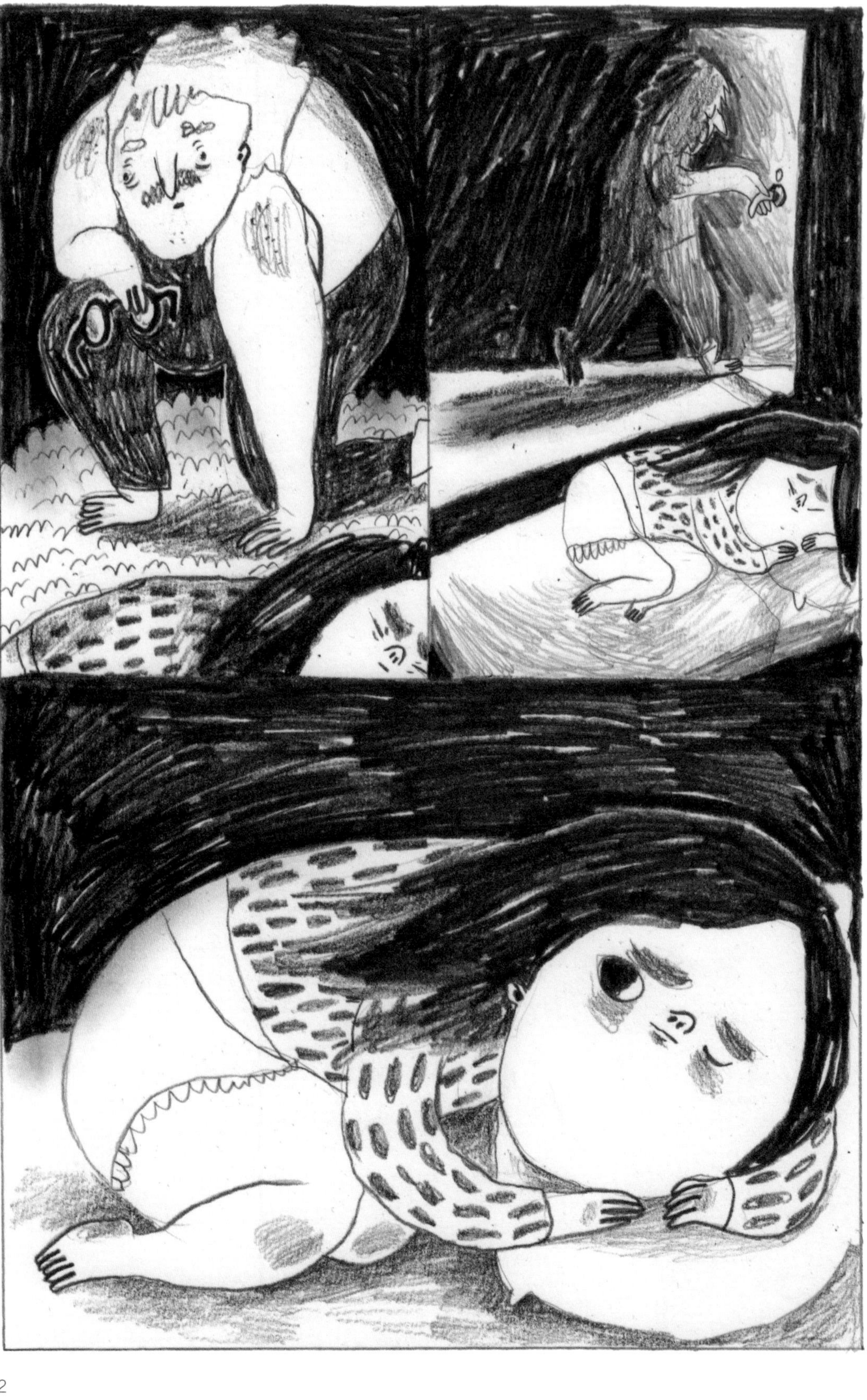

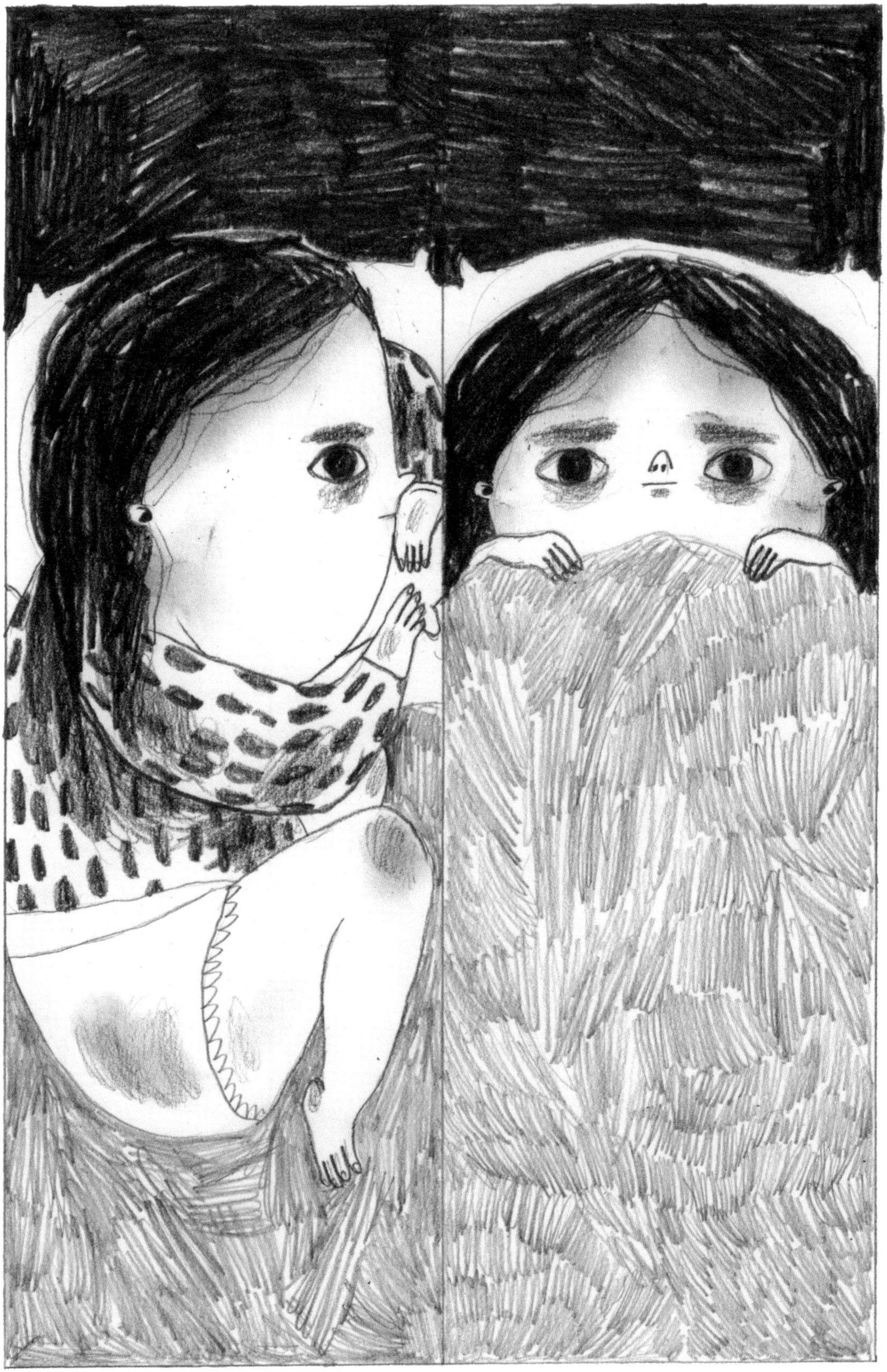

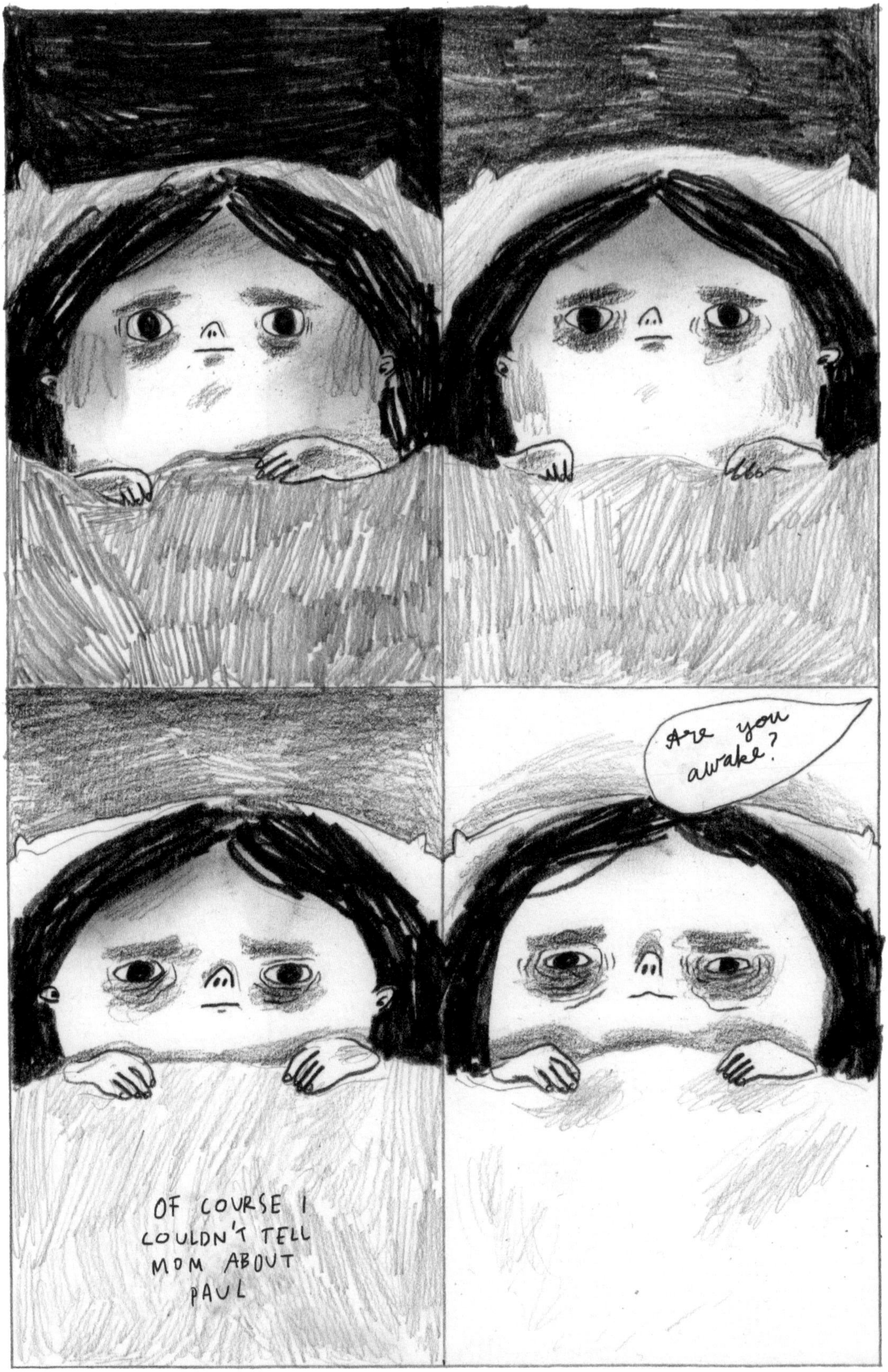
OF COURSE I COULDN'T TELL MOM ABOUT PAUL
Are you awake?

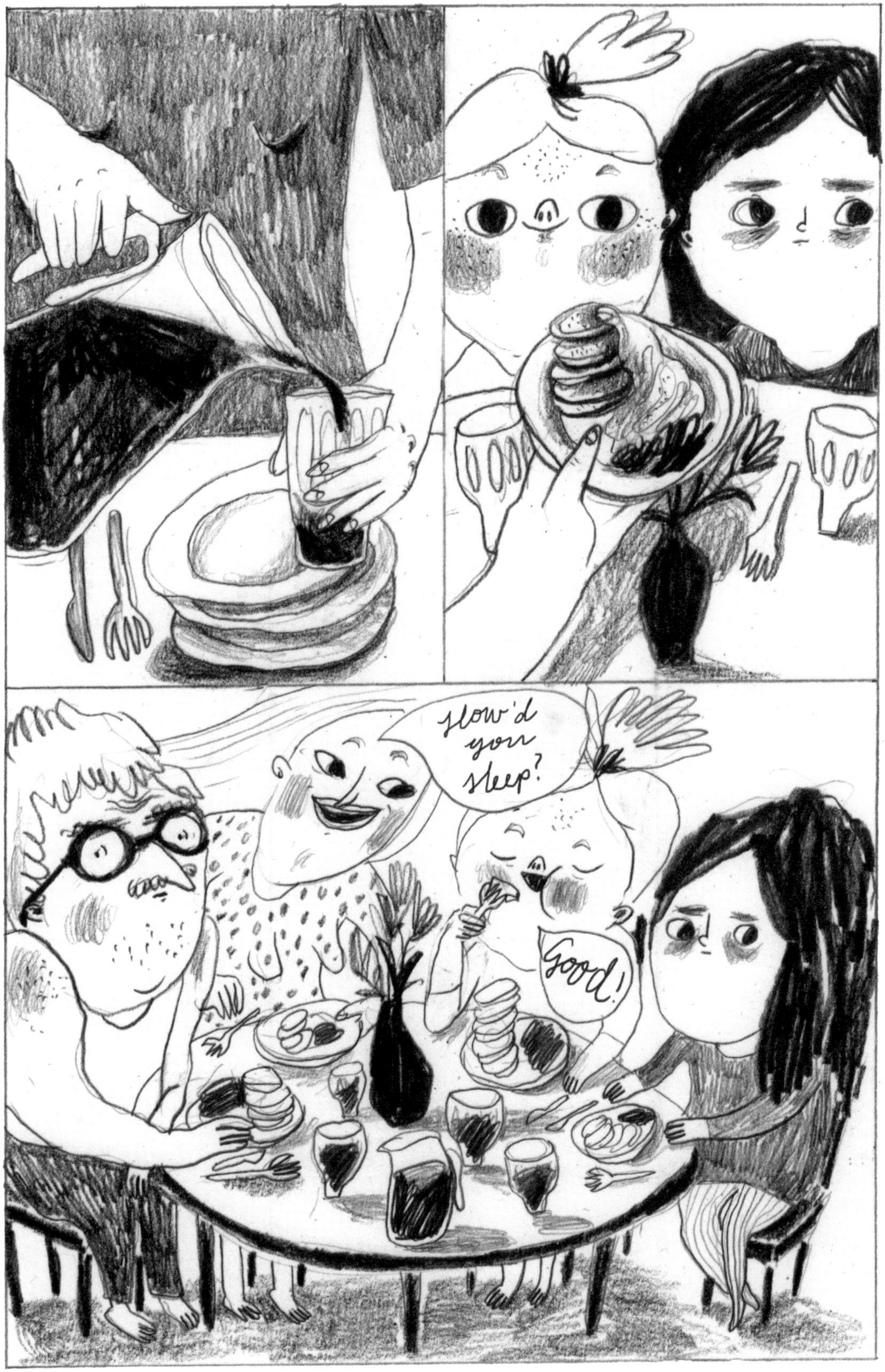
How'd you sleep?
Good!

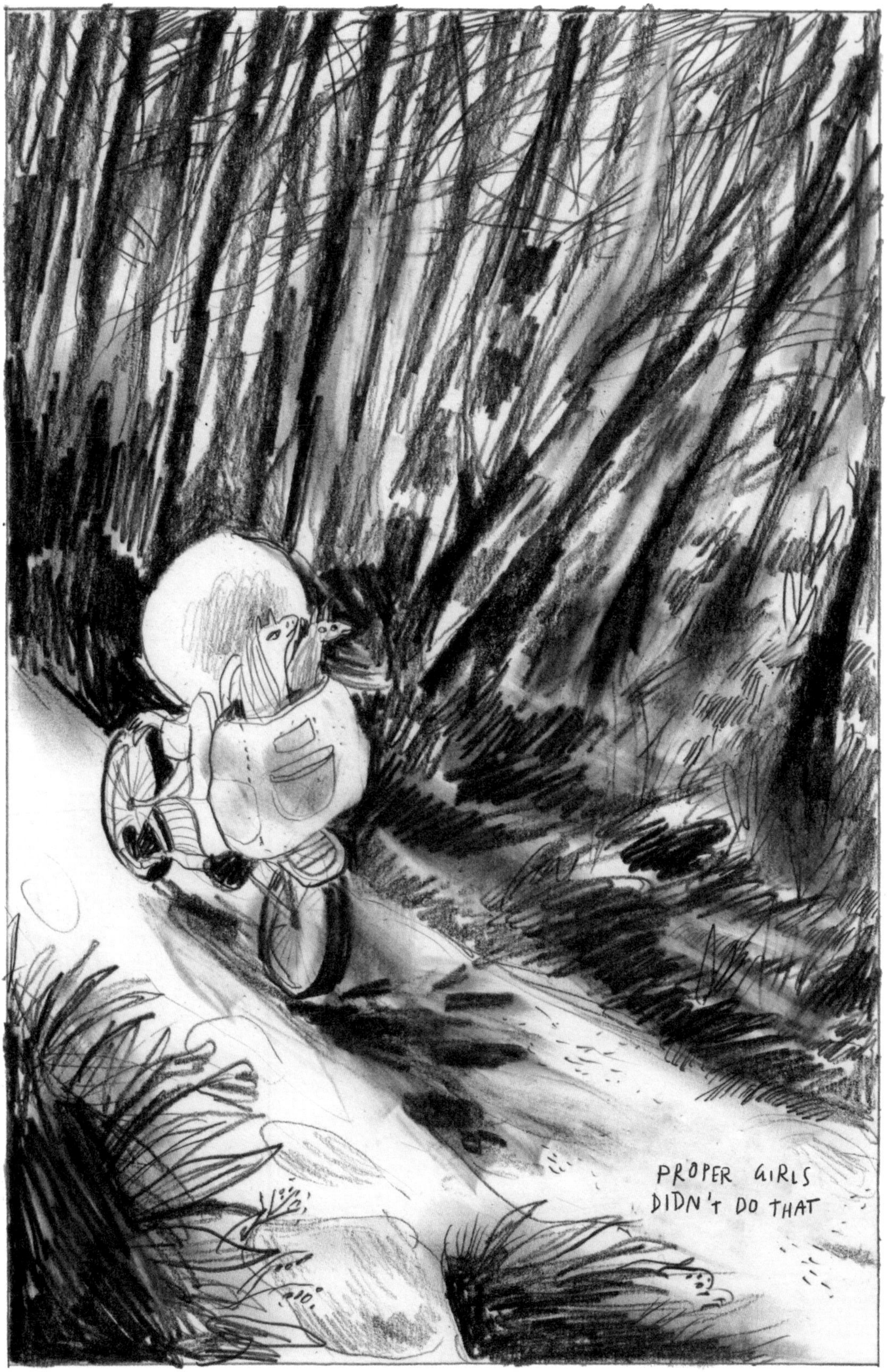
PROPER GIRLS
DIDN'T DO THAT

THE
NIGHTINGALE
THAT NEVER
SANG

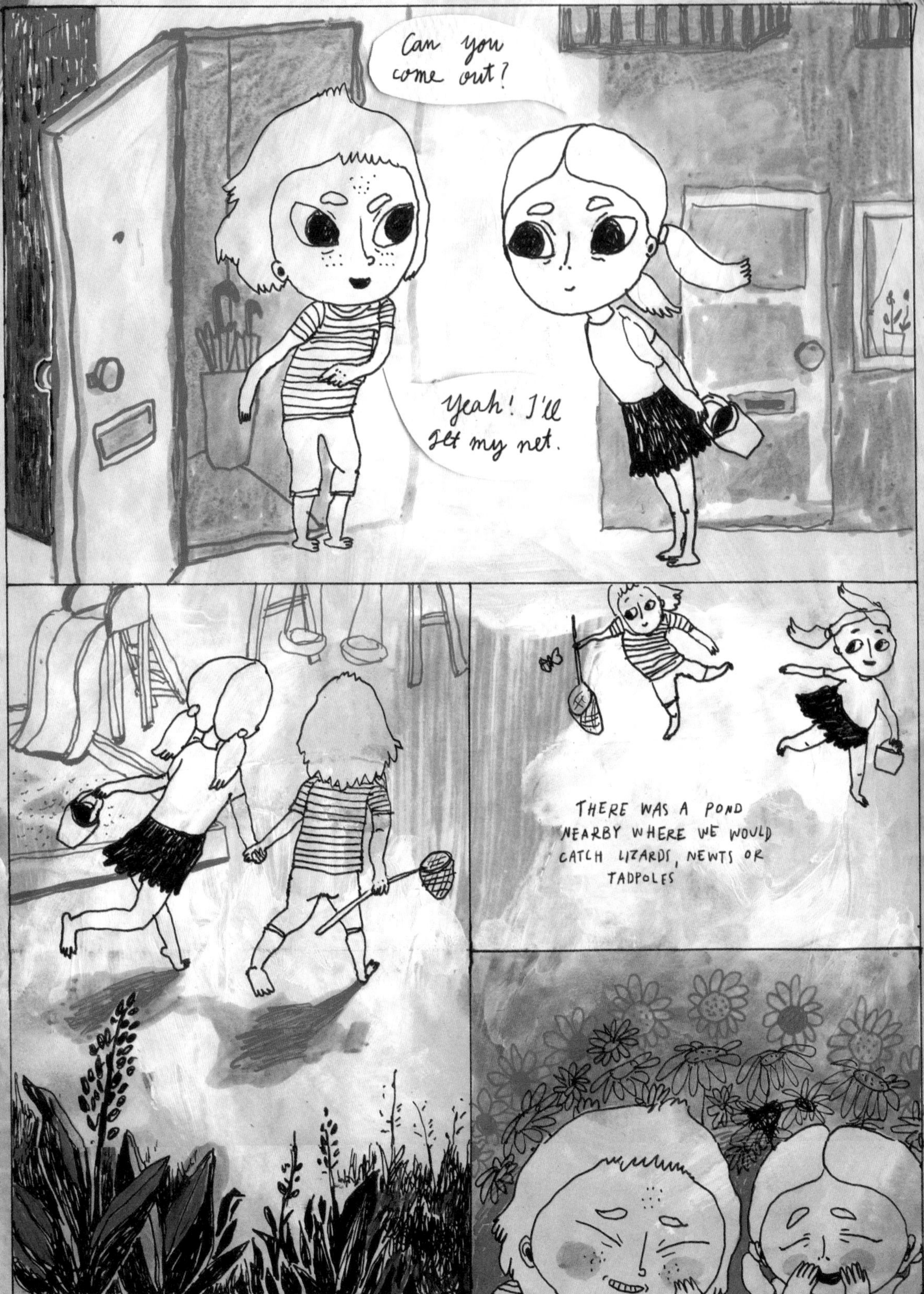
Can you come out?
Yeah! I'll get my net.
THERE WAS A POND NEARBY WHERE WE WOULD CATCH LIZARDS, NEWTS OR TADPOLES

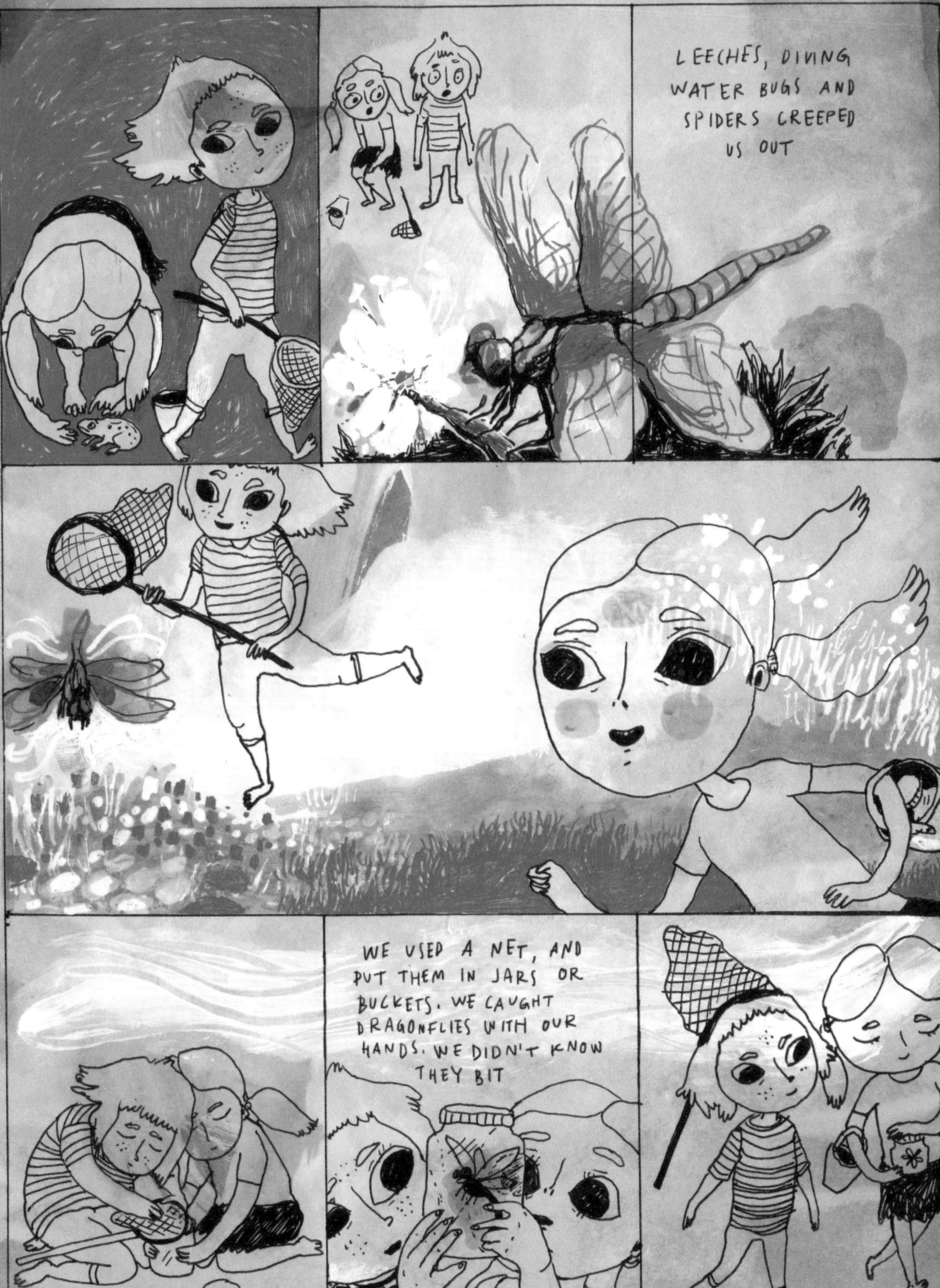
LEECHES, DIVING WATER BUGS AND SPIDERS CREEPED US OUT
WE USED A NET, AND PUT THEM IN JARS OR BUCKETS. WE CAUGHT DRAGONFLIES WITH OUR HANDS. WE DIDN'T KNOW THEY BIT

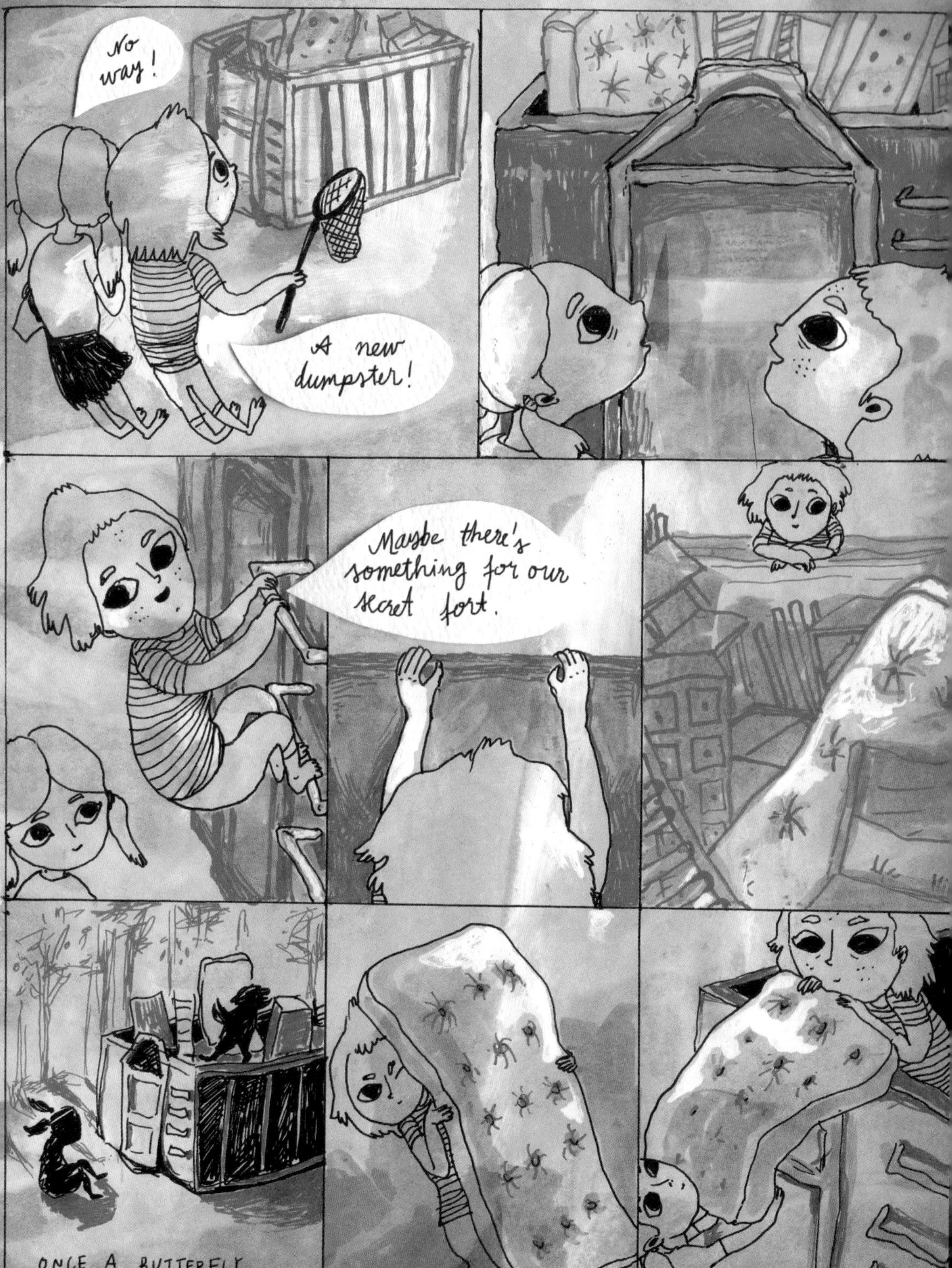
No way!
A new dumpster!
Maybe there's something for our secret fort.
ONCE A BUTTERFLY STARTED TO BLEED AND WE HAD TO LET IT GO

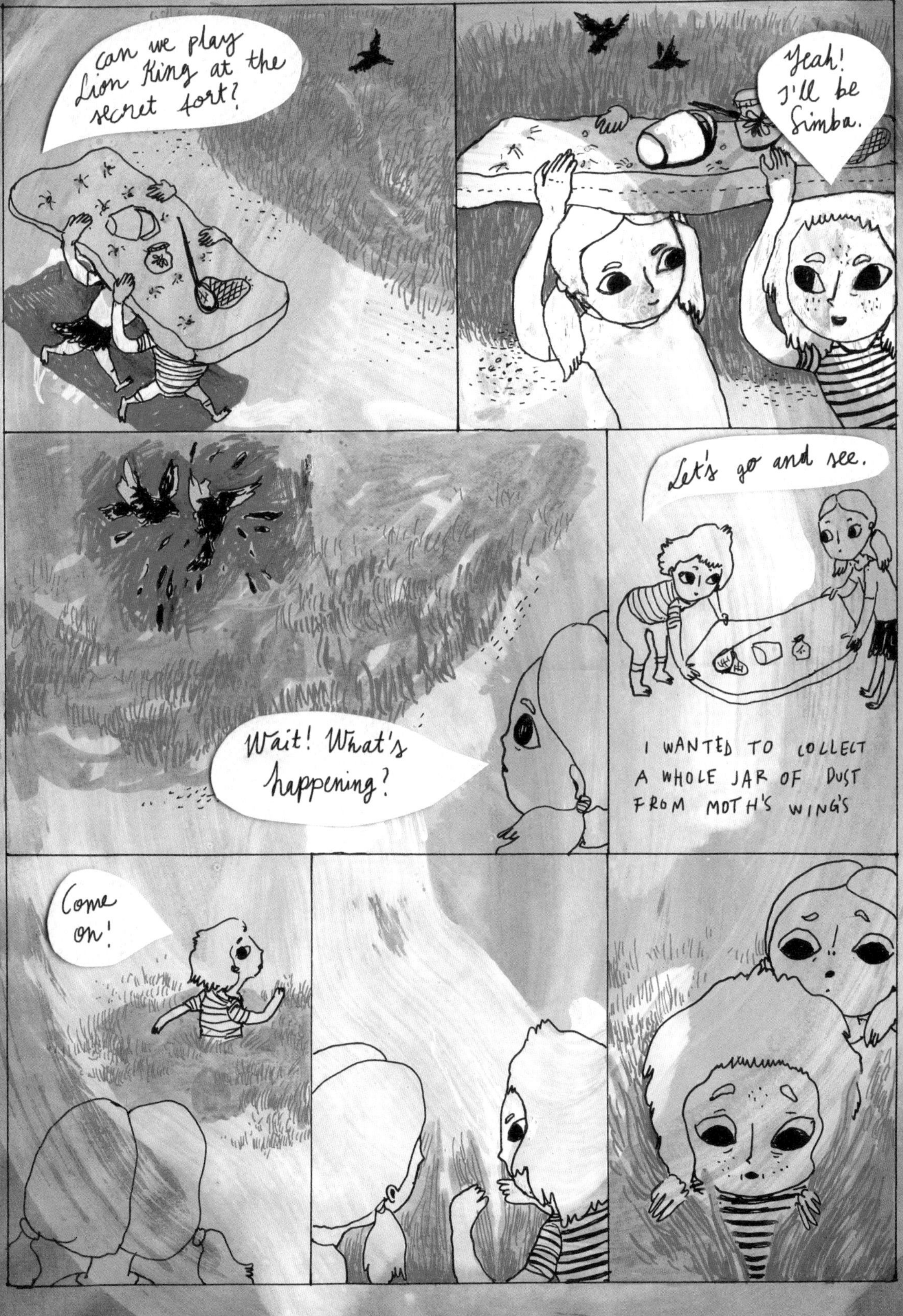
Can we play Lion King at the secret fort?
Yeah! I'll be Simba.
Wait! What's happening?
Let's go and see.
I WANTED TO COLLECT A WHOLE JAR OF DUST FROM MOTH'S WINGS
Come on!

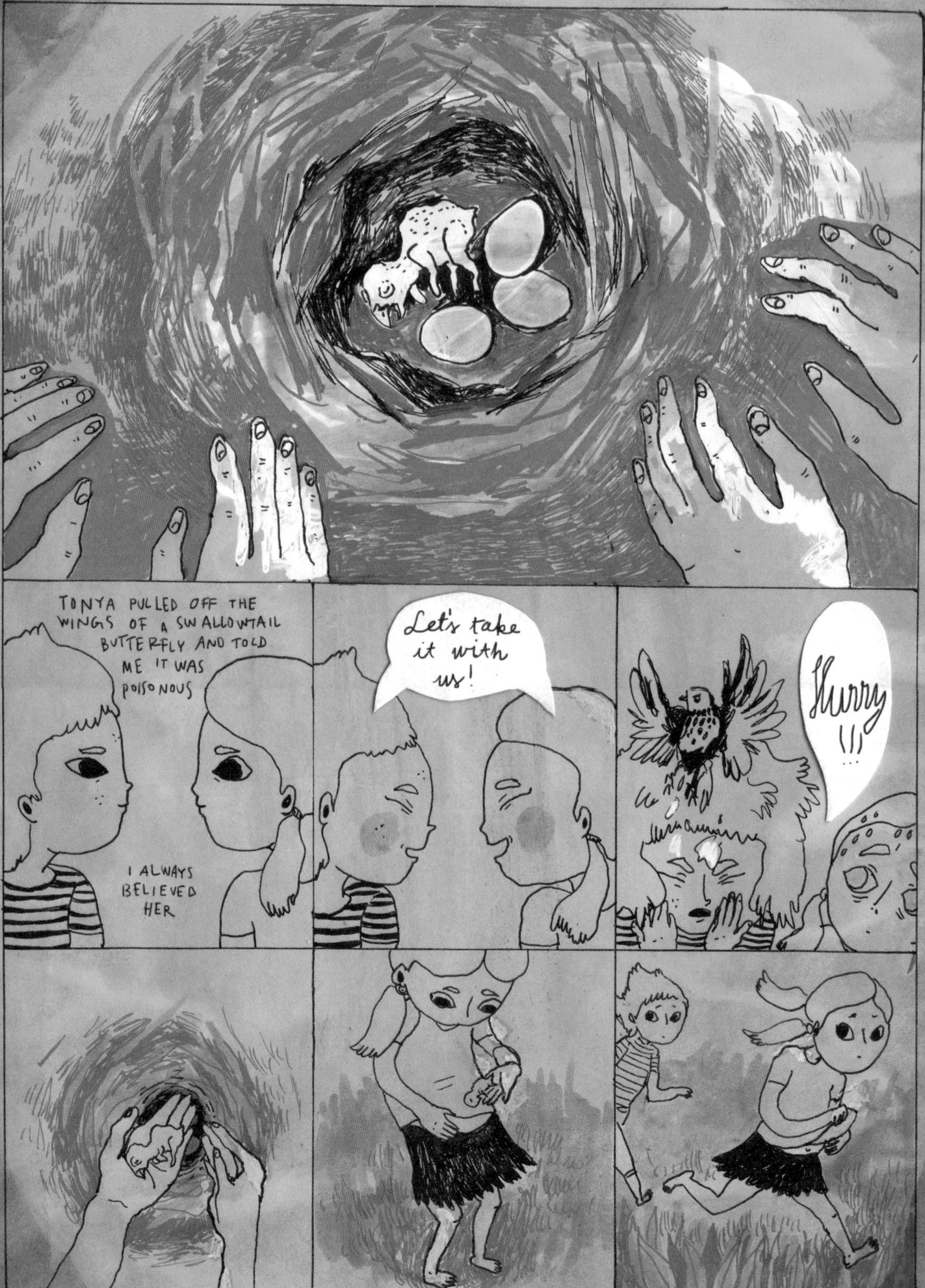
TONYA PULLED OFF THE WINGS OF A SWALLOWTAIL BUTTERFLY AND TOLD ME IT WAS POISSONOUS
I ALWAYS BELIEVED HER
Let's take it with us!
Hurry!!

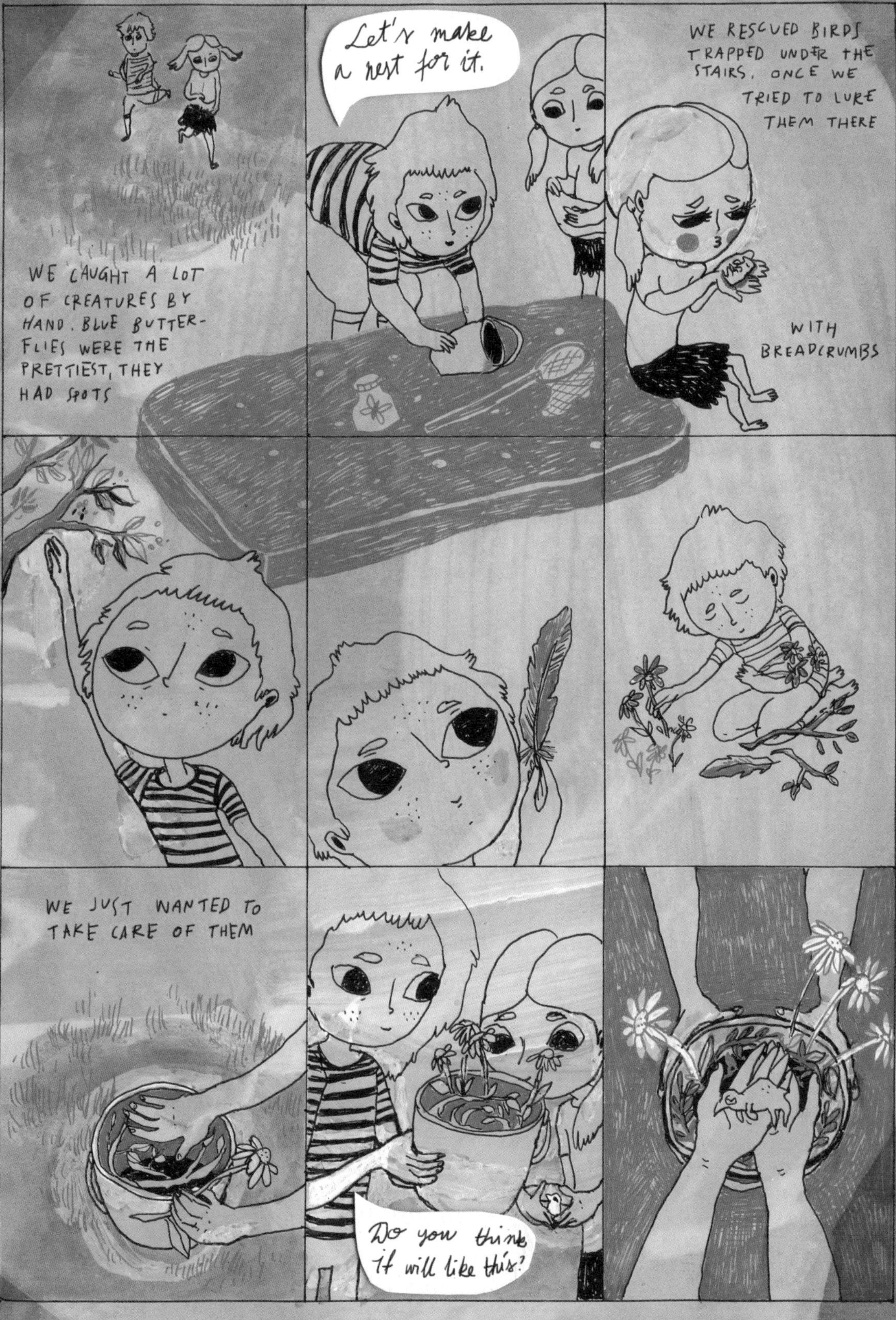
WE CAUGHT A LOT OF CREATURES BY HAND. BLUE BUTTERFLIES WERE THE PRETTIEST, THEY HAD SPOTS
Let's make a nest for it.
WE RESCUED BIRDS TRAPPED UNDER THE STAIRS. ONCE WE TRIED TO LURE THEM THERE
WITH BREADCRUMBS
WE JUST WANTED TO TAKE CARE OF THEM
Do you think it will like this?

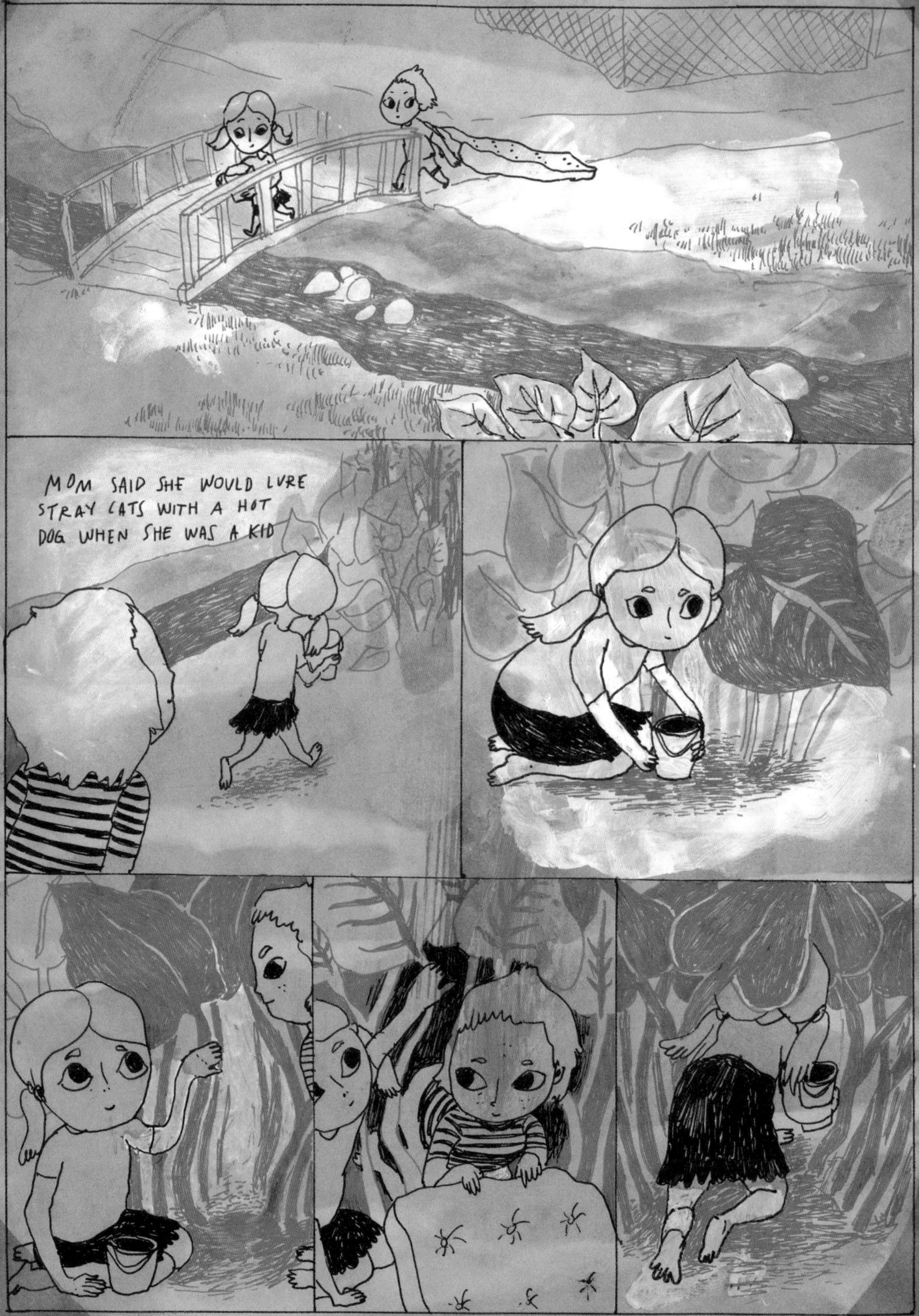
MOM SAID SHE WOULD LURE STRAY CATS WITH A HOT DOG WHEN SHE WAS A KID

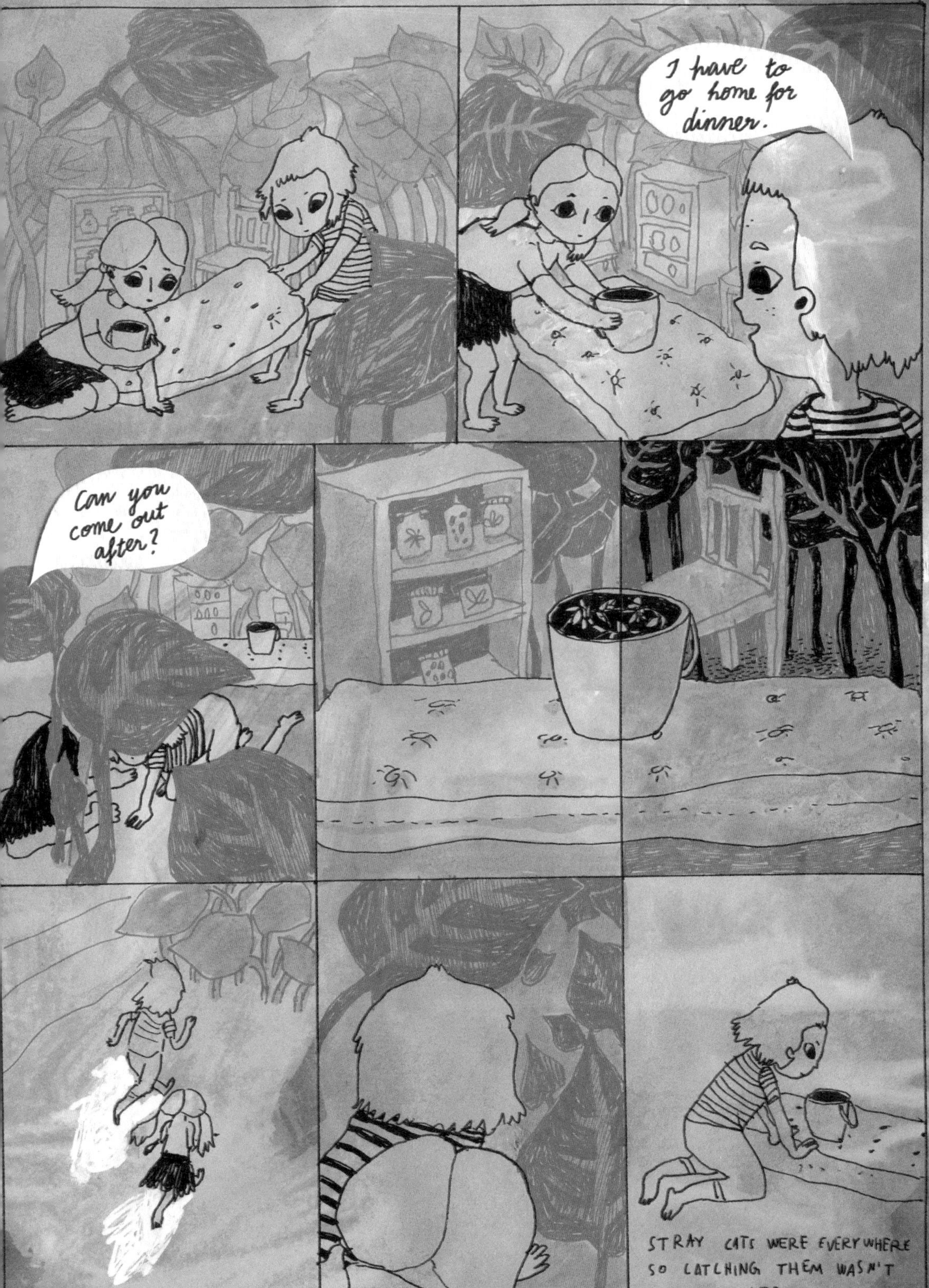
I have to go home for dinner.
Can you come out after?
STRAY CATS WERE EVERYWHERE SO CATCHING THEM WASN'T HARD

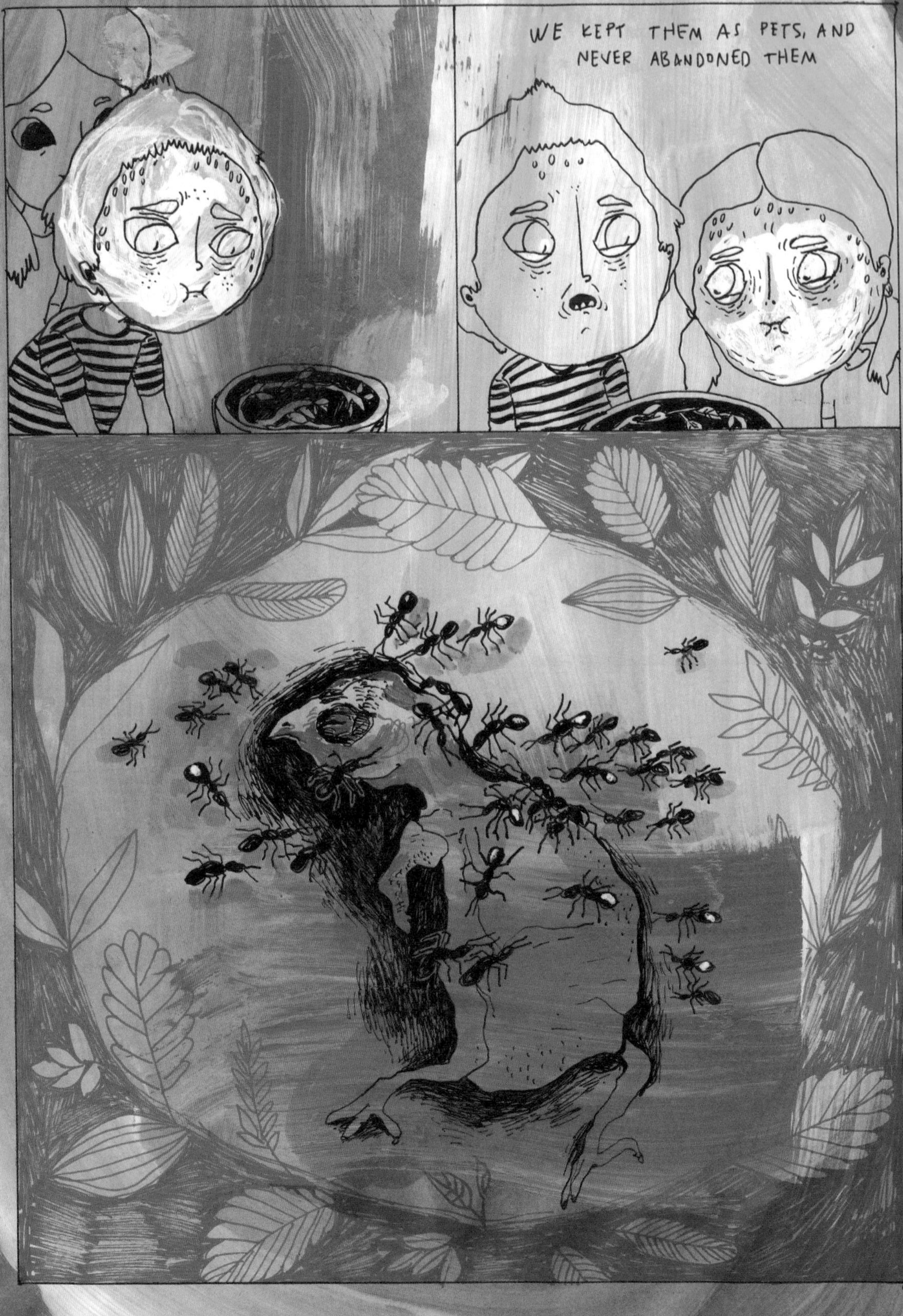
WE KEPT THEM AS PETS, AND NEVER ABANDONED THEM

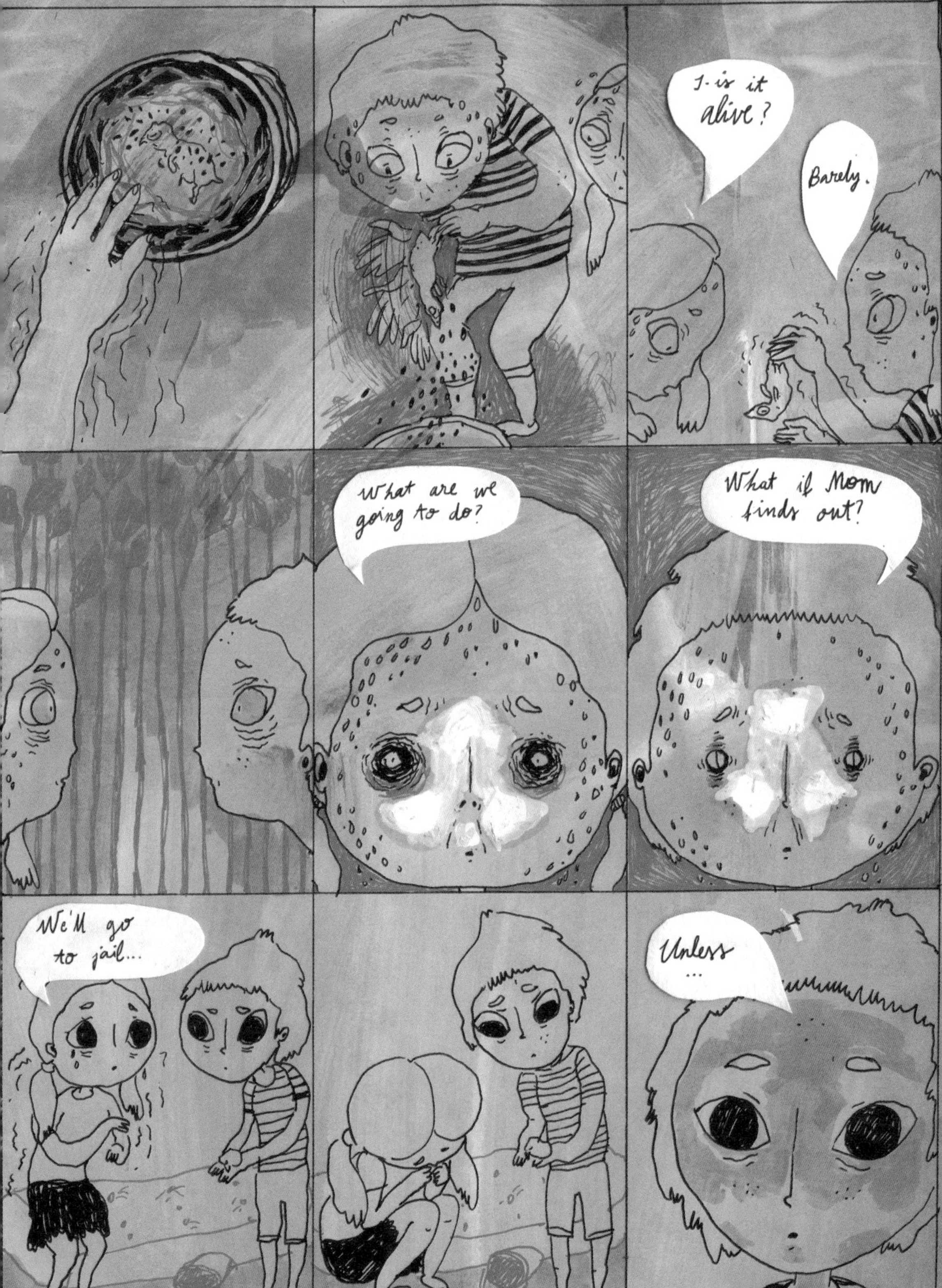
I-is it alive?
Barely.
What are we going to do?
What if Mom finds out?
We'll go to jail...
Unless
...

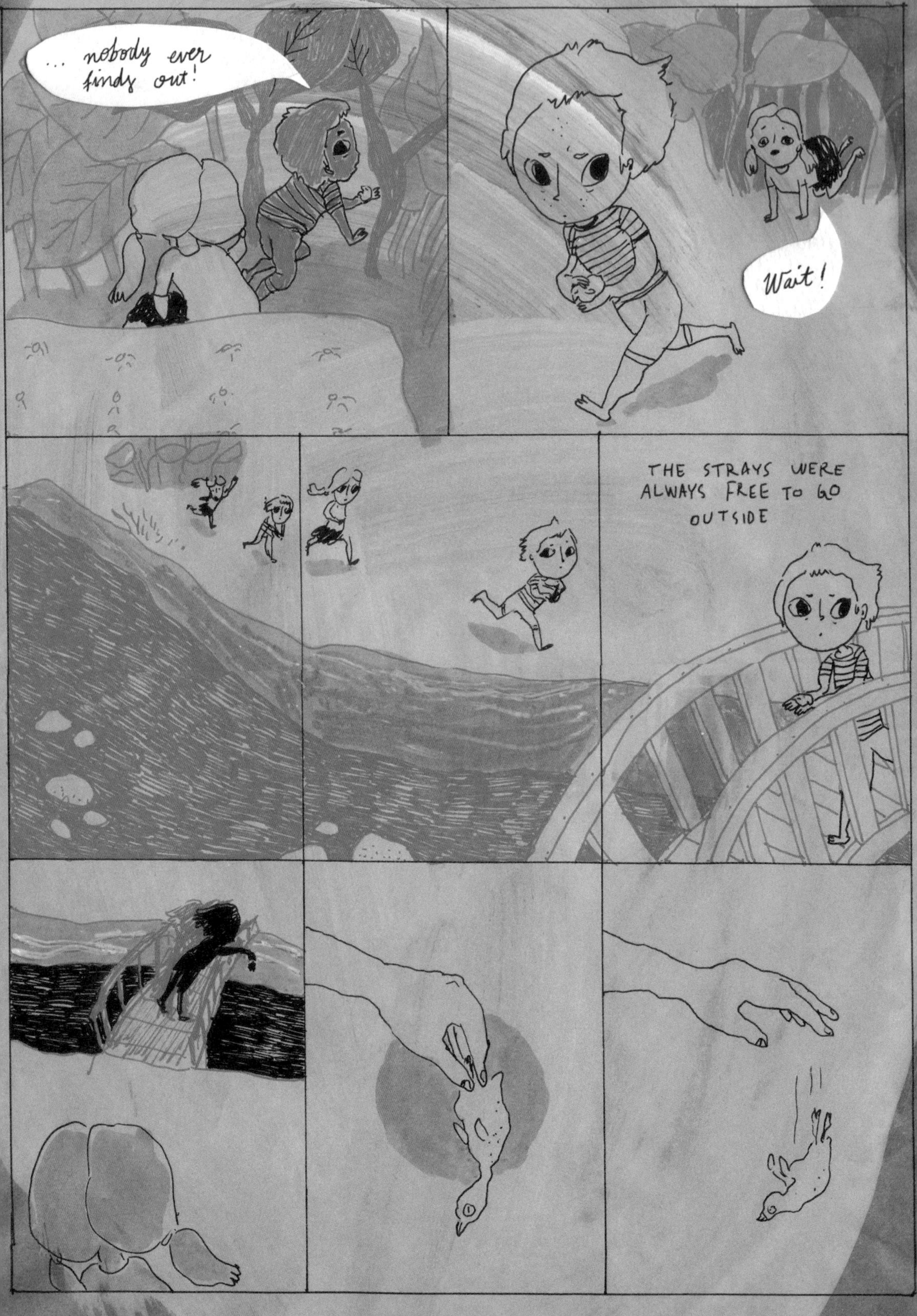
... nobody ever finds out!
Wait!
THE STRAYS WERE ALWAYS FREE TO GO OUTSIDE

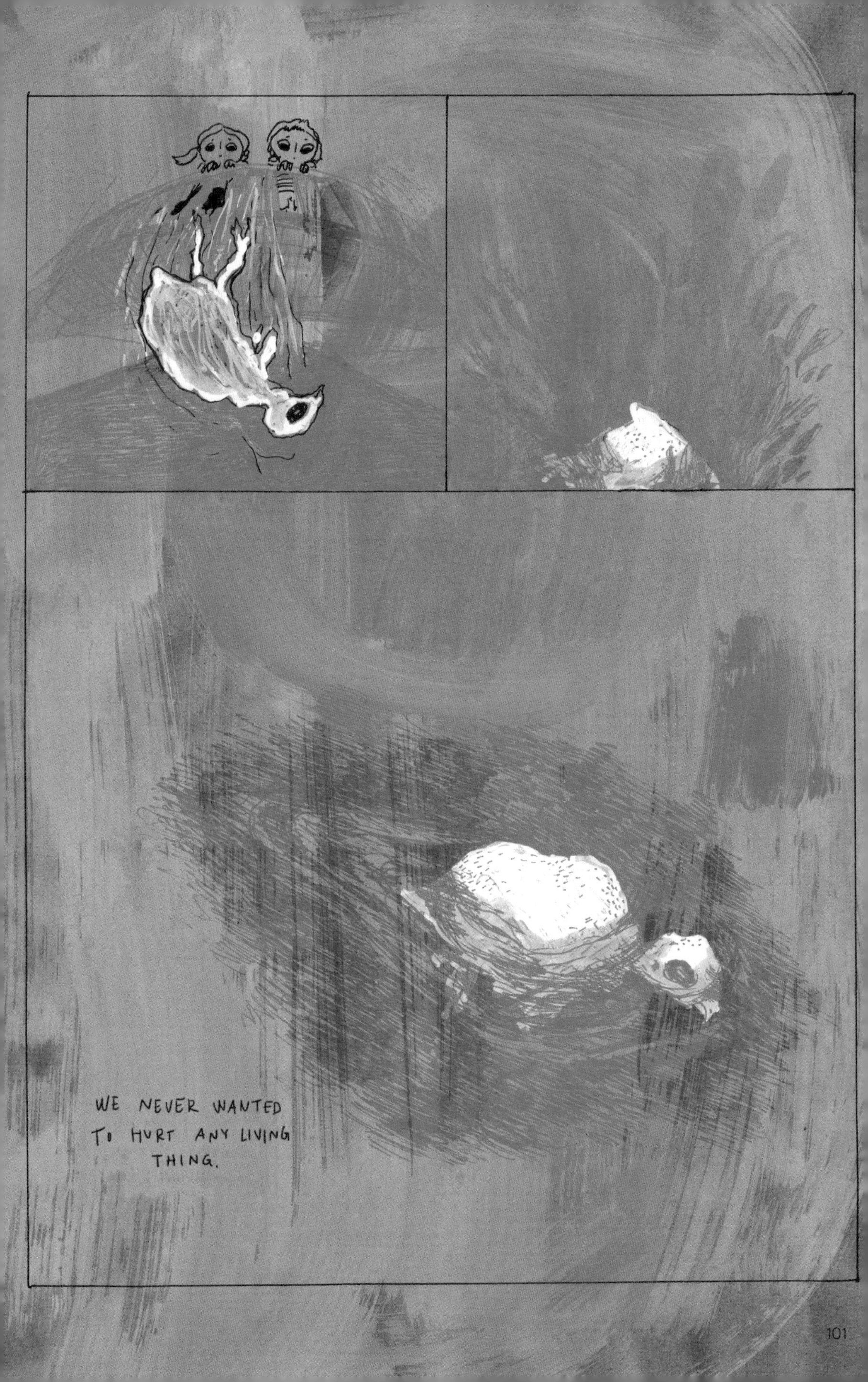
WE NEVER WANTED TO HURT ANY LIVING THING.

BEING SELFISH
IS A SIN

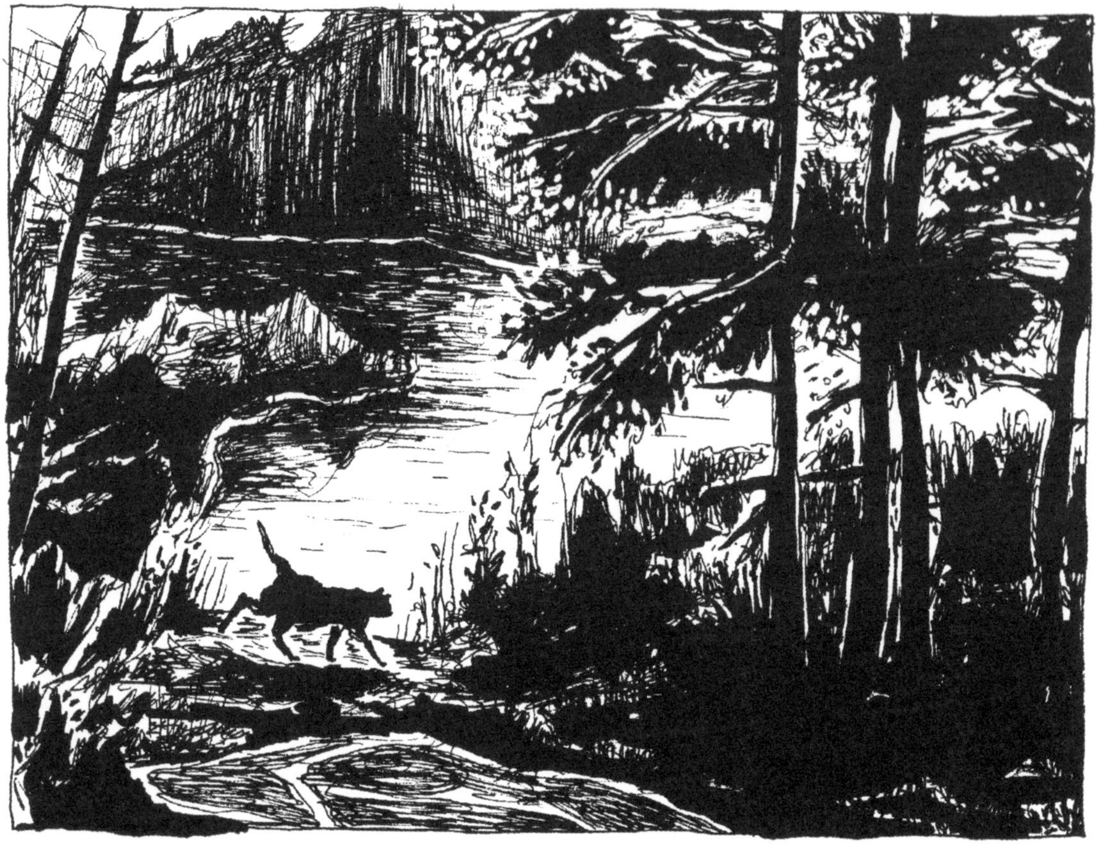

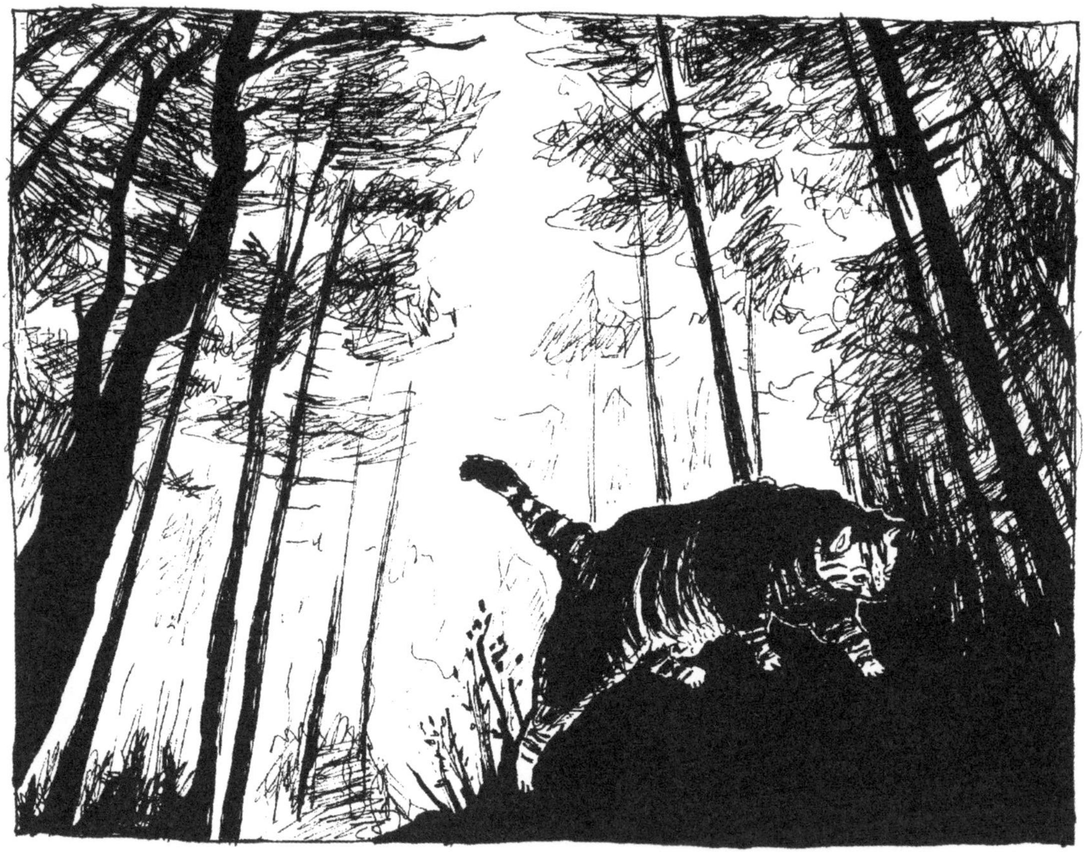

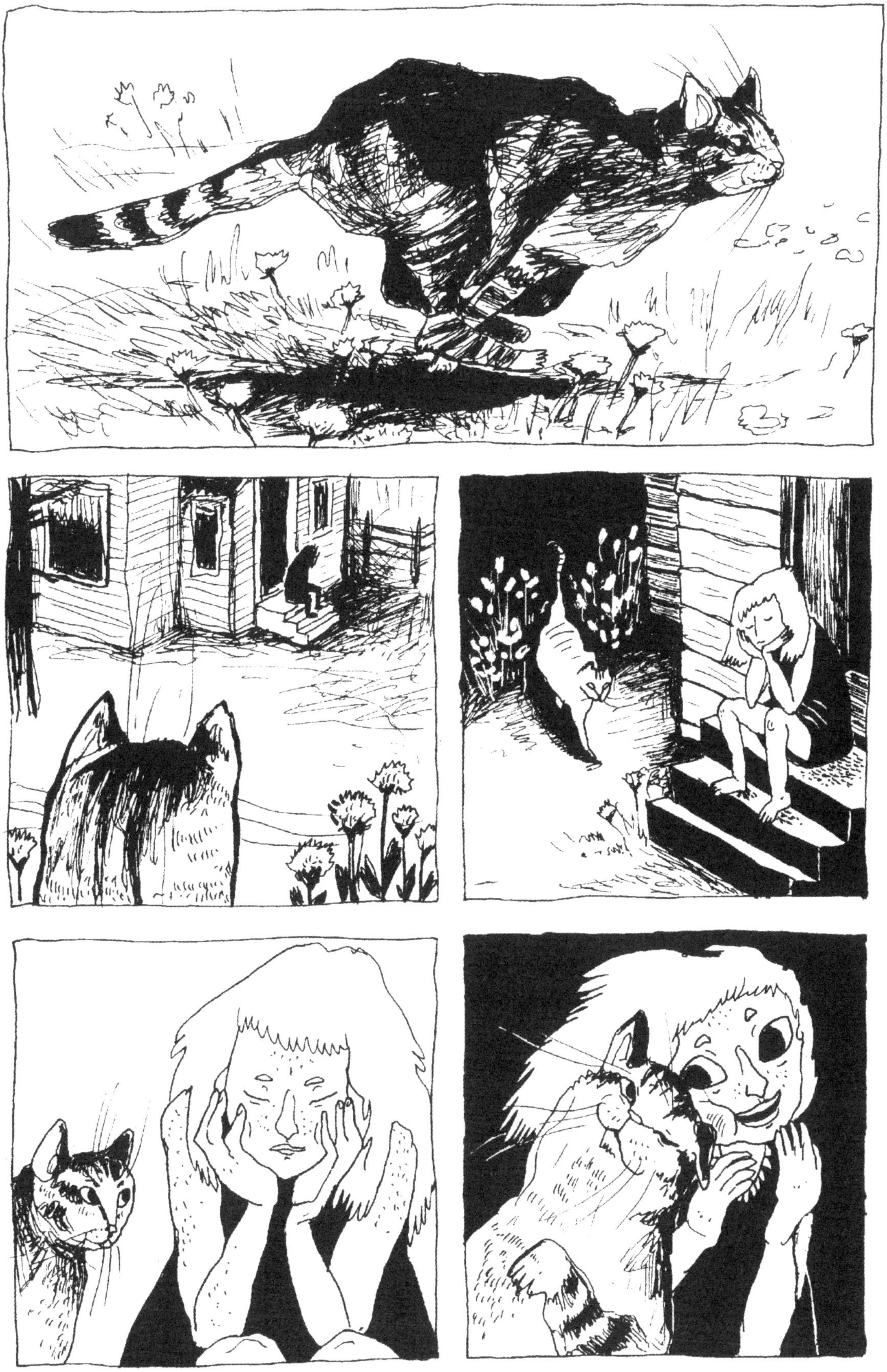

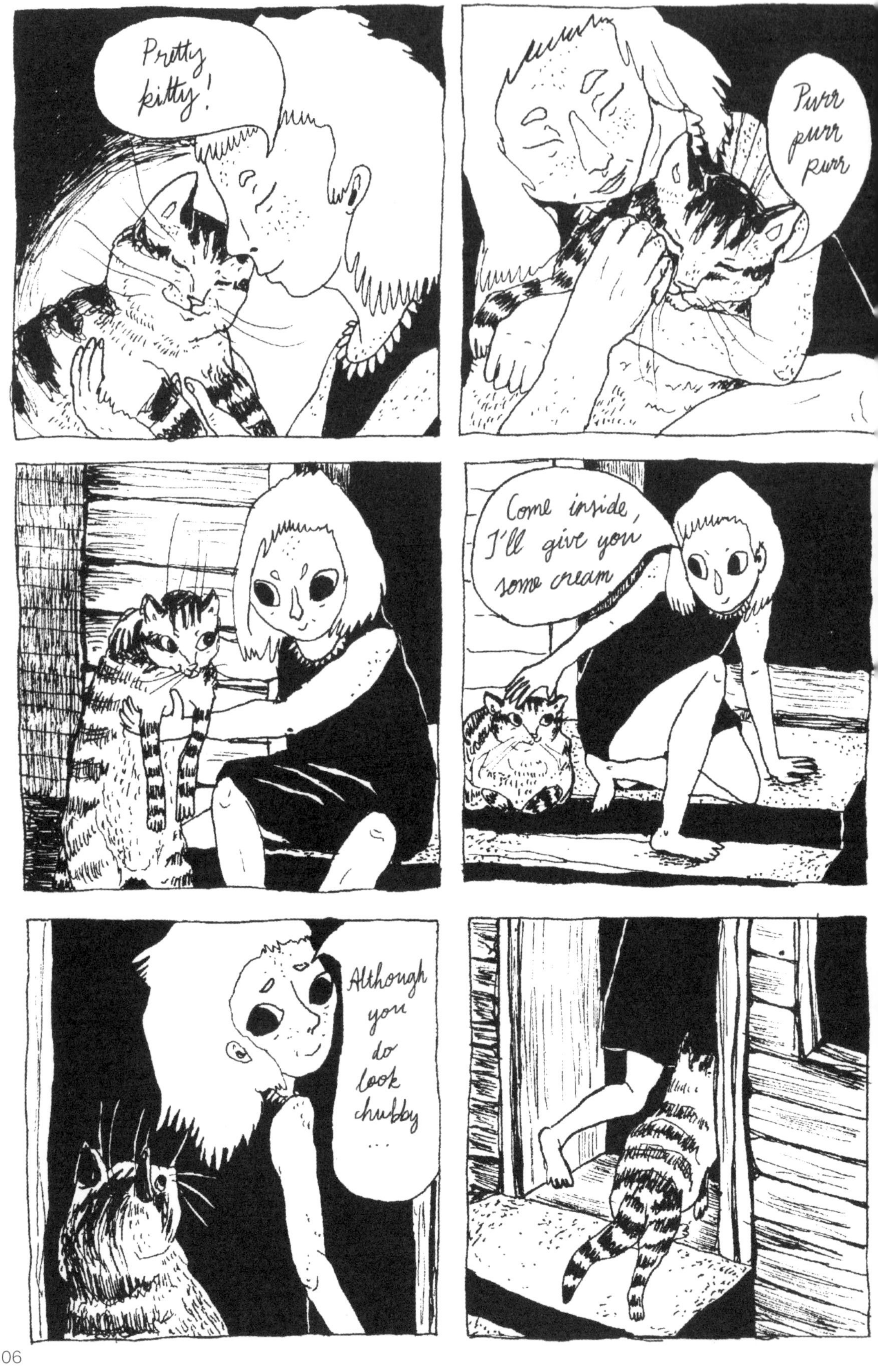
Pretty kitty!
Purr purr purr
Come inside, I'll give you some cream
Although you do look chubby ...

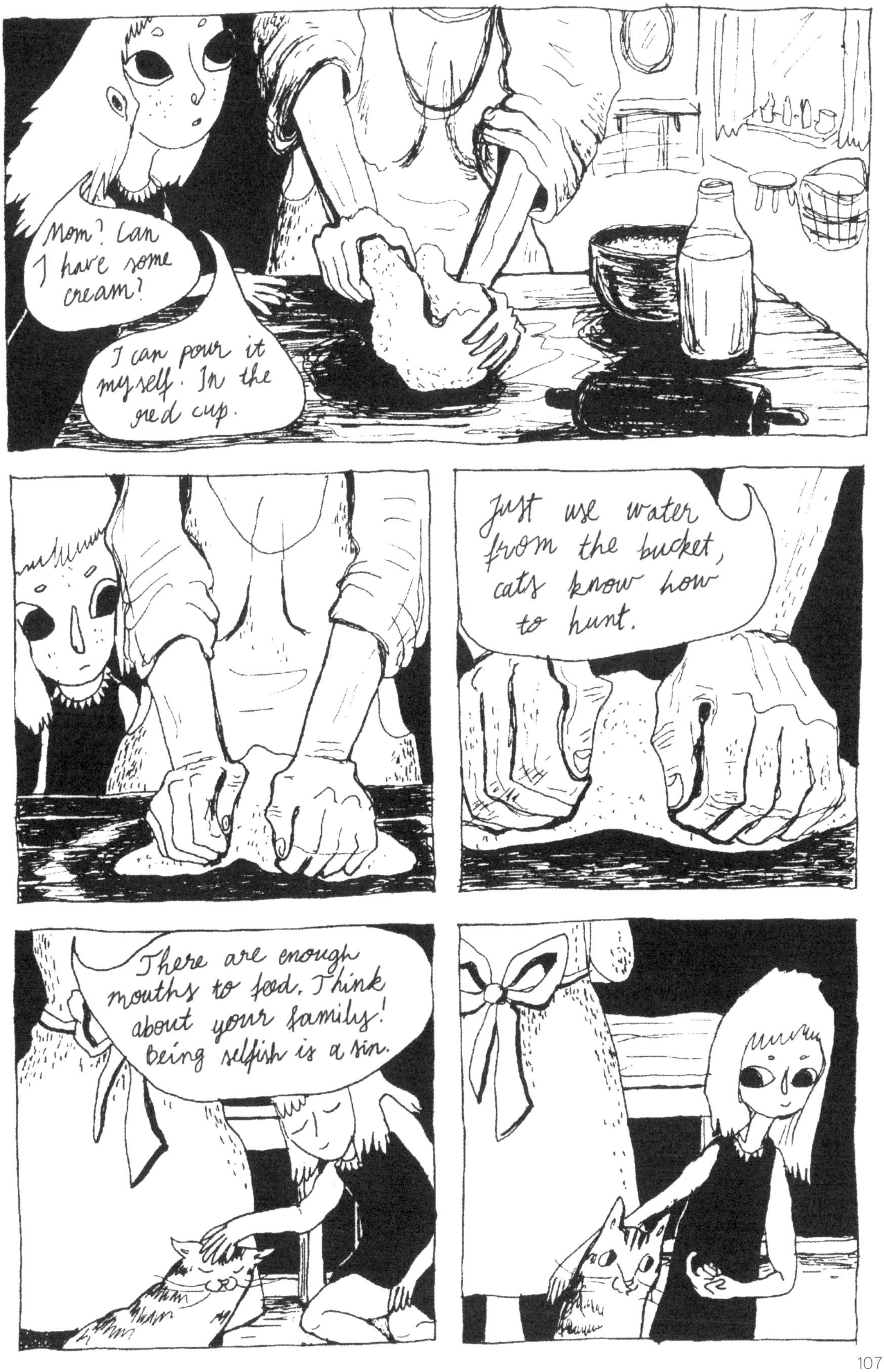
Mom? Can I have some cream?
I can pour it myself. In the red cup.
Just use water from the bucket, cats know how to hunt.
There are enough mouths to feed. Think about your family! Being selfish is a sin.

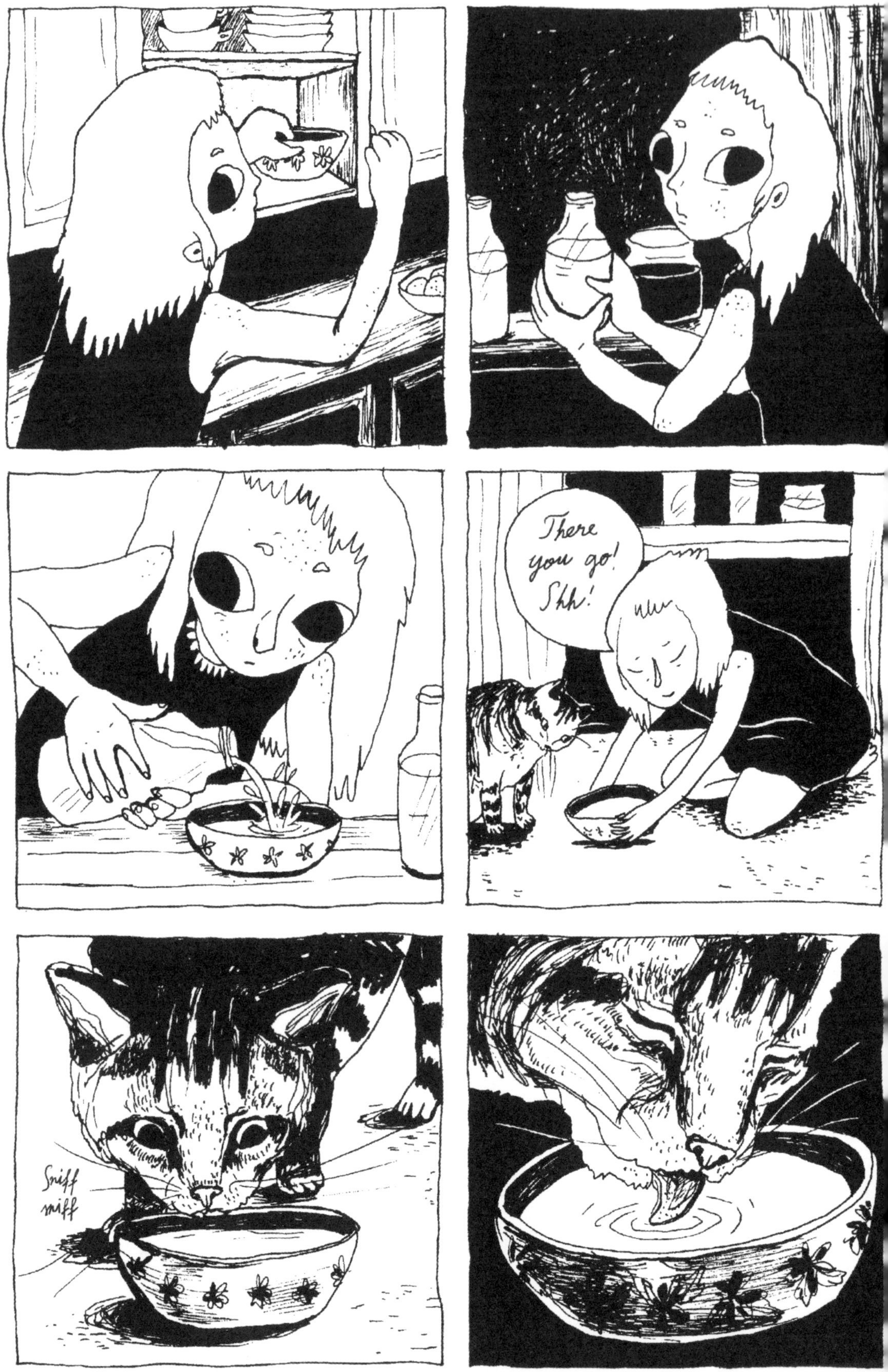
There you go! Shh!
Sniff sniff

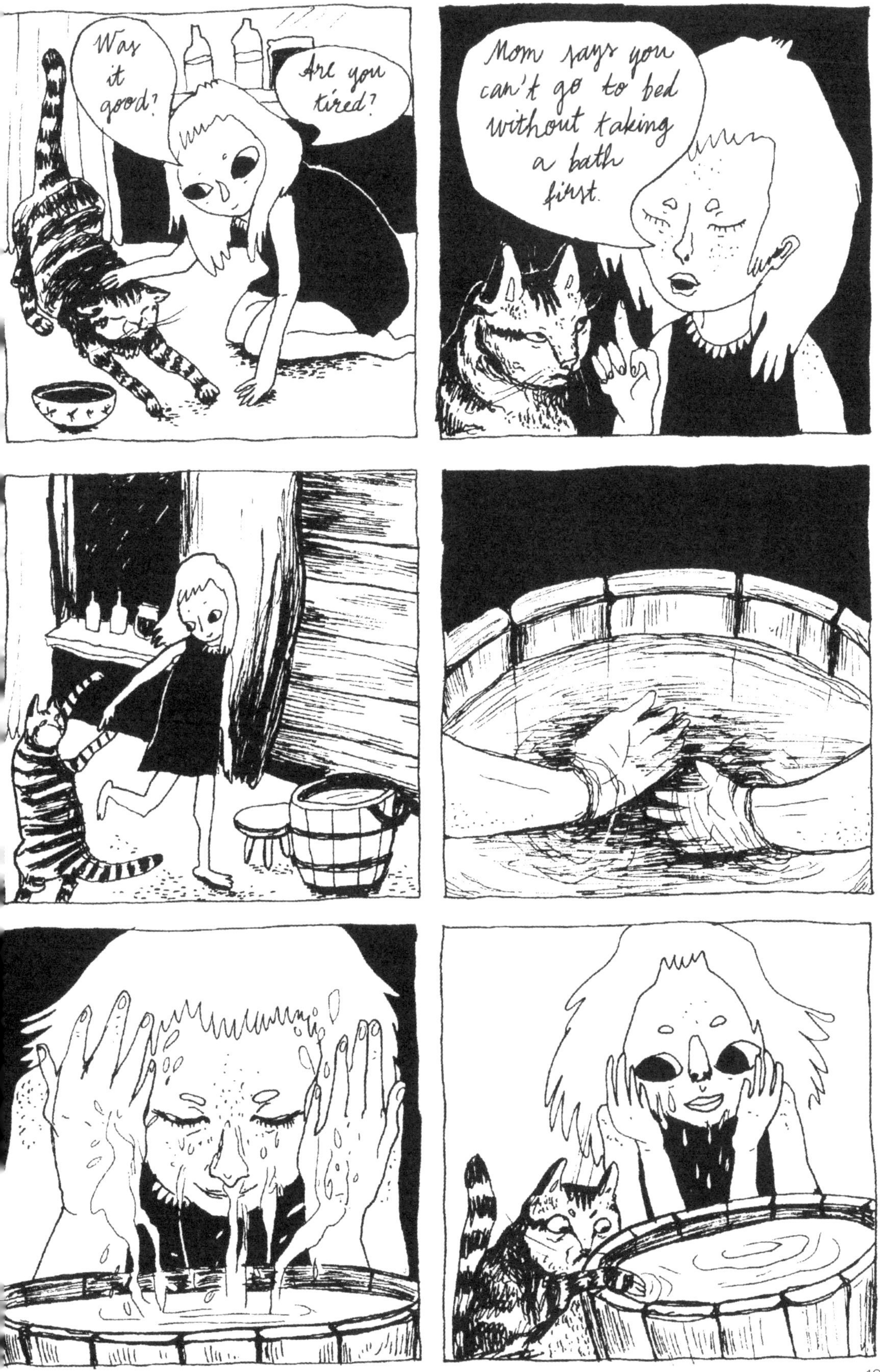
Was it good?
Are you tired?
Mom says you can't go to bed without taking a bath first.

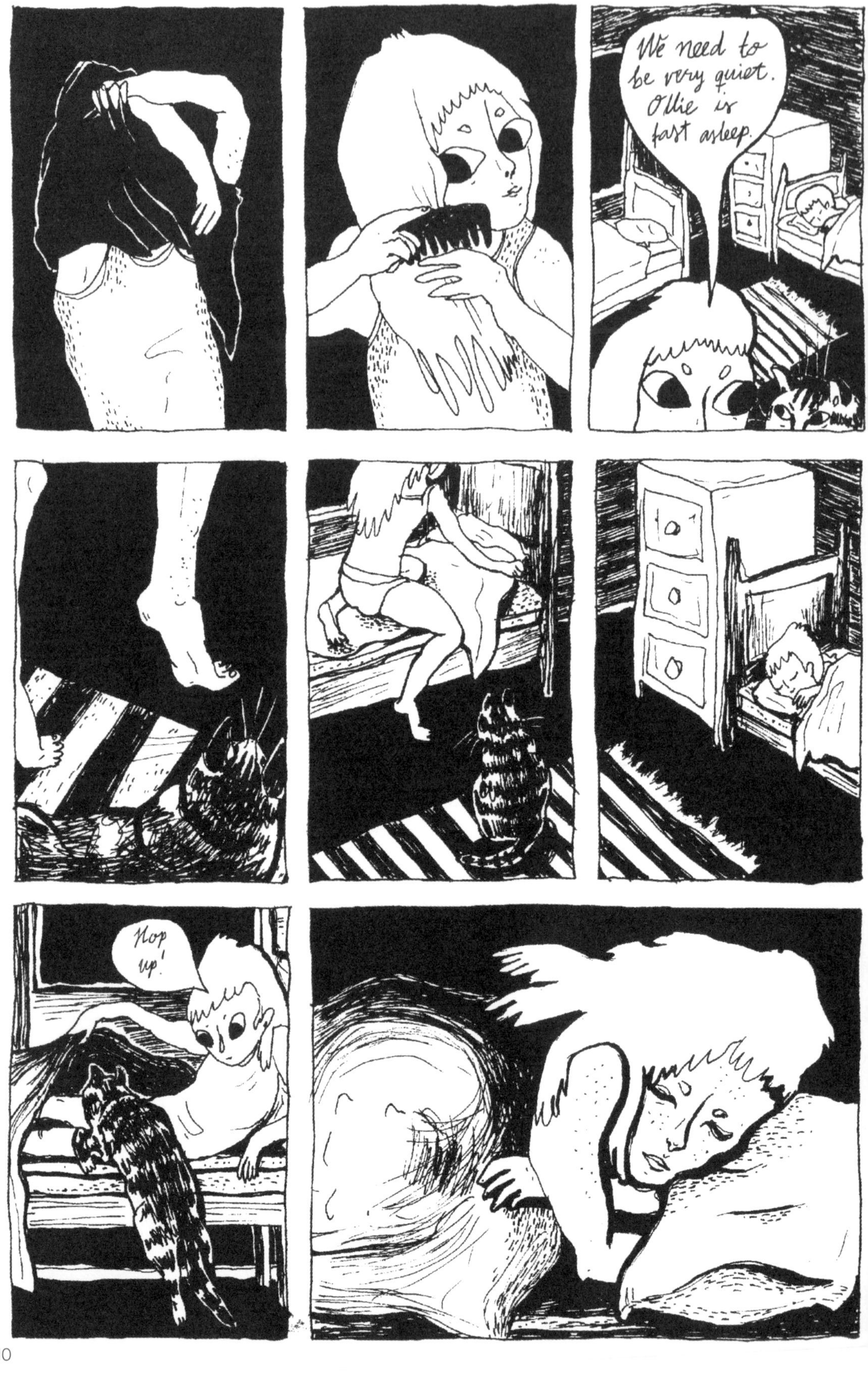
We need to be very quiet. Ollie is fast asleep.
Hop up!

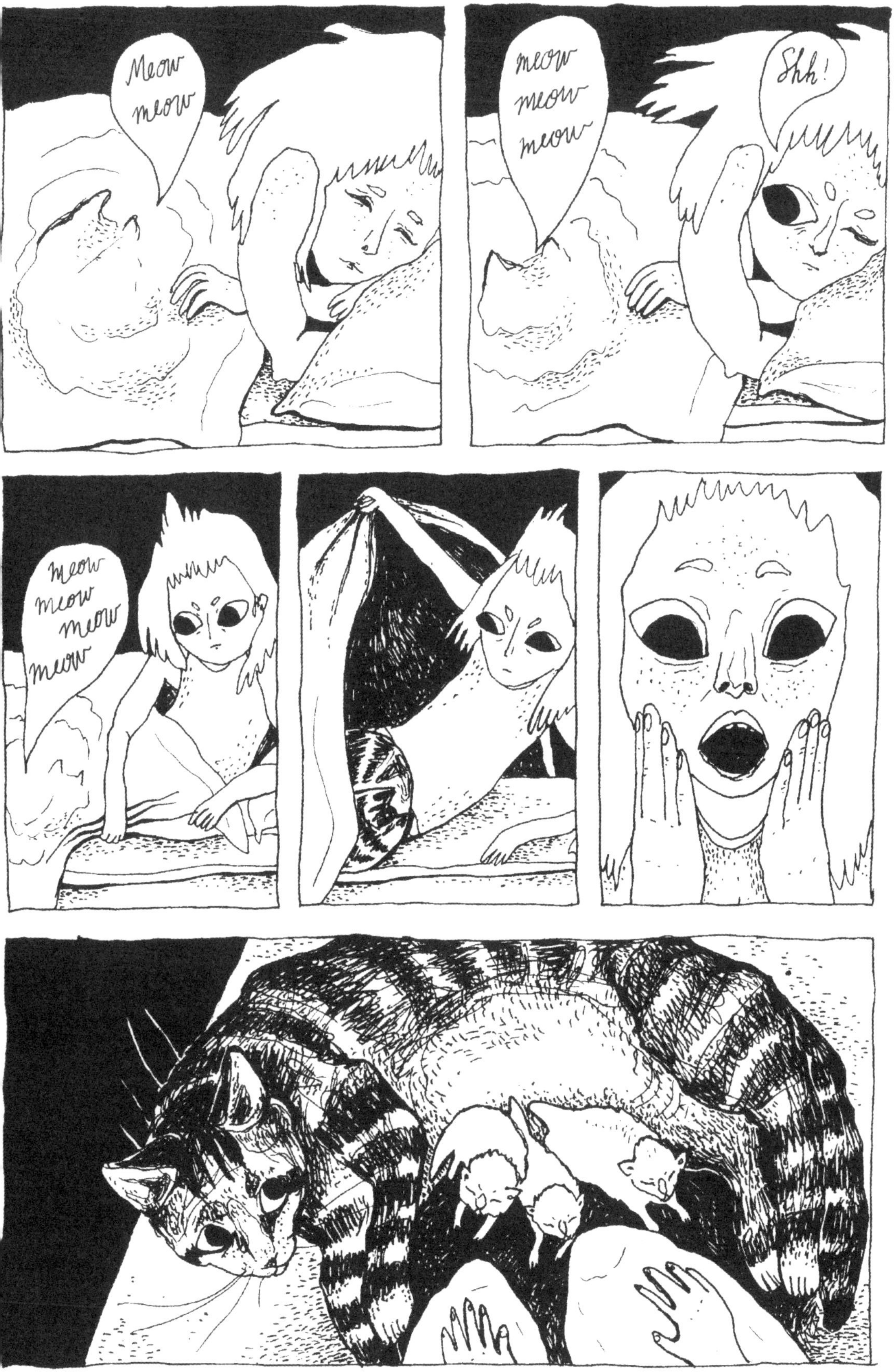
Meow meow
meow meow meow
Shh!
meow meow meow meow

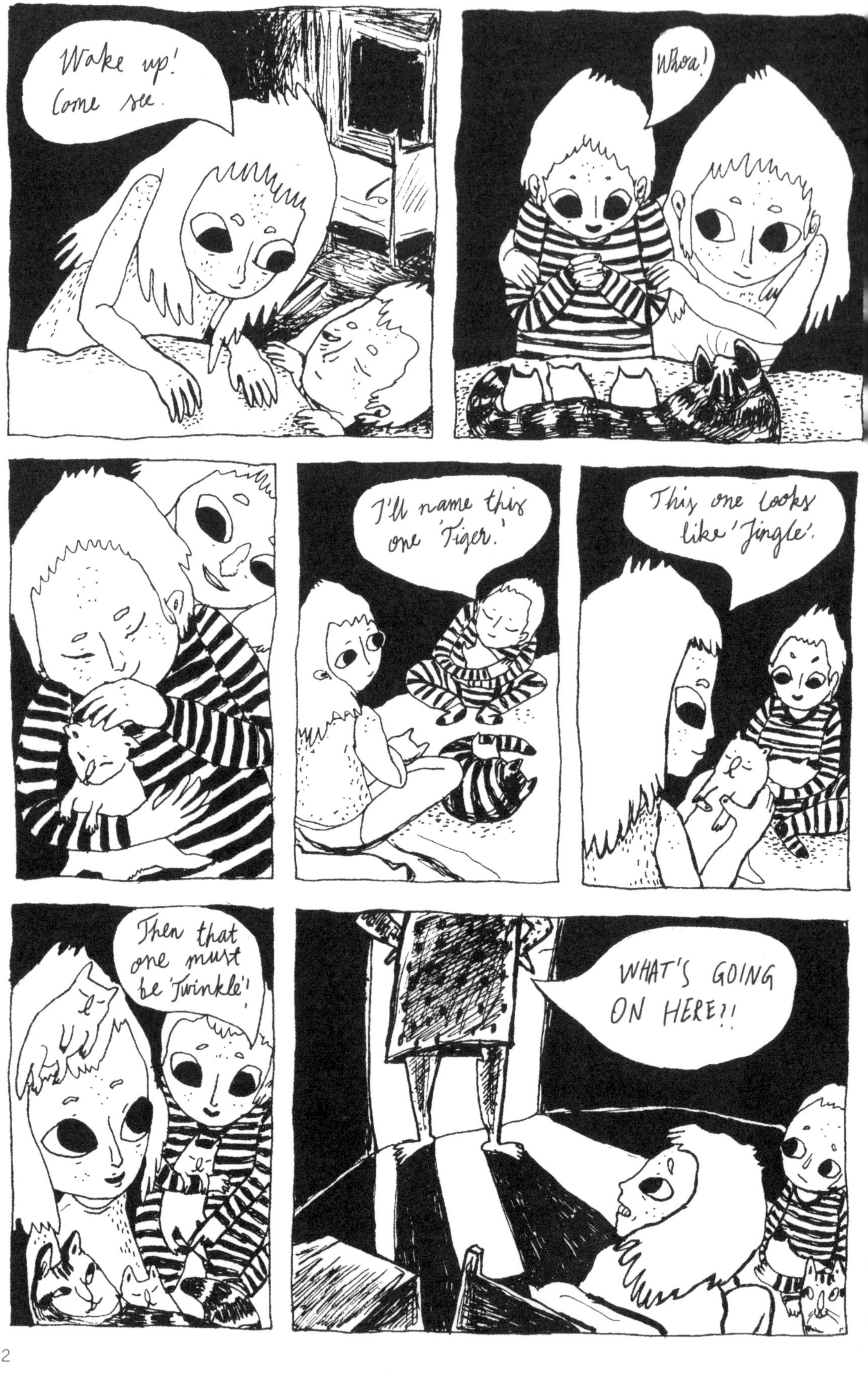
Wake up! Come see.
Whoa!
I'll name this one 'Tiger.'
This one looks like 'Jingle'.
Then that one must be 'Twinkle'!
WHAT'S GOING ON HERE?!

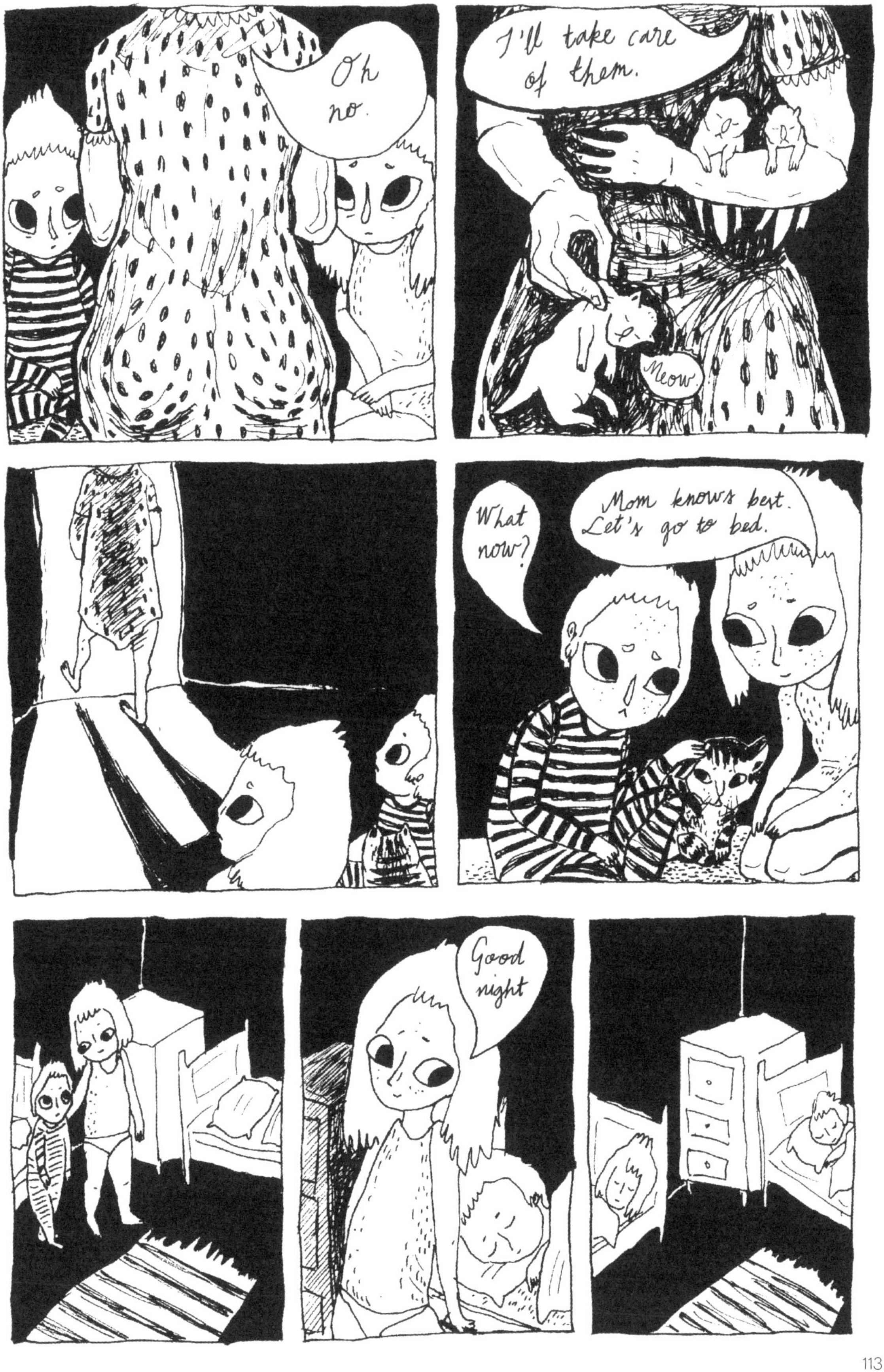
Oh no.
I'll take care of them.
Meow.
What now?
Mom knows best. Let's go to bed.
Good night

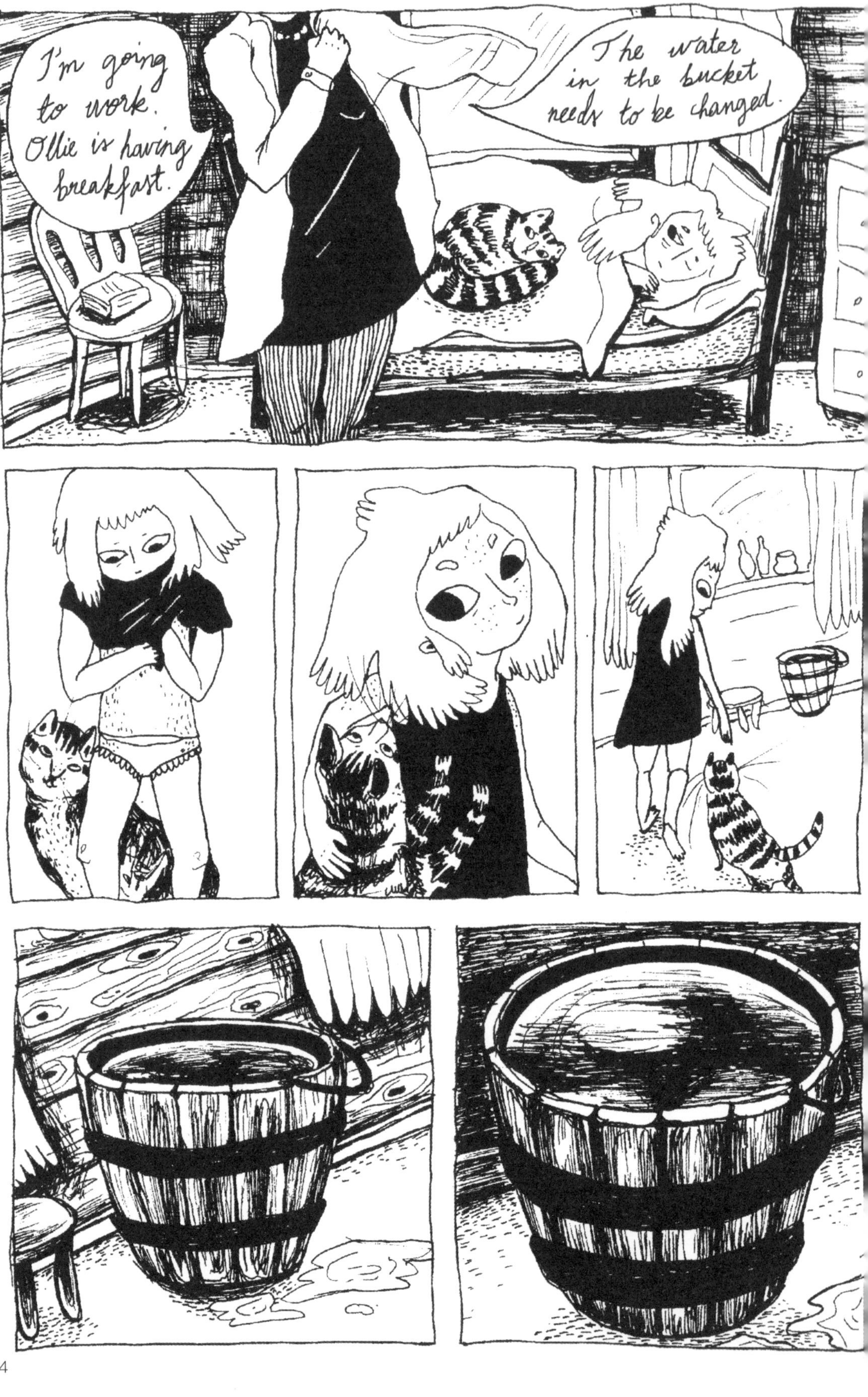
I'm going to work. Ollie is having breakfast.
The water in the bucket needs to be changed.

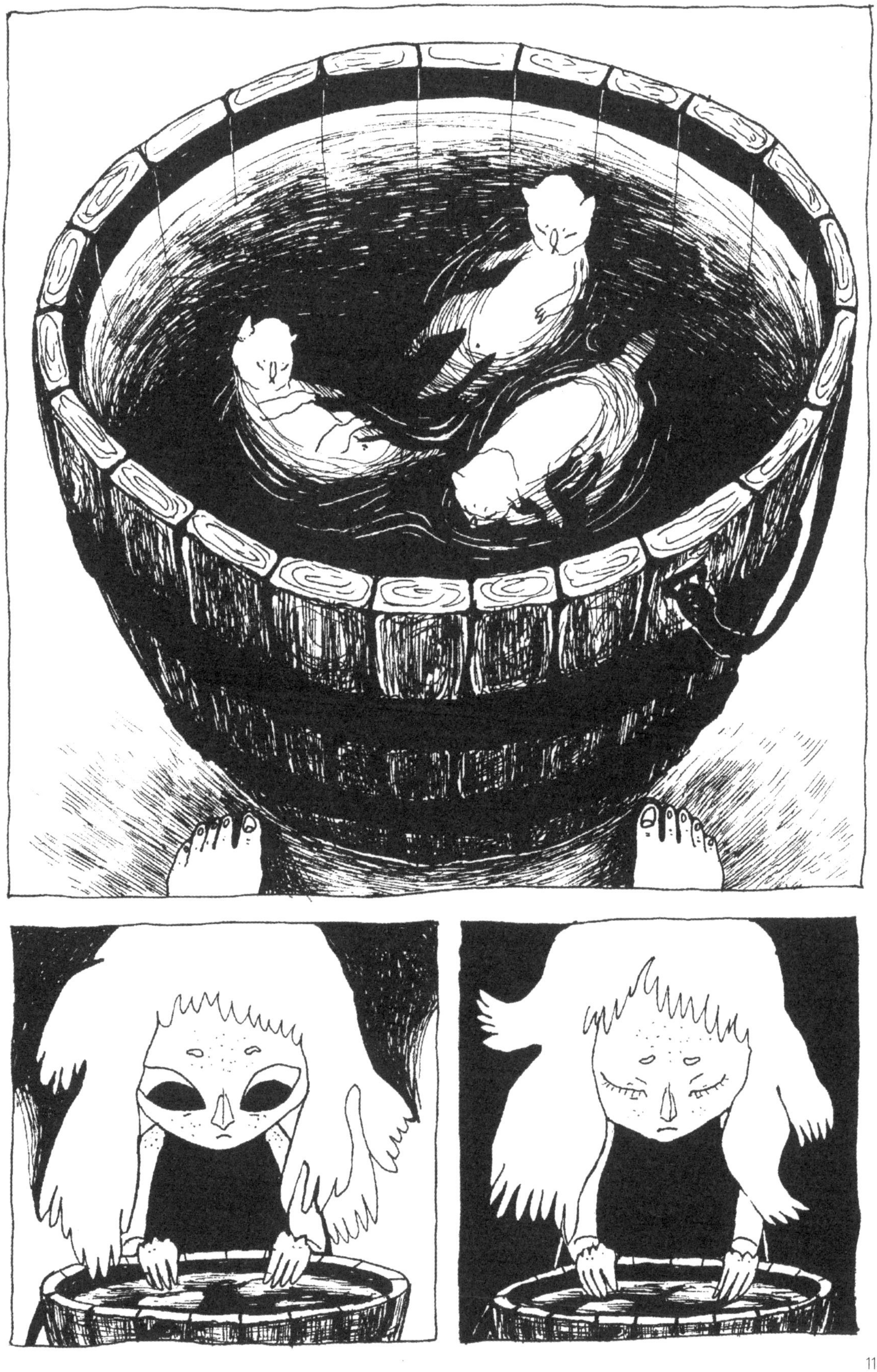

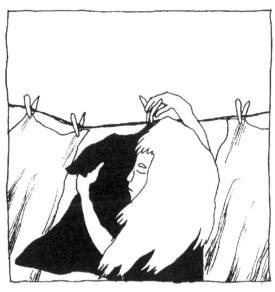

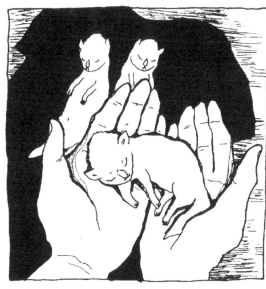

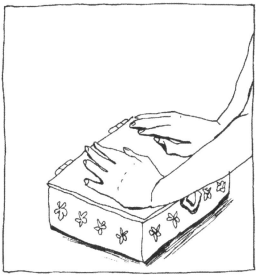

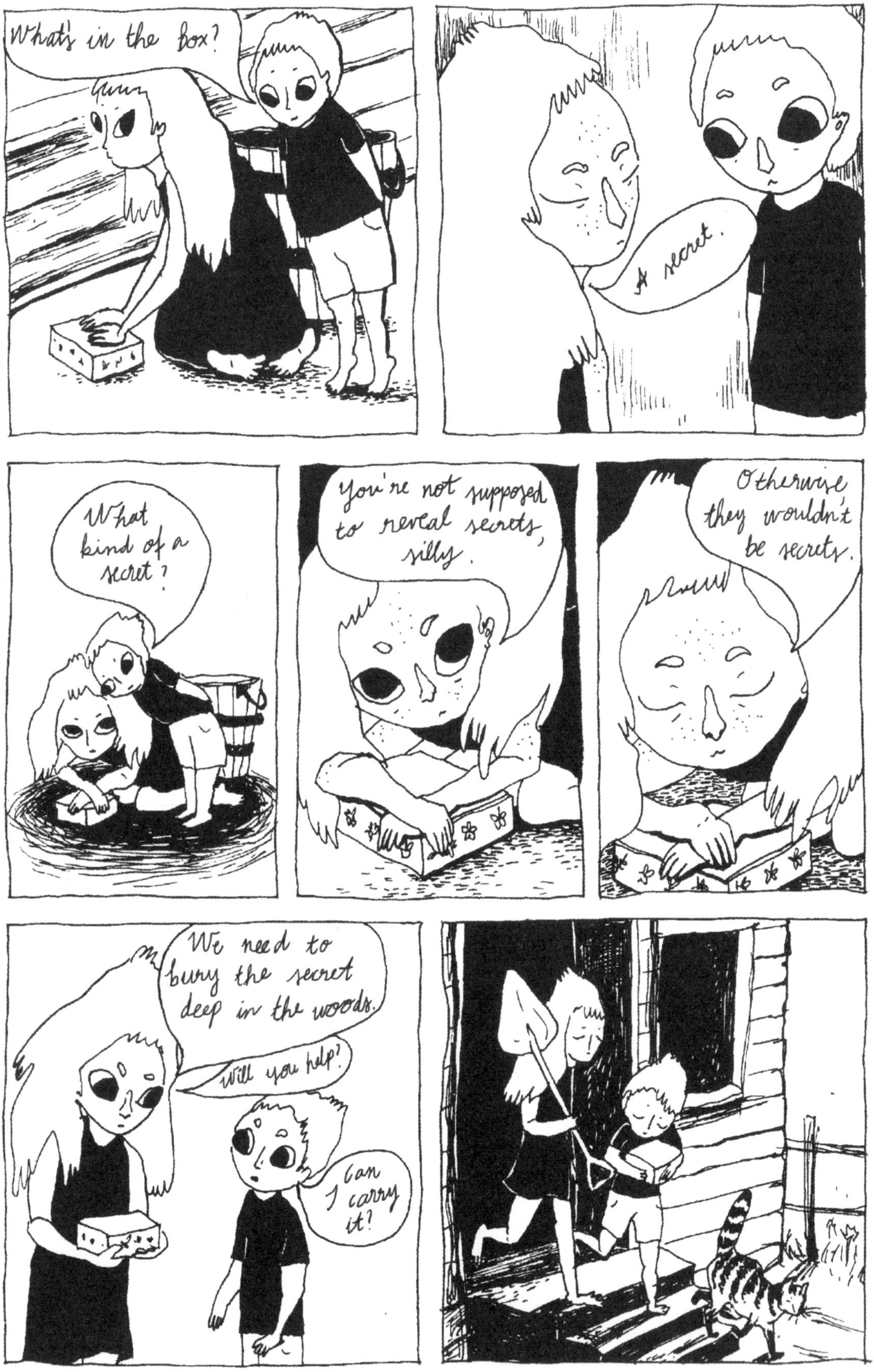
What's in the box?
A secret.
What kind of a secret?
You're not supposed to reveal secrets, silly.
Otherwise they wouldn't be secrets.
We need to bury the secret deep in the woods.
Will you help?
Can I carry it?

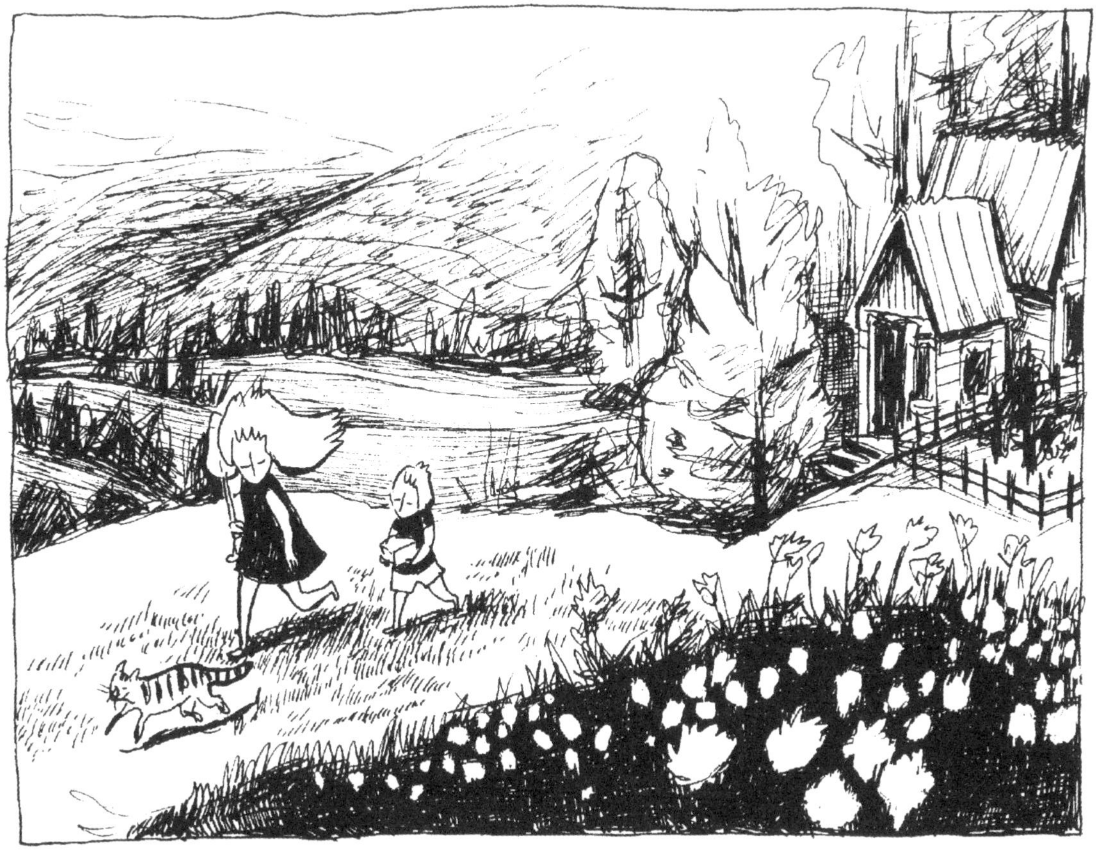

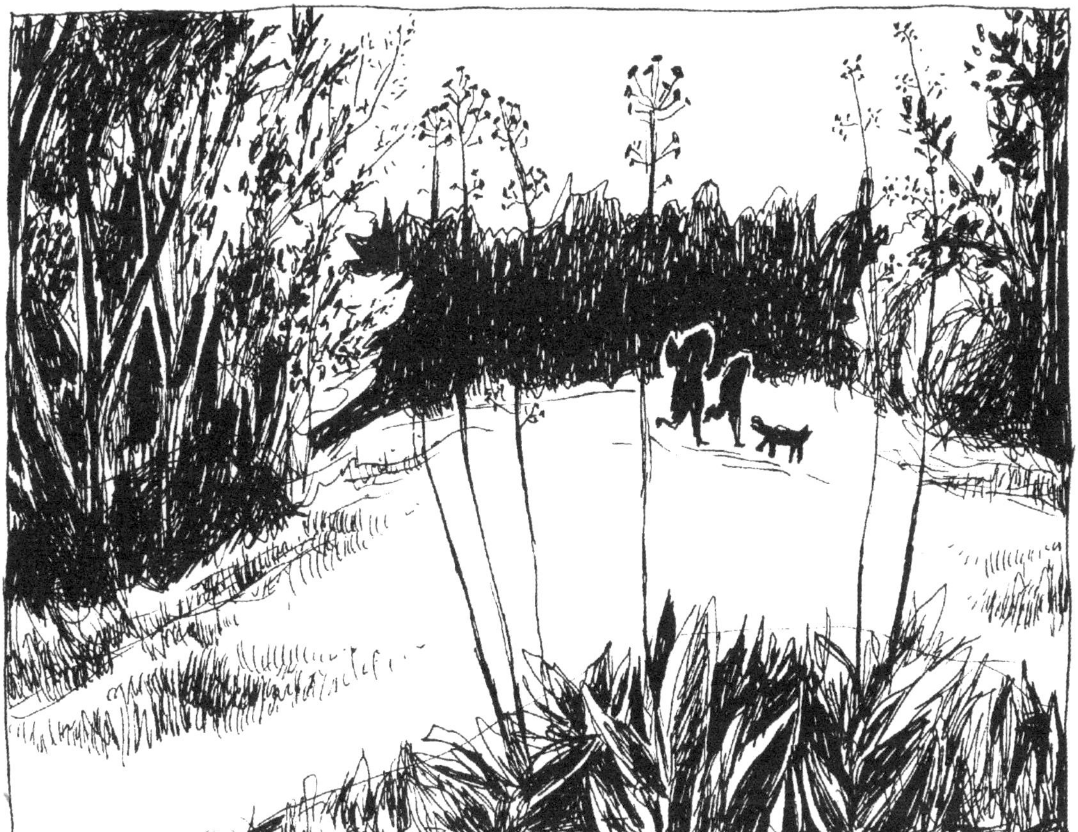

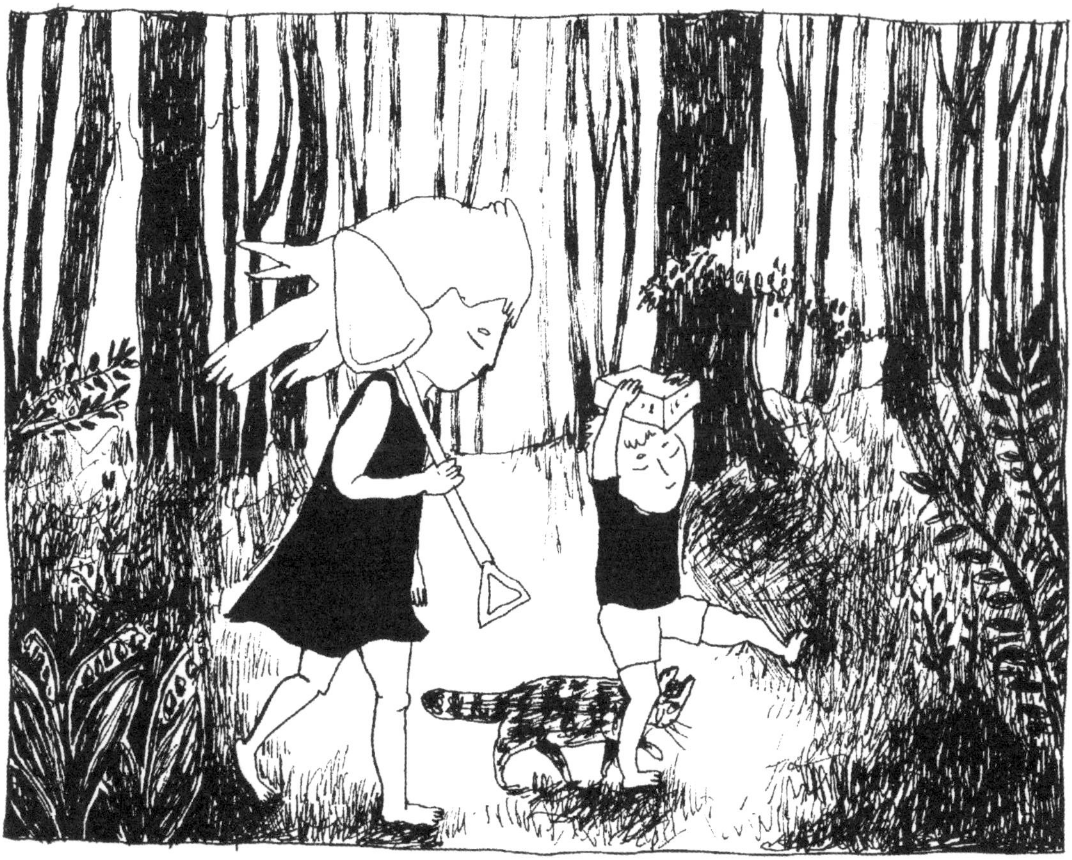

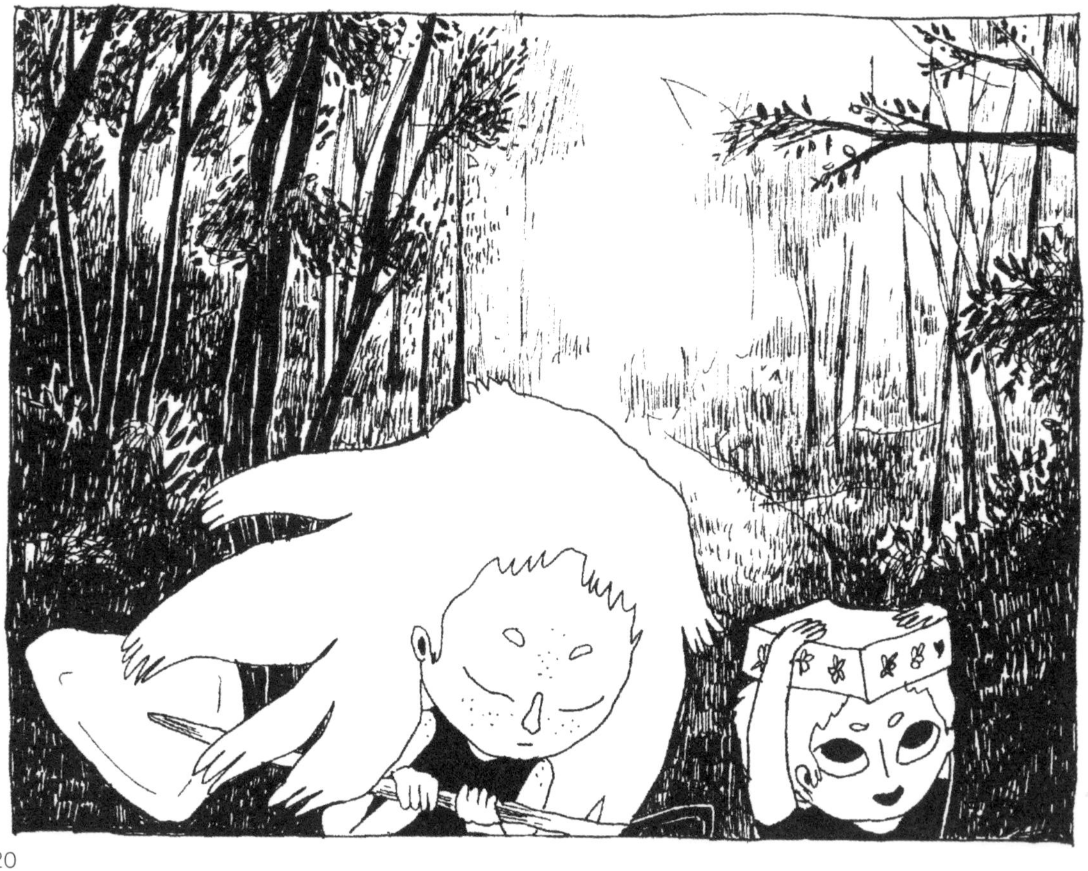

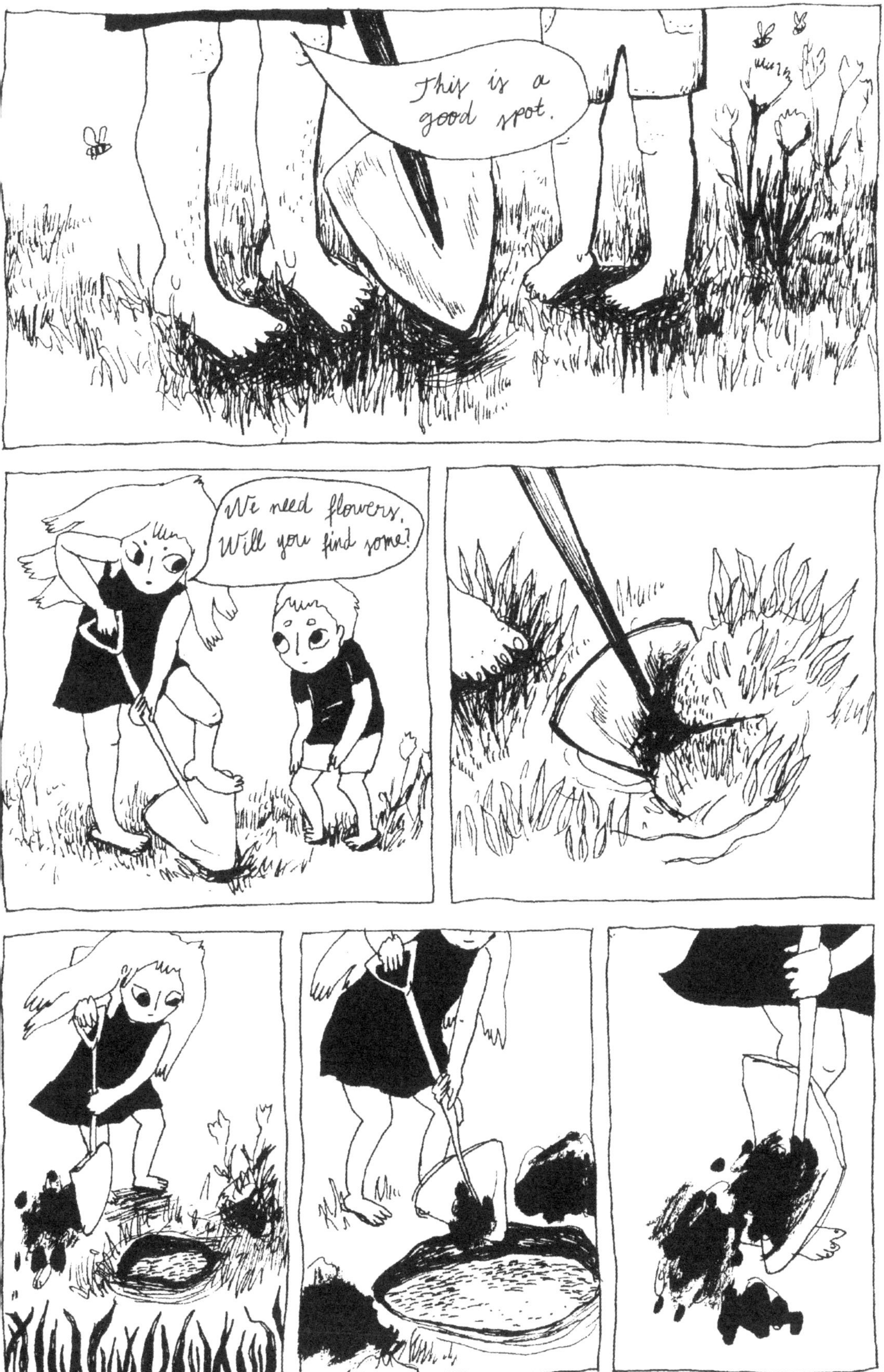
This is a good spot.
We need flowers. Will you find some?

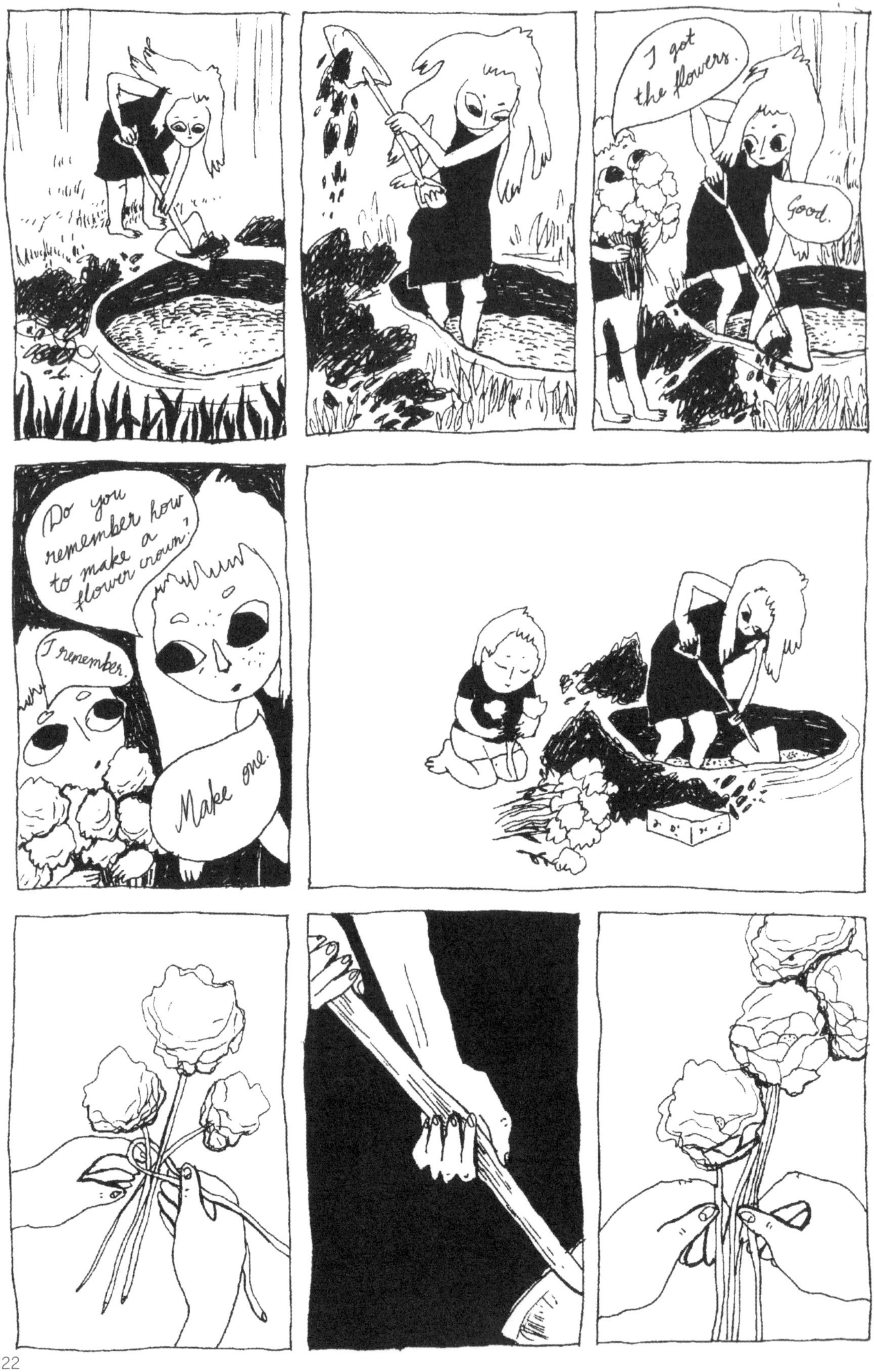
I got the flowers.
Good.
Do you remember how to make a flower crown?
I remember.
Make one.

Done!

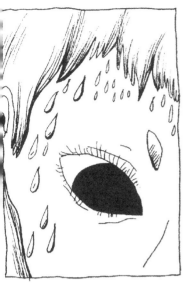

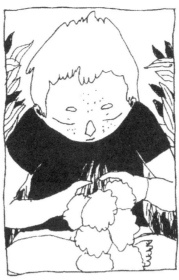

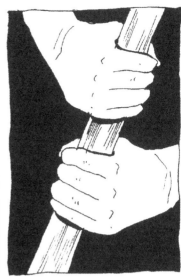

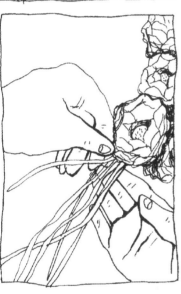

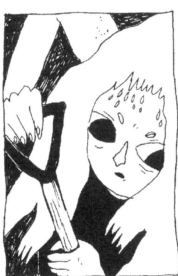

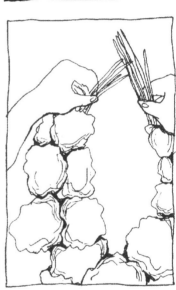

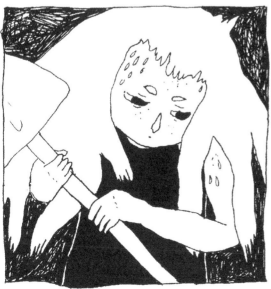

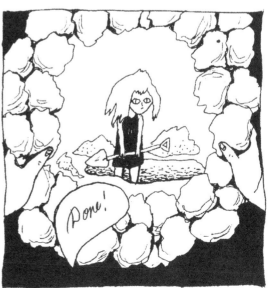

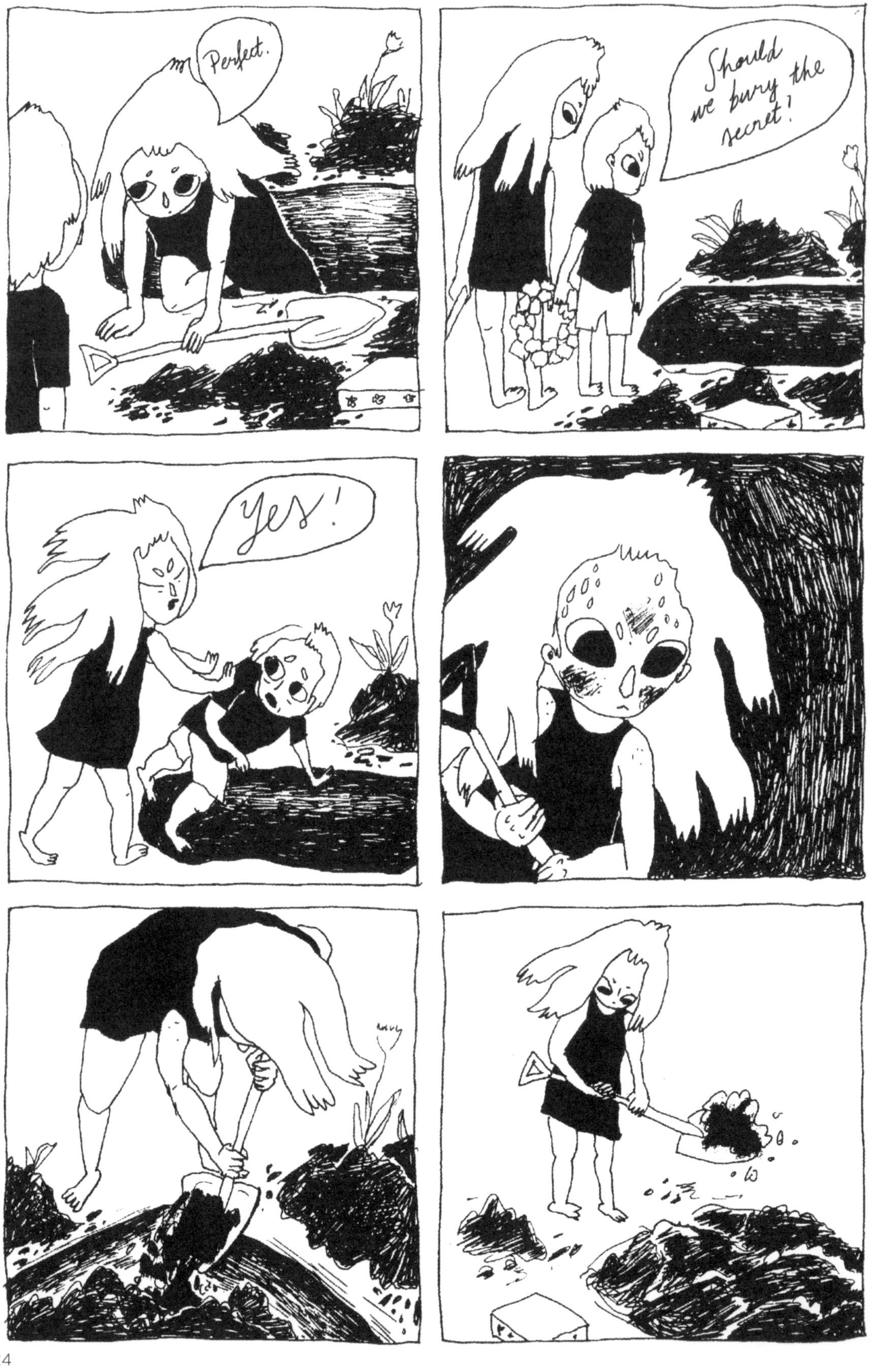
Perfect.
Should we bury the secret!
Yes!

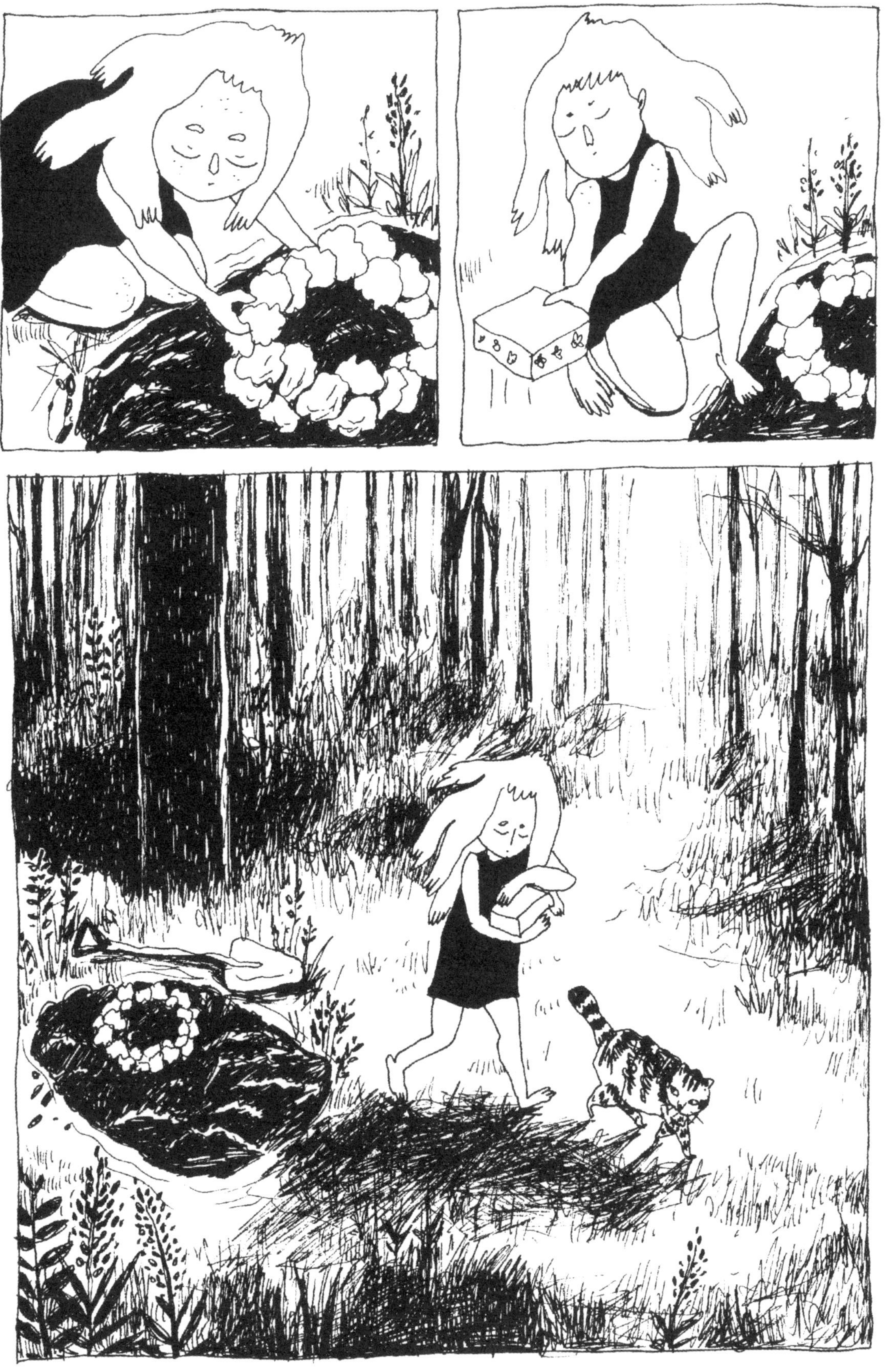

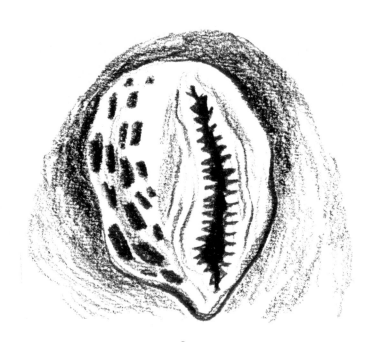

THE
CLAMBOX

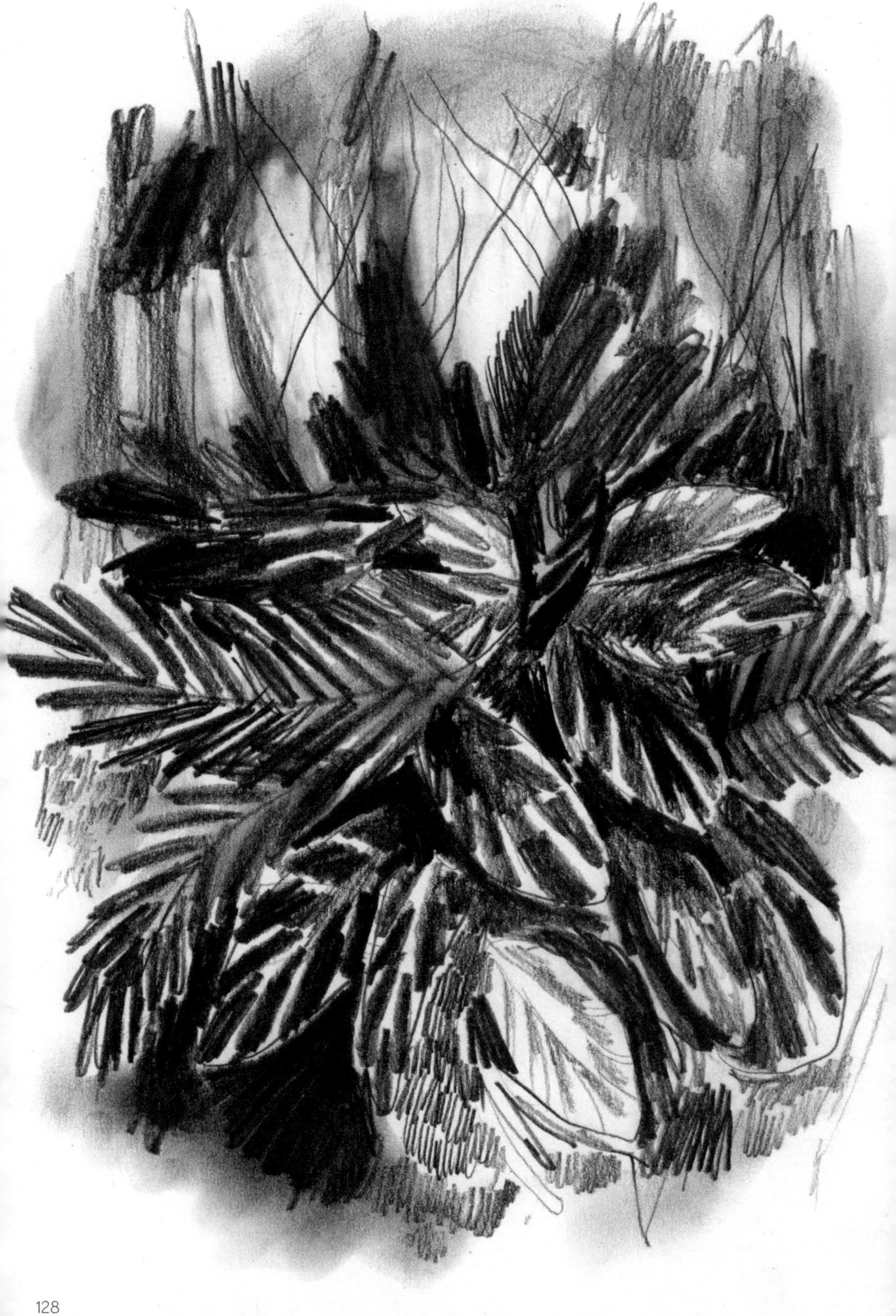

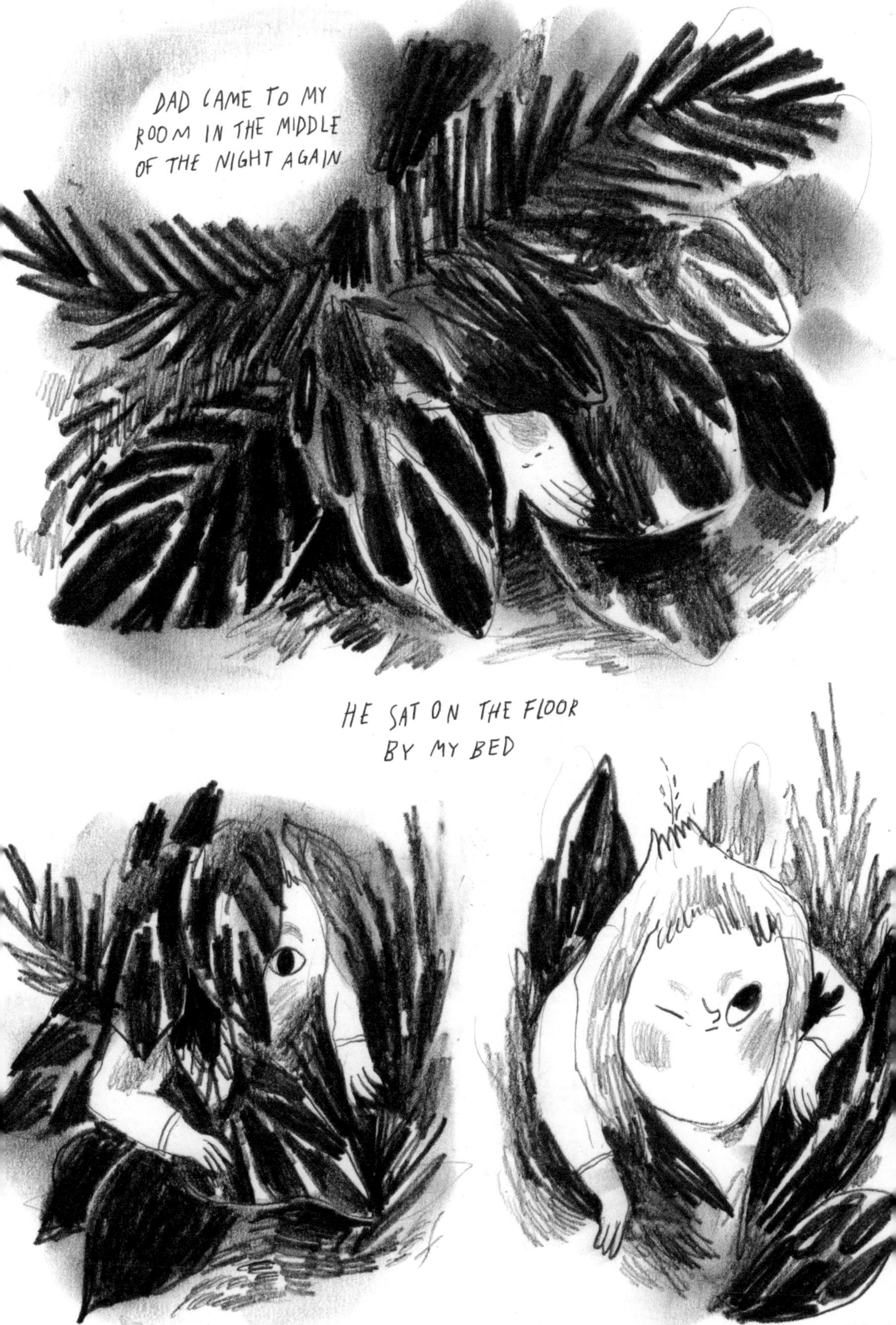
DAD CAME TO MY ROOM IN THE MIDDLE OF THE NIGHT AGAIN
HE SAT ON THE FLOOR BY MY BED

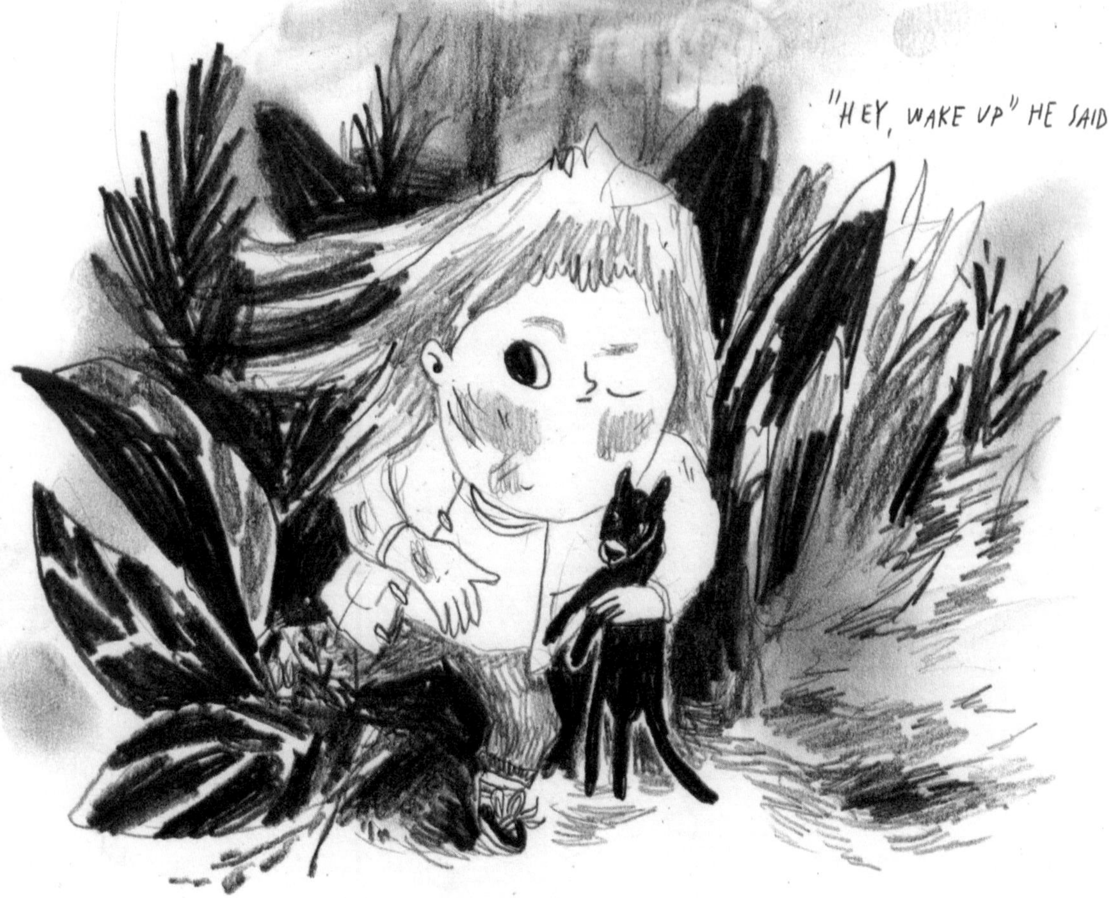
"HEY, WAKE UP" HE SAID

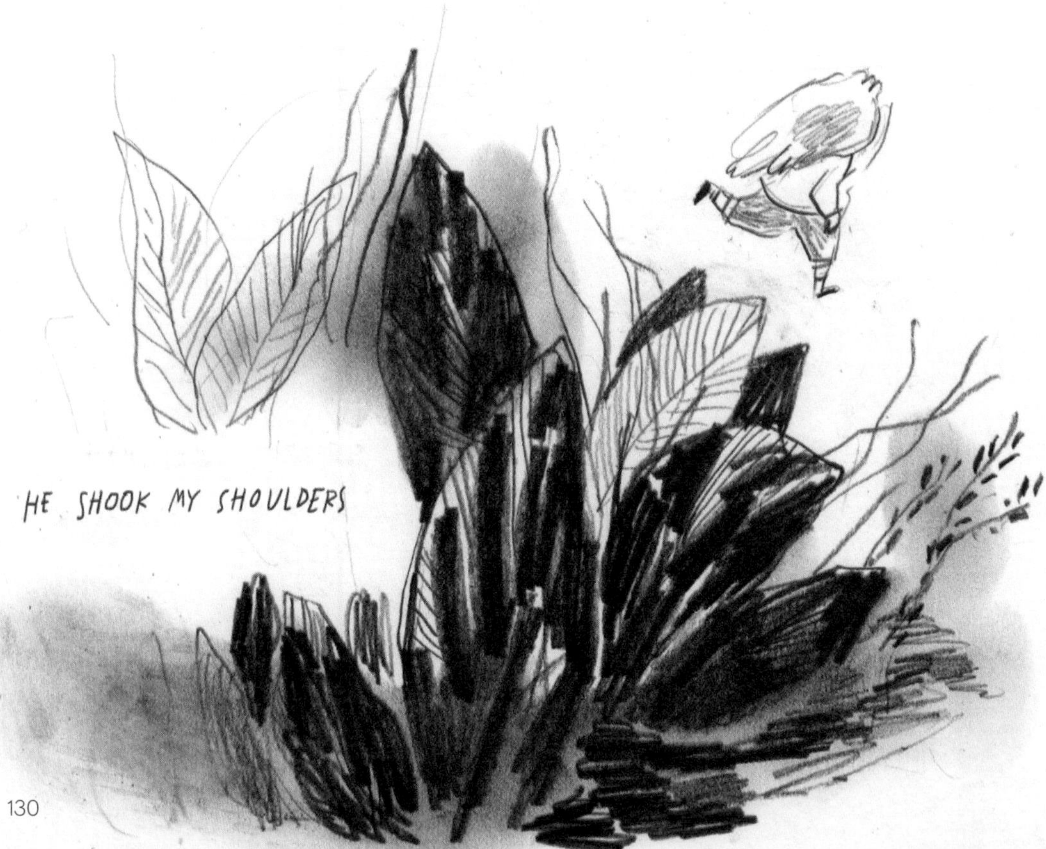
HE SHOOK MY SHOULDERS

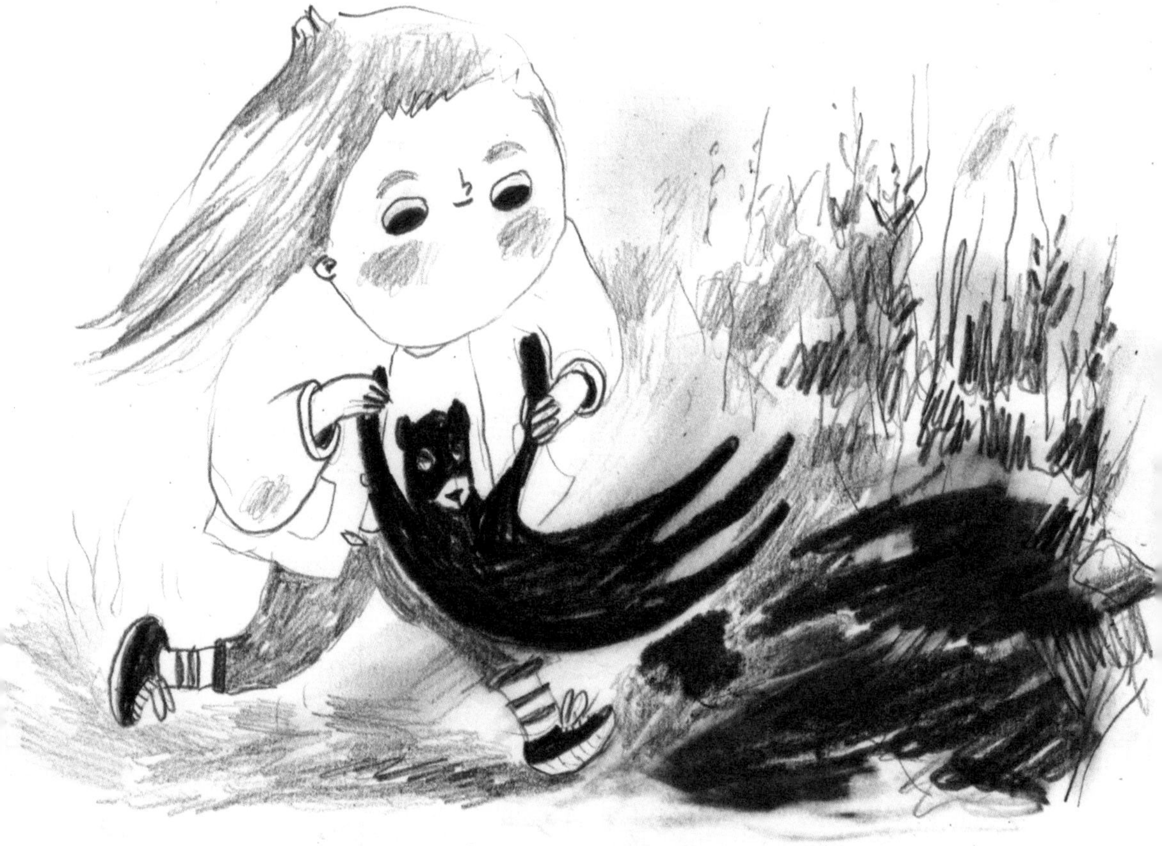

HE WAS FEELING BAD
AND WANTED TO TALK
TO SOMEONE

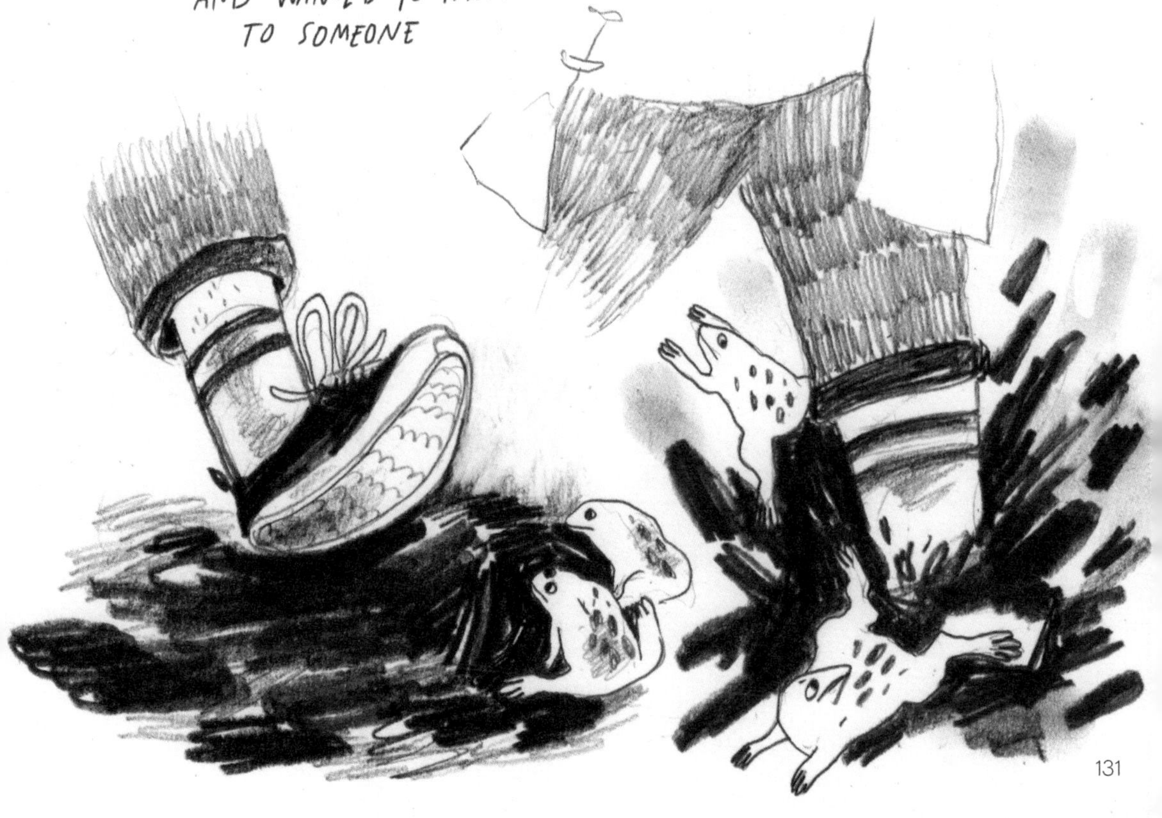

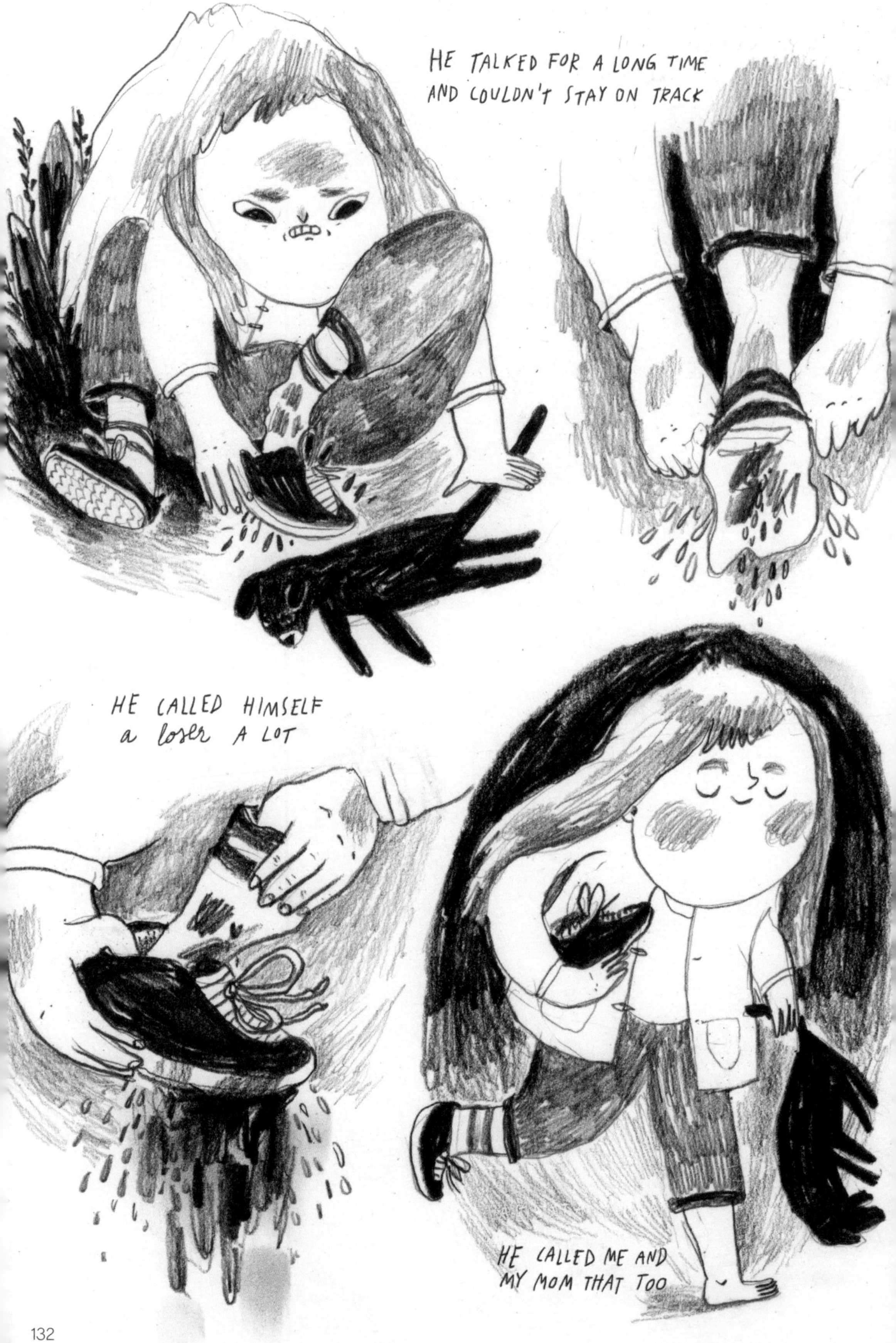
HE TALKED FOR A LONG TIME AND COULDN'T STAY ON TRACK
HE CALLED HIMSELF a loser A LOT
HE CALLED ME AND MY MOM THAT TOO

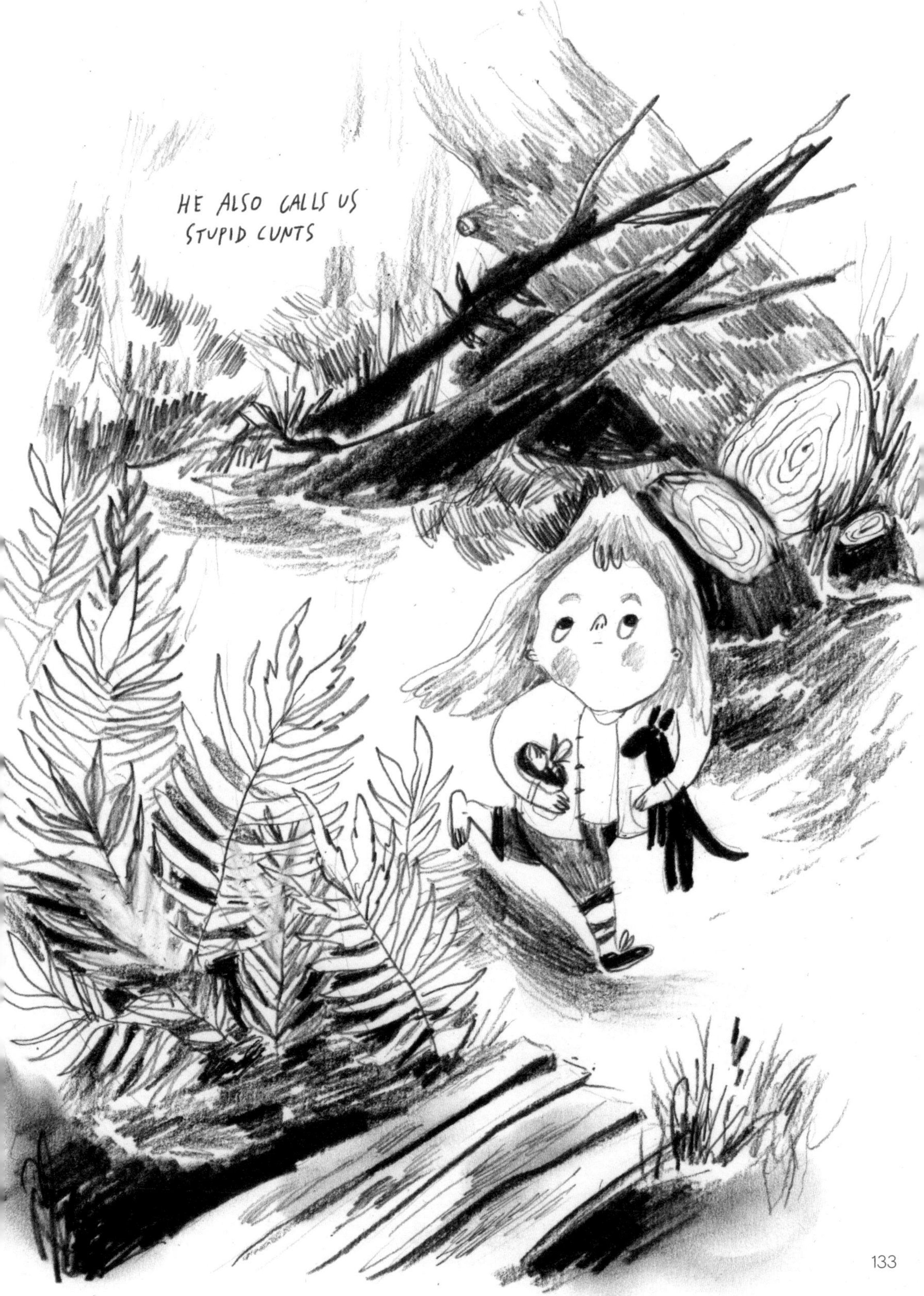
HE ALSO CALLS US
STUPID CUNTS

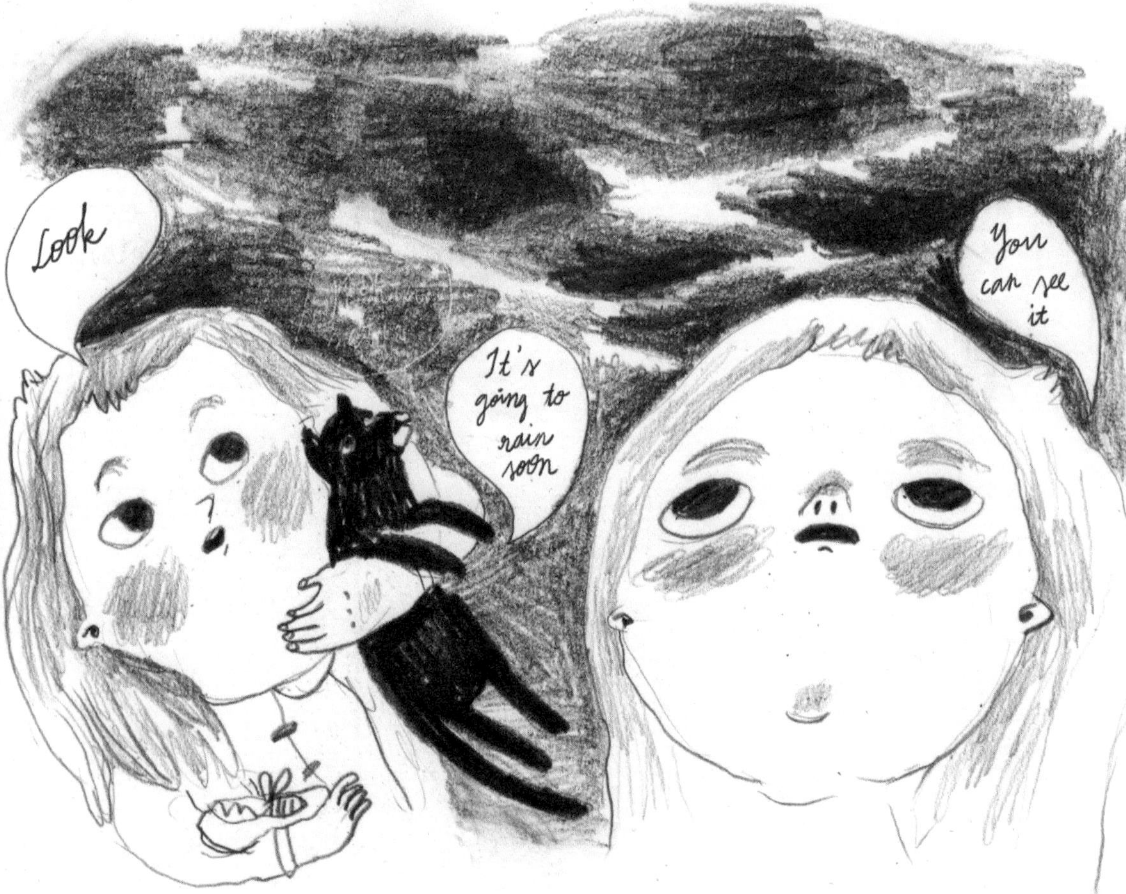
Look
It's going to rain soon
You can see it

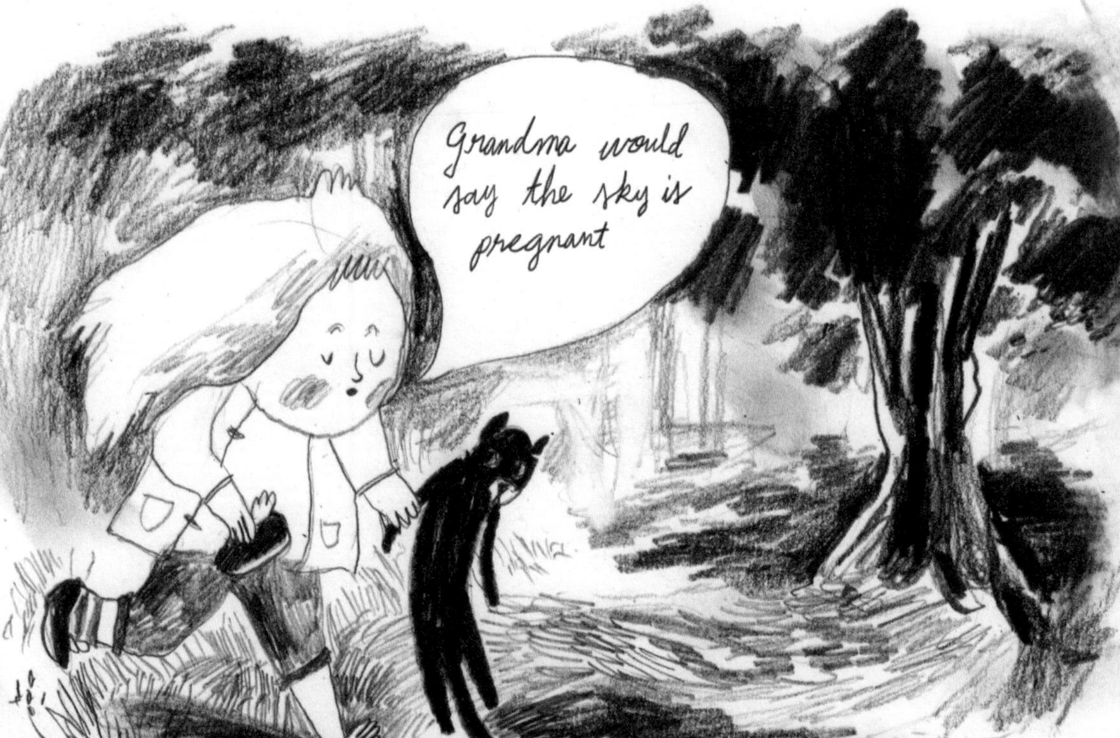
Grandma would say the sky is pregnant

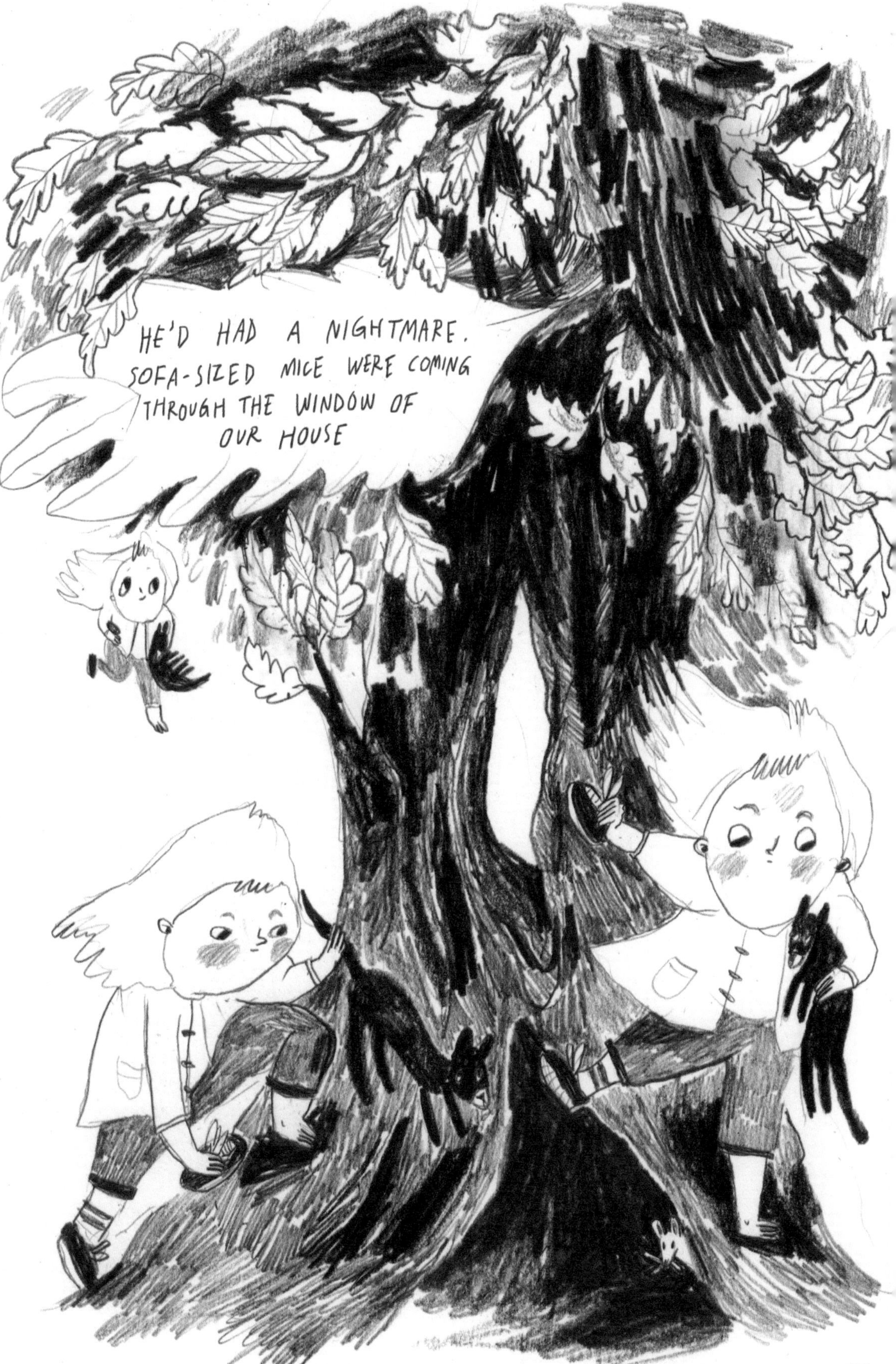
HE'D HAD A NIGHTMARE. SOFA-SIZED MICE WERE COMING THROUGH THE WINDOW OF OUR HOUSE

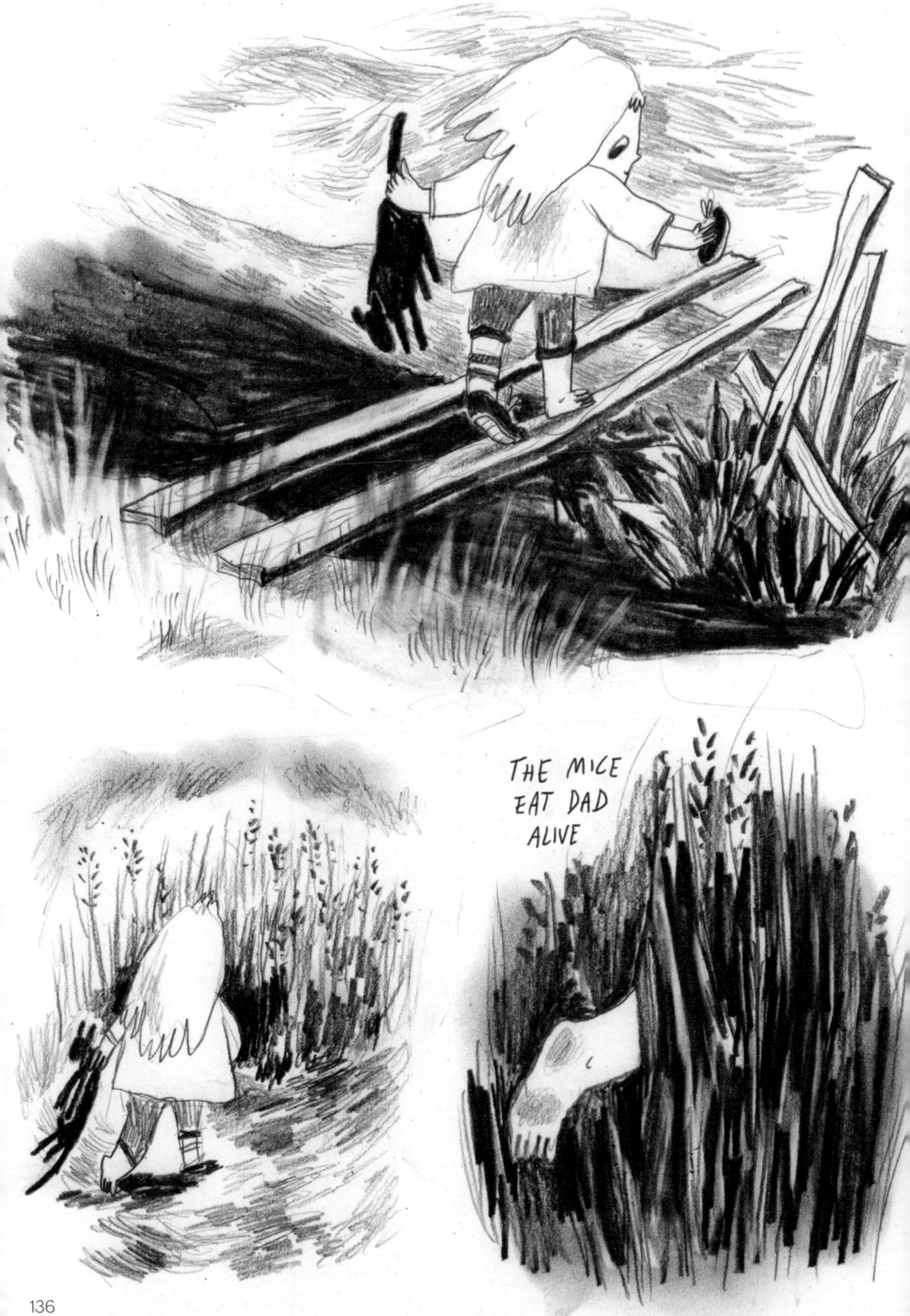
THE MICE
EAT DAD
ALIVE

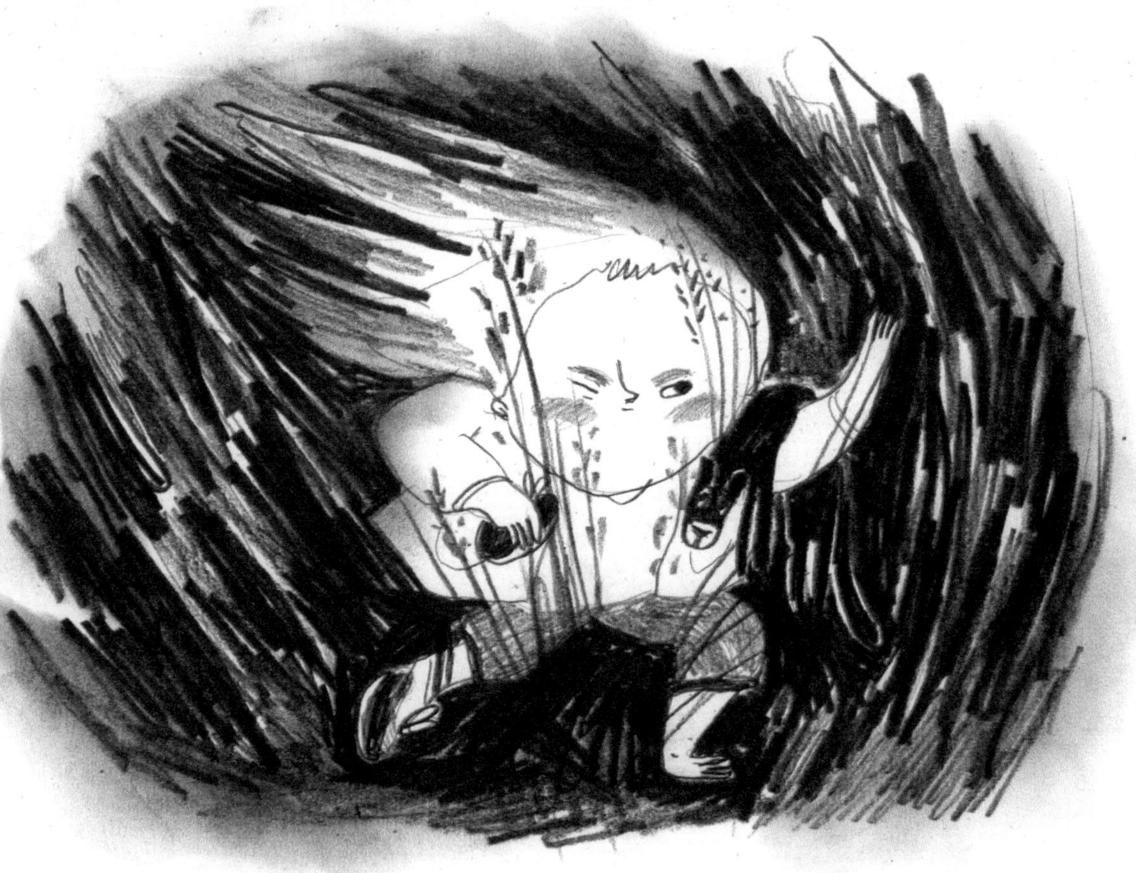

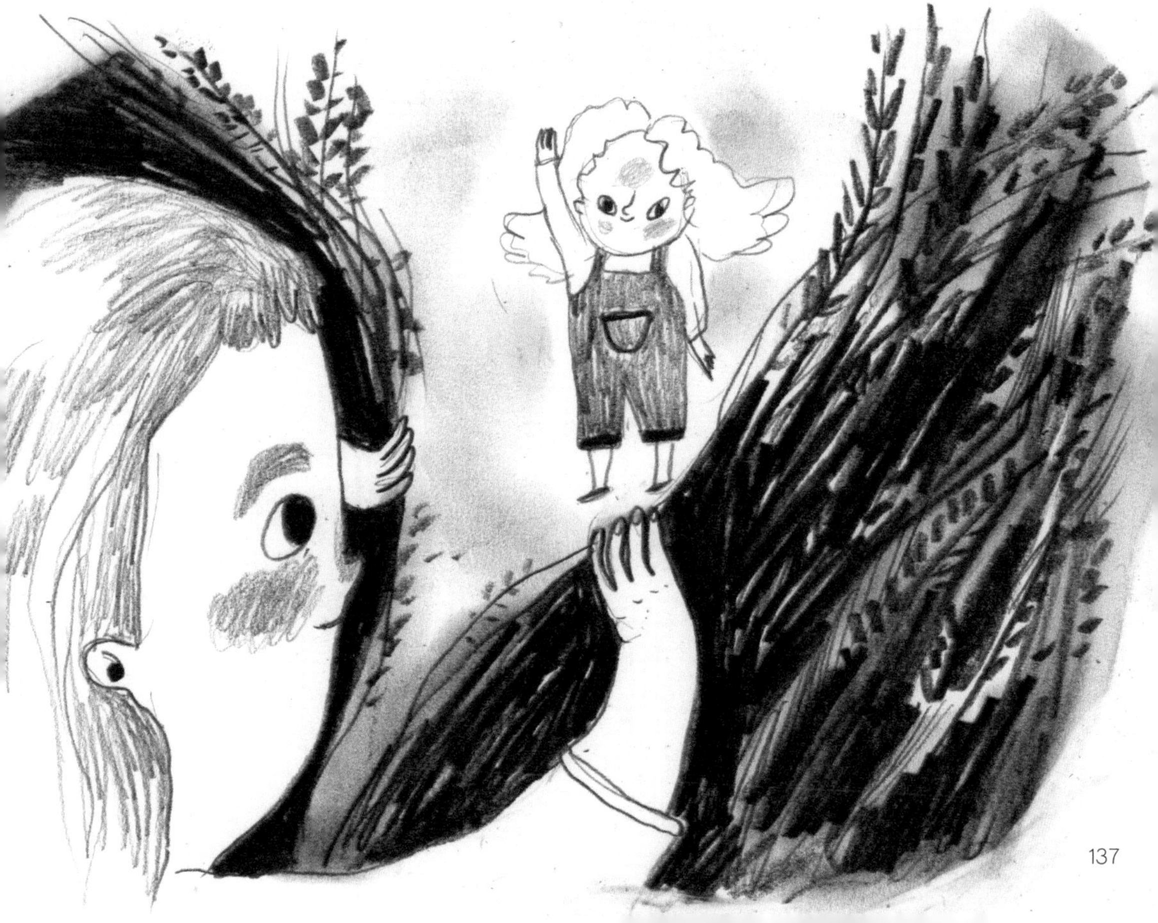

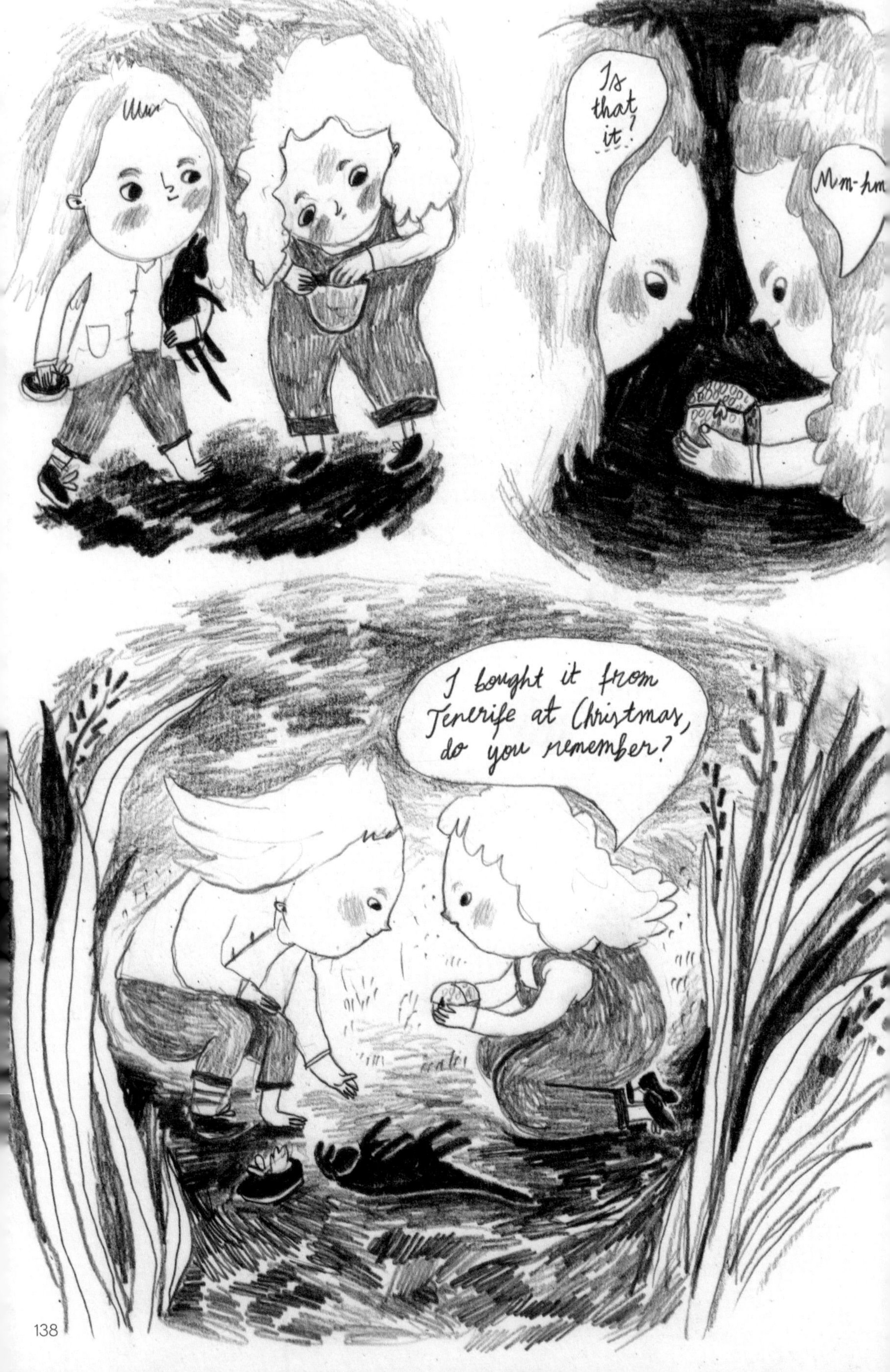
Is that it?
Mm-hm
I bought it from Tenerife at Christmas, do you remember?

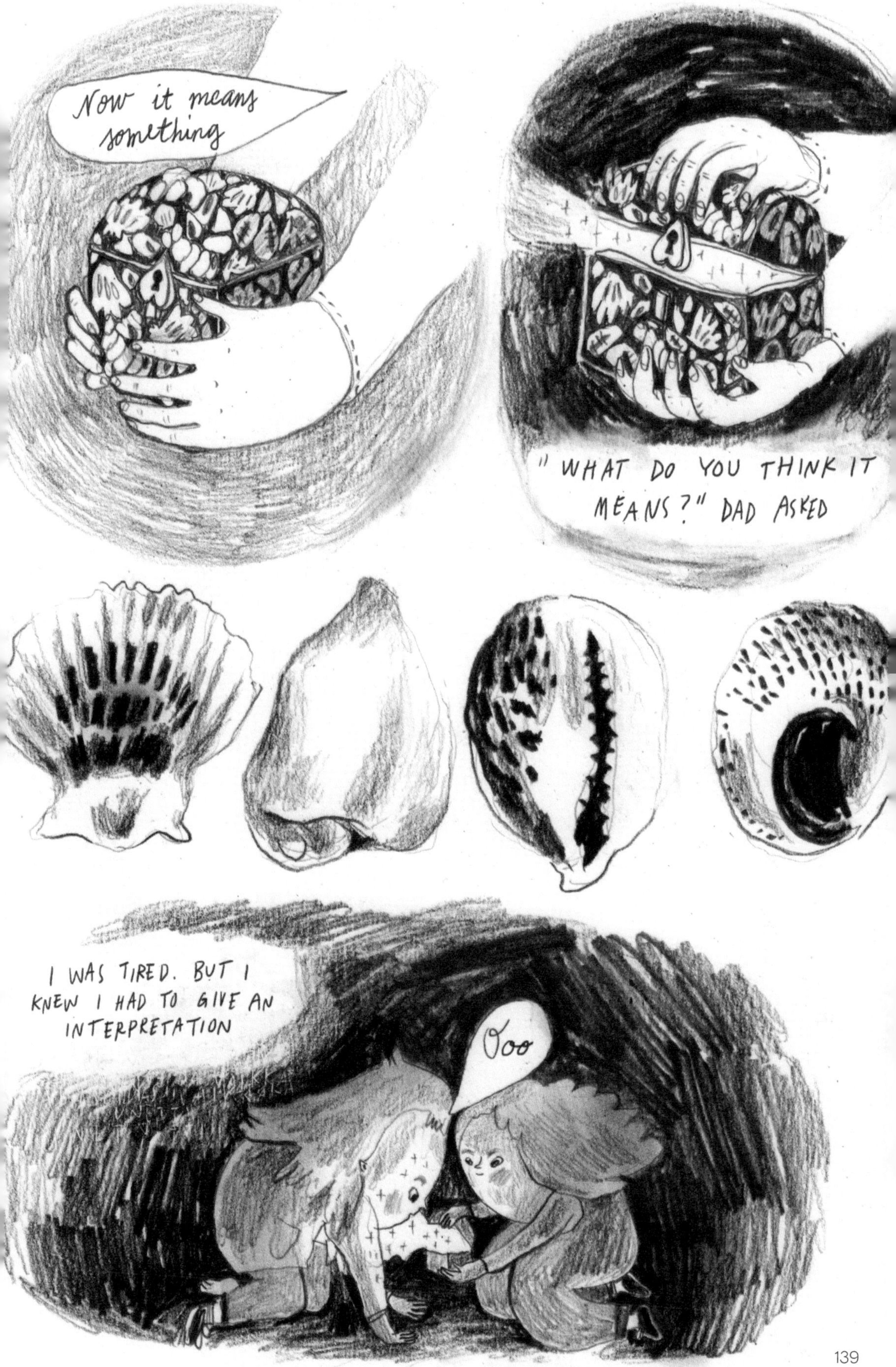

Now it means something
"WHAT DO YOU THINK IT MEANS?" DAD ASKED
I WAS TIRED. BUT I KNEW I HAD TO GIVE AN INTERPRETATION
Ooo

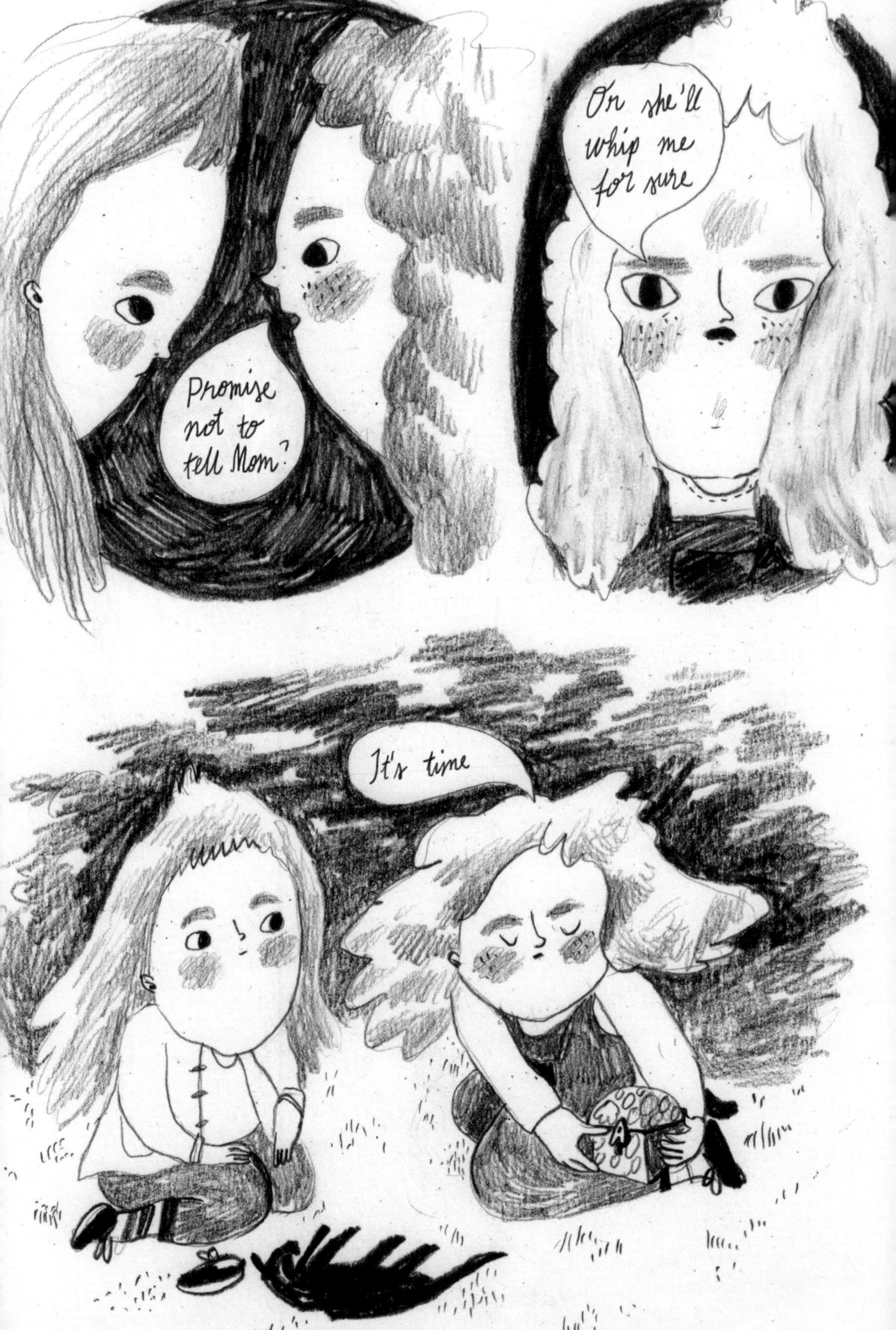
Promise not to tell Mom?
Or she'll whip me for sure
It's time

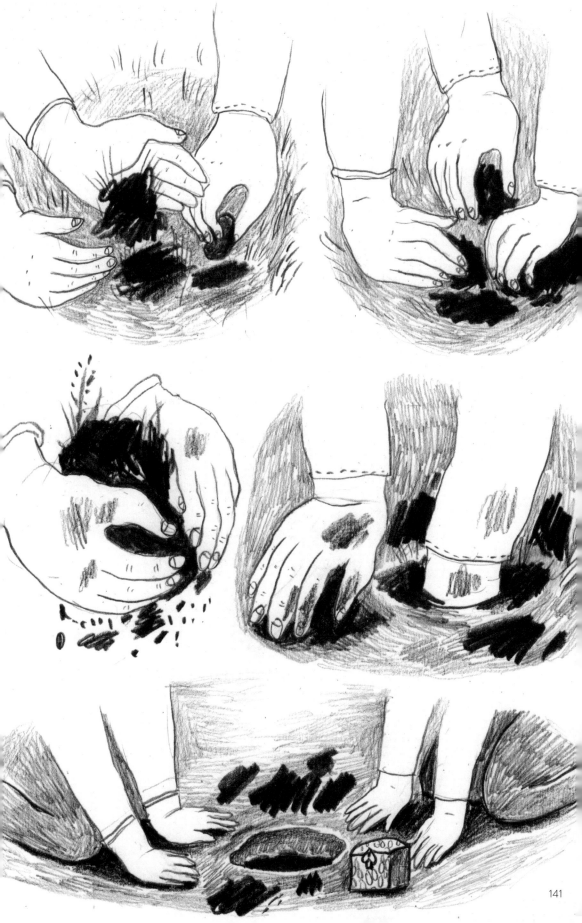

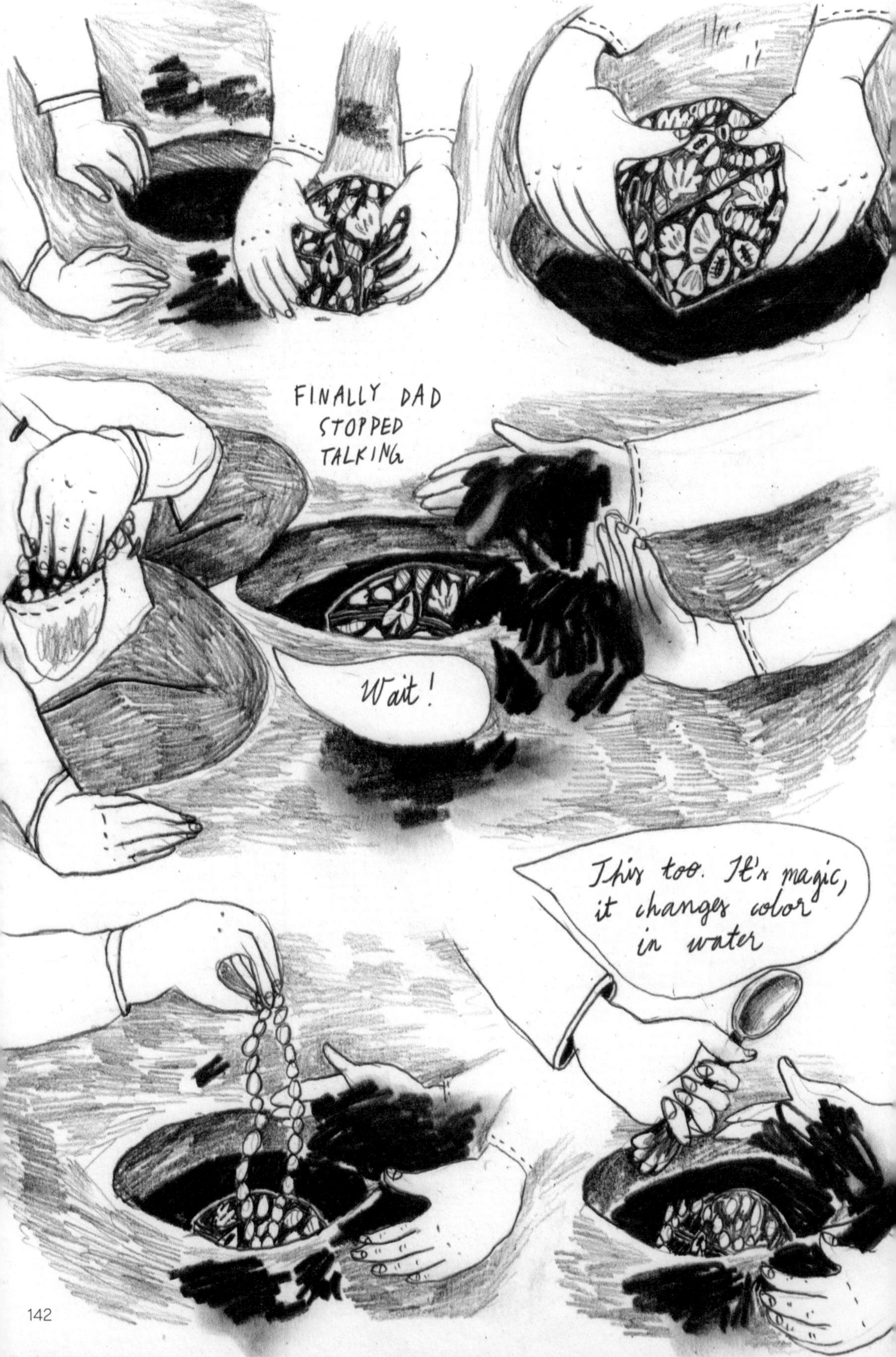
FINALLY DAD
STOPPED
TALKING
Wait!
This too. It's magic,
it changes color
in water

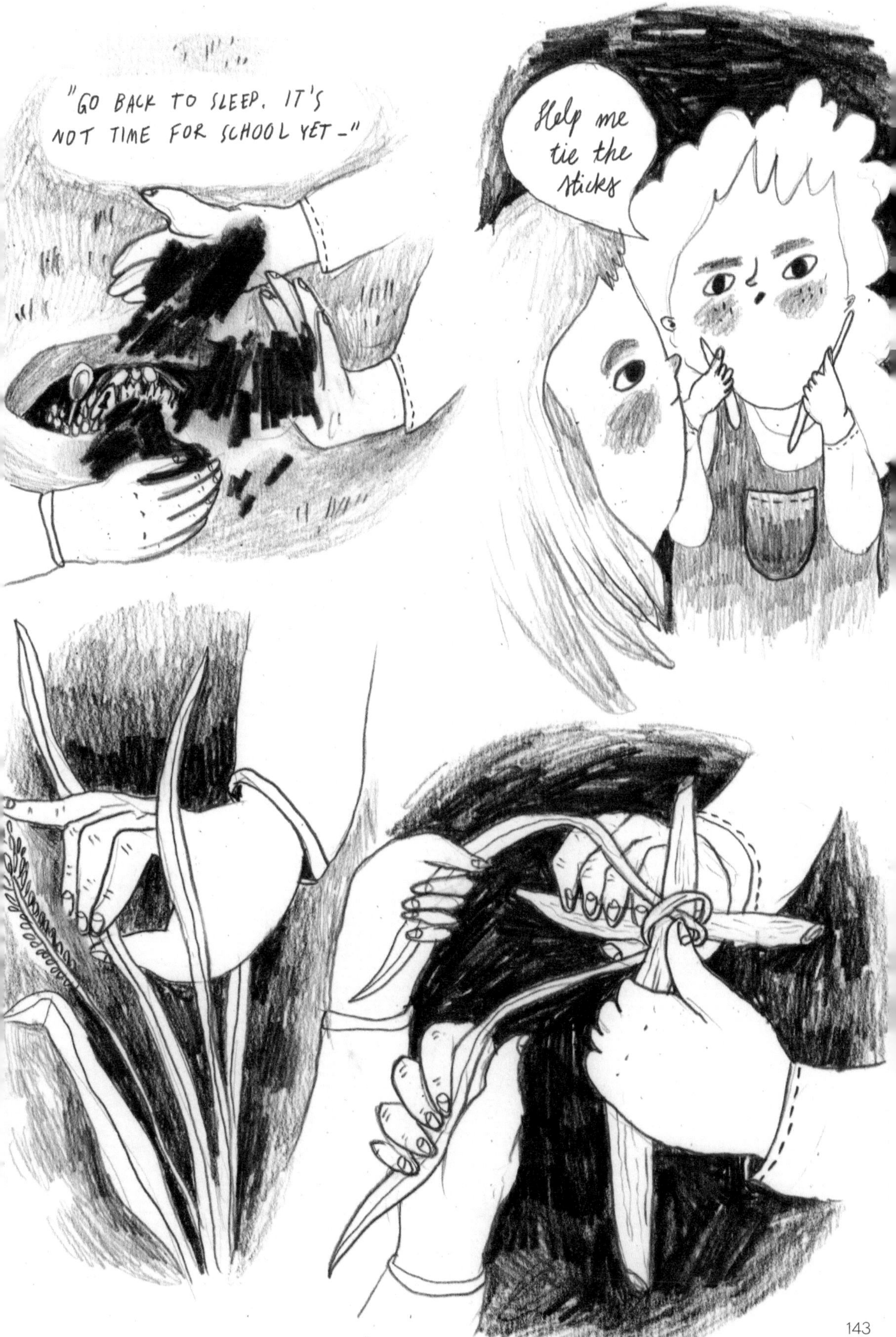
"GO BACK TO SLEEP. IT'S NOT TIME FOR SCHOOL YET -"
Help me tie the sticks

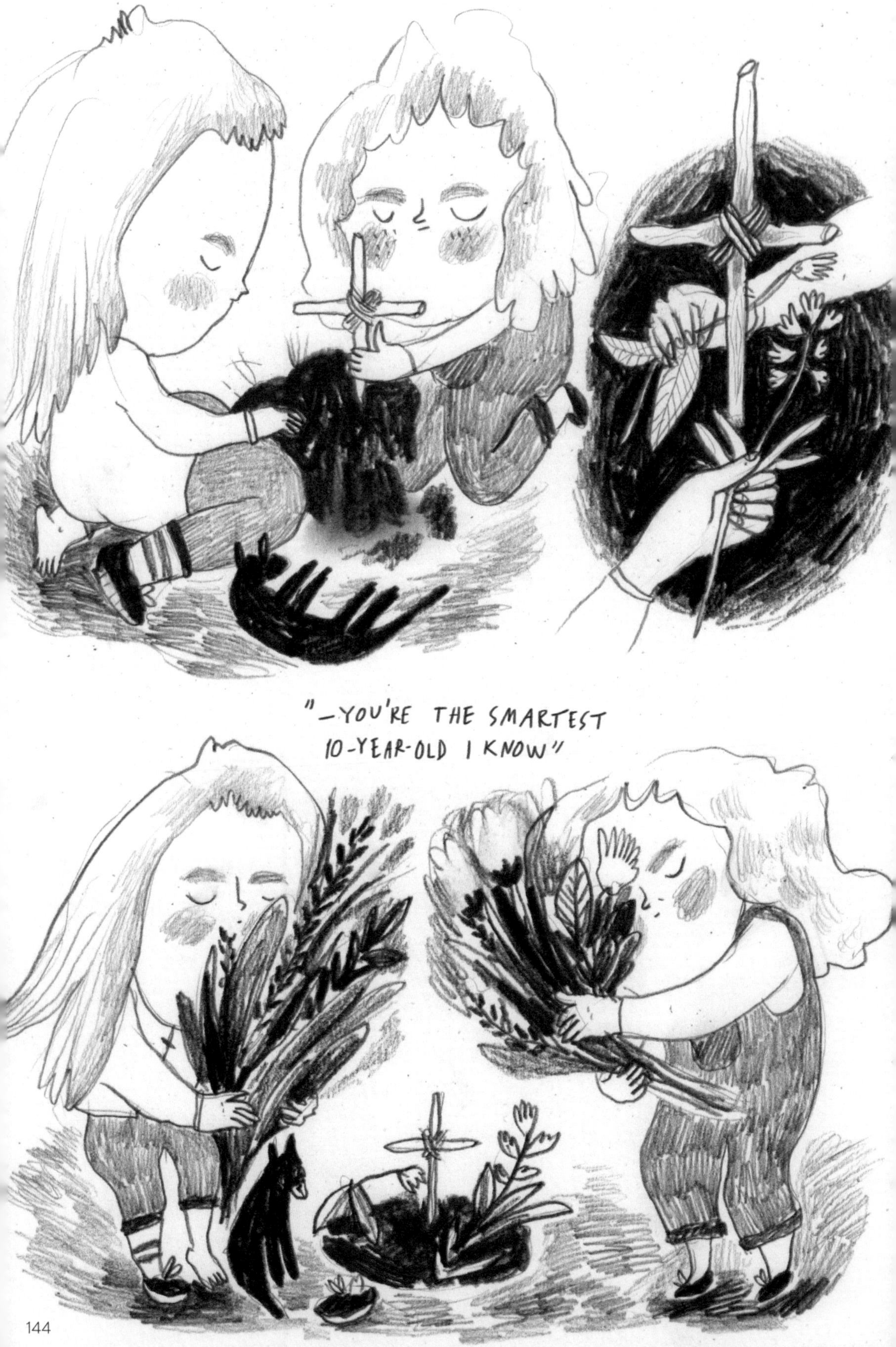
"—YOU'RE THE SMARTEST
10-YEAR-OLD I KNOW"

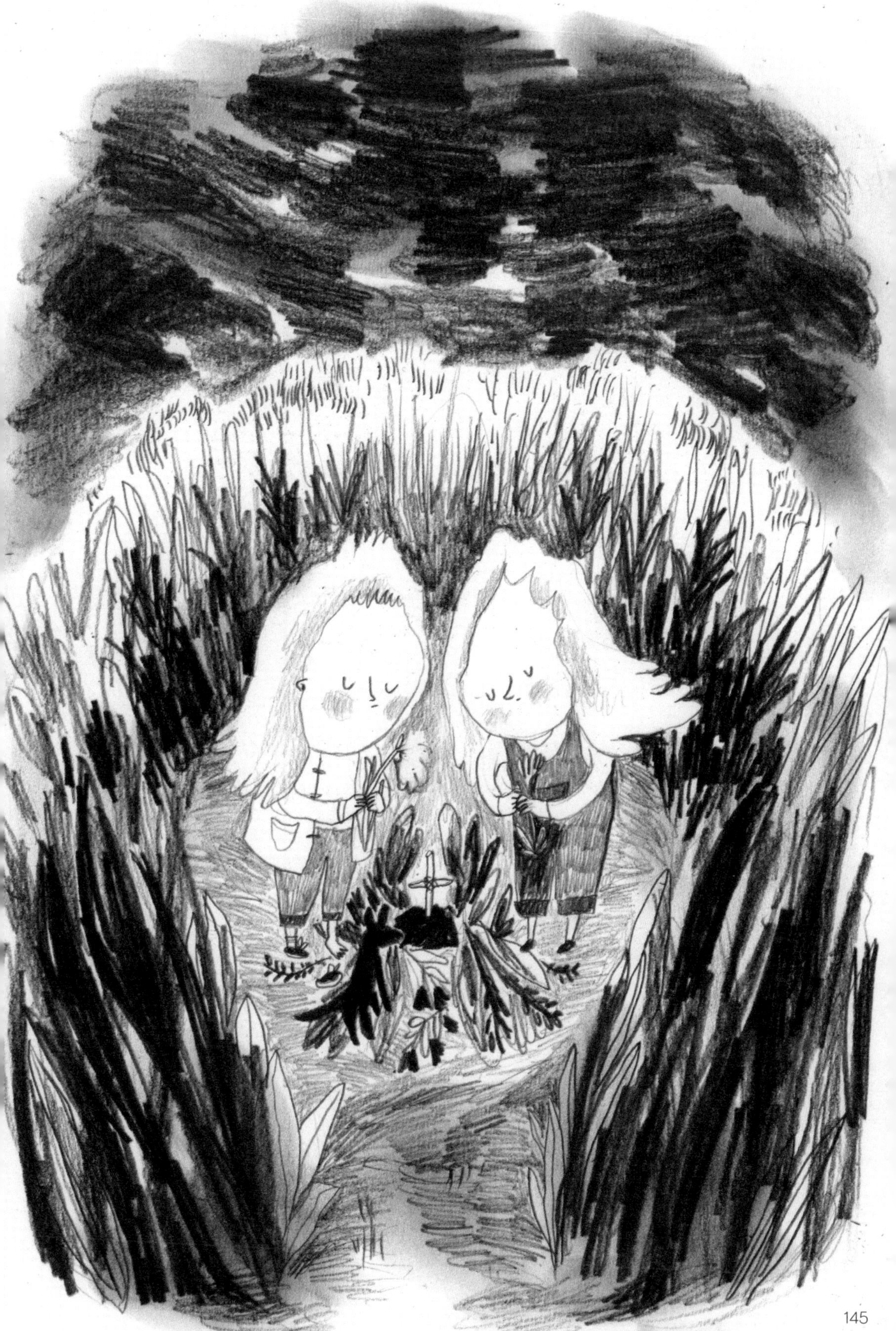

Special thanks for all the help, support and patience to
Matti Hagelberg, Zach Dodson, Konsta and friends.

This book was funded by the Arts Promotion Centre Finland,
Finnish Literature Exchange (FILI), the Kone Foundation,
and the WSOY Literature Foundation.

Taiteen edistämiskeskus
Centret för konstfrämjande
Arts Promotion Centre Finland

FINNISH
LITERATURE
EXCHANGE

KONE FOUNDATION

WSOY:n
kirjallisuussäätiö

Juliana Hyrri was born in Kohtla-Järve, Estonia, and moved to Helsinki, Finland, when she was little. In addition to being a cartoonist, Juliana is a painter, illustrator and experimenter. Her work has been exhibited in Finland and internationally, and includes public artworks such as murals and spatial comics. Juliana's artistic work extends in many different directions, but she sees it as a strength and a way to maintain curiosity, creativity and sensitivity.

This book, her debut, was widely acknowledged in Finland. She was named one of the most talented cartoonists of her generation (Ville Hänninen, *Aamulehti*) and was awarded the Critics' Award by the Finnish Association of Critics (SARV), given annually to just one artist of any field for the best artistic breakthrough of the year.

Juliana loves collecting old kitsch porcelain animals and plants.
Her home jungle is inhabited by two ferocious cats—Kimmo and Poopy.

julianahyrri.com

featherproof BOOKS

Publishing strange and beautiful fiction and nonfiction
and post-, trans-, and inter-genre tragicomedy.

Available in bookstores everywhere,
and direct from Chicago, Illinois at
www.*featherproof*.com

fp29 HISTORY IN ONE ACT: A NOVEL OF 9/11 by William M. Arkin $24.95

fp28 TINY by Mairead Case $14.95

fp27 WEEPING GANG BLISS VOID YAB-YUM by Devendra Banhart $17.95

fp26 ON THE BACK OF OUR IMAGES, VOL. I by Luc Dardenne $21.95

fp25 THE SPUD by Brielle Brilliant $14.95

fp24 MAMMOTHER by Zachary Schomburg $17.95

fp23 FROM THE INSIDE by John Henry Timmis IV $14.95

fp21 I'M FINE, BUT YOU APPEAR TO BE SINKING by Leyna Krow $15.95

fp20 THE INBORN ABSOLUTE by Robert Ryan $60

fp19 MAKE X by various artists $30

fp18 THE TENNESSEE HIGHWAY DEATH CHANT
by Keegan Jennings Goodman $13.95

JNR170.3 ALL OVER AND OVER by Tim Kinsella $14.95

fp17 SUNSHINE ON AN OPEN TOMB by Tim Kinsella $16.95

fp16 ERRATIC FIRE, ERRATIC PASSION by Jeff Parker & Pasha Malla $14.95

fp15 SEE YOU IN THE MORNING by Mairead Case $13.95

fp13 THE MINUS TIMES COLLECTED: TWENTY YEARS / THIRTY ISSUES
(1992—2012) edited by Hunter Kennedy $16.95

fp12 THE KARAOKE SINGER'S GUIDE TO SELF-DEFENSE by Tim Kinsella $14.95

fp11 THE UNIVERSE IN MINIATURE IN MINIATURE by Patrick Somerville $14.95

fp10 DADDY'S by Lindsay Hunter $14.95

fp09 THE AWFUL POSSIBILITIES by Christian TeBordo $14.95

fp08 SCORCH ATLAS by Blake Butler $14.95

fp07 AM/PM by Amelia Gray $12.95

fp05 BORING BORING BORING BORING BORING BORING BORING
by Zach Plague $14.95

fp04 THIS WILL GO DOWN ON YOUR PERMANENT RECORD
by Susannah Felts $9.95

fp03 HIDING OUT by Jonathan Messinger $13.95

fp01 SONS OF THE RAPTURE by Todd Dills $12.95

fp00 THE ENCHANTERS VS. SPRAWLBURG SPRINGS by Brian Costello $12.95